The Black Spiral: Twisted Tales of Terror

Robert Weinberg and Tina L. Jens—"ELVIS CAN'T DANCE"

Gnashing his teeth, Elvis pushed open the lid of his coffin and sat up. Angrily, he reached over and shut off the nearby radio, cutting off the song in mid-play. There was a limit to what even the dead could stand. And a rap group sampling his songs was two steps over the line.

F. Paul Wilson—"CUTS"

LA screenwriter Milo Johnson is having a bad day. The studio is busting his chops over his latest adaptation of a horror novel. More sex and violence they say. And even worse, he awakens to find his body riddled with abrasions and welts. Before his doctor can make a psychiatric referral for self-mutilation, Milo discovers the awful truth ... revenge is the dish best eaten cold.

Tim Lebbon—"FELL SWOOP"

Jack groaned and raised himself up on one elbow, closing his eyes to try to purge his mind of hallucination and pain. When he opened them again the man was still there, hands resting on knees, long hair hanging over one shoulder in a ponytail. His eyes were black and he was staring directly at Jack.
    "Wake up," the naked man said. "It's going to be a hell of a day."

    ... and Jack turned and ran back down the sideroad he had emerged from, seeking the sightless, soundless blank oblivion of the previous night.
    "I'll find you," Rook had said. The stranger who wore his face.

The Black Spiral: Twisted Tales of Terror

Richard Weber—"DEAD HEAT"

If looks could kill, they'd look like Madison Chase; blonde, appealing, deadly:

As the speedometer needle shivered past ninety, Madison squinted anxiously through the bug-splattered windshield of the stolen Shelby Mustang Cobra. The tour bus loomed on her right...

The driver turned toward her, sunlight glinting off his Ray-Bans, and suddenly pulled hard left. The bus careened across the centerline—pummeling the side of the muscle car with a glancing blow.

>Her teeth shook with the force of the collision.

>Tortured sheet metal shrieked and buckled.

As the steering wheel was nearly ripped from Madison's hands, she wrestled it and held tight as the pony car lurched onto the shoulder, kicking up gravel that sprayed noisily against the undercarriage. The steering wheel shook, sending bone-numbing vibrations up her arms.

>Time and the world blurred into slow motion.

Don't hit the brakes, foot off the gas, her mind coached matter-of-factly as experience overruled panic.

Regaining control, Madison hitched the wheel to the right and plunged back onto the blacktop. She stood on the gas, double-clutching through the gears, sending all 390-ft. lbs. of torque to the rear axle, which caused the Mustang's tail end to whip violently as she closed the distance in seconds.

The Black Spiral: Twisted Tales of Terror

Frantically, her eyes searched the dash gauges. They read normal. "Good boy, Frank," she said, praising the Cobra's stamina. "Now let's frag their ass!"

As she tucked the Mustang tight on their butt and eased off the gas, the throaty bark of the dual exhaust empowered her. With *un*blinking eyes, she took in the red, custom-painted letters scrawled across the back of the bus that read:

LEGION

"WOMAN-CHILD"

Now, as she lay in bed, her button-down nightshirt riding high on her firm thighs, her legs propped up, she gave Capt. Wiggly a horsy-back ride. "Ride a cock horse to Mulberry bush . . . ride a cock horse on . . ." she sang.

With each bounce of her knees, the inseam of the little clown's pants bulged slightly at the crotch.

She yawned and reached over, extinguishing the light.

"Good night, Capt. Wiggly."

As she began to drift into sleep, Phoebe pulled her legs into the fetal position, snuggling the clown firmly between her thighs. Concealed by the cloak of darkness, Capt. Wiggly smiled like the serpent in the Garden of Eden. His form shape-shifted, elongating, stretching, rippling beneath the covers.

The Black Spiral: Twisted Tales of Terror

PRAISE FOR BLACK SPIRAL:

"BLACK SPIRAL is a wonderfully 'twisted' book which takes the reader on a spiraling descent into terror, I recommend it for any connoisseur of the nightmare world of suspense."
Charlee Jacob: six time Stoker nominee and author of THIS SYMBIOTIC FASCINATION, HAUNTER, and DREAD IN THE BEAST

"The Black Spiral: Twisted Tales of Terror" Copyright©2003 by Richard D. Weber

Also by Richard D. Weber

PROTOCOL-17

The Black Spiral: Twisted Tales of Terror

THE BLACK SPIRAL:
TWISTED TALES OF TERROR

**EDITED BY
RICHARD D. WEBER**

The Black Spiral: Twisted Tales of Terror

A Cyber-Pulp

Published by Cyber-Pulp eBook Publishing,
13430 Whitchurch Way, Houston, Texas 77015-1316.

http://come.to/cyberpulp

Artist/Partner for this project was *Eric Banderson* visit his website at-
http://www.ericbandersoncreative.com/posters.html

FIRST EDITION
First Trade Paperback Printing December 2003.
Copyright © 2003
All Rights Reserved by the Editor and Author Partners

International Standard Book Number: 1-897013-22-1

E-Book ISBN: 1-897013-23-X

The Black Spiral: Twisted Tales of Terror

Copyright Notices

"Elvis Can't Dance" Copyright©1994&2003 by Tina L. Jens, originally published in "Shock Rock II," a collaboration with Robert Weinberg, edited by Jeff Gelb, from Pocket Books, 1994 with expanded version first published in "The Black Spiral." "Mom" Copyright©2002 by Karen Sandler. "Youth Not Wasted"Copyright©1991 Nancy Kilpatrick, published in Cold Comfort, Dark Tales. "Gillian's Eyes" Copyright©2003 by Julie Novais. "Meeting the Author" Copyright©1999 by Ramsey Campbell reprinted from "Waking Nightmares" with author's permission. "Woman-child" Copyright© 2003 by Richard D. Weber. "Fell Swoop" Copyright©2002 by Tim Lebbon, originally published in story collection "As the Sun Goes Down" by Night Shade with revised version first published in "The Black Spiral." "Dead Heat" Copyright©2003 by Richard D. Weber. "Cuts" Copyright©1998 by F.Paul Wilson, originally published in "SILVER SCREAM," edited by David J. Schow, Dark Harvest, 1998. "The Best Fishing Ever" Copyright©2003 by Jan S. Strnad. "Elvis and Me" Copyright©2003 by Richard D.Weber. "Famous House" Copyright©2003 by Michael Rimar. "Megan's Spirit" Copyright©1991 by Nancy Kilpatrick, published in Cold Comfort, Dark Tales. "The Gargoyle Sacrifice" Copyright© by Tina L. Jens 1994 &2003, originally published in "100 Creepy Little creatures,"(Barnes&Noble),1994,expanded and revised version first published in "The Black Spiral." "Picnic" Copyright©2003 by Kevin Anderson. "Minimum Human Interest Levels" Copyright©August,2003 by Thomas Deja. "Organic" Copyright©2003 by Sara Merlene. "The Serpent Said" Copyright©2003 by William D. Gagliani. "The Dance" Copyright©2003 by L. Marie Wood a collaboration with Richard Weber. "Light, Reign O're Me" Copyright©2001&2003 by Sephera Giron, originally published in 2001 WFC program CD, edited by Nancy Kilpatrick.

The Black Spiral: Twisted Tales of Terror

"The Black Spiral: Twisted Tales of Terror"
Copyright©2003 by Richard D. Weber
Writers Guild of America Registration Number: 946843
"Introduction: Now That's Horror" Copyright©2003 by
Mort Castle

All rights reserved. No part of this book may be reproduced or transmitted in any form or by any means, electronic or mechanical, including photocopying, recording, or any information storage and retrieval system, without the written permission of the copyright holder and the publisher, except where permitted by law.

This book is a work of fiction. Names, places, characters, and incidents are products of the author's imagination or are used fictitiously. Any resemblance to actual locales, events or persons, living or dead, is purely coincidental.

The Black Spiral: Twisted Tales of Terror

For the wee ones: Stacy and Erick.

And a very special thanks to Nancy Kilpatrick for her support and voice of experience. To the established authors who gave unselfishly. And, of course, to all the contributors. To Mrs. Norma White for her keen eyes. The real Uncle Elvin. But most of all to Punky and Mum for their patience and support.

The Black Spiral: Twisted Tales of Terror

CONTENTS

INTRODUCTION 12
   Mort Castle

ELVIS CAN'T DANCE 18
   Robert Weinberg & Tina L. Jens

MOM 31
   Karen Sandler

YOUTH NOT WASTED 38
   Nancy Kilpatrick

GILLIAN'S EYES 42
   Julie Novais

WOMAN-CHILD 56
   Richard D. Weber

FELL SWOOP 74
   Tim Lebbon

MEETING THE AUTHOR 90
   Ramsey Campbell

DEAD HEAT 102
   Richard D. Weber

CUTS 120
   F. Paul Wilson

THE BEST FISHING EVER 138
   J. Knight

The Black Spiral: Twisted Tales of Terror

ELVIS AND ME 143
    Richard D. Weber

FAMOUS HOUSE 160
    Mike Rimar

MEGAN'S SPIRIT 178
    Nancy Kilpatrik

THE GARGOYLE SACRIFICE 188
    Tina L. Jens

PICNIC 195
    Kevin Anderson

MINIMUM HUMAN INTEREST LEVELS 203
    Thomas Deja

ORGANIC 210
    Sara Merlene

PREVIEW FROM NEKRomantik Erotic Tales:

THE SERPENT SAID 215
    William D. Gagliani

THE DANCE 227
    L. Marie Wood

LIGHT, REIGN O'RE ME 236
    Sephera Giron

AUTHOR BIOGRAPHIES 245

The Black Spiral: Twisted Tales of Terror

INTRODUCTION

NOW THAT'S HORROR!
Nine Musings on The Nature of Horror
(With Several Droll but Snappy One Liners)

You write horror? They (readers, students, writing colleagues, telephone solicitors, the FBI, etc.) ask me.

Do you buy horror? I ask them.

If they say yes, I say, "I write horror."

Stands to reason, then, that I'd have handy-dandy, even a facile definition of horror.

I don't.

But I know it when I see it.

Just like Nixon's Supreme Court knew porno.

2. Author, editor, attorney Doug Winter wrote in his 1982 anthology *Prime Evil*, "Horror is not a genre... It is not a kind of fiction, meant (for)...a special shelf in libraries or bookstores. Horror is an emotion."

This quotation is widely bandied about in the "horror community," despite its being a) wrong and b) ponderously obvious.

To begin with b) why, yes, horror is an emotion. Got it. Had not thought it was one of the prime food groups or a means of vulcanizing rubber.

The Black Spiral: Twisted Tales of Terror

But step into Barnes and Noble or Borders, visit the Info Desk and ask to be directed to the *Disgusting* books section ... No matter how detestable, with its bumper sticker religion and 17th century medical knowledge, Dr. Sagi Cobra's latest Oprah endorsed tome, *Starvation for Spiritual Salvation* is on the "Self-Help" shelf.

Ditto the other emotions.

But hot damn, horror is too a genre.

Because it says so right on the spines of the books you'll find on the shelves underneath the HORROR sign!

It was horror when for a dozen or so years it was disguised as *Dark Fantasy* or *Supernatural Thriller* or *Crypto-Modern Gothic* or *Bleak and Baleful Suspense* or what the hell.

But it's horror.

So there.

3. So here comes Kurtz after peering right at/into the *Heart of Darkness*: "The horror. The horror."

Nobody thought to ask him what the hell he was talking about.

Someone did ask Joseph Conrad.

He answered in Polish.

4. "But I guess people read horror to release their deep-seated fear of death, provide a cathartic purging." That's a line from a note recently sent me by... Richard Weber, that self 'n' same fella who edited *this volume*!

The Black Spiral: Twisted Tales of Terror

Logic would say that. "People write horror to release their deep-seated fear of death, provide a cathartic purging."

Maybe Logic would and maybe Richard would, but not this guy.

Here's what I had to say in "Dani's Story," which appeared in the *horror* magazine *After Hours* and was reprinted in the horror collection *Moon on the Water*:

Our narrator, a fictional guy named Mort Castle, is trying to write up fictional Dani's story:

> (So…) why don't I just get on with it? Her story. Just charge into the beginning, chainsaw through the middle, and then, Tah-dah!
> At last!
> The End!
> That will be IT!
> That will take care of it. I know that is what she hopes in a vague and inexpressible way that manages to irritate the hell out of me.
> So, hey, why doesn't she write it?
> No, no thank you, Mort. I lived it. That takes care of my obligation, yes?
> Dani thinks I have magic. Mort the Writer. Published and everything, published in languages I do not even speak.
> Okay, maybe … to Dani, and a few others, I am Mort The Shaman
> And I can do magic
> Get HER story into print.
> That will give purpose to the horror.
> Purpose. Not catharsis.
> Catharsis? Doesn't happen. And I cannot will not
> will not tell her
> that it is just there

The Black Spiral: Twisted Tales of Terror

the horror
will always be

Whoo, I got pretty carried away there, I guess…. Hoo-and hah.

5. So what is your definition, what is horror about, whatchoo talkin', anyway?

From "Dani's Story" once more.

> Horror is WHAT IF? Above all, and forget the bullshit metaphysics, horror is the impossible to control hurting we do to ourselves. If the toothache eases, hey, we just have to stab the old tongue in there to get it fired up and screeching again, don't we?

6. Horror is when I fall on the icy sidewalk and chip a bone in my ankle and the ankle will always hurt when it gets cold and I will always remember that there are icy sidewalks waiting, icy sidewalks and worse.

Of course, comedy is when you fall on the icy sidewalk.

Except when I am chock-ful of Buddha compassion.

7. Alice Sebold's *The Lovely Bones* is masterfully written horror.

Joe Schlepper's *Humongous Groto-Ugly Face Eating, Snot Sucking Lumpy Puke Pus Monster* is also horror and it's every bit as well written as you might imagine.

To some readers, it doesn't matter.

8. Akira Kurosawa said, "It is the role of the artist not to look away."

The Black Spiral: Twisted Tales of Terror

Joseph Conrad said (in English), "My task which I am trying to achieve is, by the power of the written word, to make you hear, to make you feel-it is, above all, to make you see. That-and no more, and it is everything."

Mort Castle said, "Too damned many alleged horror writers can't see and they invite you to share their vision."

9. A true gentleman and a superb writer named Gary Braunbeck said, "...before there can be fear, before there can be terror... there first must be a held breath of sadness and longing..."

Sadness and longing.

Here is the start of a story...

A five-year-old girl was abducted from outside her apartment house in California. She was molested and murdered.

That really happened. That really happens. It's terrible, and if you are one of the rare people who actually do cluck their tongues, then you might register this as a three clucker. *What a world...*

But that is *not* horror. We do not get horrified at each new face on a milk carton. *The milk carton kids! Collect them all!*

Now, here's something else you need to know. And this, too, is true.

The little girl was carried off by a man who lured her with a request for help in finding his puppy dog.

That sort of cruelty, that calculated wickedness that understands childhood so well ... *A puppy is soft and funny and nice and kids love puppies.*

The Black Spiral: Twisted Tales of Terror

And now we start to see it. *He needed her assistance because he was kind of a heavy guy, couldn't bend down to look in all the places a puppy might hide. He told her, though she knew on her own, that the puppy would be lonely. The puppy wouldn't know where it was. The puppy would be frightened. The puppy would get hungry. The puppy would starve or eat something bad and maybe it would die and that was why she had to help him and when they found the puppy, he would give her a reward: five dollars.*

Now, look at her face as she gets in the man's car.
You're starting to feel it, aren't you: This is the horror part, buddy boy.

It gets worse. I'm talking horror here. Look at his face. Look at his face. Look at his face.

And now, here is the horror.

Later, after he did what he did, after the child was dead, he had some good luck.

His missing puppy had found its way back home.

The dog, a terrier mix, one black ear and a droopy white ear, was waiting for him at the back door.

And the man was very glad that his puppy was home and safe.
Now, for me, that's horror.

And you?

Mort Castle
Sept. 14, 2003

ELVIS CAN'T DANCE

Robert Weinberg and Tina L. Jens

Gnashing his teeth, Elvis pushed open the lid of his coffin and sat up. Angrily, he reached over and shut off the nearby radio, cutting off the song in mid-play. There was a limit to what even the dead could stand. And that crap was two steps over the line.

Eyes that didn't blink surveyed the mausoleum. At least, they had followed the instructions of his secret will to the letter. Much as he wanted to be buried at Graceland, the thought of grave robbers digging up his body and holding it for ransom had been too much for him. That was the reason for this special, secret tomb on the other side of Memphis. Here, he could rest in peace, undisturbed for all eternity. And, because even in death he wanted to keep an ear on rock and roll, he specified a radio tuned to a Top Forty rock station be left playing in the crypt.

He climbed shakily out of the pink, gold-trimmed coffin. It was nicely put together, though there were no racing stripes on the sides as he requested. It hardly mattered. He had been a pretty easy-going guy in life as well as in death.

Being the King meant putting up with a lot. There had been those incredibly bad covers for some of his greatest hits. Not to mention Presley classics slowed down as ballads, sung by British rockers with Mersey accents, or done as disco soundtracks. None of it had bothered him.

Dimly, he remembered laughing at some of them while he was alive. Just dimly though. He had been dead so long that his brain didn't work that well anymore. His memory wasn't the best anyway, considering all those damned pills he had been taking right before his death. The pills that finally killed him.

Then there had been the impersonators. Hundreds of them, thousands of them now if the radio could be believed. Young men and old, white and black, even Asian and Latino, dressing like him, acting like him, trying to sing like him. Calling their acts, "Tributes to Elvis" and things like that. Personally, he felt anyone with a decent voice should be trying to make a career on his own instead of living off the King's image. Even

The Black Spiral: Twisted Tales of Terror

though he'd never written any of his own songs, "I always did them My Way," he croaked, testing out his long-dormant vocal cords.

What the impersonators did with their lives was fine by him. They were, after all, his fans and treated his songs with more reverence than he had toward the end.

He could even tolerate the commercials using his songs to sell cars and candy bars and power tools. And the velvet paintings of him they sold at flea markets. Not to mention the latest indignity, the post office vote on the fat or skinny Elvis stamp.

He blanched at the thought of the week-long movie marathons on TBS, wondering how anyone could sit through some of those turkeys. He accepted it all as part of the legend of the King of Rock and Roll. Besides, being dead, he didn't care much. Still, he did have a legacy to protect, and this new group had pushed him too far.

According to the disc jockey, the group called themselves K.I.D. Stupid! which stood for the "King is Dead, Stupid!" It was a rap group.

Elvis hated rap. Everyone had a right to his own kind of music, but rap wasn't rock and roll. And it didn't belong on top-forty stations. He was sorry now that he hadn't requested the radio in his tomb be set to an oldies station. But, there hadn't been such outlets when he was alive and any dial spinning now would surely be noticed by the caretaker.

There were enough stories about him in the tabloids without him providing new material. He trusted the groundskeeper but big money meant big temptation. Just look at all those miserable biographies by his suck-up friends. He was just glad he'd never revealed to any of them his secret will.

At times, it seemed everyone he'd ever met had written a book about him. There was a virtual library of Elvis books. And they kept on coming. Like that really gruesome account of his death and autopsy published recently. Damned thing had been grisly enough to kill him a second time.

He shook his head, trying to clear the cobwebs. Nobody had any respect for the dead these days. Not like when he was a kid and you showed proper reverence for the dearly departed. If he had been capable of crying, a tear would have trickled down his cheek. But there was no time for crying in the chapel.

New York City was home to K.I.D. Stupid! The disc jockey had mentioned they were playing a concert in Madison Square Garden a few days from now. Elvis sighed heavily, though his lungs no longer needed

The Black Spiral: Twisted Tales of Terror

air. He remembered playing the Garden on his come-back tour. It seemed *sacrilegious* having rap there, especially rap by K.I.D. Stupid! mocking his music. Elvis knew it was his sacred duty to make sure that didn't happen.

Stiffly, he walked to the door of the tomb. As per his final wishes, the door could be opened from the inside as well as out. He had always worried about being buried alive. Unfortunately, that turned out to be the least of his problems.

He usually woke up three or four times a decade. When he did, he'd sneak out of the tomb and head across the street to the Gas and Go Mart.

A quick karate chop got him inside, even though it broke a bone or two. He hit the frozen food cases first, popping a cheeseburger and a chili burrito into the counter microwave. He couldn't eat food anymore—his teeth were too loose and his digestive tract didn't work. But he still liked to smell it.

Next, he cleaned out the cash register. Then he shuffled down the aisle, opening and sniffing candy bars, bags of chips and cans of Pepsi. His senses satisfied, he cleared out before the police arrived.

Afterwards, he headed to the Saulmon & Daughter Bookstore. Another karate kick got him in. He stopped first at the magazine rack, grabbing anything with his name or alleged picture on the cover. He was amazed that with all the fake photos the tabloids ran, no one ever caught him on his midnight excursions.

Grabbing a handful of comic books, he moved on to the entertainment and biography section for the new books featuring him. Guarding his legacy required that he stay current with everything written about him. Then he browsed through the nonfiction and history aisles.

His shopping spree always ended in the same place. Over the years, the section bore the labels "Philosophy," "Religious Studies," "Metaphysics," and most recently, "New Age." He laughed at the latest label. "New Age" implied that the truths had just been discovered. Many of the books were hundreds of years old.

He'd been into this stuff since the early sixties. In death, it was more relevant to him than ever. For the hundredth time, he wondered why his spirit still remained on Earth. No book had an answer to that one.

At the end of each visit, he bagged his selections and paid for them with the money taken from the convenience store. He could justify

The Black Spiral: Twisted Tales of Terror

taking the cash from the Gas and Go Mart, with what they charged for gas and cheeseburgers, but Mr. Saulmon had been a friend. He'd special-ordered the religion books for Elvis and kept quiet about it when word that the King was into Eastern mysticism would have ruined his career. Heck, it had been a closely guarded secret that Elvis knew how to read. Being a bookworm didn't fit the public image the Colonel had created.

But there was no time for a book run tonight. Carefully, he turned the inner handle of the tomb door and peered out into the darkness. No one was around. The King smiled, his dry mummified lips crackling like peanut brittle. Tonight he was after that big old pink Cadillac stored in the garage about a mile away. He was the only one who knew of its existence.

Back in his paranoid days, he'd stashed cars with a ready supply of cash all over town. They stayed gassed and ready to go in case he needed to make a quick getaway. Over the years, he had sold or given away most of them, but a few remained. One was all he needed to make it to New York.

At the garage door, he spun the dial on the combination lock, working the rust out of the mechanism. His fingers were creaky from disuse and he fumbled with the lock trying to hurry. The overhead streetlight made him all too conspicuous to passing traffic. Finally, the lock popped open. His memory wasn't great but the combination took no thought. It was Priscilla's phone number when she was in Germany.

He pulled the dustcover off the car and climbed in. The keys and cash were undisturbed in the glove compartment. Holding an unneeded breath, he turned the ignition key and held it as the engine turned over, started, and coughed. Nodding with satisfaction, he gunned the motor, checked his mirrors and backed the pink monster onto the street.

Elvis headed toward North Main. It wasn't the fastest way to get to the Interstate, but he was feeling nostalgic. He wanted to cruise past the old Sun Records Studio - "the chicken shack with the Cadillacs out back"—where it all began.

Once he hit I-40, he settled in for some serious driving. He had 1,100 miles to cover and sunrise wasn't far off. The King was on his way to New York to take a bite out of the Big Apple.

Percussion and a bass drove the rap beat.
"...Love me tender and love me true
The Hound Dog's dead so don't be blue

The Black Spiral: Twisted Tales of Terror

Whiteys can't dance, you know it's so
So they stold our music and copped our dough.

"The King is dead, make no mistake
Cry no tears for the white, fat fake
He stold our music, and that's a fact
But we're K.I.D. Stupid! and we're takin' it back."

"You're listening to WRAP Radio and that was the title track off K.I.D. Stupid!'s debut album, Elvis Can't Dance (Cause He's Dead). It's just two nights till their big concert in Madison Square Garden. We're here in the studio with two of the members of the band. Say hello to DoJo, the lead rapper—and Reemy, who handles the sampling tapes.

"DoJo, I don't think there's anyone in the country that doesn't know that K.I.D. Stupid! stands for the "King Is Dead, Stupid!" But can you tell us how you came up with that name?"

"Since the day the slavers put our African brothers in chains and shoved them onto the ships, the white man has hated and feared us. They broke up our families, tried to keep us down by denying us an education...."

"And they're still doin' it now," interrupted Reemy, "with the big-city slums and inner-city schools. And that's a fact!"

Dojo continued, "They tried to strip away our culture. Look at the music, dance and fashions of any decade. It's a rip-off from us. Any music you want to listen to—gospel, blues, rock or rap...."

"Elvis, he was the worst—a white boy who wanted to be tan." This was Reemy again. "He never had an original thought in his life. Just stoled black songs, sang black, danced black, and declared himself King of Rock and Roll."

The DJ protested. "Don't you give him credit for being the first white man brave enough to integrate rock and roll?"

"Brave, shit! He was poor white trash that had nothin' to lose. He..."

With a snarl of disgust, Elvis punched the radio button. He preferred static to the garbage Dojo was spouting. "Son, I never stole nothing in my life," he muttered, "'cept for a few dollars from a certain convenience mart."

He vowed to pay that money back when he returned to Memphis. Assuming he hadn't used up all the funds in the glove box.

The Black Spiral: Twisted Tales of Terror

It was true he had listened to and admired the musicians on the black radio stations when he was young. And he had incorporated gospel sounds into his music. He'd been singing that music with his mama and daddy in the church choir when he was two.

But he'd also created a sound never before heard on any radio station or sung by any choir. It was a sound only in his head—the animal in him. It was the animal that made him growl and purr, bump and grind, turn soulful ballads into the hot sultry music that thrilled the teenagers and frightened the parents. And gave rise to his self-chosen nickname, "Crazy."

Turning the radio on again, he searched for a gospel station. Though he had only recorded four gospel albums during his career, it had been his music of choice when he and his friends gathered around the piano. It seemed to tame the animal in his soul.

He wondered again why he was still on Earth. In private, he had turned away from organized Christianity, though he still believed in a Supreme Being, heaven and hell. However, sixteen years after his death, his spirit hadn't gone anywhere. Unknown, nameless chains held him captive.

The first signs of daylight were streaking across the sky. It was time to hunt for cover. He had always been a night person, traveling after dark and sleeping by day. Even at home he had stuck to his nocturnal schedule.

For a few short months during one of his many dieting and shape-up regimes, Priscilla had lured him out into the sun to ride horses and hold group karate lessons in the yard. But then Priscilla had taken off with the karate instructor. Elvis had banned the sport from his house and returned to his late night hours.

"We'll have to charge you for a full night, Mister, uh, Crazy. It's house policy. If you're in a band, how come I never heard of the Blue Moon Boys?"

"It's like this, honey. We've been out of circulation for a while, but we're making a comeback."

Quite a while. It had been almost forty years since he done the Memphis club circuit with Scotty and Bill, trying to find his sound.

"So I guess you have to stay in your stage makeup whenever you're out in public, huh?"

The King kept quiet. He was glad his appearance didn't scare

The Black Spiral: Twisted Tales of Terror

the girl. He'd sure frightened himself when he first looked in the rear view mirror. The desk clerk was a pretty young thing, the type he'd always liked. She couldn't be any more than eighteen, with long blond hair pulled back in a ponytail. And she hadn't cussed once.

In his better days, he might have made a move on her. Now, five minutes in his room and she'd discover he wasn't wearing any stage makeup.

"Could you send me up a ham and cheese omelet, fried in bacon grease, a peanut butter and banana sandwich with mayo, a bag of chips, a pot of coffee, a chocolate malt and a hot fudge sundae," he said, figuring he owed himself one sort of treat if denied another. "And a box of aluminum foil."

The clerk looked at him oddly. "Aluminum foil? You planning to wrap up the left-overs?"

"Shoot, darlin," the King drawled, "the foil is for the windows. I like it dark, real dark, when ah sleep."

Driving all through the night again, Elvis made it to New Jersey in plenty of time to make a necessary stop on one of the back streets of Newark. Even after hearing story after story on the radio, he was amazed how easy it was to purchase drugs. Not that the hardcore addicts considered Dexedrine—speed—very dangerous. On the road, he had formulated a plan for his encounter with K.I.D. Stupid! Another stop in New York would provide his costume. The only other requirement, a Colt .45 ACP semi-auto wrapped in grease paper and plenty of fresh ammo he'd "borrowed" on another recent nocturnal outing, came from beneath the front seat of his car. All his life, he believed in being prepared for emergencies.

He spent the daytime in a small motel outside of Newark. The sun was touching the horizon as he steered his car onto the Jersey Turnpike. He'd gotten an early start. The concert was a few hours off, and he had another store to visit.

Cruising through the Lincoln Tunnel, he debated for the last time whether he was doing the right thing. Some folks would say he was doing wrong, practicing censorship of the worst kind. But the King knew he had to stop K.I.D. Stupid!

If they were sampling his songs for some pop dance number, he could overlook it. Instead, they were using his music and his voice on

The Black Spiral: Twisted Tales of Terror

"All Pigs Must Die" and "One Bag of Crack for Sale." Those songs advocated the murder of lawmen and the sale of illegal drugs.

During another radio interview, Dojo stated that "the harassment of blacks by the police and other government agencies made the sale of drugs the only economically *viable* career choice available to people of color."

Tell that to the black lawmen, the King thought angrily. Elvis had been named an honorary deputy by police and sheriff's departments all over the country. President Nixon had even made him an honorary narcotics agent. And President Carter had appointed him as special advisor on the youth of America. The King knew his critics laughed at that, but he took those honors and responsibilities seriously. Very seriously. Even after death.

He knew his critics called him a drug abuser and pill popper. But, every one of his pills had been prescribed. He shrugged. He had paid the price for his mistakes. And the members of K.I.D. Stupid! were going to pay the price for theirs.

He cruised through the theater district looking for the right store. Elvis had been avoiding mirrors—his vanity hadn't deteriorated at the same rate as his body—but he knew he looked pretty bad. The clerk at the motel last night had made that clear, especially when a hunk of rotten flesh had dropped off his arm as he was registering. Double the price of the room, in cash, had paid for the man's silence. But bluffing his way into the Garden wouldn't be so easy, looking the way he did.

It didn't take long to find the shop. It was only a few doors wide, but eight stories high. "The Show Must Go On!" read the sign in the window. "Period Costumes: Prehistoric to 25th Century. Flats, Risers, Backdrops and Props. Everything You Need for Any Show on Earth!"

Elvis had known from his earliest days in Memphis that he was destined to leave his mark on American pop culture, so he was sure the store would have an Elvis costume. He assumed it would be the studded white jumpsuit from his Aloha Concert, broadcast live worldwide via satellite. He turned to the caped jumpsuits when he could no longer get his weight down for tours. He'd gotten the idea from his comic book hero, Captain Marvel.

He was not prepared to discover that he had an entire section in the store's dead rock star department. It looked like they had a copy of his entire life's wardrobe on the rack. There were white capes and gold

The Black Spiral: Twisted Tales of Terror

lame, as well as the leathers from his comeback TV Special. (Elvis figured he was the only singer in the world who had more comebacks than Bob Dylan.) There were silk scarves, karate suits, country western fringed shirts, even the army uniform complete with dog tags and stripes. And all with appropriate wigs to match.

Burrowing in the racks, he came upon an unexpected treasure. His face broke out into a childish grin, the skin at the corners of his mouth cracking alarmingly. Pink-striped black pants, pink shirt, and drape-shaped pink sports coat, the outfit dated back to his truck-driving days. Wearing it would put him in the proper mood for tonight's festivities.

His last stop was the makeup counter.

"Scuse me, missy. Y'all got anything to cover up a skin condition?"

The clerk had her back to him, and started to answer before she turned around. "What's the condition, si-iiir!"

"Well, lack of it, mostly," Elvis told her.

"I think you want," she whispered, avoiding looking at his nearly fleshless face, "a heavy, *heavy,* pancake."

Fighting to maintain a professional attitude, she piled together a stack of water-based cake makeup, blush, eye-brow pencil, eyeliner and shadow, and hair dye. "Will there be anything else?"

She gulped as part of his lip peeled away and dropped to the counter. They both stared at it for a moment.

"Sugar," asked Elvis, "you got anything for chapped lips?"

Three hundred-dollar bills had gotten him past a security clearance, plus a glimpse of the evening's schedule. K.I.D. Stupid! should be taking the stage right about now. Which suited the King fine. Heading for the washroom to change, he could hear the rappers launch into their first song.

Stripping off his tattered shirt, he dropped it into the trash. He turned on the water in the sink and ducked his head under the faucet, not waiting for it to warm up. Anxious to finish, he squirted some soap into his hair and worked it in. A whole clump pulled loose when he tugged at a tangle. He reckoned he'd better be a little more careful. Rinsing out the soap, he applied the black dye.

Black foam, strands of hair, and bits of skin clogged the drain, causing the water to form an inky cloud in the sink. As Elvis watched, the mixture swirled into the distinct image of a smoking gun. A feeling of relief swept through him. A strong believer in visions, he'd often seen angels and demons in his dreams when he was alive. He felt sure this latest sign came directly from above.

After changing his clothes, he applied his makeup. Ready for action, Elvis bowed his head in prayer. Lifting his folded hands to touch his forehead, he intoned, "Send me some light—I need it bad."

He'd said the same prayer before every concert, as long as he could remember. It was a habit he wouldn't break now.

K.I.D. Stupid! concluded its third number as Elvis walked up the underground ramp behind the stage. In a clear attempt to control the crowd, the stage was raised ten feet off the auditorium floor. The rappers hated police of any type, and this arrangement enabled them to perform without any security guards on stage. There was only one officer patrolling the tunnel. He was leaning on an old photo machine, watching the show. Silently, the King strolled up behind him.

"Pardon me, friend," said Elvis, tapping the man on the shoulder. "You got change for a fifty?"

Startled, the guard turned. Catching sight of the King close up, the man's eyes widened to the size of saucers. Silently, he collapsed to the floor in a dead faint.

"Nice," commented Elvis and ran his fingers through the guard's pockets. Fishing out four quarters, he slipped the man a fifty in exchange.

Depositing the money, the King hurried into the booth and mugged for the camera. A few minutes later he nodded his approval. Not having an envelope, he removed a pen from the unconscious guard's pocket and wrote on the back of the strip, "Please send to the *National Enquirer*." Then he wrapped the man's hand carefully around the pictures. He wondered what type of story the paper would come up with to explain these.

K.I.D. Stupid! had just finished a song when Elvis climbed onto the rear of the stage. Dojo spouted propaganda after each number and the King figured the rapper would follow the same routine throughout the night. It was time for him to make his move.

The band was set up in typical formation. Dojo stood front and center, with his drummer slightly behind and to the right. Lead guitar was front far left; bass player, front far right. Reemy was farther back,

The Black Spiral: Twisted Tales of Terror

behind his table full of turntables and tape equipment ready to play recordings of other people's music instead of making some of his own. While Dojo rambled, the other band members crowded around Reemy, passing around a bottle of scotch.

A recording of Elvis singing "Bossa Nova Baby" swelled beneath Dojo's monologue. The King had never been fond of that song, despite the fact it had been a top-ten Hit. In a moment's reflection, Elvis decided he had made the same mistake with managers as with doctors. He never sought a second opinion. When the Colonel declared rock and roll dead and ordered Elvis to record more middle-of-the-road stuff, the King had done as ordered. But, he often wondered what would have happened if he had told the Colonel to find a different carnival and played the music he wanted.

As the King strode across the stage, "Bossa Nova Baby" faded into "All Shook Up." It wasn't his best, but Elvis liked it better. Dojo spotted him just as he reached the bass player's mike.

"Who the fuck do you think you are?" Dojo screamed.

Elvis grabbed the mike, stand and all, and swung it around. Southern pride welling up inside him, he drawled, "Wel-l-l-l, son, ahm El-vis."

Startled, Dojo looked around for help. But, strictly following the rap star's orders, there wasn't a policeman in sight.

"You boys been pickin' mah music to pieces," Elvis said, grinning the fleshless smile of the long dead. "Now ahm here to do a little sampling of mah own."

Screaming obscenities, the bass player rushed forward, eager to regain control of his position. Dropping the mike, Elvis bent at his knees and brought his arms up in karate stance. The musician, his instrument still slung around his neck, charged closer. If he managed to get his hands on the King's brittle limbs, it would be all over.

The King waited motionless until his target was in range. Pivoting a quarter turn, Elvis bent at the waist and kicked his heel into the punk's nose. Cartilage slammed into the musician's brain, killing him instantly. Elvis felt a thrill of satisfaction, recalling innumerable karate kicks performed in his stage act during his "middle years." All of that practice finally paid off.

Not understanding what was happening, the drummer ran to his friend's aid. Elvis saw him coming. Reaching down, he pulled the instrument free from the corpse. Holding the guitar like a Louisville

The Black Spiral: Twisted Tales of Terror

Slugger, the King swung for the cheap seats. The bat connected solidly with the drummer's head. The crack of his neck snapping was louder than a home run.

The lead guitarist almost got him, but the King's luck held true. The musician tripped over the bodies of his bandmates. He dropped to his hands and knees. Instantly, Elvis straddled him. With a sureness of movement dating back to his Las Vegas days, he whipped the pink silk scarf from around his neck and looped it over the guitar player's. The King gave it a quick twist and watched the jerk's face turn blue. It only took a few seconds for him to die.

Elvis spotted Reemy cowering behind his table full of equipment. Reaching the tape setup in three strides, the King hauled the rapper across the table. Grabbing him by the hair, Elvis pulled Reemy's head back. Digging into his pocket, Elvis pulled out a handful of pills and forced them down the runt's throat. A second dose, just for good measure, followed.

The first convulsion hit Reemy as he collapsed to the floor. He gurgled once as the speed lit up his system. Remembering the rapper's comments on drug dealing, Elvis considered the boy's death poetic justice.

Dojo had almost made it to the wings, screaming for the police. Elvis stopped a few feet away, beside the nearest mike stand. Calmly, the King pulled the microphone out of its clamp.

"Turn around, son. Ah don't like to kill a man when his back's turned."

The rapper stopped screaming and swung around, his face crowned with disbelief. With slow, deliberate movements the King dropped the microphone, picked up the stand, and rushed his nemesis. Thrusting savagely, he impaled Dojo through the stomach with the pole of the mike stand.

There was no time to savor the moment. Security guards and policemen were climbing onto the stage. Reaching into his pocket, Elvis pulled out his nickel-plated semi-auto. Then hesitated, realizing he was about to fire on policemen.

He had been forced to kill K.I.D. Stupid! They had been corrupting the youth of America - encouraging them to use drugs, sell narcotics, and kill lawmen. And, they had been using his songs to do it. Standing there, Elvis wondered if maybe the ones who bought the music, made the rappers famous, weren't equally to blame. Turning, he aimed

The Black Spiral: Twisted Tales of Terror

his .45 at the crowd.

It was then that he heard the faint strains of a gospel Hymn. For a second, the King thought one of Reemy's tape recorders was playing. But where were those colored lights coming from? Time froze, and he saw his mother.

"Mama?"

She was walking down a golden stairway. His mama, young and beautiful and thin, just like she'd always wanted to be. The one woman he'd worshiped all his life. And with her was a young man in a pure white suit, looking like Elvis had back when he was young and handsome.

"Elvis, it's time to come home, son."

"Who's that with you, Mama?"

"It's Jesse, son," said his mother. The twin who had died at birth. "I've been waiting a long time to introduce you to your twin brother."

Elvis looked at his body in shame. The pink suit hid the splintered bones and withered flesh. But he knew they were there.

"I can't come looking like this, Mama," he mumbled. "Besides, I've been stuck here for sixteen years. Heaven don't want me."

"That's cause you're stubborn as a mule," said his mother. "You got to stop holding on, son. Forget about that horrible Colonel, and protecting your legend. Let go of the fame. Stop fussing and fuming about how you're going to be remembered and let it go."

"C'mon, El," said Jesse. "Pa's waiting."

Elvis suddenly felt himself rising into the air. But there was a weight holding him down. The gun. He dropped it to the stage. And floated up toward the light.

Madison Square Garden was filled with the gentle strains of "How Great Thou Art." And Elvis was singing lead.

A few days later the new issue of the *National Enquirer* hit the stands, headlines screaming.

Massacre at the Garden!

The King Returns!

Elvis Raptured: Ascends Stairway to Heaven!

see photos page 5

But, of course, that version of the story was not reported by any other paper.

The Black Spiral: Twisted Tales of Terror

MOM

Karen Sandler

Benjamin Hagen raced pell-mell down the school's front steps, taking the stairs two at a time. He shrugged into his backpack as he ran, the heavy books smacking against his back in syncopation with his stride. Waving to his friends, he turned the corner onto his block.

The man was there again. Leaning against a tree in front of the liquor store across the street. As he had been three times last week, four times the week before. The man raised a hand and shouted, "Hi!" But Benjamin ignored him just as he had those other times. He kept his face straight ahead. Mom wouldn't like him talking to strangers.

Benjamin counted as his feet pounded the pavement; one hundred eight steps from the corner and he was at his front gate. Twelve more and he was at his front door, his feet slapping against the concrete porch. Benjamin pulled the string holding his key from around his neck.

Inside the house, Benjamin threw the deadbolt on the door, leaving the key in the lock. He dumped his backpack on the entry table, then snatched an apple from the fruit bowl on the table. It was probably too close to dinner to have a snack, but he was starving. His fifth-grade teacher had kept them late, drilling them in math word problems.

School was a pain, except in the fall and winter. Mom got up early then. She would make dinner, then help him with his homework. She had time sit and talk to him before she left for her night job.

He padded into the living room and was just reaching for the TV remote when the doorbell rang.

Benjamin paused, his mouth still open to take a bite of the apple, his hand resting on the remote. Mom hadn't told him anyone was coming over. She always let him know when to expect visitors. Benjamin hesitated, staring at the locked door.

Whoever it was knocked, first lightly, then pounded loudly. Benjamin moved closer to the door. "Who is it?" he shouted.

"Everett Air Freight. Got a delivery," a muffled, male voice shouted from beyond the door.

The Black Spiral: Twisted Tales of Terror

The voice sounded familiar; maybe it *was* the deliveryman. Mom hadn't said anything about a package today, but Benjamin thought he remembered she'd sent away for something.

Benjamin stood on tiptoe to look out the peephole. The deliveryman was standing off to the side and Benjamin couldn't get a good look at him.

"Leave the package on the porch," Benjamin yelled.

"Can't. You gotta sign for it."

Benjamin glanced at the shut door to his mother's room, then back to the front door. Resolute, he slipped the chain lock into place. For extra security, he planted his foot close to the threshold.

Benjamin eased open the deadbolt, turned the doorknob, and opened the door to the extent of the chain. "Pass it through," he said, trying to see the man.

There was a blur, then a brief, frozen moment when Benjamin saw the man's face, the face of the man from the liquor store. Then with a thud and a splintering of wood, the door crashed open, breaking the chain, banging into his foot. Benjamin went sprawling as the man lunged inside and slammed the door shut behind him.

"Well howdy, Benjy," the man said hoarsely, grinning.

Benjamin scrambled backward, putting space between the man and him before he rose to his feet. His left big toe throbbed, twanging with pain.

"How do you know my name?"

Keeping his eyes on Benjamin, the man threw the deadbolt back into place, pocketing the key. "Been asking about you."

The man's ruddy face stared, his eyes shone wildly, and a rough stubble of whiskers covered his cheeks and thick neck. His black hair was straight like Benjamin's. For a single, crazy moment, he thought the man might be his father, come back at last.

"I don't know you," Benjamin said. "My mom wouldn't like you being here."

"She gone?" The man took a few more paces into the house, looking around. "Seen you a lot. Never seen her."

Behind the man's back, Benjamin flicked a glance at Mom's closed door. "Yeah, she's gone. I can't have people over when she's not here. Not even friends."

The man smirked. "We're gonna be friends. Good friends."

The Black Spiral: Twisted Tales of Terror

Benjamin backed up against Mom's door, trying to remember where she kept her key. "Look Mister..."

"Name's..." The man paused, smiled thinly, his gaze slowly drifting toward Benjamin. "Joe. Call me Joe."

"Mister, I mean Joe, I've got homework and chores to do before my mom gets home, so if you could just tell me what you want..."

"Been watching you," he said, moving closer. "Figure you have to live here with someone "

"My mom works nights, sleeps days," Benjamin said, then continued quickly, "but she's out running errands now."

Joe stood so close Benjamin could smell the sour odor of the man's breath, could see the greasiness of his denim jacket. When his fingers rose to stroke Benjamin's cheek, it was all he could do to keep from throwing up on the man's filthy shirt.

"Don't do that," Benjamin said hoarsely, squirming away from the door. His aluminum baseball bat was leaning against the entry table. He grabbed it. Gripping it tightly with both hands, Benjamin waved it menacingly. "You have to leave now."

Joe laughed, snatching the bat from him. Grinning, he extended the bat and poked at Benjamin, butting him in the chest, the shoulders, the arms, and finally, a hard butt to his privates.

Benjamin gasped, bending over to protect himself, tears welling in his eyes. He turned to wipe them away unseen. Joe, guffawing, tossed the bat to one side and wandered around the living room.

He stopped at the upright piano and studied the photographs displayed there. He picked up the only one of Mom, holding Benjamin as an infant. "Pretty," Joe sneered, skimming Mom's image from throat to ankles with a grimy finger. Benjamin felt a sick hotness in his belly and his hands itched for the bat again.

Joe replaced Mom's picture, then scanned the others, all of Benjamin by himself. Mom had arranged them carefully, from age one to ten, the last one his soccer picture.

Joe looked from the photographs to Benjamin's image in the mirror above the piano. Inadvertently, Benjamin made eye contact with Joe in the mirror. He tore his gaze away and stared fixedly at the clock on the wall.

Another hour at least. If he couldn't make the man leave...

"Are you hungry?" Benjamin asked. He swallowed back the bile burning his throat. "I could get you something to eat."

The Black Spiral: Twisted Tales of Terror

Joe moved closer to place a moist hand on the back of Benjamin's neck. "Sure, Benjy," he said, gripping tightly until his fingernails bit into Benjamin's flesh.

Benjamin gritted his teeth against the pain, his eyes tearing again. He started moving toward the kitchen, but Joe stayed with him. The hand clenched, tighter, tighter, until Benjamin felt something wet trickling down his neck, until he felt nearly numb with pain. Then abruptly, Joe released him.

Benjamin raised a shaky palm to his neck, then held it out to see the red, wet stain. Trembling, he muttered, "Excuse me." Moving to the sink, he held a paper towel under the faucet. He cleansed his neck, rubbing it again and again, but he couldn't make it feel clean.

Joe poked around in the refrigerator, pulling out a bottle of wine and a hunk of cheese. He sat down at the kitchen table, opened the bottle and slung it to his lips.

"Mom gonna be home soon?" he asked, crumbs of cheese falling to the table.

"I really don't know. She didn't say how long "

"She'll like me," he said suddenly, licking Benjamin's blood from his fingertips. "You will, too. It'll hurt some"—Joe's callous features screwed up in a curiously bemused smile—" but you'll ask for more."

Numbed and confused, Benjamin stared blankly, feeling the throbbing in his neck, in his foot where the door had struck. Then with a sudden flash of insight, he edged toward the kitchen counter, to the knife drawer.

"D-do you have kids?" he asked inanely, his fingers behind his back, reaching for the drawer pull.

Joe grinned. "Had lots of kids. Some even younger than you."

Benjamin shuddered. He curled his fingers around the handle, opened the drawer. "I mean are you married?"

Taking a long swallow of the wine, Joe stared into space, his red-rimmed eyes narrowing. "Was."

Benjamin's hand snaked into the drawer, closed around a knife handle. "Where's your wife now?"

Black marble eyes fixed on Benjamin's face. "Tried to leave me. So I beat her. Think I killed the bitch."

Looking back toward the living room, Benjamin said, "Is that my mom?" When Joe tuned away, Benjamin swept the knife from the drawer with agonizing clumsiness. He bolted across the kitchen floor, hiked the butcher knife high above his head, and stumbled at the last second, raking the blade against Joe's arm instead of plunging it into his chest. A scarlet swath of blood seeped through Joe's sleeve as Benjamin hoisted the knife again. Instinctively, Joe's free hand shot out and grabbed Benjamin's wrist. The boy gasped as he heard his wrist bones snap. The knife clattered to the floor.

With a cruel backhand that connected with the side of Benjamin's head, Joe slammed him across the room. Benjamin hit the refrigerator, his broken wrist caught between his hip and the metal door. Bright lights danced before his eyes, then everything went black.

He woke, cheek still pressed to the refrigerator door. Frantically, his gaze shot to the wall clock. Maybe fifteen minutes, surely no more. Joe was not in the kitchen, but Benjamin could hear him in the living room ransacking through drawers. Benjamin staggered to his feet, moved to the kitchen door.

"What do you want?" he rasped.

Joe spared him a glance. "Whatever I can find, Benjy. You got any drugs?"

Benjamin shook his head, trying to clear it. "Drugs?"

Joe jerked up the piano lid, scattering the pictures. "All you kids use 'em   pot, coke. Where you keep 'em?"

The room had grown dimmer; Benjamin switched on the light. Only ten minutes now, maybe five. He wasn't sure. Joe had tossed the clock onto the floor somewhere. It was definitely darker. Or was he passing out again?

"What's this?" Joe said triumphantly as he finally found the revolver. He clicked open the cylinder, then satisfied that each chamber was loaded he flicked it shut. With a grin, he looked up at Benjamin and finally saw Mom's bedroom door.

"What's in there?" he asked, moving across the floor.

Benjamin sprang forward, blocking the door. "N-nothing. Just storage."

Joe tapped Benjamin on the side of the neck with the barrel of the revolver. "For what?"

"Sheets ... towels and things. It's just a closet."

The Black Spiral: Twisted Tales of Terror

"We'll see about that," Joe said, trying the knob. When it didn't give, he raised his foot and kicked hard against the door. The reinforced doorframe groaned, but held. "What the hell?"

He backed up a few paces, slammed into the door with his shoulder, with the same result. Then at short range, he raised the handgun.

"No!" Benjamin shouted, grabbing Joe's gun hand, pulling it away. Deflected, the round splintered the doorsill. Joe kneed Benjamin in the stomach and he fell.

With one last effort, Benjamin scrabbled along the floor and braced himself against the door. Joe leveled the handgun dead on Benjamin's forehead.

"Wanted to have a little more fun with you, first," he said with a trace of regret.

Benjamin squeezed his eyes shut, scrunching himself down, back sandwiched to the door panel. The door knifed opened. Benjamin tumbled backward. The cold, comforting smell of *earth* from Mom's room poured outward.

He landed in a ball at his mother's feet.

"Benjamin?" she asked, her voice still liquid from sleep. Her long hair still hanging loose around her face, she gazed down at him. She took in his pain, then turned on the intruder, her eyes bristling with rage.

Joe must have sensed the threat because his hand swung up, firing off two rounds, pointblank into her chest.

She recoiled and staggered backwards briefly then lunged, tearing the man's arm neatly from its socket.

Joe's face contorted then constricted into something resembling a misshapen Halloween mask. He swayed, the blood rushing from his shoulder, his mouth opening and closing like a fish. Then he slumped and fell to the floor.

Mom tossed the dismembered limb on top of Joe's writhing body and turned to gently examine Benjamin's wrist. "I'll take you to the doctor," she said softly.

Benjamin nodded, his face tight with pain. "I can wait. You must be hungry."

She smiled, brushing a shock of hair from his forehead. "I am."

Benjamin studied the bright, sharp eyeteeth creasing her lower lip. "Go on, Mom. I can wait," he repeated.

The Black Spiral: Twisted Tales of Terror

    She pressed an icy kiss to his cheek, then turned, pulling Joe's shirt collar down to expose his neck. "I am so very hungry," she said.
    Her canines growing impossibly long, she lowered her mouth to feed.

The Black Spiral: Twisted Tales of Terror

YOUTH NOT WASTED

Nancy Kilpatrick

Tummy rumble. This is dicey, Reta thought.
"Stretch it and meltdown!" The aerobics goddess out-grated the ghetto blaster. Reta crushed her eyelids together and hoisted a lumpy calf. The amplifiers belched bass. Muscles hungered for deliverance.
Shake.
Pound.
Squeeze.
Chop.
Famished, Reta thought half an hour later. She elbowed past a limp twenty something stuffed into silver-blue spandex then blasted through the swinging door, nearly creaming a dishy Madonna-clone with thighs the size of Reta's humerus. Youth, she sighed. What a waste.
She crawled into the sauna and, thank God, it was empty for once. The top bench sizzled her butt. Reta forced herself to chill. Waves of heat from electrically cooked rocks pulsed toward the ceiling, microwaving her sinuses. She stripped off the corn-colored leotard, lemon wrist-and-head bands and lay back. What the hell, she thought. No pain, lotsa gain. At her age beauty was a ravenous bitch.
Before she fried, Reta treated her cellulite to a knife-point shower. She bandaged her torso in terry cloth until she resembled a turkey wrapped in cheesecloth then dragged her blow dryer and makeup bag out to the communal vanity. Only one stool was left—way at the end where the glass had spiderwebbed. The girl who'd been wearing teal spandex perched on Reta's right chatting to the sun-ripened Madonna look-alike on *her* right.
"So I bought it anyway," the one two seats away said. "But I can lose a few, ya know? Color's dynamite. Matches." She raised a tube of lipstick.
"What shade?"
"Candy Apple Red."
Meat red, Reta thought, and glanced at herself. Three hairs the color of shiny cow's brains glinted among strawberry strands and she plucked them out. The new contacts, fabulous—chestnut—contrasted

The Black Spiral: Twisted Tales of Terror

with her hair. She'd need another lash extension soon, though, and she'd better book electrolysis fast for those brows. Shit! That fat mole on her chin had just been chopped six months ago and already it was sprouting again. At least the face-lift held. Taut miracle. Evaporated laugh lines. Melted crow's feet. She caught the shadow of a double chin in a pie slice of mirror and her spirits fizzled. Time for a major overhaul.

The one two seats down giggled. She had the dark, sultry looks of the girl pictured on cans of tomato paste. Lush, pouty lips. Naturally crimson. Reta watched her outline those tomato lips in creamy Candy Apple Red. The fine brush slowly rounded the edge where firm flesh kissed the lip line.

Famished, Reta thought, and turned away.

When she had coiffed and colored, she struggled into skin-sticker cow-hide pants. It was like *they* had been shrunk by the steam instead of her flab.

She abandoned the gym by the alley exit. Night air cold enough to freeze mineral water slapped her cheeks until they burned but she refused to cover the skin. She wanted the get-it-while-you-can look.

Once on the street she avoided *The Doe-Nut Shoppe, Costa's Souvlaki Den* and *Hamburger Shangri-la*. A taxi with neon tubing whipped past: *Deep and DangerousPizza*. Reta's three-inch spike heels speared candy wrappers and fast food cartons as she hurried away.

The trendoid eatery was jammed. She cut toward the stand-up bar, on route sizing up a scrumptious dude fingering his chocolate brown tie. Reta grinned his way.

"... no chicken!" he mumbled, looking past her to scan the room.

Chicken.

Dark meat.

Famished.

The black leather crowd packed the window, undyed suede owned the opposite wall. Like the middle shelf of a refrigerator, the center of the room was crammed with a nauseating mix of goods; fruity-colored tie-dies, rough Tibetan lamb's wool and gobs of shot silk the color of uncooked rice noodles. The air reeked of sour grapes. Thank God the lighting was deco and dim but it was hot as a barbecue and she felt like a sow roasting on a spit.

She reached the bar and checked out the far end. Chubby spandex was squished into an armed bar stool, gnawing the fat with a loser in an eggplant jacket. Tomato mouth clutched the brass rail while

The Black Spiral: Twisted Tales of Terror

chocolate tie zeroed in to leave his order in her ear. The cherub's cherry tomato lips compressed into a delicious little pout. When she escaped to the can, Reta followed.

The ladies' was cramped and mildewy. It stank of urine and half digested food stuffs, but what could you do. The Mediterranean princess took one stall, the other john was occupied by somebody puking up dinner.

Reta slipped the sign from her bag—a stick figure in a skirt, encircled, red line carved through the body—and stuck it on the outside of the door over *Women*.

A toilet flushed then a pasty-faced girl staggered out and rinsed her mouth. As she exited, Reta's eyes brushed up her fashionably ripped jeans to a broccoli designer top that exposed ribs.

Ribs.

Ummmm.

Reta shoved the tangerine trashcan against the door and waited.

Her stomach churned.

She caught gaunt features in the glass.

When the Madonna replica swirled out, she seemed rattled to see Reta. The black-haired angel ran her fingertips delicately under the faucet, took the lipstick and a brush from her pigskin purse and made repairs.

"Nice color." Reta's tummy growled.

The girl's honeydew eyes skipped from the tube to Reta's stomach to Reta's face. Her expression proclaimed Reta overdone. "Thanks," she mumbled, turning back to the glass.

"Pretty enough to eat."

The tomato shriveled. Reta caught sight of her own potato-skin orbs.

Fodder.

Feeder.

FAMISHED.

Items were jammed back into the purse and the tidbit was already slicing by when Reta wrung her neck. The sweet treat dropped like a slab of mutton hitting a butcher's floor.

Poor starving *bambino*, Reta thought, meaning herself. She licked those delicious ripe beefsteak lips. Hard. Harder. Juice dribbled and gushed. She nibbled for a few seconds, then indulged.

The Black Spiral: Twisted Tales of Terror

The breast was divine. The dark meat heavenly. By the time she had devoured the rump and moist organs and was left with only bones to chomp on, Reta was ecstatic. Youth was never hard to swallow.

She tidied up, tore the sign from the door and dabbed Candy Apple Red onto her freshly washed tomato lips. Then she headed back to the bar, a new woman.

"So, how about dinner?" chocolate tie slurred in her new ear. "My place."

"Just ate."

"Dessert?" Crème de cacao breath braised her cheek. "Not too much, not too little. Tasty, know what I mean?" Through two sets of clothing, firm flesh nudged her stomach.

Digestive gas lurched from her tummy and blasted out. She managed an embarrassed grin and checked her bulging gut then his bulging pants. Yeah, she was stuffed. Even a bit was bound to show. But, what the hell. You're only young and hot and female for so long.

"Maybe just a bite." Reta licked her chops. Youth *is* irresistible, in any flavor. No sense wasting it.

GILLIAN'S EYES

Julie Novais

"You can open your eyes now, Gillian," a female voice whispered softly through a cottony fog.

I ignored her, half asleep, drifting in and out.

More sounds, muffled and distant, floated toward me. The soft clanging of metal as slick, oily wheels turned and slid across newly waxed floors. The sharp click and slap of heels, the squeak of soft-soled shoes on linoleum. Urgent static-filled voices crackled over a faulty PA system. People were shouting in hushed tones. A siren's wail was dying in the distance.

Strange scents lathered the air. The pungent, piney odor of disinfectant mingled with the rancid, once lovely aroma of my untouched dinner: congealing meatloaf, garlic mashed potatoes, cinnamon applesauce and a chocolate-fudge brownie. Hospital food.

I felt the crisp linen sheet beneath my curled fists, the taut blanket cocooned around my body, the faint breath of the heater pumping wisps of warm air across my sweat-chilled face.

"Gillian, wake up. Open your eyes." Again came the soft whisper.

I pretended to sleep, eyes shut tightly, breathing deeply.

My mind drifted to yesterday morning. I'd awoken in my own bed, in my own apartment. I'd gone about my usual morning routine. Thirty minutes of exercise followed by a hot shower with my favorite tangerine body scrub, a hurried blow dry and make-up. A quick cup of coffee, furious brushing of teeth, a few swipes of lipstick and I was ready to go.

The phone rang as I was closing the door.

"Gilly, you're still there?" I heard the familiar voice of my mother as I picked up.

"Yeah, Mom, just on my way out the door."

"I'm worried, honey. Are you okay with all this?"

The Black Spiral: Twisted Tales of Terror

"Mom, it's a routine procedure. They perform the thing every day. I've told you . . . on thousands of people. It's no big deal. Listen, I'm late. I need to go. I'll call you tonight. Okay?"

"Sure, honey. I love you. Good luck."

Why'd she say that, I wondered. Luck had nothing to do with this. I'd researched my condition and the corrective surgery, extensively. I'd selected the clinic and my physician, Doctor Millicent, with care, contacting referrals and thoroughly reviewing the history and success rate of the clinic. Still something was now bugging me, spurred by my mother's worry no doubt.

"Gillian..." The voice rang out louder, bringing me crashing back to the present.

"Yes?" I muttered, straining to break the crust sealing my eyes. Then they slowly opened, as if on rusty hinges, gluey threads of mucus connecting upper and lower lids. I blinked several times, attempting to clear my vision. Success. I saw a young nurse hovering above me, her worried frown quickly replaced with a welcoming smile.

"Great! You're awake," she said, introducing herself as Mary. "What can you see?"

My eyes took in a softly lit, tranquil hospital room with pale green walls, an empty bed beside me, and flower arrangements on a wooden credenza. Purple irises commingled with blood-red roses, bright sun-yellow marigolds and snowy babies breath. Strange, the flowers couldn't be for me, I thought. This was outpatient surgery. Scanning the room again, I took in a small window overlooking a mostly deserted parking lot, the dim twilight illuminated by sodium-vapor lights. Then my gaze panned to a tray of surgical instruments at the foot of the bed: the steely glint of sharp scalpels, tweezers of varying sizes, fluffy rolls of white gauze and small bottles of multi-hued liquids with unfamiliar labels. I tried to speak but my throat was parched and raw. It screamed for a taste of the cool water in the pitcher on my bedside table. I pointed, licking my cracked lips.

Nurse Mary held a glass to my mouth. The water spilled over my lips and trickled down the side of my face, wetting the pillow beneath me.

"How do you feel?" Mary asked.

"Not great."

"Well, let's have a look," Mary said, turning on the bedside lamp. And that's when I noticed it; the light speared my eyes with needle-sharp pain, a glassy pain that bored straight through to the back of my skull.

My hand flung to my eyes.

She flicked off the light and sat down.

"Sorry, dear. It may take a while for your eyes to adjust. You've been out a long time. We've been worried about you. I'm so glad to see you coming around," she said. "Doctor Millicent will be in to check on you soon."

I blinked, my eyes tearing slightly, grateful for the soft jaundice glow that poured through the window.

Mary rose to leave. That's when I noticed the blood. It pooled in the chair she'd just vacated. It flowered redly across the stark white backside of her uniform as she slipped through the doorway. Frantically, I turned my head. Muddy-red fingerprint smudges dotted the empty water glass, which I'd drank from moments before. A scream formed in my throat. I blinked again. The chair was now clean with an ordinary, aqua-colored plastic seat. The glass was smudge-free.

I vaulted from the bed, feet hitting the slippery floor, a dizzying wave surging through my head. I steadied myself against the bed, willing the wave to subside and staggered toward the bathroom while scanning the room for my clothes. There they were. My beige khaki's and blue sweatshirt were neatly folded on the armchair by the bed. Grabbing them as I crossed the room, I opened the door to the bathroom. When I flicked the switch, the tiny room exploded in a flash of florescent light. It was as if millions of tiny ice-carved shrapnel had blinded me. I caught my reflection through tear-glazed eyes in the mirror above the sink. A disheveled image stared back at me: messy caramel-colored hair, greasy and tangled; my pale, thin face was the color and texture of curdled milk. And my black eyes were encased in deeply bruised pockets of flesh. I did scream then, though the sound was gargled, a mere whisper. I leaned closer, staring into the eyes I no longer recognized—dark as the inky dank pool of oil accumulated on the concrete drive under my car. The whites, once clear, were now spiderwebbed red with burst capillaries, swollen and excruciating to touch as I attempted to rub the tears away.

What the hell did they do to me, I wondered, as I hurriedly struggled into my street clothes, intent on escape.

Leaving the bathroom, I found my room as empty as I'd left it. I gathered the remainder of my things, hurried toward the door. I halted as

The Black Spiral: Twisted Tales of Terror

I heard the booming voice of Dr. Millicent approaching from the hall, conversing with a soft-spoken female.

I pulled on my hospital gown and jumped back into bed, clutching the sheet close to my face. I remembered his broad mahogany face looming over me just before the surgery, the look of concern in his mud-brown eyes before he'd given me the anesthetic, his whispered assurance, "It'll be okay, Gillian. Better than before, you'll see."

I heard them approaching, his footsteps heavy, hers barely audible in the hallway outside my room. I could smell their combined scents as they entered the room—the musky darkness of Dr. Millicent, the light feathery perfume of his companion.

I closed my eyes, again pretending to sleep. I hoped they'd hurry. I hoped they'd soon leave so I could be on my way.

I felt the heat of Dr. Millicent as he stood beside the bed, leaning his face close to mine. His heavy, onion-scented breath assaulted me in puffs of scorching, acrid air that blasted across my cheeks. I nearly jumped when I felt his palm, sticky and slickly coated with sweat, press against my forehead. Meaty fingers brushed stray strands of hair from my face. Apparently satisfied that I wasn't awake, he continued his conversation.

"This is Gillian," he said. "One of the volunteers I told you about. Had a bit of a problem with her reaction to the anesthesia. It knocked her out cold; She's been unresponsive for several days. Not completely unexpected given the dosage required, but surprising, nonetheless. She was the perfect candidate for this operation ... young, active with no previous vision problems other than the nearsightedness we talked about. No known allergies to medication or previous surgeries."

"Do you think she'll make it?" the female voice asked.

"Certainly. Gillian's a fighter. She'll be one of our success stories. We haven't failed yet, have we?" He cleared his throat and paused. "We should move on to the others, though, Lydia," Dr. Millicent said quickly. "The longer term transplants. Jeremy and Carolyn. They'll be able to tell you what they've experienced, how their lives have changed. You'll be pleased." He seemed to be hurrying Lydia.

"Dr. Millicent, as you know, your continued funding for this experiment rests upon one condition. My being pleased with the results," Lydia said. " I'd like to see the others again, of course. But I was satisfied when I spoke with them the last time. They seemed to be responding to the eyes you paired them with, and were already exhibiting the anticipated reaction. They see things they'd probably never have been capable of before the surgery. They seem to have visions of things somehow imparted by the donors. I'm concerned about Gillian, though. You took a bigger risk with her, right? Who was her donor? I don't think you said."

My heart pounded in my ears as I strained to hear his response.

"Mr. *Harvey*. Remember him?"—Dr. Millicent paused a beat—"He was more of a risk, an older male with a more colorful past than the others. It will be interesting to see how Gillian responds."

"Oh yes, I remember Mr. Harvey. I also remember I was concerned whether he'd make a suitable candidate the first time his name came up. And I remember telling you as much. When will I be able to see Gillian again?"

"We'll keep her here a bit longer . . . for observation. When you're back on Friday, she'll still be here," Millicent said.

"I'll count on that," Lydia said impatiently. "Let's move on. I'll meet you in the hall."

I heard the scrape of her chair as she pushed it back, heard her voice diminishing as she excused herself to visit the restroom and left Dr. Millicent to finish up with me.

Before departing, he pressed his heavy thumb against my eyelid, raising it. When his thumb flicked on the pen-like flashlight, it blazed with white-hot light. Starbursts exploded behind my corneas. Searing pain. Blackness crowded inward, surrounding his face. Then, obliterated it entirely.

I woke to an empty room, the dull pain gone, disturbing questions replacing it.

The visit from Dr. Millicent and the woman named Lydia. A dream? Reality? Who was she? From the conversation I'd heard, I gathered she was a colleague, a contributor of funds to the clinic, someone with an interest in the procedures being performed here. But I'd come in for routine lazar surgery, to correct my nearsightedness and to remove an advancing cataract-like substance in my right eye. What was this about others and transplants? Who was Harvey? And how was he connected to me? Could this have something to do with the murky color of the eyes I'd seen staring back at me in the mirror when the eyes I knew, like my mother's, were the rich blue of a summer sky? Whatever the answer to these questions, one thing was clear to me. I needed to get out of this hospital, and now.

However, the busy sounds of the clinic in full motion during the early evening hours kept me pinned to my bed temporarily. Smarter to bide my time, wait until later, I decided, when patients would be sleeping, my escape less likely to be interrupted by those with an interest in keeping me here. So I waited.

Throughout the evening, weird visions haunted me as the prickle of pain in my eyes intensified: a rat scurrying across the hospital room floor into the hall; the crisp hospital sheets snug and cozy one moment, then transforming into a smothering fetid corpse pinning me to the bed the next. Each time, a blink of the eyes restored my vision to "normal."

I picked up the bedside phone, hoping to reach my mother. I dialed only to receive her usual cheery recorded greeting. I tried my own number, my similar sunny greeting responded.

Finally, later that night when I was sure other patients would be asleep and the hospital staff heavy-eyed and uninterested, I rose. Still clothed, I shed my gown. Grabbing my purse, I peeked into the empty corridor and raced down the hall toward the exit door, pushed and exploded into the frigid dark of the night beyond.

I scrambled across the parking lot, my eyes darting left then right.

My car was there, the key fit, the engine sparked.

As I backed out, I was startled by the molten blur of an image to my left. A woman in white—Nurse Mary. Her faced loomed, wide-eyed and panic stricken. Her fists pounded the widow. She screamed, "Gillian. Gillian, take me with you!" I dropped it into drive, cranked the wheel hard, and jammed the accelerator. At first the tires slipped, then grabbed pavement, catapulting me forward. I sped away, the vision of her tormented face slowly shrinking in my rearview mirror.

Leaving the parking lot, I stole a glance at the room I'd just left. The lights were on and an enormous black man stood silhouetted at the window, watching my escape.

As I pulled onto the narrow two-lane blacktop that would lead me home, the blinding lights of an approaching truck cut through my head, eliciting intense pain. Finally as the truck sped on, past my line of sight, the pain subsided and my vision cleared. The route, normally

The Black Spiral: Twisted Tales of Terror

beautiful in daylight—a country road meandering through miles of expansive Texas flatland populated with horse ranches—was dark and desolate at night. When I'd driven to the clinic, days before, visions of vast golden fields, the sleek, glistening coats of stallions and mares grazing, and large houses with their adjacent stables had accompanied me. But as I returned, the darkness was complete. Streetlights were nonexistent in the country, and ranchers had turned off any lights illuminating their homesteads.

I traveled in silence, focused on my goal—getting home. There was no traffic on the road at this hour, other than that initial truck. I drifted peacefully into a state of drowsy calm, miles accumulating, closer and closer to home. The rhythmic thump, thump, thump of the tires rolling over the rough road hypnotized me. As I began to veer over the raised lane dividers, their wash-board effect jerked me fully awake, forcing me to crank the wheel hard, pulling the car back into my lane. On the side of the road, a man stood with a vacant gaze, bloody and tattered, disheveled and ancient, holding out a grimy thumb. A hitchhiker. I sped on, narrowly missing him.

What was he doing here, in the middle of nowhere, trying to get a ride at this hour? Or was he another vision, not there at all? Would he have vanished immediately in the blink of an eye?

My eyes were itching now, weeping. The feeling began as a mild tickle, quickly escalating to a burning sensation, a screaming demand for attention. I wanted to scratch. God, how I needed to scratch. The fiery daggers of fresh agony my fingers sent slicing through my head when I attempted to relieve the itching, however, left me unwilling to try again.

The road stretched on, mile after mile. The drive that should have taken thirty minutes extended into endless night.

As I approached a railroad crossing, florescent red-and-white-striped wooden arms lowered, halting my progress. My eyes screamed with the assault of flashing lights. The clanging of bells and the hollow whistle of an approaching train in the distance echoed through the night. The rhythmic hum of the machine's wheels clicking across the railroad ties, combined with the idling vibrations of my car and the heat spewing from the floor vents, lulled me toward sleep. The blast of the air horn as the train passed wrenched me back.

Directly in front of me stood a young boy, dressed in soiled clothes, no bigger than my ten-year-old nephew, David. His face was grimy and wore a weary smile, despite the look of sadness and fear and

The Black Spiral: Twisted Tales of Terror

despair in his eyes. He lifted his small hand and waved, then started toward the passenger side of my car. Only after releasing the lock and leaning across to open the door, did I pause to wonder if this was such a good idea. Letting a stranger, no matter how small, into my car on a dark, deserted road, late at night was something I would normally never have considered doing. However, the child's disheveled appearance, his resemblance to David, and the sight of him alone, huddled against the cold, tore at my heart. I couldn't leave him here on his own. My ache and desire to reach my own home suddenly seemed less urgent than helping this small boy.

As he slid onto the seat next to me, the pungent aroma of ripe, freshly laid sod filled the car. Stifling the urge to gag, I faced the boy, attempting a smile.

But it was David who smiled back. That same blue-black shock of hair fell over his forehead and into his eyes. Those same eyes, startling green. David's eyes. His cheeks were flushed, chapped from the cold Texas night, streaked with what I had initially thought was dirt but which now more closely resembled the muddy crust of dried blood. He was crying, tears washing clean, vivid streaks through the rust-colored terrain of his cheeks. Dressed in torn jeans, a fraying gray sweatshirt with no coat despite the frigid cold of the night outside, he leaned toward the heat pulsing from the floor before him and rubbed his small hands together.

"D-David?" I asked.

"No, Ma'am, my name's Jake," he responded in a timid whisper. "What's yours?"

"Gillian. You can call me Gilly, though, everyone does. What're you doing out here, all alone at night?"

"I don't rightly know, Ma'am. I been wanderin' around for a while, can't seem to find my way home." He withdrew his warmed hands from the heat and wrapped them tightly around his body.

I asked if he knew his address, a number to call. He didn't. He expressed vague recollections of a house at 33 Farmer's Lane, his grandparents' home. They had no telephone, he told me, since his grandparents were old fashioned and had never seen the need to have one installed.

"I think I can find the turnoff, though, if we drive a bit," he said. "It's just ahead. I know it is."

The Black Spiral: Twisted Tales of Terror

The train passed, the wooden arms lifted. Wanting nothing more than to speed home, but now burdened with the responsibility of the boy and the challenge of finding his home, I accelerated slowly, allowing him to lead the way.

A dark stretch of road extended before us. No turnoffs in sight. I drove, searching for the next exit.

"Jake, how'd you end up out here?" I asked.

"My brother, Billy, and me had a fight over whose turn it was to muck the horse stalls. He said it was mine but I know I did it last. He didn't believe me, said he'd tell Granny. Said he'd make me do it. He pushed me, hard. He does that sometimes. He's older, thirteen. I fell and hit my head on the barn floor. It hurt bad and I cried. Then he laughed at me, called me a baby. He does that a lot. Said he'd hit me again if I didn't stop crying. I couldn't stop, it hurt too bad. I got up and ran to one of the empty stalls in the back of the barn. To get away from him." His eyes cast downward briefly then rose, staring into space. " I just kept running, as far I as I could get. Later, once I stopped, I got scared and all I wanted to do was get back home, but I couldn't remember the way. I met a man. He said he'd help me."

"Met a man? Where?" I asked.

"He was at the road. I'd run all the way there. He was trying to hitch a ride somewhere. He was old, really old, and really nice. His name was William. Looked kind of familiar. Said he'd help me get home, or try anyway. But he had his own problems. William was blind and I think he was lost, too."

"Where's he now?"

"Don't know. We were together for a while. Told me he'd take me with him when he got a ride, have the driver take me home first. I went into the bushes by the road to go pee while he stayed out by the road. When I came back, he was gone. I never saw no lights, didn't hear no car come but he must've got a lift, must've forgot about me. I looked and looked and couldn't find him. I sure hope he got home. He was real sad, said his wife would be missing him and worrying something awful."

The elderly hitchhiker I'd passed a while back flashed through my mind. Had he been the same man? Had to be. But, if so, he'd not been picked up and delivered safely home as the child wanted to believe. He was miles behind us, still searching for a ride, apparently further away from his intended destination than he'd been when he was with Jake.

The Black Spiral: Twisted Tales of Terror

Because I chose not to tell the boy that I thought I'd seen his companion, and because I didn't want to crush his hope that the man had reached his destination, I asked if he recognized anything, if he thought we were nearing his turnoff. He assured me we were close, that it must be around the next bend.

We traveled several more miles and still we passed no exit roads, no signs indicating upcoming crossroads. I hit the button on my watch, illuminating the face, checking the time: 1:30 AM. A quick trip home that should have taken half an hour, maybe forty-five minutes with the delay of the train crossing, had extended to close to an hour.

My eyes began to tear again, clouding my vision. They left salty wet snail-trails as they ran down my face, accumulating and dripping from my chin. The pain had subsided to a dull background chorus, humming in the dark, awaiting a bright flash of light to bring it back to a piercing, operatic crescendo.

"Gilly, look," Jake shouted, pointing out the windshield to the right. "It's my road, up ahead."

My headlights washed over a narrow dirt lane, one I'd never noticed before. No street signs identified the unpaved, narrow path that appeared hardly big enough for my car.

"Are you sure, Jake," I asked, not at all sure I wanted to venture down this desolate road.

He assured me this was it. I reluctantly turned off the main road, and started the slow creep through brush. Overgrown tree limbs pressed and scraped at the sides of my car as I edged the vehicle forward. After several cautious miles, I saw the bulk of a large farmhouse emerge from behind dense foliage. A two-story clapboard dwelling with a weathered wooden frame. Cracked and scaled over with peeling paint. Moonlight haloed its edges as if captured by its faded yellow skin. The house was dark and the surrounding grounds were choked with weeds. I'd expected this. What I hadn't expected was a complete lack of any sign of life: an empty driveway, an open garage scattered with parts of old automobiles, trash and discarded broken furniture piled high on the porch. Broken windows stared outward as I cut off the engine and turned to face Jake.

"Honey, are you sure this is it? It doesn't look like anyone's home, that anyone's been here in a while," I said.

"I'm sure, Gilly. It looks different, but I'm sure this is our house. Come on, Granny'll be inside waiting, I know she will."

The Black Spiral: Twisted Tales of Terror

We left the warmth of the car, quickly covering the short distance to the porch, stooping against the cold wind that buffeted our faces, dried my eyes, and lifted our hair. As we climbed the porch steps, our weight encouraged splintery creaks and groans from the parched wooden slats. Arriving at the front door, I pressed the doorbell, heard no sound from within. I rapped on the door, the hollow wooden knock sending echoes of pain through my arm, up to my eyes. No response. I tried the doorknob. The door was unlocked.

Pushing forward, Jake and I proceeded into a small living room. The musty scent of moldering cloth, rotting wood, and the ripe odor of fresh animal droppings greeted us. I heard the faint, scurrying sounds of rodents fleeing the surprise of our entry. I felt for a light switch, pushed the nub on the wall, to no avail. The dim light of a full moon strained through the age-warped windowpanes and revealed the shadowed outlines of furniture as the vague shapes of cobwebs stretched above us.

I rummaged in my purse for a flashlight. As its bright beam sprayed across the room, it confirmed what I'd feared. The house looked to have been deserted long ago, occupied now only by rats and squirrels. Dark, furry, green flowers of mildew spread over the fading pink of the peeling wallpaper, faded red velvet curtains dripped off the rails in decaying strands, couches and armchairs were covered with ripped fabric, their innards exposed and exploding onto the floor. And the hardwood floorboards were marred with deep scratches and puddles of dark liquid and festering stains.

I heard Jake gasp beside me.

"It didn't look this way when I left this morning," he cried. "It was pretty. Granny loves this room. She takes care of it. The sofas ain't ripped, the curtains ain't falling, the walls ain't moldy—they're covered with flowers. The room smells like Granny. Always. Like her perfume—flowers and spice."

I couldn't believe this house could have been all that different just this morning. The room wore the signs of years of decay and neglect, like an old spinster pining her lost youth. How could Jake have been here just this morning?

My eyes were throbbing, aggravated by the beam of the flashlight and the burning sting of the stench–lathered musty air.

"Jake, I don't know what's going on here but let's sit down, talk for a while, think a bit. My head's hurting, my eyes, too. Okay?" I asked, leading him over to a small couch in the corner of the room that looked to be mostly intact. A small oil lamp, salvaged from one of the end tables appeared to be undamaged. I lit it, filling the room with a faint yellowish glow. I wanted to see Jake, despite the pain the glare would undoubtedly cause my eyes. There was a desk calendar on the table beside us. I glanced at the date—November 30, 1955—almost fifty years ago.

When he faced me, he was David again, a small and scared-looking boy, one I wanted to hug and protect, to save from what was to come, what had already happened.

"Sure, we can sit," he said. "But, Gilly . . . what's wrong with your eyes?"

"What do you mean?"

"They look weird ... all dark and puffy ... red and watery. Were you in an accident?"

"No, Jake," I said, my voice croaking slightly. "I had an eye operation a couple of days ago. It was supposed to be no big deal, but there were problems and they're hurting me pretty bad right now. I was on my way home from the clinic when I picked you up. They look pretty bad, don't they?" I stole a glance at him.

"Yeah, like they hurt a lot. Plus they're moving all over the place," he said, turning from me to stare again at the devastated room.

They were, in fact, moving, darting around in their sockets, something I'd never experienced before. Back and forth, up and down, my vision swam in and out of focus as my eyes skittered. Next they bombarded me with a rapid procession of flickering images, like a montage of old and new movie clips spliced together into a continuing reel of seemingly unrelated events, which together—suddenly made sense . . . .

A teenager prodding the body of a small boy I recognized as **Jake** *into an empty horse stall, covering the body with loose straw, then turning to run away. The teenager,* **Billy,** *screaming, "An accident, an accident, I didn't mean to kill him," as he ran, sobbing, to a place far from the farmhouse he'd shared with Jake and his grandparents.*

Billy *again, an old man now, so they call him* **William Harvey,** *enters a tiny brick house, greeted at the door by an elderly, overweight woman. William, silently pouring whisky into a glass tumbler as the woman talks nonstop. William—emptying crushed sleeping tablets into the woman's coffee when her back is turned, later bludgeoning her with a baseball bat while she sleeps. William—standing over the bloody* *corpse of the old woman as he raises his drink, thinks of his murdered brother, his murdered wife, and downs the liquid gold in a gulp, washing a mouthful of tablets down his throat. Lying beside the bloody corpse of his wife, fatal slumber approaching, William cries, hugs the bludgeoned body beside him and closes his eyes for the last time.*

My eyes fluttered as more visions flickered on the screen of my eyelids.

*A pretty woman in white, Mary, in her nurse's uniform, rummaging in a laboratory, pushing aside clear glass jars filled with opaque liquid the thickness of molasses, suspending gelatin orbs of varying colors. Eyes. Labels affixed to the jars, with names proceeded by the word "***Transferor.***" Mary, shuffles through a metal file cabinet, apparently searching for something. Mary, lifting a folder labeled Gillian Andrews, opening it, scanning a sheet entitled "***History of Transferor.***" The name, "***WILLIAM HARVEY***" typed precisely at the top. Then someone, a looming familiar figure—Dr. Millicent, interrupts her. Mary—scattering papers, knocking jars to the floor, turning to run, to flee his wrath and the punishment she is sure to receive. Mary—screaming as she's thrown to the ground, as she's beaten and raped, as she is pummeled into the world of eternal silence by a furious Dr. Millicent, as hundreds of pairs of suspended eyes watch, William Harvey's among them.*

The visions continued.

A young woman I recognize as myself lying on an operating room table. Drugged, asleep. Dr. Millicent approaching, joking with his comrades. He's lifting my eyelids, wrenching my eyes from their sockets. He deposits them in gelatinous fluid, while a nurse hands him their replacements from a jar labeled **William Harvey.** *They are giving his eyes to me—the eyes of a murderer. I see my body convulsing, rejecting the unwelcome intrusion, see my spirit lifting, beginning to move on as Dr. Millicent and his staff fight to bring me back.*

Suddenly, I knew what was happening . . . I was seeing the world through William Harvey's guilt-ridden eyes.

And I was dead.

I knew that Jake and I were on a journey; not to the homes we'd come from, as we knew them, but instead to our ultimate home, the home we'd share with those we'd loved and who would love us for all eternity. I knew now that fate had ordained for me to pick up Jake and leave his brother, the hitchhiker, William Harvey, to walk the night for eternity, until he reached his final stop—Hell.

I thought about Dr. Millicent and the crimes that he'd committed against me, against Mary and perhaps many others. Rage consumed me. I wanted to return to the clinic, wanted to stop him from hurting anyone else, but ultimately I knew that his punishment would be decided at a later time, by someone far superior and less personally involved than I was. This comforted me, the sudden understanding that eventually he would receive the maximum penalty, be sentenced to an infinite walk through time without end as another wandering— hitchhiker.

And most of all, I knew we'd not be traveling alone, knew with certainty that there was at least one additional lost soul waiting somewhere out on the road, waiting for us to find her, to rescue her and to take her with us to our final *destination.*

I stood, gently pulling the boy up beside me, leading him from the house, down the steps to my car. He smiled up at me through tear-washed eyes and I hugged him close.

"Let's go, Jake. Mary's waiting. Once we find her, we're going home."

WOMAN-CHILD

Richard D. Weber

Phoebe couldn't sleep. She was too excited, too lovesick, and on a deeper subconscious level—too frightened. Her mind was haunted by phantasms that shifted about like smoke, searching for a way to escape into the open air.

And if they had escaped it would have been the certainty of defilement that terrified her, more than the night visitor himself, more than his disembodied voice, more than his lustful need.

Sally, her Afro-Cuban nanny, had peeked into her bedroom on the hour like clockwork. Now she stood at Phoebe's bedroom door frowning. She shook an admonishing finger, finally relenting with a dimpled smile.

"Princesa Phoebe, it's past midnight. Young lady needs beauty sleep, or you turn into wrinkled old prune like Ms. Sally."

Princesa Phoebe was her nickname, Sally's endearment for her seventeen-year-old charge. Tall, lissome, strikingly beautiful, Phoebe Snow possessed a feminine grace that seemed far beyond her tender age. A wave of auburn hair—pure to the roots—fell back past the line of her tanned shoulders, framing a face of exquisite features. The shape of her mouth was clearly defined, a sensual mouth until she smiled, restoring childhood and innocence.

Phoebe marked her spot in the paperback romance novel she was reading with her finger and met Sally's eyes. "Just another twenty minutes, please? I promise. Besides, tomorrow's Tuesday."

"So? Tuesday not holiday, girl!"

"But it is. It's my birthday."

"Birthday?"

Rolling her big liquid brown eyes like a typical teenage girl, she said, "Like I'm sure you forgot, you sly old nanny goat. Let's see your game, lady."

Sally was a large Marge. She smiled wide and gestured toward her huge bosom with a cocked thumb. "You want a piece of me, girl?"

Before Phoebe could answer, Sally bounded into the room with surprising speed and agility, grabbed a stuffed clown from the chair, and threw a jump shot into Phoebe's outstretched arms, which now formed a makeshift basketball hoop.

"Pretty fast moves for old nanny goat, ehh? Sally teach Michael Jordan all his best game, you know."

The sight of her dribbling an imaginary basketball about the bedroom, her circus-tent-size muumuu swishing around her piano legs, was enough to make a televangelist come-to-Jesus. Maybe even swear off hookers, gay bashing, and popcorn-tub-sized collection plates. At least that's what Papa had said the last time he saw Sally's pendulous, doughy underarms swaying as she beat the pancake batter for their traditional Sunday morning breakfast.

Phoebe doubled over with laughter. She had spent more quality—and quantity time with her nanny than her mother or father, the Ambassador. Even tonight, the eve of her birthday, they were out of town. She loved Sally. Sally had become her surrogate mother.

Pulling herself upright and catching her breath, Sally wheezed, "Young girls. Same all over. Think of nothing but boys, boys, boys. You crazy for boys, Phoebe. Nanny can read your mind, you know. Okay, read your trashy love book, but no more 'please, Sally' tonight. Understand?"

Phoebe winked and threw herself back on the bed, tossing the book into the air as Sally closed the bedroom door. She turned off the bedside lamp and lay thinking of young Mr. Jeffrey Dagon her senior classmate at the exclusive St. Martin's prep school in Bethesda, MD. Yes, she could see him, crystal-blue-persuasion eyes, flaxen blond hair and a perfect smile. Brad Pitt in miniature.

In the darkness a sound crept to her ears.

A hissing. Then a vague rustling of fabric.

Phoebe sat up in bed. Squinted into the surrounding darkness, saw nothing, cocked her head, and listened.

Where was it coming from? She strained to hear, her breath tightening in her chest. Phoebe felt the first pinprick of fear.

Then it came again. A tiny sigh.

From beneath the bed.

She groped blindly for the flashlight she kept nestled in her bookshelf headboard. Found it and eased toward the edge of her bed.

Probably just the cat, she thought.

"Mr. Muffins?" she called out.

Silence.

The Black Spiral: Twisted Tales of Terror

    A scraping noise, followed by soft mewling, disturbed the stillness.
    The uncanny feeling that the thing under the bed sensed her awareness washed over her.
    "No. That's just silly."
    Phoebe swooped over the side of the bed, flashlight in hand and hung upside down. Blood rushed to her head. When she flicked the switch, the narrow beam of the flashlight blazed to life, arcing through murky shadow, spraying across dust bunnies and one old grass-stained tennis shoe.
    She laughed, picturing how foolish she'd look if one of the girls from school saw her like this.
    Pulling herself upright and plopping against her pillow, she puffed out her cheeks and sighed.
    Something brushed against her arm. Quick and furtive.
    She jolted and the flashlight flew from her hand, tumbling end-over-end and clattering to the floor. It spun like a revolving pointer in a board game, casting luminous spirals over the polished hardwood flooring. As the spinning flashlight slowed to a stop, its beam fell upon a tiny figure. A brief flash of eyeshine. The glint of fangs. And it was gone. It darted away, catlike.
    "Damn, cat!"
    Then she remembered: Mr. Muffins was at the Vet.
    More sounds. Like the scampering of tiny feet moving away from her and across the room.
    "All right. I've had it . . . knock it off!"
    She reached for the switch on her bedside lamp. Couldn't find it. Fumbled. Finally her fingers found the lamp base, then the knob.
    The room pooled with a fragile light. Warm and welcoming.
    She panned the room, but nothing moved. Shadows were only shadows. Searching again, her eyes fell upon the rocking chair in the corner. Eyes fixed, a slightly sardonic grin creasing his face, sat Capt. Wiggly. The clown. Bedecked in a black-and-white satin costume. A mop of bright red hair flamed from beneath his tasseled cap.
    Phoebe chuckled to herself.
    "Shame on you, Capt. Wiggly. Scaring a poor girl like that." Swinging her lithe tanned legs from the bed, she scampered across the room and stood before the clown. "How'd you get over here?"

The Black Spiral: Twisted Tales of Terror

The door creaked behind her. She spun toward the sound. There in the doorway stood Sally. Her hair snarled in a tangle of rollers. Face smothered in cold cream. Clutching something furry in her large hand.

"You lose something, Princesa?" Sally asked.

Phoebe shook her head. "Ozzy, you little devil, you!" She took her pet ferret in her arms, snuggled him, and scurried across the room where she placed him gently back in his cage.

Sally laughed. "I think Ozzy's been lookn' for Sharon again. He was prowling around my room."

Phoebe bit her lower lip and avoided Sally's eyes.

"I guess we shoulda' left them together, but they make so much noise during the night."

"Then tomorrow night they can make all the racket they want. I'm putting them both in the kitchen."

"But—"

"No buts, girl. Sally has spoken. And who's Sally?"

In as deep a baritone voice as Phoebe could muster she said, "She who must be obeyed."

"And don't you forget it." Having gotten in the last word, Sally whirled about and was gone.

Phoebe snatched the clown from its roost, pounced into bed, and lay on her back, holding Capt. Wiggly at arm's length. She lowered him to her pouting lips and placed a quick peck on his cheek.

"Some gentlemen you are, Jeffery Dagon. Giving me such a rascal." She giggled and stroked the clown's forehead, caressing him with her fingertips.

As she stared into those lifeless eyes, she was transported back to the summer carnival. It had been two weeks ago. Their first date. It was evening and a sickle moon ornamented the night. Cicadas droned in the trees. When they crested the hill walking from the parking area, the carnival appeared to rise from the sea of sawdust like a mirage. Twinkling lights and the sound of a calliope beckoned. As they were strolling arm and arm down the midway, the scent of fresh-made candied apples, corn dogs, and the musky odor of circus animals drifted through the throng.

"Come one, come all. Mr. Dollar's ring toss. Every throw a winner," barked a carny as they passed.

Phoebe shook her head.

"Win that lil' girl a prize, says Mr. Dollar to the scholar."

The Black Spiral: Twisted Tales of Terror

Jeffery bit the hook and dragged her toward the booth.

A toad-faced carnival barker with hooded eyes and a slightly green-tinged complexion stood waiting. A cigar saluted from the corner of his mouth.

"How much?" Jeffery asked.

"The price, a mere five dollars. Three rings for *repeat* customers, every throw a winner," he said, his mouth leaking smoke.

Jeffery plunged his hand into his pocket and pulled out a crisp bank note.

Mr. Dollar plucked the five-dollar bill from Jeffery's hand with the speed of a sticky-tongued bullfrog snatching bottle flies in mid-flight. As he pressed the plastic rings into the boy's hand, he drew a flask from his vest pocket and took a hard pull. But just as Jeffery clasped the rings, the carny's gnarled, liver-spotted hand clamped down hard around his wrist. Phoebe remembered how his face tightened, as he winced with pain.

"Hold on there, boy," he half-whispered, half-gurgled in a raspy phlegm-filled voice.

Jeffery turned ashen-white. He swallowed audibly.

The barker leaned across, pressing his vein-marbled bulbous nose to within inches of Phoebe's face. Rancid breath, reeking like a fish market, poured over her. He spat out his cigar. His pockmarked cheek puffed out as his tongue pressed against the inside of his mouth. Then his tongue slowly emerged from the corner of his mouth, crawling along his weathered lips like a black slug across a rotting leaf.

Phoebe shuddered. With his free hand, the barker reached out. At first her eyes locked on his dirt-encrusted fingernails as his hand drew closer and closer. She cringed. But then she noticed the whole hand. It was webbed, the fingers woven tight—deformed. Ever so gently, the slightly scale-encrusted fingers stroked her auburn hair, pooling it behind her ear.

Phoebe's eyes pleaded with Jeffery. He responded. His body stiffened as his face became a blotched rictus of unbridled rage. Twisting his wrist hard and lashing out cobra-quick, he took the barker by surprise, driving a roundhouse punch to the man's temple. Mr. Dollar teetered backward, off balance and fell to the ground with what Phoebe could only describe as a liquid thud. At this moment Phoebe didn't know who she feared more, the old lecherous sonofabitch—Mr. Dollar or Jeffery. Although she admired his quick action, his defense of her honor, and although she found this new "bad boy" side of him quite seductive, she was frightened.

Seemingly sensing her confusion, Jeffery gripped her firmly about the waist, pressed her firm but ample breasts to his chest and kissed her hard. That's all it took. *And besides,* she thought, *the little toad deserved it.*

Mr. Dollar rose, dusting the dirt from his overalls.

On pudding legs, he walked to the prize rack, reached high with a long pole, and snaked down a clown. He slapped the five-dollar bill into Jeffery's hand and said, "No charge there, young fella. No harm, no foul, ehh?" Rubbing his temple briefly, he winced and turned to Phoebe.

"Now, lil' lady, here's a very special prize just for you." Phoebe took an involuntary step back.

"Nah, now go on an take it. A peace offering." He shook an admonishing finger. "As Mr. Dollar says, a winner every time."

Phoebe turned to Jeffery. He shrugged.

She studied the clown. "Well . . . he's kinda cute." Her eyes brightened. "Does he have a name?"

Mr. Dollar and Jeffery exchanged side-glances.

A wide gap-toothed grin creased Mr. Dollar's face. "Yes, indeed he has. Call 'em . . . Capt. Wiggly."

She reached out and took the clown.

They walked on. Past the swaybacked ponies plodding in a lazy circle. Past freckle-faced boys racing and roughhousing their way through the crowd while firmly gripping tuffs of cotton candy in their outstretched hands. Beneath a string of overhead bulbs they had kissed again. Longer. Deeper. Harder.

Now, as she lay in bed, her button-down nightshirt riding high on her firm thighs, her legs propped up, she gave Capt. Wiggly a horsy-back ride. "Ride a cock horse to Mulberry bush . . . ride a cock horse on . . ." she sang.

With each bounce of her knees, the inseam of the little clown's pants bulged slightly at the crotch.

She yawned and reached over, extinguishing the light.

"Good night, Capt. Wiggly. And my sweet, Jeffery Dagon."

As she began to drift into sleep, tendrils of cloud vapor glided across the full moon framed by her windowpane. A lone nighthawk screeched somewhere in the darkness.

The Black Spiral: Twisted Tales of Terror

Phoebe pulled her legs into the fetal position, snuggling the clown firmly between her thighs.

Concealed by the cloak of darkness, Capt. Wiggly smiled like the serpent in the Garden of Eden. His form shape-shifted, elongating, stretching, rippling beneath the covers.

Black. Everywhere black.

A black ceiling overhead. Recessed lighting dimly pooling on the black marble floor below. Cool black satin sheets on the bed beneath him. Black window drapes.

All four walls were an ocean of mirrored glass. A myriad of reflected images encircled him, leering back with their cold winter gaze. Reflecting the image of his naked form as he lay upon the silken, sable waters. Arms tucked behind his head—thinking. Becoming.

He closed his eyes.

Concentrate.

Become.

He'd visited her and others before her many times. But tonight would be different. In the past he'd lost control, leaving nothing but the inert, battered bodies of his midnight work ... his playthings. However, his skill was increasing, growing, gaining in strength and power.

Becoming.

It was the word he chose to describe the physical, emotional, and mental transformation that was taking place within him.

But traveling on the astral plane or "Visiting," as he preferred to call it was difficult and dangerous. He'd learned that lesson the hard way and now had adopted one cardinal rule. Never wander aimlessly. Choose a specific destination, a subject. Meditate long and hard before hand.

Concentrate.

Become.

In his mind's eye he pictured a ball of thread hovering just over his solar plexus. Glowing, throbbing, pulsating with energy. Gently he would begin to unravel the golden thread. As it floated higher and higher, uncoiling, he attached the imprint of his other self, his doppelganger to it.

But hitching a ride into the ether could be just as dangerous as hitching a ride down some deserted two-lane blacktop; never knowing what demented crazed lunatic would come crawling down the highway, shielded by the harsh glare of headlights. And on the other side there were plenty of Hannibals. He thought he could imagine the horrors of Hell and its denizens. Father Kennedy had described them in detail in school, drummed them into his head. But one glimpse of these swarming demons and elementals would have sent the good Father into the abyss of madness, never to return.

    Eyes. Thousands of eyes. Groping hands, groping tendrils that clawed and tore at your spirit as you floated onward. No. Crossing the abyss required study, patience. Courage. He studied long and hard. His father had taught him well. And yet, sometimes he feared. At first he mentally painted a talisman on his chest. The magical Trident of his ancestors—the Dagon. However, he soon learned that these beings could not harm him. He learned to ignore their wailing cries, their seductive siren's song. Their offers of power, of friendship. Yes, sometimes he still feared, because if you weakened or succumbed to their flattery, invited them in or lost control, they might hitch a ride down the golden thread and into your sleeping body. And they'd never leave willingly. They made loud obnoxious dinner guests who feasted on your soul.

    The darkness whispered to him.

    Beginning with his feet, he moved progressively up his body, tensing and releasing his muscles as he focused; to his legs, tensing and releasing; to his chest . . .

    The darkness soothed him.

    Tensing and releasing.

    He was becoming.

    And tonight he would take his bride.

    Phoebe slept fitfully, tossing and turning, drifting in and out. Somehow she sensed her dream ghost was coming. She used to welcome him with open arms but no more. Now he frightened her.

    And somehow she knew tonight would be different. A rite of passage. Phoebe often sensed things; saw things that no one else seemed to see. She knew she was different. But it had been this way as long as she could remember. It only scared her sometimes. And tonight, even in her sleep, was one of those times. Tonight—like many nights before—a reoccurring nightmare began to unfold, groping through a moist seedbed of pubescent urges and fancy.

    She moaned.

The Black Spiral: Twisted Tales of Terror

Her thighs pressed tighter.
Squeezed.

His intent was formed. Crystal clear. His spirit rose higher and higher. Drawn upward by the swift-pulling flue of the moon goddess herself—Phoebe. Also known as Diana.

Airborne now, he soared over rooftops, cityscapes, and woodlands. Rushing past the perched owl, the howling wolf; airborne like cold silk brushing against the cheeks of clouds and heroes and gods frozen in the constellations. Higher and higher he rose, swooping over the outstretched hands of lost souls and black-hearted necromancers. Over leaping flames and capering demons that resembled quivering masses of raw liver.

He inhaled deeply. Filling his center with her scent.

Dead on target like an enormous bird of prey, wings back, using the force of gravity like a slingshot, he dove toward her as she lay asleep in her bed.

He studied her.

She was so beautiful there in the dark, on the bed, alone and unaware of how soon she would be his. A sliver of moonlight spilled across her flesh. When it met her body it become golden, and her porcelain skin seemed faintly luminous, as though she pulsated with an inner fire.

A woman-child.

She lay on her back, her chest rising and falling in silken-smooth rhythm. The sloping curve of her breast and the dark pigment of her areola peeked out from beneath her unbuttoned nightshirt taunting him. Bewitching him. Sleeping beauty waiting to be awakened by the kiss of a prince.

He became aroused.
Pulsating. Hard.
Insatiable.

Phoebe, goddess of the moon, he whispered.

She rolled onto her stomach, clutching Capt. Wiggly to her breast. She moaned in dreamless sleep.

Phoebe!

No reaction.
He seethed with anger.
Rage coursed through his veins.

The Black Spiral: Twisted Tales of Terror

If she sensed his presence she showed no signs. Didn't seem to care.
Stop it! I need you.
Still no reaction, only a gentle sigh. Anger welled within him and exploded in a burst. *You damn whore! I'll give you something to dream about.*
Then Capt. Wiggly convulsed as though stuck with an electric cattle prod. He stretched. His scales glistening in the ambient moonlight, he began to uncoil and slowly slither over her neck, down her back, gliding lower and lower.

Phoebe murmured peevishly and stirred, pawing at the rumpled sheet with her slender sun-bronzed foot, all fathom-deep dreaming now. She was too young, too innocent to realize that she could break anyone's heart.
Dreamscapes: her dreams becoming hot and swift, a phantasmagoric amalgam of flight and pursuit.

A mad carnival, a midway of catastrophe, pulsed and blazed, burning images of terror onto the retina of her mind's eye. Spinning Ferris wheels of white-blue lights spewed silver sparks. Spinning round and round. Faster and faster. Blurring now into a stroboscopic afterimage that coalesced with the blackness. A boy dressed in a bright-colored clown costume sits before a gigantic calliope, playing a dissonant circus melody.

Baa Bup Buppa Buppa BaBa Buppa

Out of the darkness, floodlights ignite. Illuminating a bannerline that thrashes in the wind. And it reads:
Colonel Tod Browning's Traveling Sideshow!
Circus of Scars!
A spotlight tracks The Tall Man, the impresario of the strange, the unusual, FREE-AKKS, the bizarre, as he seems to float across the stage. Dressed in a black suit with white shirt and bola tie, his shoulder-length blondish-white hair frames his death-mask face. He gazes sightlessly from cataract-filled eyes. His long arm extends outward from his gaunt and stoop-shouldered body. In his hand, he clutches a glass eyeball. It stares un-blinking.

The Black Spiral: Twisted Tales of Terror

"Gaze into the hypnotic eye, lil' lady. Inside my dear, it's all inside."

A tent appears behind him. He opens the flap and beckons with his long tapered finger.

Phoebe tossed and turned. She kicked and struggled. A long golden thread began to rise from her navel, twisting higher and higher. Simultaneously, something cold and wet was slithering against her inner thigh. Exploring.

She floats through the opening in the canvas.
The Tall Man is at her side. "What'll it be first, lil' lady?"
As she stares into his face it morphs, transforming into the face of Mr. Dollar. But now his eyes are bulging and enormous with a vaguely oily sheen, and he, too, stares fish-eyed, raping her with his gaze. His face is scaled over. Long tendrils whip from his walrus-like face. He glides across the floor on a slithering mass of octopus-like legs, leaving a wet trail as he moves.
He intones with a slurping sound and says, "Hurry along now. We can't be late for the show!"
A star field bursts on the screen of Phoebe's eyelids.
The Tall Man reappears.
"Idiot, fool. He doesn't know a thing.
"Lots of cleavage. Lots of chairs.
"Plenty of time. Plenty of time."
Haunting Middle-Eastern music drifts towards her. A crowd of Boy Scouts sits before a stage; cheering and caterwauling, as a troupe of belly dancers perform. The dancers' pheromones drift through the air like hot, sultry smoke.
Rolls upon rolls ripple in undulating waves up and down their obese stomachs. Rivers of stretch marks and craters of cellulite adorn their bodies. Their eyes are lined with crow's feet, their hair thin and graying. They cackle from between blackened lips and toothless grins.
The Tall Man hurtles Phoebe into the crowd where the lusting scouts propel her towards the stage like a crowd at a rock concert.
Young fingers grope and maul her, ripping at her nightshirt as she moves over the wave of hands.

Darkness surrounded him.

The Black Spiral: Twisted Tales of Terror

He lay immobile on the bed.

His nude body glistened with the sheen of perspiration. Sweat rolled off his body, drenching the satin sheets. He shifted his attention to his groin. What was once flaccid grew hard. White-heat tingled in blood-engorged tissue.

His lungs bellowed in deep, ragged breaths.

His pulse quickened with anticipation. **Need.**

He studied her. So lovely. So young and firm. So lovely in her terror.

A faux flute sounds.
She's transported.
Phoebe stands cold and shivering upon a mountaintop. A wind gust tears across her cheek and flames her auburn hair. Gooseflesh stipples her forearms and legs. The air is so thin and razor-edged it seems to score her lungs as she struggles to breathe.

In the distance, she sees the gaping maw of a cave. It throbs with glimmering pulses of light. As she stumbles forward barefoot and frightened over uneven ground, jagged rocks lash the soles of her feet.

The cave beckons.

She stands at the mouth of the cave. A bright purple haze pours over her. She enters, her eyes panning right then left. The walls gleam as if wet. They undulate with a barely detectible rhythm. Breathing.

As her true self lay snuggled a tangle of sheets, his Peeping Tom apparition took in the exquisite concavities and convexities of her young ripe body. A tiny river of saliva flowed from the corner of her mouth as she gave an involuntary kick with one long mocha-colored leg. He focused his consciousness into the shape-shifting clown, husking himself within it. Phoebe's sweat-chilled body convulsed as he slowly coiled around her supple thigh.

A firefly appears from nowhere, hovering inches from her face. Studying it, she notices its luminous abdomen, each blazing segment. Another lands in her hair. In tandem the tiny wings of a third breezes past her cheek. Another scrambles into her ear. She claws, catching it in the palm of her hand. A faint purple-tinted light leaks from between the fingers of her fisted hand. It grows in intensity until bright rays fan

The Black Spiral: Twisted Tales of Terror

out. It tickles, tingly and pleasant at first with a slight burning sensation—then glassy pain. She squeezes her hand tight, crushing it.

Like a thundering colony of bats, fireflies shoot from the walls of the cave, congealing into a dark mass that swarms over her.

In the black room he squirmed on the mattress; his heels drummed the sheets. Pain speared through his head, through his groin. His manhood became flaccid.

He battled with his childlike alter ego for control.

Concentrate.

He shuddered.

Bitch-child.

No! Focus. Become.

But he could smell her fear, bathe in it.

So lovely in her fear.

Ignore me, laugh at me will you!

His neck corded. Veins bulged at his temples, swelled on his forearms as his hands fisted at his sides.

You're all nice enough at first, aren't you? Then you snicker behind my back, compare notes about me with the other girls at sleep-overs, about my problem, my impotency. Buzz and gossip like a bunch of fuckin' bees.

His head snapped to one side—

NO! Focus ... deep relaxing breaths.

—then snapped back to the other.

Lying fucking whore. I'm gonna tear you a new ...

The room around him grew cold. Then came a gray fog, and things; Lurkers crept in the fog, crept and crouched and waited to be recognized as they hid in the creases of shadows. Waited until the time was right.

Now Phoebe twisted and thrashed in a knot of sweat-drenched sheets. Even in sleep she sensed his presence. His face was blurred and out of proportion, like a hulking giant peering through the tiny window of a dollhouse. But she recognized it. It was Jeffery Dagon. His eyes blazed cold with the bland power of a hungry shark.

Grief and confusion racked her. *How can he torment me like this?* She sucked in a deep breath, steeling herself. A cold sense of reason washed through her. *Maybe if I can just wake up?* In her mind's

eye she struggled, floating upward from the fathomless depths of sleep. Her consciousness was thrown backward as it rammed headlong against an invisible barrier hard as cold steel while something equally hard and cold and wet crept up her thigh, pressing its flat head against the threshold of her virginity.
Sally, help me!

Inside the cave an angry buzzing fills the air. The lightning bugs clamored up her thighs on tiny wiry legs. Metal legs that seemed to slash at her soft flesh like a thousand razor cuts. As she paws at her thighs, the swarm splits and rushes in a wave beneath her nightshirt, over her flat stomach, the swell of her breasts, and finally pours upward toward her face. She screams.

Scuttling tiny wire-brush legs crawl over her chin, her lips, and rush into her mouth. Phoebe clenches her teeth and grinds their crisp little bodies into a bitter mash. She gags and spits tiny crunchy fragments of legs and cellophane wings to the ground. With gnarled fingers, she tears at her cheeks and throat, ripping the fireflies from her skin.

Below, the insects condense and form an oblong shape that feels like a stainless-steel finger as it probes and thrusts. Feelings of violation and repulsion drown in a sea of molten pleasure, rippling up and down her body.

But as her eyes roll back in ecstasy, another flood of fireflies pours into her mouth and down her throat, suffocating her. Frantic for air, she redirects her breathing, inhaling deeply through her nose. But then they swarm into her nostrils. A sublime mixture of terror and wanton abandon courses through her. She staggers, choking and gagging for air. And then for the first time in her life she climaxes, shuddering with pleasure, again and again. The consuming enticement of death by craving vs. the will to live battles within her. Self-preservation wins out.

Forcing her finger down her throat causes a gag reflex and she disgorges a burning fountain. Doubled over with dry heaves now, her legs still tingling with pleasure, she stumbles forward. Fresh cool air fills her lungs.

In the distance, she hears a familiar voice.
"Princesa, Princesa . . . this way."

The Black Spiral: Twisted Tales of Terror

Having regained her strength, she picks up the pace and breaks into a run. Fueled by adrenaline, desperation, and fear. She's a little girl now, and as she runs the grown-up urges and desires are replaced by a child's primary needs: love and the safety of a mother's embrace.

The fireflies shrink back and retreat.

The cave floor beneath her ripples and morphs into carpet. The damp air and darkness are replaced by warmth and light. She's sprinting down a hallway. Up ahead, a large figure looms, silhouetted by a welcoming glow. Large outstretched arms anticipate. She falls into them.

"Princesa Phoebe, my baby," Sally said as she cradled her in her meaty arms. "Honey, come on back to bed now. You've been having another bad dream, walking in your sleep."

"Oh God, Sally—it was so real." Phoebe blotted her tears on the sleeve of her nightshirt. Because she was weak and confused, and because she wasn't sure now if it really had only been a dream, Phoebe didn't argue or protest. Instead she walked arm in arm with Sally, down the hallway to her room.

After placing her in bed, Sally pulled the covers snugly beneath Phoebe's chin, kissed her gently on the forehead, and lumbered out of the room.

Flickering candlelight sent hobgoblin-like shadows capering over the walls of Sally's bedroom. In the corner stood a tall black lacquered cabinet. Sally unlocked the double doors and swung them open. Inside were rows of statues: The Blessed Virgin, well-known Catholic Saints, and some not-so-well-known figures—*Orisha*—the idols and gods of Santeria, which was the somewhat voodoo-like faith of Sally's ancestors the *Yoruba*, slaves brought to Cuba from West Africa, now known as Nigeria. Sally's father and grandfather were *Babalawo*—high priests.

The rhythmic beating of drums pounded from the CD player.

Rivulets of hot wax dripped from funeral candles. Mirrors lined the sides of the cabinet. And in the center, swaying slowly back and forth hung a figure—Capt. Wiggly. The clown was suspended upside-down. Where his legs should have been was a glistening mass of tendrils, bound with red ribbon and rosaries. The clown face was now youthful with deep blue eyes and a mop of blond hair. It was Jeffery's face.

The Black Spiral: Twisted Tales of Terror

Sally's muumuu spilled off her shoulders, pooling onto the floor. As she stood nude, her obsidian flesh gleamed with the sheen of perspiration in the candlelight.

She extended her hands, palms upward, and chanted, thanking her ancestors and placating the *Eggun*—spirits of the dead. Next she filled a pot with a santera's brew: India ink, goat excrement, a cat's tooth, a scorpion, mugwort and cemetery dirt. Lastly adding ground glass, the blood of a black rooster, and a dried bat's head.

The honed point of the dagger's blade sliced into the clown's belly. The *ebo'* or sacrifice.

Sally's sausage-like fingers poked and prodded until finally pulling out a thread. Further and further the filament stretched. As she dipped the end of the thread into a pot filled with the dark gelatinous liquid, intoning an incantation, something shifted beneath its surface, something not inert. The charry mass within the pot quivered and lurched in unnatural spastic bursts with each syllable muttered.

Slowly, the dark liquid congealed and took form. One by one tiny misshapen figures grew limbs and climbed up and along the thread. If you looked closely you could almost make out tiny sinewy backs and shoulders straining as they climbed hand over hand along the string. As they edged closer and closer to the gutted clown, Sally heard the faint whisper of a pleading cry escape its lips.

A scowl creased her dark moon face as she said, "To Hell with you, Jeffery Dagon. Prepare to be 'mounted!'"

Black. Everywhere black.

A black ceiling overhead. Recessed lighting dimly pooling on the black marble floor below. Cool black satin sheets on the bed beneath him.

Jeffery's eyes swam in terror. A cruel smile melted off his face, revealing the bereft, self-pitying mask of an unloved child. He thrashed and twisted trying to free himself from the invisible bonds that held him tight. No use. He'd lost control while "Visiting."

Tears began to well in his eyes. A series of tiny tugs pulled in cadence at the golden cord extending from his navel. He stared fixedly at the cord. With each tug of the cord, his heart hammered, sending a deafening roar of rushing blood to his ears. A syncopated death march.

Tug ... Lub dub ... whoosh
Tug ... Lub dub ... whoosh

The Black Spiral: Twisted Tales of Terror

He squinted, straining to see. Down they came; an endless stream of Lurkers with fiery Hell-lit eyes, sharp gnashing teeth, and tiny leathery wings sprouting from their scabrous, scaled backs.

Closer.

He wet himself, the musk of urine and fear-scent lathered the air.

Closer still.

Soft whimpers bubbled from his lips.

Sheer terror drove a spike deep into the frozen reaches of his heart.

Trembling and casket-eyed, he stared as the Lurkers reached his navel. Like millions of red-hot pokers their barbed feet seared his flesh; some entered his bellybutton, cutting deep with straight-razor-edged incisions, sharp as a stingray's spine. Others washed over his entire body, cocooning him. They probed and poked as Lilliputian tongues, slimly as raw liver, licked his ear lobes and prune-puckered scrotum. Then, burrowed deep into every orifice, clogging them.

He writhed with revulsion. Suffocated in fear.

He bucked as if shocked by a live wire.

While on the trembling edge of dissolution, he prayed to the gods of his ancestors—The Ancient Ones—the Lords of Dagon.

I'm becoming ... I'm a God! Concentrate. Focus.

With these words, his body began to change. Hair follicles drew inward; his skin rippled, changing to a mottled green-gray-yellow. With moist and oozing noises—like the sound of a boot being drawn from the muddy bottom of a swamp—Jeffery's skull cracked and swelled to three times its normal size. Bloated and bulging, his eyes finally slid from their sockets taking root at the sides of his deformed head. His features imploded and reformed into the bulbous goose-egg-shaped head of an *Octopus*.

Next as if made of wax, his torso and limbs thickened and elongated, morphing into tentacles dotted underneath with suction pads.

The throbbing mass of Lurkers became absorbed in the congealing flesh and blood, in the bone marrow and sinew and cartilage, as his tendrils whipped and flailed.

The Jeffery-thing lay still, in quiet repose. His reptilian eyes stared outward sightlessly. The rapture of conquest and a sense of power filled him. He'd harnessed a power like the raw fury of the storm.

With an ironclad will, he commanded his body to transform back to its original form.

The Black Spiral: Twisted Tales of Terror

He felt a slow change in his tissues, but not enough of a change, and then a sliding away, so he tried again and again, but with each attempt came nothing, no shift at all.

His mind reeled in stark terror, denial, and again he willed himself to revert to his born identity.

No change. Something was terribly wrong.

Even worse: he began to suspect that he was trapped, locked forever in a prison of cold glistening flesh; he was incarcerated in a cell comprised of his own transformed tissue.

Time passed.

As he lay there for hours—days, continuing his struggle to resume human appearance, he became dehydrated; cracks began to marble his flesh, and breathing became more and more difficult. Even though cephalopods had evolved and ruled the earth over 465 million years ago—before fishes swam the seas, before land plants developed spores, before vertebrates came ashore, their hemoglobin-derived blood was a poor oxygen carrier.

Life slowly ebbed from him.

His twin gills fought in vain to supply his three hearts. With his elliptical eyes gradually sinking shut, his mind drifted into stark madness and chaos. One thought played over and over in his mind, echoing with a maniacal resolve:

I'm becoming. I'm becoming. I'm becoming.

His thoughts slowly wound downward into oblivion.

I hav-e b-e-c-o-m-e...

Be—com . . .

FELL SWOOP

Tim Lebbon

Sometimes when he looked in a mirror, Jack saw someone else.

If he really concentrated he would see himself as others saw him. Subtle irregularities jumped out at him, so familiar that they normally went unnoticed: the scar above his right eyebrow from a stone thrown when he was a child; acne pocks around his cheeks; his left eyelid drooping just a little more than his right. Instant recognition was sometimes a curse. Occasionally it did him good to see himself as a distinct person, a human being . . . not just as *him*.

He always thought it was simply a matter of perception. He never truly believed that he was seeing a stranger wearing his own face.

He never expected to meet that stranger.

Something made him open his eyes. A noise, or a sensation, or a smell whatever, it must have been major. With a nuclear hangover going meltdown in his skull, it was a miracle he could experience or sense anything at all.

Hearing was the final sense to go when you died, he'd heard that somewhere, and now it was the first to return. All he could hear was his own ragged breathing. Vision pulsed in and out with his heartbeat, a slow strobe. At first there was only shadow, and then outlines sharpened and color found its rightful place. He saw a wall sprayed with graffiti; a pavement smeared with vomit and shit; a naked man sitting cross-legged in the road.

Jack groaned and raised himself up on one elbow, closing his eyes to try to purge his mind of hallucination and pain. When he opened them again the man was still there, hands resting on knees, long hair hanging over one shoulder in a ponytail. His eyes were black and he was staring directly at Jack.

"Wake up," the naked man said. "It's going to be a hell of a day."

"Who are you?" Jack muttered. His mouth felt as though it had been fired with a blowtorch. He felt a sudden urge to piss and scrabbled at his zipper, groaning at the pulsing pain in his head. He managed to free himself just in time, and a puddle of urine spread across the pavement in front of him.

The naked man stood and watched the pitiful display. "How glad I am that I'm no longer a part of you," he said.

Jack put himself away and stood up, slowly, using the wall behind him to support his sodden weight. He tried to recall what had happened last night: an argument with Jane, he thought; a quiet corner in a noisy pub; glass after glass from the end of the bar, and a bottle from his pocket later on. He could not recall the argument, he remembered only her mouth opening and closing, all the bad things she had to say about him bubbling out. He guessed he'd said them right back at her. As usual.

A cloud of shame settled slowly around him. His memories of the night were episodic at best, and in truth he could have gone anywhere, done anything, with anybody. He wondered how many people other than Jane had cause to hate him this morning.

"Who are you?" he asked again. He realized at last that it was daylight and this guy was hanging naked around the streets. He was tall and muscular, fine skin, long hair, big dick ... if Jack went that way at all, he'd have to say that he was gorgeous.

And more to the point, he was strikingly familiar.

"I'm who you've always wanted to be," the man said. "I'm who you could have been. You could have been called Rook, so that's my name, if it pleases you."

Jack could not help staring at the man's body.

"Prefer me clothed?" Rook asked. He pirouetted on the spot, Jack blinked, and a second later the naked man was naked no more.

"What   ?"

"No time. As I said Jack, things will happen today. Lots of things. Shall we go see?"

"I have to go home."

"Home? That odious little house where you live, where Jane is waiting for you even now, the worst rebuke you could ever imagine on her lips? Home is a state of mind, not a place, Jack. Home is where your heart is."

Jack did not answer, could not. He tried to think of Jane but it hurt too much. Even breathing hurt.

"Heartless bastard, aren't I? Come on."

The Black Spiral: Twisted Tales of Terror

They walked side by side along the street, Jack staring down at his feet, the man striding and whistling as if competing with the birds. It seemed to Jack that the stranger Rook walked without his feet actually touching the pavement, but alcoholic fallout fuzzed his brain and he tried to see no more.

It was only as they came onto the main street, and Jack caught sight of himself and his mysterious companion in a shop window, that he realized why he looked so familiar. Perhaps because Rook's mirror image was all Jack had ever seen before.

The stranger could have been his own twin brother.

"I'll leave you for a moment," Rook said. "There's something here you need to see, it'll give you more of an idea about me. But be warned   however far you choose to run, I'll find you."

Jack watched him turn and step through a wall ... not into it, *through* it. And he shook his head and reveled in the bursts of pain, because it convinced him that he was seeing and hearing things. He wondered how such a statement could sound like a threat, a promise and a reassurance, all at the same time.

Alone, he stared along the street at the hundreds of people, milling and driving and aiming themselves to work. He had worked once, many months ago, but then things had gone downhill and he'd used his own bad luck as an excuse to convince Jane to pay his way. For some strange reason she'd agreed. Maybe she still loved him more than he thought. Whatever ... they'd been arguing ever since.

You spend all your fucking money on drugs, Jack.
Why don't you go out and get a job?
There's more to life than TV and beer and jerking off all day.
Bitch. What did she know?

Nobody seemed to notice him, or if they did they ignored him, perhaps fearing he may be about to ask them for a handout. He wondered whether any of them had seen the stranger, Rook.

As he went to ask a passer-by, fifty people across the street spun, flipped, screamed and dropped down dead.

For a terrible second blood tainted the air, sprayed and slashed at it like the brushstrokes of an insane graffiti genius, planted on the visual reality of things before gravity pulled it down to the pavement, the road, the upturned, wide-eyed faces.

The Black Spiral: Twisted Tales of Terror

Then, the screams; the metal on metal as cars crashed; the frightened shouts; a young child pushing at its dead mother; panicked mumblings, smashing windows, sobbing, pounding feet . . .

. . . and Jack turned and ran back down the side-road he had emerged from, seeking the sightless, soundless blank oblivion of the previous night.

"I'll find you," Rook had said. The stranger who wore his face.

Jack ran along the street and tried to dodge the screams. They came from the main shopping precinct behind him, ahead where this side street branched into two, the open office windows above him . . . they came from all around. In the run-down shops and the low-rental offices, screeches and bangs and cries and groans filled the air with a most unnatural chorus. Jack wanted to add to the noise—he wanted to scream—but he was too short of breath.

He could not run very far. His blood was slow and thick, his breath forced out by the weight of the pain in his head, his limbs, his guts. His arms ached almost to the point of uselessness; even swinging them at his side hurt. Minutes after starting out he was huddled in a boarded-up shop doorway, hugging his knees and whimpering and dying for another piss. *Your time will come*, someone had scratched into the wood of the doorframe years ago. Fresh blood had recently been wiped across the gouging to bring out the words once more. It was so fresh, Jack could smell it.

He felt suddenly sick, and as he leaned forward to puke he fell onto his side.

More screams. More shouts.

He'd seen people dying. He'd seen them dead. Blood splashed across fresh window displays, a string of guts glistening in the early morning sun, a child wrenched from a pram and beaten hard against a wall . . . with no visible cause for any of it. There had been no madman, no murderer, no knifeman—had there?

Perhaps he was still pissed. Still stoned. Maybe he'd taken something from someone in one of the grotty pubs he'd visited last night. He'd had bad trips before, but hell, this one was—

"Hell . . . oooo!"

He tried not to hear the voice. "Still pissed," he muttered, then he said it again, louder, to muffle the sudden cries of dreadful shock

The Black Spiral: Twisted Tales of Terror

coming from an open first-story window across the street. "Still pissed, get back to sleep—"

"You talking to me?"

Jack started. A face pressed out of the crumbling brickwork opposite.

"I said, you talking to me? Huh?"

"Rook," Jack said, though the man had changed since a few moments before. His face was leaner; his eyes—if it were possible—were darker, madder. His hair was cropped into a clumsy Mohawk.

"Who the fuck you think you're talking to?"

"Rook, I . . ." But Jack could not go on. He closed his eyes. He wished he could close his ears, because then—

"I don't see anyone else here."

—he would shut out all this craziness, and when he woke—

"Wake up, you fool," Rook's voice drawled.

Jack opened his eyes.

Rook stood before him, back in his neutral clothes now, his face pudgier, his hair more wispy where it still clung to the pocked scalp.

"Those people," Jack said. "We have to help—"

Rook changed. There was no transmutation, no morphing from one man into another. He simply flipped, like a film moving from one frame to the next. He grew taller, a long coat appeared, and Jack was sure he saw the glint of a gun in the shadows.

"You wanna stay alive, you stay with me."

Rook laughed his way back to himself.

"Oh God, what's happening, what's going on?" Jack could smell his own puke, the rich stench of sweat, the stale miasma of alcohol and cigarettes. They repulsed him but they were smells he recognized, so he hugged them close. Rook was people he recognized, as well. His favorite characters. The actors he'd wanted to be, when he'd had anything like ambition left in his heart.

How could he know?

"Oh Jack," Rook said, and a note of sympathy crept into his voice. "It's the end of the world. Face it."

"Who are you? Are you doing all this?"

Rook looked genuinely offended. "Of course not! I'm here to help you. Give you a little time. Guide you through as best I can."

"But what . . ." Jack could find no words.

". . . am I?"

The Black Spiral: Twisted Tales of Terror

Jack nodded.

"I'm . . .I'm your guardian angel. Your fairy godmother. Your lucky charm. Your black cat and chicken's claw and *piskie*, all rolled into one big fat me."

"But you're . . . you're me."

Rook shrugged. "Well I look like you, granted. And there are other . . . distasteful similarities. For instance, I am well aware of the sordid little acts that you passed your time performing last night. But at this present extraordinary moment in time, I smell much better. Now follow. Places to go, things to see." He smiled. "You may be surprised."

Rook walked and Jack had to follow.

There were sirens now, blaring from the distance and bringing an upset sense of normality and control to the terrible scenes. But still he heard screams and sobs and the disbelieving words of a hundred people mixing in the air, a soup of terror, tainting the bright morning with fears that should never exist. That *could* never exist.

"What the hell's happening?" Jack asked, but Rook merely giggled theatrically and strode on. "Where are we going?" Again that affected shrug, a twitch of the shoulders that changed Rook's coat into a cloak and sent it shimmering in an invisible breeze.

Jack reached out and grabbed the man's shoulder. He felt fingers digging into his own shoulder as well, but he could not turn around to see who had a hold of him, he simply could not. Because Rook had turned and was staring at him, and it was like looking into a mirror. It was not a flattering mirror, this one, certainly not one that would tell him he was the fairest of all. It threw memories back at him, things he had wanted to forget for so long: a stinging palm from where he had slapped Jane; the sinking shame of seeing her sprawled on the floor in a nightclub, his hand still extended from the push; the warmth of splashed blood on his chin after he had accidentally mashed her lip into her teeth—

—*accidentally? Really Jack? Accidentally, are you sure?*

. . . and the voice was Rook's.

"Accidentally, Jack?"

"Of course it was an accident!"

"Ah," said Rook, turning away again. "Look, there's dear old Piccy!"

Jack saw a man jogging along the street, long hair flowing behind him, his face a determined frown.

"Can you see it following me?" the man screamed, but he said no more. One second his throat was stretching and twisting around his own particular dialect, the next it was spread across a baker's window, speckling Jack's view of the cake trays with a strawberry redness.

"Oh Jesus!"

"No, just Piccy. Hi Piccy!" Rook shouted.

The man was still twitching on the pavement. Jack hoped—in fact, he *knew*—that this was not who Rook was referring to. On the windowsills above, pigeons cooed in interest at the mess they saw below them. Thankfully they were biding their time. As Jack looked closer he saw something ... something dark but not a shadow, more a stain upon his vision. It held the vague shape of a human. It kicked the dying man in the chest. He groaned. And then it was not there any more, and Jack was unsure whether he had even seen it at all.

"I'm going mad," Jack said.

"No, in fact, you're more sane—"

"Going mad and I'll wake up and I'll be in bed, hungover and a little worse for wear, maybe with someone in bed with me, what's her name? God what's her name? Let's hope I remember in time, nothing more embarrassing—"

"Earth calling Jack! Hello, reality check, Jack!" Rook grasped his cheeks roughly, squeezing until the bones in his face felt ready to crunch and crumble. He spoke directly into his mouth, and Jack could taste his breath. It was sweet. It was succulent. It was rich and potent, not sour and rancid as he had expected. Perhaps this man really was a guardian angel, if rather different to what Jack could have ever imagined.

"Who's Piccy?"

"That dead man. And his murderer. Bit of a demon, really."

"You were *waving* to him?"

Rook looked thrown for the first time in the few minutes that Jack had known him. His confident outer coating slipped a fraction to show the potential of turmoil beneath, like a sheet of thin ice covering a boiling lake. "Don't ask about what you can't understand," he said at last, and he turned and stalked away.

Jack followed because he did not know what else to do. He tried to think of Jane but it hurt too much, he had hurt *her* too much, and she had hurt him back by threatening to leave. His arms still ached. His hands stank of cigarette smoke and pine forests. He tried to breath deeply but the fresh air twinged his hangover. He told his legs to stop . . . but he kept on following Rook. He truly did not know what else to do.

They came to a small park surrounded by tumbled walls and overturned trashcans, the trees more used to drunkards' piss then lovers' knives. Rook appeared keen to enter, and for Jack it was respite from the terrible sights in the streets all around. Panic and chaos had settled down over the town, and while the ambulances and police cars flitted to and fro, still a great sense of disorder tainted everything. Normality had slipped; dead people lay everywhere, nightmares now lived in daylight. In one place, blood flowed along a gutter.

But the park, though no escape from the noise and the shouts and screams, offered some shelter from the sights. Initially, at least.

Rook led him straight to its centre, where four stone benches were arranged around a central statue. Jack thought the image was of a soldier from one of the wars, but on closer inspection it could just as easily have been a miner, or a sailor, or a person who was meant to look like someone else. He searched for a plaque, but there was none. He had been here many times before, but he had never paid this monument any attention. Just like any town dweller, he rarely looked up.

Rook leaned against the statue, raised an eyebrow and nodded at one of the benches.

Jack looked. There was a shape there, insubstantial but defined. It was a man, long hair flowing in an unseen breeze, his face moving like heat haze, distorting the rose bed behind him.

"Keene," Rook said, "long time no see."

Jack heard no reply, but he did sense some subtle communication. It felt like a fly trapped in his ear, struggling to get out, beating its wings against his drum as it described impossible, mad circles around and around. The shape was looking up at Rook. A shadow twisted where its mouth should be, a hole in the air.

"Really?" Rook said. "Wow! And I thought I was having fun with this one!" He nodded at Jack. "I'm just taking Jack here to see his."

"See my what?" Jack asked.

The fly began to laugh.

"Over there," said Rook, "is another body. Come on, I'll show you." He reached out quickly, grabbed Jack's shoulder before he could turn away, almost dragged him between two of the benches and behind a wild stand of shrubs.

There was indeed a body there, freshly dead, blood still flowing from an open artery in its forehead. Its eyes had been removed. "Only the good die young," Rook said. "You believe that? Well, it's bollocks. This man was not good—"

"How do you know all this, unless—?"

Rook raised a hand, palm out, a silent "shut up." "As I say, this man was not good. A year ago he punched his wife, six months ago he stole from his mother. He could have been better. He could have been someone valuable to society, someone with ideas instead of hatred, positive thoughts instead of rancid dreams. He was a dreamer, you know; he had such dreams! He could have been a philosopher. And now . . . now, he *is* that person for the first time. He's Keene, as Keene has never been before. Death, my friend Jack, becomes some people."

Jack stared down at the body. His hangover kicked at the base of his skull as the sun revealed itself, and he tried to think again about last night. Vodka, he thought, he was sure he could still taste it under his tongue and in his teeth. But what else? What else had left this sour taste in his mouth?

"So," he said, "I suppose you'll tell me . . . is this the Keene who's sitting out there?"

Rook raised his eyebrows, mouth dropping open in a feigned show of admiration. "My Jack, alcohol hasn't totally pickled your brain after all!"

Jack glanced back at the square of seats and that uncertain statue, trying to see the wraith that had been sitting on one of the benches. All four stone seats were empty.

What he did see, though, was that the statue now resembled something inhuman . . . or something more than human. It held a perfection that he could not quantify.

Jack closed his eyes. "We have to tell someone about this body," he said. "Why did you show me? Why show me a ghost? Why bring me here to . . .?" He trailed off because his thoughts were leading in circles. Ever-decreasing circles with madness at the hub.

"No ghost," Rook said, "just a truer reality. I'm keeping you from yours for a time. Feel honored. You're seeing what most people never will. Follow me, Jack."

The Black Spiral: Twisted Tales of Terror

And of course, like all the best rats, Jack could do nothing but comply.

The streets had changed.
There was the slew of bodies, cut down by some grotesque random harvest, and the people attending them and crying over them. There were cars parked curb side or buried in shopfronts, some of them with bloodied shadows pressed against windshields, other still burning or sitting with open doors, their owners fled somewhere else to die. Not normality, perhaps, but something understandable, identifiable.
But there was also something wrong with the buildings.
A pub on the corner of two streets—perhaps one which Jack had frequented the previous night—was out of focus. Whichever angle he viewed it from, however much he winced or stared or rubbed his eyes, all lines were losing definition and hard edges were softening. He could almost see the clarity of the place being stripped, and here and there misplaced shadows clung to the walls, like patches of wavy moss.
A takeaway had slumped down without any of its structure cracking. Its sign was bowed out but the words were not distorted, and its window, although not broken, had taken on a shattered edge. Birds flitted in and out with cold chips in their beaks, passing through the glass and leaving tiny ripples in its previously solid surface. It moved like flesh, shook like a face being struck with an open palm . . . Jane's face, his palm.
"Things are looking much better already," Rook said. "Don't you agree? Yes indeed." He bent down so that his nose was inches from Jack's. "Things are moving on apace, my friend. Come on, let's hurry." Then he looked up at the sky, smiled and said: "Oh-oh, hang on a minute. Here comes another one!"
Jack was watching three firemen trying to extract a body from a crashed car. Two of them dropped down dead—one with his head twisted on his shoulders, the other with ribs shattered and protruding through his uniform like blood-streaked ivory.
The survivor stood there for a long time; looking, staring, not seeing. Shadows buzzed him. He seemed unaware of them.
More shouts. A car crashed somewhere across the river and a pall of smoke puffed up into the still air. On the town bridge Jack saw a dozen people drop like felled wheat, a dozen more run to their aid in

shocked silence or with a useless shout. Others wandered aimlessly, talking into thin air, looking around them as if surrounded by phantoms.

The bridge parapet lifted slowly into the air, solid metal sheets splitting in equal patterns and stretching as well, opening up into metallic rose sculptures, the road bowing in the middle and rising to mimic the transformation of its surroundings. The bland gray metalwork took on new, wonderful colors—oily green and blood-red and the brightest, lightest blue Jack had ever seen, the blue of a ten thousand year old glacier—and it was gorgeous.

He could never have imagined anything like this. In his wildest dreams, in his most ambitious youth, he had never dreamt of anything as wonderful, nor as beautiful as this.

He stumbled back against a wall and felt it move beneath him. He spun around, his brain seeming to lag behind, and stared at . . . into the eyes of . . . something was on the wall, a shadow, a blip in the sunlight, hands scraping at brickwork and turning it slowly, impossibly into something else. The bright red bricks faded to an oaken brown colour, their aggregate lengthening into bark strips. Jack backed away and looked up at the windows as they deformed, the roof where it buckled and changed colour from a bland slate-gray, to a vibrant leaf-green. It was a building made of trees, not simply constructed but grown.

Rook nudged him. "Always wanted to be an architect, didn't you?"

"How did you know?"

"It's easy when I'm you."

Jack did not acknowledge him. He was too aghast with what he was seeing, the change being wrought over his surroundings. Some of it was slow—the bridge was still lifting, its metal flanks still stretching and warping into fantastical new shapes—some of it was fast. The shopfront changing to wood. The corpse in the gutter, flowing and melding, becoming a part of the ground even as
he watched . . .

"Let's go!" Rook said once again.

"I'm not going with you." Jack backed away, expecting Rook to leap at him, grab him in a headlock and drag him along the street. But the tall, weird stranger

The Black Spiral: Twisted Tales of Terror

(but he's not really a stranger, Jack, any more than that person you sometimes see in the mirror, the real person behind your familiar face) merely stood and watched him go, a quizzical smile on his face.

"Jack, you have to."

"Why? It's written, is it? Is that what you're going to tell me: I should follow you because it's written?"

"No," Rook shook his head. "I just thought you'd want to know what's happening to Jane."

Jack paused. Talk about a loaded comment. He could see something behind Rook's surface expression, but he didn't know exactly what it was. He wasn't at all sure he even *wanted* to know.

"Duck!" Rook shouted suddenly.

There was a shimmer in the air, a vibration with no noise or feeling, a certainty that something was happening. More screams . . . more shouts . . . in a greasy spoon café across from where they were standing, several people were thrown against the window in bloody red abandon, their dead expressions sliding down the glass, wide white eyes blaming Jack.

"You're enjoying this!" he shouted. Rook was smiling; he'd always been smiling, even behind his frowns and strange impressions.

"Yes, of course," the tall man said. "It's my time. That's why I'm guiding you around for so long. Hey look, bet you could never have designed that one!"

Jack looked to where he was pointing. A building he had never taken any notice of before—a council office, he thought— was bulging at the seams. There were several dead people on the pavement near its main entrance, and as the brickwork expanded so it shoved them aside, crushing them under and smearing their corpses across the crumpling pavement. Jack felt sick but he was also amazed, enthralled in what was becoming of things.

The building started to contract again ... then expand ... contract, expand . . .

"No need for plumbing or heating in a living building," Rook commented.

Jack shook his head. *No. Impossible.*

"Oh, I think we should go," Rook muttered, his expression suddenly serious, his hands reaching out for Jack. They kept reaching, past any chance he had to defend himself against them, into his personal space, around his neck, squeezing—

Rook backed off with what looked like a great effort.

Jack gasped.

"Let's go and see Jane," Rook said.

Jane. Jack had a lot to say to her, even now. A lot to apologize for. Things were changing. Things *had* changed. Now, more than ever, they would need each other.

But this was all impossible, he knew that. He was drunk somewhere, sleeping under a bush or in a gutter or in a cell, pissing and shitting his pants and being pathetic. Nobody was dying. Buildings weren't changing . . . buildings weren't *breathing,* for fuck's sake!

"Quickly!" Rook said. "I can only protect you for so long." He started to run.

Jack had seconds to decide; it took him only two before he followed. He'd always been weak, a sheep, a feeble man with no real control over his own life or ambitions. He knew that and accepted it, even though it had never made him proud. Now, he felt more wretched than ever.

Jane, he thought, *what did I do?* He rubbed snot from his nose as he cried, and he smelled pine forests and piss.

Whatever change was occurring it had yet to reach his street.

Rook muttered and mumbled as they walked, most of it inaudible, the bits Jack did catch confusing and frightening. He spoke of new orders and dead people and a time for change. Jack had seen corpses and change this morning—new orders, he did not want to know about.

The street brought back bad memories. He had obviously left it yesterday in an effort to flee the row he and Jane had had, the violence he may have meted out to her. He wondered what she would say at his appearance now, especially with the strange Rook leading him on. He hoped she could forgive. He looked at his hands and wondered what they had done.

Alcohol bled his memory, like a leech used to suck out bad blood. He craved a drink even now. He craved forgetfulness on a larger scale. In a way, he wanted to be that stranger in the mirror.

"Well," Rook said, "here we are. At last." He looked strangely at Jack, a glimmer in his eye that Jack could not identify.

The Black Spiral: Twisted Tales of Terror

"Jane!" Jack called. He walked forward. The house looked quiet, still. There was no movement across its masonry, no dip or rise in its roof, no change of colour. He almost believed he'd never seen those things just now—not only believed, but sought to convince himself of this belief—but then he saw the evidence, even here.

Above the house, rising in the distance, stood a solid tower, transparent and as wide as a football field. People launched themselves into the air from its heights, fell and then drifted back up and out. Gossamer wings reflected sunlight like oil on water. They spiraled up and down, catching the thermals and apparently denying gravity when there were none. One shape plummeted straight up, disappearing into the clouds before swooping back down, wings glittering with moisture and ice.

"What ...?" Jack said.

Rook spun on his heels and he was naked again, his back ridged into two spines, each split down its length and betraying the odd protruding feather here and there.

"Angels?" Jack whispered.

Rook shook his head. "Of course not, fool! We just like flying, every now and then. Hurry up, now, I'm only giving you a little more time."

"What do you mean?"

"Time. I'm giving you more time. I can only hold back . . . protect you . . . for so long, you know. Go in. Find Jane. Make your peace."

Rook was changing, subtly but certainly. His nails were longer. His face was narrower. His eyes had lost their humor, and that worried Jack most of all.

"Jane!" he called.

Someone walked out of the house. At first he thought it was Jane and he went to go to her, but then he held back. The person—the thing—had Jane's features for sure, but Jane had never had teeth that long. Jane had never possessed fingers so strong, so gnarled. Jane, Jack was positive, had never had scarlet skin.

Rook and the new woman exchanged a few quick, incomprehensible comments. He laughed. "Well," he said to Jack, "seems you had quite a row last night. Pity you couldn't remember, because then I would have known too and I could have spared you . . . well, so much heartache."

The Black Spiral: Twisted Tales of Terror

"You bastard!" the thing on the steps spat. Jack was not sure whether the comment was directed at him or Rook. Rook's laughter answered for him.

"What?" Jack asked. "Where's Jane? I need to see Jane?"

The scarlet thing's eyes opened slightly.

"Will you let him?" Rook asked. "Just let him see? He's a little hungover, you see."

"But you know what—"

"Only briefly, and then I'll finish it. I've kept him for too long as it is."

It nodded.

Jack ran up the steps and past the scarlet thing where it stood in the doorway. It had Jane's eyes. It even stood like Jane, one knee bent, one hand on one hip.

"Jane!" he called. "Jane, you alright?"

But coming back into the house—his house, his books scattered around, his clothes strewn in his own untidy patterns across the floor – brought back more of last night. Things he did not wish to see, because they were shameful. Then other things, things he had no wish to recall because they were too frightening. Too damn frightening.

—arguing, fighting, into the bathroom—

He ran upstairs.

—she'd already run a bath; they were due to go out—

He shoved open the bathroom door.

—she had yet to run any cold, it was scalding—

The air in the bathroom carried a hint of pine forests. Jane had liked bath salts. Soothed her aching muscles, she always said.

She lay in the tub, fully clothed, her exposed skin branded pink by the once-hot waters, dead. Bruises on her throat. Face submerged. Mouth open in a wet scream. Eyes wide, still seeing the final terror. Still seeing Jack.

His hands began to sting with the memory of them closing around her throat.

"Oh no!"

Rook suddenly stepped through the wall, trod on Jane's corpse and stood next to him.

Jack turned to run, not only from the awful deed he had done, but from this thing as well. It meant him no good, he knew that now, it had been playing with him, not saving him. Like a cat with a mouse before it delivers the final, fatal blow . . . .

Within a blink, Rook was blocking the doorway. The disturbed bathwater swilled behind Jack, as if Jane were still alive.

"And now," said the tall thing with Jack's face, "I can make good all the potential you ever lost, wasted or forgot." It reached for him, ripped open his shirt, hissed. Its nails were long.

Jack's chest was vulnerable.

And his heart, as he had always known, was weak.

The Black Spiral: Twisted Tales of Terror

Meeting The Author

Ramsey Campbell

I was young then. I was eight years old. I thought adults knew the truth about most things and would own up when they didn't. I thought my parents stood between me and anything about the world that might harm me. I thought I could keep my nightmares away by myself, because I hadn't had one in years—not since I'd first read about the little match girl being left alone in the dark by the things she saw and the emperor realizing in front of everyone that he wasn't wearing any clothes. My parents had taken me to a doctor who asked me so many questions I think they were what put me to sleep. I used to repeat his questions in my head whenever I felt in danger of staying awake in the dark.

As I said, I was eight when Harold Mealing came to town. All my parents knew about him was what his publisher told the paper where they worked. My mother brought home the letter she'd been sent at the features desk. "A celebrity's coming to town," she said, or at least that's what I remember her saying, and surely that's what counts.

My father held up the letter with one hand while he cut up his meat with his fork. " 'Harold Mealing's first book *Beware of the Smile* takes its place among the classics of children's fiction,' " he said. "Well, that was quick. Still, if his publishers say so that's damn near enough by itself to get him on the front page in this town."

"I've already said I'll interview him."

"Robbed of a scoop by my own family." My father struck himself across the forehead with the letter and passed it to me. "Maybe you should see what you think of him too, Timmy. He'll be signing at the bookshop."

"You might think of reviewing his book now we have children writing the children's page," my mother added. "Get some use out of that imagination of yours."

The letter said Harold Mealing had written "a return to the old-fashioned moral tale for children—a story which excites for a purpose." Meeting an author seemed an adventure, though since both my parents were journalists, you could say I already had. By the time he was due in town I was so worked up I had to bore myself to sleep.

The Black Spiral: Twisted Tales of Terror

In the morning there was an accident on the motorway that had taken the traffic away from the town, and my father went off to cover the story. Me and my mother drove into town in her car that was really only big enough for two. In some of the streets the shops were mostly boarded up, and people with spray paint who always made my father angry had been writing on them. Most of the town worked at the toy factory, and dozens of their children were queuing outside Books & Things. "Shows it pays to advertise in our paper," my mother said.

Mrs. Trend, who ran the shop, hurried to the door to let my mother in. I'd always been a bit afraid of her, with her pins brisling like antennae in her buns of hair that was black as the paint around her eyes, but her waiting on us like this made me feel grown up and superior. She led us past the toys and stationery and posters of pop stars to the bookshop part of the shop, and there was Harold Mealing in an armchair behind a table full of his book.

He was wearing a white suit and bow tie, but I thought he looked like a king on his throne, a bit petulant and bored. Then he saw us. His big loose face that was spidery with veins started smiling so hard it puffed his cheeks out, and even his gray hair that looked as if he never combed it seemed to stand up to greet us. "This is Mary Duncan from the *Beacon*," Mrs. Trend said, "and her son Timothy who wants to review your book."

"A pleasure, I'm sure." Harold Mealing reached across the table and shook us both by the hand at once, squeezing hard as if he didn't want us to feel how soft his hands were. Then he let go of my mother's and held on to mine. "Has this young man no copy of my book? He shall have one with my inscription and my blessing."

He leaned his elbow on the nearest book to keep it open and wrote "To Timothy Duncan, who looks as if he knows how to behave himself: best wishes from the author." The next moment he was smiling past me at Mrs. Trend. "Is it time for me to meet the little treasures? Let my public at me and the register shall peal."

I sat on the ladder people used to reach the top shelves and started reading his book while he signed copies, but couldn't concentrate. The book was about a smiling man who went from place to place trying to tempt children to be naughty and then punished them in horrible ways if they were. After a while I sat and watched Harold Mealing smiling over all the smiles on the covers of the books. One of the children waiting to have a book bought for him knocked a plastic letter-rack off a shelf and broke it, and got smacked by his mother and dragged out while nearly everyone turned to watch. But I saw Harold Mealing's face, and his smile was wider than ever.

When the queue was dealt with, my mother interviewed him. "A writer has to sell himself. I'll go wherever my paying public is. I want every child who will enjoy my book to be able to go to the nearest bookshop and buy one," he said, as well as how he'd sent the book to twenty publishers before this one had bought it and how we should all be grateful to his publisher. "Now I've given up teaching I'll be telling all the stories I've been saving up," he said.

The only time he stopped smiling was when Mrs. Trend wouldn't let him sign all his books that were left, just some in case she couldn't sell the rest. He started again when I said goodbye to him as my mother got ready to leave. "I'll look forward to reading what you write about my little tale," he said to me. "I saw you were enjoying it. I'm sure you'll say you did."

"Whoever reviews your book won't do so under any coercion," my mother told him, and steered me out of the shop.

That evening at dinner my father said, "So how did it feel to meet a real writer?"

"I don't think he likes children very much," I said.

"I believe Timmy's right," my mother said, "I'll want to read this book before I decide what kind of publicity to give him. Maybe I'll just review the book."

I finished it before I went to bed. I didn't much like the ending, when Mr. Smiler led all the children who hadn't learned to be good away to his land where it was always dark. I woke in the middle of the night, screaming because I thought he had taken me there. No wonder my mother disliked the book and stopped just short of saying in her review that it shouldn't have been published. I admired her for saying what she thought, but I wondered what Harold Mealing might do when he read what she'd written. "He isn't entitled to do anything, Timmy," my father said. "He has to learn the rules like the rest of us if he wants to be a pro."

The week after the paper printed the review we went on holiday to Spain, and I forgot about the book. When we came home I wrote about the parts of Spain we'd been to that most visitors didn't bother with, and the children's page published what I'd written, more or less. I might have written other things, except I was too busy worrying what the teacher I'd have when I got back to school might be like and trying not to let my parents see I was. I took to stuffing a handkerchief in my mouth before I went to sleep so they wouldn't hear me if a nightmare woke me up.

At the end of the last week before I went back to school, my mother got the first call. The three of us were doing a jigsaw on the dining-table, because that was the only place big enough, when the phone rang. As soon as my mother said who she was, the voice at the other end got so loud and sharp I could hear it across the room. "My publishers have just sent me a copy of your review. What do you mean by saying that you wouldn't give my book to a child?"

"Exactly that, Mr. Mealing. I've seen the nightmares it can cause."

"Don't be so sure," he said, and then his voice went from crafty to pompous. "Since all they seem to want these days are horrors, I've invented one that will do some good. I suggest you give some thought to what children need before you presume to start shaping their ideas."

My mother laughed so hard it must have made his earpiece buzz. "I must say I'm glad you aren't in charge of children any longer. How did you get our home number, by the way?"

"You'd be surprised what I can do when I put my mind to it."

"Then try writing something more acceptable," my mother said, and cut him off.

She'd hardly sat down at the table when the phone rang again. It must have been my imagination that made it sound as sharp as Harold Mealing's voice. This time he started threatening to tell the paper and my school who he was convinced had really written the review. "Go ahead if you want to make yourself look more of a fool," my mother said.

The third time the phone rang, my father picked it up. "I'm warning you to stop troubling my family," he said, and Harold Mealing started wheedling: "They shouldn't have attacked me after I gave them my time. You don't know what it's like to be a writer. I put myself into that book."

"God help you then," my father said, and warned him again before cutting him off. "All writers are mad," he told us, "but professionals use it instead of letting it use them."

After I'd gone to bed I heard the phone again, and after my parents were in bed. I thought of Harold Mealing lying awake in the middle of the night and deciding we shouldn't sleep either, letting the phone ring and ring until one of my parents had to pick it up, though when they did nobody would answer.

The Black Spiral: Twisted Tales of Terror

Next day my father rang up Harold Mealing's publishers. They wouldn't tell him where Harold Mealing had got to on his tour, but his editor promised to have a word with him. He must have, because the phone calls stopped, and then there was nothing for days until the publisher sent a parcel.

My mother watched over my shoulder while I opened the padded bag. Inside was a book called *Mr. Smiler's Pop-Up Surprise Book* and a letter addressed to no one in particular. "We hope you are excited by this book as we are to publish it, sure to introduce Harold Mealing's already famous character Mr. Smiler to many new readers and a state-of-the-art example of pop-up design" was some of what it said. I gave the letter to my mother while I looked inside the book.

At first I couldn't see Mr. Smiler. The pictures stood to attention as I opened the pages, pictures of children up to mischief, climbing on each other's shoulders to steal apples or spraying their names on a wall or making faces behind their teacher's back. The harder I had to look for Mr. Smiler, the more nervous I became of seeing him. I turned back to the first pages and spread the book flat on the table, and he jumped up from behind the hedge under the apple tree, shaking his long arms. On every two pages he was waiting for someone to be curious enough to open the book that little bit further. My mother watched me, and she said, "You don't have to accept it, you know. We can send it back."

I thought she wanted me to be grown-up enough not to be frightened by the book. I also thought that if I kept it Harold Mealing would be satisfied, because he'd meant it as an apology for waking us in the night. "I want to keep it. It's good," I said. "Shall I write and say thank you?"

"I shouldn't bother." She seemed disappointed that I was keeping it. "We don't even know who sent it," she said.

Despite the letter, I hoped Harold Mealing might have. Hoped! Once I was by myself I kept turning the pages as if I would find a sign if I looked hard enough. Mr. Smiler jumped up behind a hedge and a wall and a desk, and every time his face reminded me more of Harold Mealing's. I didn't like that much, and I put the book away in the middle of a pile in my room. After my parents had tucked me up and kissed me good night, early because I was starting school in the morning, I wondered if it might give me nightmares, but I slept soundly enough. I remember thinking Mr. Smiler wouldn't be able to move with all those books on top of him.

The Black Spiral: Twisted Tales of Terror

My first day at school made me forget him. The teacher asked about my parents, who she knew worked on the paper, and wanted to know if I was a writer too. When I said I'd written some things she asked me to bring one in to read to the class. I remember wishing Harold Mealing could know, and when I got home I pulled out the pop-up book as if that would let me tell him.

At first I couldn't find Mr. Smiler at all. I felt as if he was hiding to give me time to be scared of him. I had to open the book still wider before he came up from behind the hedge with a kind of shivery wriggle that reminded me of a dying insect. Once was enough. I pushed the book under the bottom of the pile and looked for something to read to the class.

There wasn't anything I thought was good enough, so I wrote about meeting Harold Mealing and how he'd kept phoning, pretty well as I've written it now. I finished it just before bedtime. When the light was off and the room began to take shape out of the dark, I thought I hadn't closed the pop-up book properly, because I could see darkness inside it that made me think of a lid, especially when I thought I could see a pale object poking out of it. I didn't dare get up to look. After a while I got so tired of being frightened I must have fallen asleep.

In the morning I was sure I'd imagined all that, because the book was shut flat on the shelf. At school I read out what I'd written. The children who'd been at Books & Things laughed as if they agreed with me, and the teacher said I wrote like someone older than I was. Only I didn't feel older, I felt as I used to feel when I had nightmares about books, because the moment I started reading aloud I wished I hadn't written about Harold Mealing. I was afraid he might find out, though I didn't see how he could.

When I got home I realized I was nervous of going to my room, and yet I felt I had to go there and open the pop-up book. Once I finished convincing my mother that I'd enjoyed my day at school I made myself go upstairs and pull it out from under the pile. I thought I'd have to flatten it even more to make Mr. Smiler pop up. I put on the quilt and started leaning on it, but it wasn't even open flat when he squirmed up from behind the hedge, flapping his arms, as if he'd been waiting all day for me. Only now his face was Harold Mealing's face.

It looked as if part of Mr. Smiler's face had fallen off to show what was underneath, Harold Mealing's face gone gray and blotchy but smiling harder than ever, straight at me. I wanted to scream and rip him out of the book, but all I could do was fling the book across my bed and run to my mother.

She was sorting out the topics she'd be covering for next week's paper, but she dropped her notes when she saw me. "What's up?"

"In the book. Go and see," I said in a voice like a scream that was stuck in my throat, and I was afraid of what the book might do to her. I went up again, though only fast enough that she would be just behind me. I had to wait until she was in the room before I could touch the book.

It was leaning against the pillow, gaping as if something was holding it open from inside. I leaned on the corners to open it, and then I made myself pick it up and bend it back until I heard the spine creak. I did that with the first two pages and all the other pairs. By the time I'd finished I was nearly sobbing, because I couldn't find Mr. Smiler or whatever he looked like now. "He's got out," I cried.

"I knew we shouldn't have let you keep that book," my mother said. "You've enough of an imagination without being fed nonsense like that. I don't care how he tries to get at me, but I'm damned if I'll have him upsetting any child of mine."

My father came home just then, and joined in. "We'll get you a better book, Timmy, to make up for this old rubbish," he said, and put the book where I couldn't reach it, on top of the wardrobe in their bedroom.

That didn't help. The more my mother tried to persuade me that the pop-up was broken and so I shouldn't care about not having the book, the more I thought about Mr. Smiler's face that had stopped pretending. While we were having dinner I heard scratchy sounds walking about upstairs, and my father had to tell me it was a bird on the roof. While we were watching one of the programs my parents let me watch on television a puffy white thing came and pressed itself against the window, and I almost wasn't quick enough at the window to see an old bin-liner blowing away down the road. My mother read to me in bed to try and calm me down, but when I saw a figure creeping upstairs beyond her that looked as if it hadn't much more to it than the dimness on the landing, I screamed before I realized it was my father coming to see if I was nearly asleep. "Oh dear," he said, and went down to get me some of the medicine the doctor had prescribed to help me sleep.

My mother had been keeping it in the refrigerator. It must have been years old. Maybe that was why, when I drifted off to sleep although

The Black Spiral: Twisted Tales of Terror

I was afraid to in case anything came into my room, I kept jerking awake as if something had wakened me, something that had just ducked out of sight at the end of the bed. Once I was sure I saw a blotchy forehead disappearing as I forced my eyes open, and another time I saw hair like cobwebs being pulled out of sight over the footboard. I was too afraid to scream, and even more afraid of going to my parents, in case I hadn't really seen anything in the room and it was waiting outside for me to open the door.

I was still jerking awake when the dawn came. It made my room even more threatening, because now everything looked flat as the hiding places in the pop-up book. I was frightened to look at anything. I lay with my eyes squeezed shut until I heard movements outside my door and my father's voice convinced me it was him. When he inched the door open I pretended to be asleep so that he wouldn't think I needed more medicine. I actually managed to sleep for a couple of hours before the smell of breakfast woke me up.

It was Saturday, and my father took me fishing in the canal. Usually fishing made me feel as if I'd had a rest, though we never caught any fish, but that day I was too worried about leaving my mother alone in the house or rather, not as alone as she thought she was. I kept asking my father when we were going home, until he got so irritable that we did.

As soon as he was in his chair he stuck the evening paper up in front of himself. He was meaning to show that I'd spoiled his day, but suddenly he looked over the top of the paper at me. "Here's something that may cheer you up, Timmy," he said. "Harold Mealing's in the paper."

I thought he meant the little smiling man was waiting in there to jump out at me, and I nearly grabbed the paper to tear it up. "Good God, son, no need to look so timid about it," my father said. "He's dead, that's why he's in. Died yesterday of too much dashing about in search of publicity. Poor old twerp, after all his self-promotion he wasn't considered important enough to put in the same day's news."

I heard what he was saying, but all I could think was that if Harold Mealing was dead he could be anywhere—and then I realized he already had been. He must have died just about the time I'd seen his face in the pop-up book. Before my parents could stop me, I grabbed a chair from the dining suite and struggled upstairs with it, and climbed on it to get the book down from the wardrobe.

The Black Spiral: Twisted Tales of Terror

I was bending it open as I jumped off the chair. I jerked it so hard as I landed that it shook the little man out from behind the hedge. I shut my eyes so as not to see his face, and closed my hand around him, though my skin felt as if it was trying to crawl away from him. I'd just got hold of him to tear him up as he wriggled like an insect when my father came in and took hold of my fingers to make me let go before I could do more than crumple the little man. He closed the book and squeezed it under his arm as if he was as angry with it as he was with me. "I thought you knew better than to damage books," he said. "You know I can't stand vandalism. I'm afraid you're going straight to bed, and think yourself lucky I'm keeping my temper."

That wasn't what I was afraid of. "What are you going to do with the book?"

"Put it somewhere you won't find it. Now, not another word or you'll be sorry. Bed."

I turned to my mother, but she frowned and put her finger to her lips. "You heard your father."

When I tried to stay until I could see where my father hid the book, she pushed me into the bathroom and stood outside the door and told me to get ready for bed. By the time I came out, my father and the book had gone. My mother tucked me into bed and frowned at me, and gave my forehead a kiss so quick it felt papery. "Just go to sleep now and we'll have forgotten all about it in the morning," she said.

I lay and watched the bedroom furniture begin to go flat and thin as cardboard when it got dark. When either of my parents came to see if I was asleep I tried to make them think I was, but before it was completely dark I was shaking too much. My mother brought me some of the medicine and wouldn't go away until I'd swallowed it, and then I lay there fighting to stay awake.

I heard my parents talking, too low for me to understand. I heard one of them go out to the dustbin, and eventually I smelled burning. I couldn't tell if that was in our yard or a neighbor's, and I was too afraid to get up in the dark and look. I lay feeling as if I couldn't move, as if the medicine had made the bedclothes heavier or me weaker, and before I could stop myself I was asleep.

When I jerked awake I didn't know what time it was. I held myself still and tried to hear my parents so that I'd know they hadn't gone to sleep and left me alone. Then I heard my father snoring in their room, and I knew they had, because he always went to bed last. His snores broke off, probably because my mother had nudged him in her sleep, and for a while I couldn't hear anything except my own breathing, so loud it made me feel I was suffocating. And then I heard another sound in my room.

It was a creaking as if something was trying to straighten itself. It might have been cardboard, but I wasn't sure, because I couldn't tell how far away from me it was. I dug my fingers into the mattress to stop myself shaking, and held my breath until I was almost sure the sound was ahead of me, between me and the door. I listened until I couldn't hold my breath any longer, and it came out in a gasp. And then I dug my fingers into the mattress so hard my nails bent, and banged my head against the wall behind the pillow, because Harold Mealing had risen up in front of me.

I could only really see his face. There was less of it than last time I'd seen it, and maybe that was why it was smiling even harder, both wider and taller than a mouth ought to be able to go. His body was a dark shape he was struggling to raise, whether because it was stiff or crippled I couldn't tell. I could still hear it creaking. It might have been cardboard or a corpse, because I couldn't make out how close he was, at the end of the bed and big as life or standing on the quilt in front of my face, the size he'd been in the book. All I could do was bruise my head as I shoved the back of it against the wall, the furthest I could get away from him.

He shivered upright until his face was above mine, and his hands came flapping towards me. I was almost sure he was no bigger than he'd been in the book, but that didn't help me, because I could feel myself shrinking until I was small enough to carry away into the dark, all of me that mattered. He leaned toward me as if he was toppling over, and I started to scream.

I heard one of my parents waken, far away. I heard one of them stumble out of bed. I was afraid they would be too late, because now I'd started screaming I couldn't stop, and the figure that was smaller than my head was leaning down as if it meant to crawl into my mouth and hide there or drag what it wanted out of me. Somehow I managed to let go of the mattress and flail my hands at him. I hardly knew what I was doing, but I felt my fist close around something that broke and wriggled, just as the light came on.

The Black Spiral: Twisted Tales of Terror

Both my parents ran in. "It's all right, Timmy, we're here," my mother said, and to my father, "It must be that medicine. We won't give him any more."

I clenched my fist harder and stared around the room. "I've got him," I babbled. "Where's the book?"

They knew which one I meant, because they exchanged a glance. At first I couldn't understand why they looked almost guilty. "You're to remember what I said, Timmy," my father said. "We should always respect books. But listen, son, that one was bothering you so much I made an exception. You can forget about it. I put it in the bin and burnt it before we came to bed."

I stared at him as if that could make him take back what he said. "But that means I can't put him back," I cried.

"What've you got there, Timmy? Let me see," my mother said, and watched until I opened my fist. There was nothing inside it except a smear of red that she eventually convinced me was ink.

When she saw I was afraid to be left alone she stayed with me all night. After a while I fell asleep because I couldn't stay awake, though I knew Harold Mealing was still hiding somewhere. He'd slipped out of my fist when I wasn't looking, and now I'd lost my chance to trap him and get rid of him.

My mother took me to the doctor in the morning and got me some new medicine that made me sleep even when I was afraid to. It couldn't stop me being afraid of books, even when my parents sent *Beware of the Smile* back to the publisher and found out that the publisher had gone bankrupt from gambling too much money on Harold Mealing's books. I thought that would only make Harold Mealing more spiteful. I had to read at school, but I never enjoyed a book again. I'd get my friends to shake them open to make sure there was nothing inside them before I would touch them, only before long I didn't have many friends. Sometimes I thought I felt something squirming under the page I was reading, and I'd throw the book on the floor.

I thought I'd grown out of this when I went to college. Writing what I've written shows I'm not afraid of things just because they're written down. I worked so hard at college I almost forgot to be afraid of books. Maybe that's why he kept wakening me at night with his smile half the height of his face and his hands that feel like insects on my cheeks. Yes, I set fire to the library, but I didn't know what else to do. I thought he might be hiding in one of those books.

The Black Spiral: Twisted Tales of Terror

    Now I know that was a mistake. Now you and my parents and the rest of them smile at me and say I'll be better for writing it down, only you don't realize how much it's helped me see things clear. I don't know yet which of you smilers Harold Mealing is pretending to be, but I will when I've stopped the rest of you smiling. And then I'll tear him up to prove it to all of you. I'll tear him up just as I'm going to tear up this paragraph.

The Black Spiral: Twisted Tales of Terror

Dead Heat

Richard D. Weber

As the speedometer needle shivered past ninety, Madison squinted anxiously through the bug-splattered windshield of the stolen Shelby Mustang Cobra. Overhead, the sky was blue and cloudless. The lemon-yellow sun was a blast furnace that blistered the desert landscape below. She rocketed down the lonely ribbon of highway that stretched through the isolated expanse of Sonoran Desert, barren and abandoned by all except the sentinel Saguaro cactuses which provided neither shelter or shade to the local inhabitants: lizards, scorpions, tumbleweeds, and the stubble of desert scrub.

AC/DC's "Highway to Hell" blasted from the car's CD player. The sheen of perspiration glistened on her sun-browned forearms as she clutched the steering wheel in a white-knuckled grip. Madison bobbed her head in rhythm with the music, hoping the pounding beat would somehow absorb her splitting migraine. She was about thirty. Encased in extra-short denim cut-offs, a white halter-top that accentuated her ample sweat-filmed cleavage, and with those powder-blue eyes peeking out from tresses of platinum-blonde hair, she was a definite ten on the Richter scale. And yet it was more than the sum of these attributes that made her so attractive to men: it was the innocence, the woman-child quality she exuded like hot steam.

Beneath that rough, street-wise facade lay a wounded sparrow. Her puckish, upturned nose and the light sprinkling of freckles on her oval face and forearms hinted at the truth. When she smiled a skeptical dimple appeared on those perfect cheeks. And her gaze turned from coolly sensual to slightly mischievous in an instant.

She never had to ask men for help—they just offered it. A long string of off-again, on-again romances, guys who wanted nothing more than to get into her pants. Now isn't that the truth, the story of my life, she thought. Just another babe in Boyland. Maybe that's what got me into this mess? She only hoped her luck would hold, that she'd draw the wild card and make off with the whole pot, with her life.

The windows were down and the raw, hot air flamed her long sun-bleached hair. A couple of miles back the temperature gauge began creeping toward the red. She'd killed the air-conditioning to avoid overheating the engine and becoming stranded in bum-fuck Egypt.

The Black Spiral: Twisted Tales of Terror

She glanced at the brown leather satchel that lay on the passenger seat. Reaching into the bag, she pulled out a bundle of crisp new bank notes, hundred-dollar bills, and blotted the perspiration from her forehead and the nape of her long neck. She took a deep whiff and sighed before pitching the money back into the bag.

With her spine melting into the seatback and her buttocks numb from the long road trip, she squirmed in the bucket seat seeking relief. That's when she spotted the convenience store, about a half a mile ahead. "Thank God, a stop-N-rob. An ice-cold drink, a little junk food, and some coolant for *Frank*," she said aloud. (Frank was her nickname for the Mustang coined after Steve McQueen's character Detective *Frank Bullitt* in the movie with the same surname.) She eased off the gas slightly, causing the throaty exhaust to pop as it backed down. "How about a three-point landing, Frank?" She cranked the wheel, braked hard, and fishtailed to a stop, nestling in dangerously close to the paint-chipped gas pumps.

She exited the car, burning her hand on the sun-baked dark highland-green metal-flake paint of the door panel as she slammed it. Then she opened the trunk, placed the money satchel in a secret compartment, and slammed it shut.

An old Indian man with a sun-leathered face, wearing a white long-sleeve shirt buttoned high at the collar and black vest, slowly raised his head as he sat at his perch alongside the entrance door, creaking to and fro in a weathered rocking chair. His filmy *un*blinking eyes peered out from beneath the black wide-brimmed hat he wore complete with an eagle feather saluting from its silver *concho* hatband.

He rose slowly and ambled toward her.

It wasn't until he stood a few feet from her that she noticed he was blind. Giving a sightless nod and looking slightly over her shoulder, he asked, "Fill her up, young lady?" She nodded in response, then catching herself, said, "Yes, please. And add some coolant. She's starting to overheat."

He scratched his chin and shrugged. "Yup, plenty hot today. Better go on inside and cool off. I'll getcha back on the road."

As Madison headed for the door, she paused and turned. "Say, how'd you know I was a young lady?"

He grunted. "Can't say you're a lady, just being polite. But my granddaughter likes that perfume your wearing, too."

The Black Spiral: Twisted Tales of Terror

As she walked, the pea-gravel beneath her feet crunched with each step. She stopped short of the door. From the north came the sound of an engine, low at first but gradually growing louder even as she cocked her head to look in that direction. On the nearby crest of the highway the curtains of heat shimmer parted to reveal a huge tour bus looming into view. It lumbered into the drive and pulled up on the other side of the pumps, its air brakes hissing as it rolled to a stop. Because it was painted satin black and lined with dark tinted windows, and because the only variation in this color scheme was a line of hand-painted skulls (half of which were slashed with red X's that dotted the side like hatch marks on the side of a WW II bomber), Madison thought it must be some touring rock band's road bus, maybe even Ozzy's. *Too bad I don't have time to stick around for an autograph*, she thought, chuckling under her breath.

A blast of artic air washed over her as she entered the store, leaching the heat from her skin. Madison made a beeline for a tub of iced beer and wine coolers. She snatched a rosé cooler from the ice, screwed off the cap, threw back her head, and chugged it down in one long pull. Next she scrambled to the junk-food display, grabbing a handful of Slim Jims, a Snickers bar, and three bags of assorted chips. She was famished and dehydrated, needing the salt and sugar boost, badly.

"Hey, hope you're planin' on paying for that stuff, lady!" a young voice shouted from behind the counter.

Madison turned, cheeks flushed and slightly embarrassed by her gluttony. A young girl, radiantly beautiful: about twelve years old, with liquid-brown eyes, delicate features, and skin as smooth and flawless as milk chocolate, stood with a quizzical look as she peered out from behind the cash register. She wore a short-sleeved white blouse, yellowed and frayed at the collar.

A smile blossomed on Madison's lips as she moved to the checkout counter, took in the beaded hand-tooled Indian belt cinched around the girl's faded jeans (just like the one she'd treasured when she was a kid), and plopped down her horde of munchies.

The girl said, "Didn't mean to be rude, ya know. Grandpa says it's 'cause I'm half Native American and half Irish. Black Irish, that is."

"Is that right?" Madison strained not to laugh.

"Never had any desire for Irish whiskey or fire water, either, though. Go figure, huh?"

The Black Spiral: Twisted Tales of Terror

Madison just stared, slightly dumfounded by the girl's remarks and demeanor. Then, collecting her thoughts, she asked, "Could I have a couple of packs of Marlboros and a six-pack of Pepsi, please?"

Turning to remove the soda from the cooler behind her, then reaching on tiptoe to pull the cigarettes from the overhead rack, she said, "By the way my name's Chyna. Chyna Pureheart. That's Chyna with a Y instead of an I, of course."

"Chyna with a Y it is, then. My name's Madison, like the city. Madison Chase."

"Guess your mom had a weird sense of humor, too." The girl giggled, took a deep breath, and continued. "Anyway, Grandpa says my mama loved it so—china that is—and that's why she collected it. We've got boxes and boxes of it upstairs." Chyna's gaze lowered to the countertop. "But she didn't take it, or *me,* with her when she left."

"Sorry, that must have been—"

"Well, it hasn't been a picnic, being named after a set of plates! But after Daddy died . . . well, I guess it was what they call a case of arrested development." Seeming to notice Madison's confusion at her use of adult terms, she added. "Oh, I'm plenty smart, ya know. Self-taught. Grandpa bought me a computer with an Internet connection and an Encyclopedia Britannica CD. Likes me to read to him, he's blind, I hope you noticed."

"Yes, that's him out at the pump?"

"None other! Now where was I? Oh, ya . . . Mama wasn't mature enough to cope with the shock. Now, me, I've got ice water in these veins." Chyna held out her inner forearm and jabbed it with her index finger.

It was then that Madison noticed the deformity. Chyna's arm was withered and twisted slightly at the shoulder.

Madison bent down and pretended to make a careful examination of her arm. She raised her head and smiled. "Guess that makes two of us. My mom took a powder, too, when I was about eight. Left me, Gunny Sgt. Chase (she never referred to him as Dad), and my three brothers to fend for ourselves."

Chyna's stare radiated empathy. "Still hurts, doesn't it?"

Madison shrugged. "I was a military brat, moving from one base to another, no chance to make any real friends." She paused a beat, her lower lip trembling slightly. With a flick of her sun-lightened hair, she shook it off. "Life is pain, get used to it, kid."

The Black Spiral: Twisted Tales of Terror

With those harsh words, Chyna stiffened slightly.

But Madison's eyes looked past the girl now, taking in the Arizona DPS Highway Patrol cruiser as it pulled into the drive and parked. Icy fingers shot up and down her spine, rising to the back of her neck. She swallowed hard. When she turned back to Chyna, she saw that the girl was also looking out the window. As Chyna's eyes met hers with a knowing look, she whispered conspiratorially, "Maybe *now* would be a good time for you to use the restroom."

Pitching a twenty on the counter, Madison spun on her heels and headed for the john. Chyna cried out, "That's trooper Bob. He makes a regular pit stop for a mocha coffee and a honey roll. He's usually outta here in about fifteen. Don't worry, I've got your back, Blondie."

Huddled in the ladies' room, quaking in her Reebocks, sat Madison. "I must be slipping. That kid read me like a cheap hooker scopin' out a john at the bus terminal in Toledo. Smelled my fear and need," she said in an angry whisper. She glared into the mirror. "Get a grip, girl!" Then she opened the tap wide and bent, letting the tepid water pour over the back of her neck. She rose, shook her head, and finger-combed her hair with long, lacquered nails. Plucked at her bloodshot eyes and sighed. "Now what? I'm trapped in this shithole, a cop's right out side the door, and I gotta depend on a crazy kid."

But somehow she knew, on a deep instinctual level, that she could indeed count on Chyna. Somehow they were sisters under the flesh. Somehow she knew that she would have to repay the favor. And sooner than she would've liked.

Sucking in a deep breath and holding it, she pressed her ear to the door. She could make out muffled voices, a laugh, the chime of the cash register and then … a gunshot. First one shot boomed, followed by a second, so loud the door seemed to vibrate against her skull. Then a scream. Chyna's scream. A struggle, broken glass, a loud thud crashed against the door. Madison leaped back, toppled over the toilet, and banged her head hard on the wall. Dazed and disoriented, she struggled to her feet.

"Jesus, I've got to get to her!" she managed in a rasping voice. She scrambled for the door, then hesitated. What am I doing? I can't go out there. The cop!

Another scream. Louder, pleading.

The Black Spiral: Twisted Tales of Terror

Instinct overcame self-preservation, doubt. Running full bore on adrenaline now, Madison yanked at the door. All three hundred pounds of trooper Bob's limp body spilled into the cramped restroom, directly on top of her, pinning her to the floor. His bulging eye stared sightlessly into hers. A bloodstain flowered on his chest. And half of his face was blown off.

Madison gagged choking back the flaming river of bile in her throat. She pushed and shoved, finally freeing herself. But as she rose on pudding legs, she stopped, bent over, and snatched the .40 S&W Beretta from the trooper's holster along with two extra magazines nestled on in leather holders on his gun belt. She tucked them into her waistband.

As she rounded the corner of the restroom doorway, she heard Chyna's muffled plea. "No! Please don't hit my grandpa again. Please!" Riddled through with anger, Madison charged through the convenience store, her eyes ticking right then left, taking in the empty cash register lying smashed on the floor and searching for targets as she moved. The air hung heavy blue, laced with the scent of cordite.

Up ahead, she spotted him as she peered through the shattered front glass door. A short little creep decked out in black PVC pants and shirt. With his broad freckled face, jug ears, moronic expression, and orange-dye-job clipper-cut hairdo, he would have looked almost comical if he wasn't whaling on the old Indian with a lead pipe, laying blow after blow across the old man's kneecaps. His partner, a tall, skinny, death-walking albino with white-blond shoulder length hair looked on.

As if the scene was being played across her mind in slow motion, Madison took in the gruesome tableau. The albino wore a charcoal-colored rain slicker whose tails whipped in the hot breeze like the Jolly Roger atop the mast of a ghost ship. He had one arm hooked beneath Chyna's throat, forcing her to watch as his pal beat her grandpa to a bloody pulp. And all the while he stroked Chyna's silken raven-blue hair with the long, tapered fingers of his free hand. He bent over and placed a gentle but nauseatingly long kiss on the top of her head.

Jacking a round into the semi-auto's chamber, Madison crashed through the entrance door and leveled her sights dead on the little carrot-top's head, just as the lead pipe began to arc downward again.

She screamed, "Drop it or I'll splatter your brains, asshole!"

Madison had been instructed in the use of handguns by her father, Gunny Sgt. Chase the ex-marine; however, just now, as she stood there, facing down these two psychos from Hell, she wasn't quite sure she could look into a man's eyes and pop a cap into his brainpan or not. She sucked in ragged breaths, commanding her wrist not to let the Beretta waver. Determined to show no fear.

But instead of dropping the pipe the little creep turned slowly, fixing her with his beady eyes, taunting her with his cackling laughter. He took a step forward.

Staring at him now, Madison decided that his Alfred E. Newman face didn't, after all, look the least bit funny. In fact, as he took another step, it looked distorted and less than human, like a freak in a sideshow.

As Madison readjusted her sweat-slick grip on the Beretta, her eyes ticked to Chyna who stood frozen with fear, trembling uncontrollably, then back to the advancing carrot-top, who still held the lead pipe high over his head.

It occurred to her that these two circus escapees were either totally *amped* out on crystal meth or more cold-blooded than a Gila monster in heat. Either way she didn't have many options and she new it.

Suddenly the albino spoke, which seemed to stop carrot-top in his tracks. "Welcome to the party, Madison. Care to join me and the little one here on our journey?" He patted Chyna on the head as he said it. He held Madison's eyes for a long beat, fixed her with those exceptional pink-bullet eyes. And when she looked closely, she saw that his face burned coldly, like the moon on a cold winter night. "Come on now, be a good girl, Madison. Put down that gun. Someone could get hurt. All we want is the *money*."

So that's what it was all about, the damn money. Money she'd earned from street racing. Risking life and limb for the last five years. One midnight run after the next, so many that the towns, the streets, even the faces had bled together, a distant blur now. All accept one face: Sonny's face, her boyfriend and son of Toni "the Bookmaker" Manzenera—boss of the Vegas mob. Sonny had died in pileup during their last race, a race she'd won. A race Toni had wanted her to loose. And to make sure—he had his hoods sabotage her car's brakes. But at the last minute she'd switched cars with Sonny. For luck Sonny had said. And now Toni blamed her, wanted to avenge his son's death by sending these two goons.

A bead of sweat began at her hairline and slowly crept down her forehead, then down the bridge of her nose. Her heart trip-hammered beneath her ribcage. Her arms throbbed with a glassy pain from extending them in the two-handed firing position for so long.

The Black Spiral: Twisted Tales of Terror

She steeled herself. "I don't give a rat's ass if *the Bookmaker* eats your liver for breakfast. The money's mine, Sonny's and mine, just like the Cobra, you bastard. But let go of the girl. Do it right now or die, motherfucker!"

The albino nodded his acquiescence and said, "As you wish."

But just as he feigned releasing Chyna, he shouted, "*Now*, Mr. Nemo!" Carrot-top lunged at her. Squeezing off two rounds at point-blank range, but shooting too low, she caught him in the kneecap and inner thigh.

He went down on his good knee, howling like a baby.

Turning to the albino, Mr. Nemo squealed like a stuck pig, "The crazy bitch shot me, Mr. Frost." Tears welled in his eyes as he extended a pouting lower lip. "She damn near shot off my fuckin' balls!" Almost as soon as he said it, Mr. Nemo was back on his feet. He grabbed his injured leg at the kneecap and twisted hard. Puffing out his cheeks and wheezing in a high-pitched voice, he said, "There now, that's better. Never had anyone clip my *huevos*, not sure if they'd snap back."

She stared in awe and disbelief for a second.

He smiled then, a dreadful smile; it was as if some strange fleshy thing was suddenly sprouting in the middle of his face as his eyes locked on Madison. "Don't worry, bitch. I've still got plenty of juice left for *you*." His hand shot to his boot, pulled a small-bladed knife. The desert sun's rays glinted off the cold steel.

"Oh, honey, only four inches," Madison taunted—

—then remembered Chyna.

But before she could turn and sight on the albino, something hot whizzed past her cheek. Spinning toward the albino, she found herself looking down the barrel of a S&W .357 magnum. Sunlight kicked off the nickel-plated steel of the revolver, which filled his bone-white hand. And just now as she stood frozen, the glaring sun burning her retinas— staring down the business end of the magnum was more like looking down the barrel of a howitzer canon on a naval gunship. She tried to shoot, but he was using Chyna as a shield as he moved toward the bus; she couldn't manage a clear field of fire.

She heard the gunshot, saw the muzzle flash, and collapsed to the ground as a searing pain speared her forehead. Darkness fell.

Carrot-top stood, leering over her. "Shit, ya missed, just winged her." His gaze followed the contours of her sweat-glazed breasts. Animal lust sculpted his face. His upper lip curled in an involuntary sneer, his nostrils flared, and the lids of his eyes drooped ominously low. He wanted to run his hands over her, probing what she had. "Okay, bitch," he said, reaching out, "now we'll see who's so tough, ehh."

The albino's voice cut him short. "Mr. Nemo, it's time we made our departure."

"But, you promised," Nemo whined, screwing up his face in a childlike pout and turning to the albino in confusion. "Mr. Frost . . . you promised I could play with her when we found her."

"Keep your filthy mitts off her, you mother-raping, crybaby! You touch her and so help me God—" Chyna screamed as her elbow shot back into the albino's midsection, her foot stomped down, raking his shin, smashing his instep. But seemingly impervious to pain he held her fast.

"The child's right. Put the knife away, Mr. Nemo. You make such a *mess* when you play," the albino said coldly as he stooped over and snuggled his cheek against Chyna's. "She's our little bargaining chip,"—he paused, holding her closer—"and as long as we have the child, Ms. Chase will follow. Let's give her time to think it over."

Carrot-top's eyes gravitated to Chyna. He shrugged, and brought the knife's blade to his lips. Licking it, he said, "Well honey, I guess you'll have to be Uncle Nemo's new playmate."

The blood drained from Chyna's face.

Mr. Frost's rough hands whirled her about. He placed his skeletal fingers beneath her chin, forcing it upward, and held her with his gaze. Chyna glared back defiantly but her lower lip began quivering uncontrollably, betraying the frightened little girl within.

"Don't worry, Chyna *precious*," Mr. Frost said softly, the ominous underlying tone of his voice moving closer to the surface as he continued, "as long as you're a good girl, you'll have nothing to fear." And his face, like his voice, once masked in polite formality with a hint of humanity, dissolved into the blotched rictus of brutal contempt as he said, "Isn't that correct, Mr. Nemo?"

Chyna stiffened and spat, "And don't call me—Precious!"

With heat blistering her cheek and a furnace blast of dry air scorching her lungs, she awoke. Slightly woozy, Madison struggled to her feet. A blurry image floated before her, gradually clearing and taking on form.

It was the old Indian.

The Black Spiral: Twisted Tales of Terror

As a burning, tingling sensation crawled across her scalp, Madison's hand shot to her head. Fingertips gently explored the scalp wound, roving over caked blood. "Bastard only grazed me, thank God!" she said aloud, her teeth clenched tightly, her face grimaced with pain. With faltering steps, like a punch-stunned fighter, she staggered toward the old man. Reaching him, she collapsed and edged to his side on hands and knees. He wheezed in short, ragged breaths. His left eye was swollen shut. Having checked his pulse (weak but steady) and applying a makeshift tourniquet to a seeping wound, she gingerly reached out and stroked his long gray hair. "Don't you die on me, old timer."

He came to with a start and managed, "Who you callin' an old timer? I'm just reachin' my prime!" He coughed, spit blood, then nodded, beckoning her closer. Tears crowded Madison's eyes as she pressed her ear almost to his lips.

As his cataract-filmed eyes stared sightlessly, he whispered in a voice that was gritty with weariness, "Not much time . . . save granddaughter, Chyna."

Blood bubbled from his lips.

Madison shuddered, shook her head. "But you don't understand. I can't . . . I'm—"

"—on the run." He finished her words. "Running no good. Money no good. Can't run from fate. She always find you."

Madison's mouth gaped wide in disbelief. "How did you know? You couldn't possibly—"

"NO TIME . . . run other way, save Chyna." His sun-weathered hand slowly rose, clasping hers and guiding it towards his neck. "Take medicine bag. Much power against evil spirits. Go west, they go west."

There around his neck hung a small soft leather pouch. With his last ounce of strength, he ripped the bag from his throat and dropped it into her palm. A soothing warmth flowed from the pouch and into her hand, slowly coursing up her arm to her chest as she clasped it firmly. Madison's silence telegraphed her confusion.

"The evil ones have her now. Go quickly. Save my—"

"But how do—"

"When the time comes, you'll know what to do."

Before she could respond his head lolled to one side and he was gone. After reaching out and gently closing his eyelids, she snatched the Beretta from the ground. Then she stood and strode toward the Mustang, her every step fueled with newfound determination, anger.

The Black Spiral: Twisted Tales of Terror

The Cobra's 390 horsepower 4.6-L supercharged V8 roared to life. The low rumble of the exhaust changed to a deafening snarl as Madison revved the metallic beast, then exploded as she backed off the gas. She strapped on her shoulder harness, slammed it into gear, popped the clutch, and put the pedal to the metal. The muscle car surged, its rear end lashing from side to side, it's 17-inch Eagle radials spewing dirt and raising clouds of dust. When it hit the roadway, its tires chirped with each up shift as she hit sixty in less than five seconds.

It was a simple matter of mechanics, she thought. The pony car's top end was one hundred and fifty miles per hour. The giant behemoth of a bus probably redlined at about ninety-five and cornered about as well as a skunk-drunk Methodist preacher driving a hay wagon filled with a caterwauling load of piano-legged fat ladies on New Years Eve. Sure they had a head start, about twenty minutes, but she could cruise at ninety all day in sixth gear and catch up in no time. Then it hit her. What about turnoffs? She fumbled for the road map. Her eyes flicking back and forth from the road to the map, she determined that there were no major arteries that intersected the highway for about fifty miles. "Yessss," she half-sang in a Gene-Wilder-like high falsetto as she patted the dash, "We bad, we bad." Puffing out her cheeks and blowing, she tossed the map and punched the CD player. Marilyn Manson's voice flooded the car.

The highway was flat, seemingly stretching into eternity with no oncoming traffic in sight, only a billboard advertising the biggest steak west of the Pecos. When the next sign proclaimed the restaurant's name—Trigger's Corral, she neighed her response.

The daylight slowly began to surrender. The bleeding sunset edged the horizon. Purple dusk painted the desert and darkened her mood. She rolled the dilemma around in her mind. What the hell am I doing? Turn this puppy around. Forget the kid. Since when do you give a damn, since when have you ever done anything right? But then she heard her father, Gunny Chase's voice echoing through her mind, repeating the words he'd said the day her mother left, "Life is pain, get used to it, kid." That was reason enough. Reason enough to *finally* do the right thing.

She'd been driving for about thirty minutes, crooning along with the dark one, her eyes scanning the roadway ahead when a horn blared from behind.

The Black Spiral: Twisted Tales of Terror

Her gaze flashed to the rearview mirror. The huge, flat, black-faced grille of the tour bus leered back. With its high beams blazing and with it's custom-painted jagged-tooth grin, it looked like a ravenous demon, screeching down upon her. Marilyn Manson's voice, still purring from the CD player, droned in her ears.

"Damn!" Somehow they'd circled back, she thought. Got behind me . . . but how? Were there any turnoffs? No, hell no!

She punched off the music.

Without thinking, she had eased off the gas. Her eyes ticked to the speedometer: seventy-five—she pressed the accelerator—eighty now—then eighty-five. The horn blasted again, jerking her attention back to the rearview mirror. The bus was bearing down on her fast like a hungry shark. Suddenly it whipped into the passing lane, steadily increasing speed until it pulled abreast of her.

"What the hell is the sonofabitch doing?" she cursed, her temples pulsing, her throat knotting. "Think, Madison. Think!"

She stole a sideways glance. The door of the bus knifed open. Mr. Nemo, the carrot-top geek, appeared and leveled a sawed-off 12 gauge right at her. Instinctively, she jammed the brakes just as shot pellets spiderwebbed the Mustang's windshield.

Raking in behind them now, she placed the Beretta in her lap, double clutched through the gears—eliciting a throaty double-tap bark from the dual exhaust with each up shift—and roared ahead, swerving sharply into the oncoming lane. In seconds she was alongside the driver's side window of the bus. She punched the armrest button lowering the passenger window, grabbed the semi-auto and leveled it. The albino's ashen profile appeared. However, since he was perched much higher than her position in the low-slung Mustang, the angle was no good. She had to drop back to get a clear shot.

Raising the weapon again, she took aim. But just as she squeezed the trigger she thought of Chyna, thought of the gigantic leviathan careening out of control with her onboard, her tiny body being tossed like a beanbag back and forth against the sides of the motor coach. Madison pulled the shot; the round sparked off the side of the bus.

Madison kept the needle steady on eighty, pacing the bus. The motor coach cast its pale shadow on the side of the Mustang. The steady hum of tires and rushing keen of the slipstream sang in chorus as they rocketed in tandem down the sideroad to Hell. Her eyes darted between the road and the bus. The albino turned toward her, sunlight glinting off his Ray-Bans, and suddenly pulled hard left. The bus careened across the centerline—pummeling the side of the muscle car with a glancing blow.

Her teeth shook with the force of the collision.

Tortured sheet metal shrieked and buckled.

As the steering wheel was nearly ripped from Madison's hands, she wrestled it and held tight as the pony car lurched onto the shoulder, kicking up gravel that sprayed noisily against the undercarriage. The steering wheel shook, sending bone-numbing vibrations up her arms.

Time and the world blurred into slow motion.

Don't hit the brakes, foot off the gas, her mind coached matter-of-factly as experience overruled panic.

Regaining control, Madison hitched the wheel to the right and plunged back onto the blacktop. She stood on the gas, double clutching through the gears, sending all 390-ft. lbs. of torque to the rear axle, which caused the Cobra's tail end to whip violently as she closed the distance in seconds.

Frantically, her eyes searched the dash gauges. They read normal. "Good boy, Frank," she said, praising the Cobra's stamina. "Now let's frag their ass!"

As she tucked the Mustang tight on their butt and eased off the gas, the throaty bark of the dual exhaust empowered her. With unblinking eyes, she took in the red custom-painted letters scrawled across the back of the bus that read:

LEGION

Spidery fingers ran up the hollow tube of her spine. She shook it off with a curt, "Goddamn metalheads . . ."

Now it was her turn to stand on the horn as she veered into the passing lane and shot along side of the bus.

"That's right! We bad, we bad—you motherfucker!" she shouted.

Mr. Frost, the albino, spun around with a start. A puzzled look played over his face as he peered out the driver's window. Their eyes locked.

Madison shot him the bird.

The raw bone of a smile creased his face as he removed his sunglasses. But his pink-bullet eyes glared. And right now, as she met his hate-filled stare, it was as if he could smell her fear right through her skin, drink it right through her eyes.

The Black Spiral: Twisted Tales of Terror

Her gaze ticked to the road, took in the arroyo on her left and the silvery blur of the guardrail as the onrushing pavement disappeared beneath the cowl of the Cobra's hood.

Then almost on cue, the motor coach slowly veered toward her, edging closer and closer. Madison's frantic gaze shot from the bus to the guardrail and back again.

"Oh, fuck—me . . . I'm pressed ham!" she said, gritting her teeth.

The giant beast snuggled in, pinning her car against the guardrail. The shriek of steel on steel filled the air as sparks showered her windshield. The crushing jolt caused her clenched teeth to slip. She winced in pain as her upper teeth cut deeply into her lip.

She swallowed salty blood.

Fought the sweat-slicked leather-gloved steering wheel as it spun through her hands.

But then: the guardrail ended. The bus hurtled past.

Madison struggled for breath as the pony car's tubular stabilizer bars failed to arrest the G-forces. The rear end broke right. *Steer into the slide.* Then, broke left, finally spinning out of control in a perfect one-eighty and lurched to a halt, cocooned in a cloud of dust.

In a blind rage, she pounded the wheel with her fists, then coughed and gagged as blood filled her throat. After cradling her head in her arms on the wheel, Madison sobbed, half in shock, half in defeat.

"Fuck, this isn't fair. I try to do something right and …"—she stiffened, blinked back tears, and lifted her head—"and bullshit, Madison! Get a grip. Life is pain, get used to it, kid."

As she reached for the ignition, she said, "Okay, Frank. Don't fail me now." Raising her crossed fingers, she cranked the key with her free hand. The big block V8 whined and sputtered. She squeezed her eyes tight, twisted a kink out of her neck, and tried again. Like an enraged lioness defending her cub, the engine let loose a deafening growl, followed quickly by a bloodthirsty roar.

Her hand shot out and rammed the gearshift into first, tromped the accelerator. The over-sized radials spun, then gripped, spraying dirt and gravel as she powered out of the fishtail and back onto the highway.

The battered Mustang shuddered violently as the needle hit eighty. Bent frame, she thought. Just hold on, Frank. You can do it, boy.

Up ahead, on the heat-bent road was the bus.

The Black Spiral: Twisted Tales of Terror

Instinctively and in one silken motion, she slapped it into sixth gear and floored it. The high-pitched whine of the Eaton Supercharger kicked in. The needle climbed to 100 . . . still whining . . . 115—

She was closing fast.

—130 mph.

The landscape melted into a Salvador Dali painting as she whipped past, balls-out in the oncoming lane.

The pony car rocketed past the motor coach with such speed it was as if the lumbering Mammoth was mired in a lava pool. But the punch-drunk Mustang quaked beneath her, seemingly ready to burst into shards of shrapnel any second.

What's the plan here, Madison? her mind taunted.

Nervously, her hand clawed at her neck as a maelstrom whirled inside Madison's head. That's when she felt it; the medicine bag the old Indian had given her.

What was it he said? In her mind's eye his face took shape, his dying, raspy voice whispered, "When the time comes, you'll know what to do."

A good thousand yards in front of them now she eased off the gas, the needle gradually dipping to seventy. She pulled the emergency brake, spun the wheel hard to the left, and executed a near perfect bootleg turn. The car lurched to a halt, now facing in exactly the opposite direction.

By the time she leaped from the car, the bus was about seven hundred yards away and closing fast, aimed straight for her.

With the totem bag clenched between her teeth, she popped the trunk and hoisted the leather satchel.

Six hundred yards and closing.

Now only five hundred—

Four, three . . .

The hulking shape bore down on her.

Hundred dollar bills filled the air, floating on updrafts as Madison continued to toss fistful after fistful of her nest egg above her head.

Two hundred yards and closing fast . . .

Air brakes screamed. Rubber barked. A loud boom rippled the air as one on the bus's tires exploded into shreds. The front bumper nosed downward; the rear end sheered to the right. Invisible hands pitched the bus onto its side, as if it was the discarded plaything of a spoiled giant. The tortured sequel of rending metal and a curtain of sparks filled the air as it slid on its side down the pavement at a thirty degree angle.

Paralyzed, Madison watched as ten tons of metal hurtled toward her. Her eyes vacant and her effect flat, she gazed outward with blank detachment. Clutching the medicine pouch firmly in her hand, her eyes sealed tight, she envisioned Chyna's sweet face, *secure and unharmed, secure and unharmed*. She repeated it like a mantra.

The totem bag burned red-hot in her hand.

Then her focus shifted to the bus. She visualized it swerving past her at the last minute.

And then it did.

Madison's eyes opened just in time to see the terror-filled face of Mr. Frost pressed to the windshield of the bus as it slung past her. All trace of personality pared away, stripped to its naked essence. Oily, foul, and malignant. A demon's face.

Then, the molten blur of the bus streamed past, so close that its slipstream flamed her hair, seemed to brush the angel hairs of her forearm. It's wake knocked her off her feet and headlong into the Mustang. Her skull cracked hard as it hit the crumpled sheet metal.

The door of the overturned bus sprung open. First a bloodied hand emerged, then an arm. Chyna Pureheart strained as she pulled herself over the lip of the doorframe and onto the side of the bus. Next she took the rope slung over her shoulder and fastened it to the door handle, slipped over the side, and lowered herself hand over hand. The fragile muscles of her withered arm corded as she moved.

Once on the ground she scanned the wreckage. Eyes screeching, heart pounding. Then she saw her; Madison lay sprawled on the pavement, her body dead-still. Sucking in ragged breaths, Chyna bolted toward her. As she knelt at her side, she took in the trickle of blood oozing from Madison's hairline.

"Madison," she shouted, in a quavering voice.

No response.

She shook her, pounded her chest with clenched fists.

Still no response.

Tears spilled down her soft cheeks.

The Black Spiral: Twisted Tales of Terror

"Don't you die on me!" she half-shouted, half-sobbed in a voice laced with hurt and anger. "Get up right now, you hear me. Life is pain, get used to it, kid!"

Madison stirred slightly and moaned with the queer and plaintive keen of a tiny wounded animal. Then her eyes winked opened. She sat up. Chyna threw her arms around her, hugged her tightly as if she'd never let go. After a brief moment, Chyna looked up and as a weak smile dimpled her cheeks, she said, "I knew you'd come. I just knew it."

Tears crowded Madison's eyes as she chewed her lower lip.

Chyna asked beseechingly, "But you'll never leave me, either . . . will ya?"

Madison reached out and gently held Chyna's innocent, tear-tracked face in the palms of her hands and looked deeply into her eyes. "No, honey. Never."

Two hours later as they were seated in a roadside diner, Chyna slurped the last of a chocolate milkshake and belched.

Madison scowled and shook her head. "Whoa, young lady. Where are your manners?"

"Sorry, but I left them under my bed. Didn't exactly have time to pack, now did I?"

Madison smiled. "No, I guess we'll have to buy you a new set."

"I could use a new wardrobe, too, but that would depend on our next port of call, wouldn't it?"

"Port of call?"

"Yeah, our next stop, silly. A thong bikini or a parka and snowshoes?"

Madison donned her sunglasses and rose from the table. "You can't salsa in snowshoes very well. So, how's about some Capri pants and a nice blouse instead? Mexico is pretty nice this time of year."

Chyna frowned. "I'd prefer Rio, but if you insist." Then she shrugged and mimicking Madison, she slipped on her matching sunglasses.

Grabbing the leather satchel with one hand and taking Chyna by the arm with the other, Madison steered her toward the register. They paid the check and as they turned for the door, the waitress said, "Nice little girl you've got there, ma'am."

A smile curled Madison's lips as she and Chyna exchanged knowing glances.

The Black Spiral: Twisted Tales of Terror

Chyna's eyes popped wide as she asked ever so demurely, "Mommy, can we get a dog?"

* * *

The Black Spiral: Twisted Tales of Terror

CUTS

F. Paul Wilson

It started in Milo's right foot. He awoke in the dark of his bedroom with a pins-and-needles sensation from the lower part of his calf to the tips of his toes. He sat up, massaged it, walked around the bedroom. Nothing helped. Finally, he took a Darvocet and went back to bed. He managed to get to sleep but was awake again by dawn, this time with both feet tingling. In the wan light, he inspected his lower legs.

A thin, faintly red line around each leg about three inches up from the ankle. Milo snapped on the night table light for a closer look. He touched the line. It was more than a line—an indentation, actually, like something left after wearing a pair of socks too tight at the top. But it felt as if the constricting band were still there.

He got up and walked around. It felt a little funny to stand on partially numb feet but he couldn't worry about it now. In just a couple of hours he was doing a power breakfast at the Polo with Regenstein from TriStar and he had to be sharp. He padded into the kitchen to put on the coffee.

As he wove through L.A.'s morning commuter traffic, Milo envied the drivers with their tops down. He would have loved to have his 380 SL opened up to the bright early morning sun. Truthfully, he would have been glad for an open window. But for the sake of his hair he stayed bottled up with the a-c on. He couldn't afford to let the breeze blow his toupee around. It had been especially stubborn about blending in with his natural hair this morning and he didn't have any more time to fuss with it. And this was his good piece. His back-up had been stolen during a robbery of his house last week, an occurrence that still baffled the hell out of him. He wished he didn't have to worry about wearing a rug. He had heard about a new experimental lotion that was supposed to start hair growing again. If that ever panned out, he'd be first on line to—

His right hand started tingling. He removed it from the wheel and fluttered it in the air. Still it tingled. The sleeve of his sports coat slipped back and he saw a faint indentation running around his forearm, just above the wrist. For a few heartbeats he studied it in horrid

The Black Spiral: Twisted Tales of Terror

fascination.

What's happening to me?

Then he glanced up and saw the looming rear of a truck rushing toward his windshield. He slammed on the brakes and slewed to a screeching stop inches from the tailgate. Gasping and sweating, Milo slumped in the seat and tried to get a grip. Bad enough he was developing mysterious little constricting bands on his legs and now his arm, he had almost wrecked the new Mercedes. This sucker cost more than his first house back in the seventies.

When traffic started up again, he drove cautiously, keeping his eyes on the road and working the fingers of his right hand. He had some weirdshit disease, he just knew it, but he couldn't let anything get between him and this breakfast with Regenstein.

"Look, Milo," Howard Regenstein said through the smoke from his third cigarette in the last twenty minutes. "You know that if it was up to me the picture would be all yours. You know that, man."

Milo nodded, not knowing that at all. He had used that same line himself a million times—maybe *two* million times. If it was up to me . . .

Yeah, right. The great cop-out: I'm a nice guy and I have all the faith in the world in you but those money guys, those faithless, faceless Philistines who hold the purse-strings won't let guys with vision like you and me get together and make a great film.

"Well, what's the problem, Howie? I mean, give it to me straight."

"All right," Howie said, showing his chicklet caps between his thin lips. He was deeply tanned, wore thick horn-rimmed glasses; his close cropped curly hair was sandy-colored and lightly bleached. "Despite my strong—and, Milo, I do mean *strong*—recommendation, the money boys looked at the grosses for *The Hut* and got scared away."

Well. That explained a lot of things, especially this crummy table half hidden in an inside corner. The real power players, the ones who wanted everybody else in the place to see who they were doing breakfast with, were out in the middle or along the windows. Regenstein probably had three breakfasts scheduled for this morning. Milo was wondering what tables had been reserved for the others when a sharp pain stabbed his right leg. He winced and reached down.

"Something wrong?" Regenstein said.

"No. Just a muscle cramp."

The Black Spiral: Twisted Tales of Terror

He lifted his trouser leg and saw that the indentation above his ankle was deeper. It was actually a cut now. Blood oozed slowly, seeping into his sock. He straightened up and forced a smile at Regenstein.

"*The Hut*, Howie? Is *that* all?" Milo said with a laugh. "Don't they know that project was a loser from the start? The book was a bad property, a piece of clichéd garbage. Don't they know that?"

Howie smiled, too. "Afraid not, Milo. You know their kind. They look at the bottom line and see that Universal's going to be twenty mill in the hole on *The Hut*, and in their world that means something. And maybe they remember those PR pieces you did a month or so before it opened. You never even mentioned that the film was based on a book. Had me convinced the story was all yours, whole cloth."

Milo clenched his teeth. That had been when he had thought the movie was going to be a smash.

"I had a *concept*, Howie, one that cut through the bounds and limitations of the novel. I wanted to raise the level of the material but the producers stymied me at every level."

Actually, he had been pretty much on his own down there in Haiti. He had changed the book a lot, made loads of cuts and condensations. He had made it "A Milo Gherl Film."

But somewhere along the way he had lost it. Unanimously hostile one-star reviews with leads like, "Shut *The Hut*" and "New Gherl Pix the Pits" hadn't helped. Twentieth had been pushing an offer in its television division and he had been holding them off—who wanted to do TV when you could do theatricals? But as the bad reviews piled up and the daily grosses plummeted, he grabbed the TV offer. It was good money, had plenty of prestige, but it was still television.

Milo wanted to do films, and very badly wanted in on the new package Regenstein was putting together for TriStar. Howie had Jack Nicholson, Bobby DeNiro, and Meg Ryan firm, and was looking for a director. More than anything else in his career, Milo wanted to be that director. But he wasn't going to be. He knew that now.

Well, at least he could use the job to pay the bills and keep his name before the public until *The Hut* was forgotten. That wouldn't be long. A year or two at most and he'd be back directing another theatrical. Not a package like Regenstein's, but something with a decent budget where he could do the screenplay and direct. That was the way he liked it—full control on paper and on film.

The Black Spiral: Twisted Tales of Terror

He shrugged at Regenstein and put on his best good-natured smile. "What can I say, Howie? The world wasn't ready for *The Hut*. Someday, they'll appreciate it."

Yeah, right, he thought as Regenstein nodded noncommittally. At least Howie was letting him down easy, letting him keep his dignity here. That was important. All he had to do now was—

Milo screamed as pain tore into his left eye like a bolt of lightning. He lurched to his feet, upsetting the table as he clamped his hands over his eye in a vain attempt to stop the agony.

Pain! Oh Christ, pain as he had never known it was shooting from his eye straight into his brain. This had to be a stroke! What else could hurt like this?

Through his good eye he had a whirling glimpse of everybody in the dining room standing and staring at him as he staggered around. He pulled one hand away from his eye and reached out to steady himself. He saw a smear blood on his fingers. He took the other hand away. His left eye was blind, but with his right he saw the dripping red on his palm. A woman screamed.

"My God, Milo!" Regenstein said, his chalky face swimming into view. "Your eye! What did you do to your eye?" He turned to a gaping waiter. "Get a doctor! Get a fucking ambulance!"

Milo was groggy from the Demerol they had given him. In the blur of hours since breakfast he'd been wheeled in and out of the emergency room so many times, poked with so many needles, examined by so many doctors, x-rayed so many times, his head was spinning.

At least the pain had eased off.

"I'm admitting you onto the vascular surgery service, Mr. Gherl," said the bearded doctor as he pushed back one of the white curtains that shielded Milo's gurney from the rest of the emergency room. His badge said, *Edward Jansen, M.D.,* and he looked tired and irritable.

Milo struggled up the Demerol downgrade. "Vascular surgery? But my eye—!"

"As Dr. Burch told you, Mr. Gherl, your eye can't be saved. It's ruined beyond repair. But maybe we can save your feet and your hand if it's not too late already."

"Save them?"

"If we're lucky. I don't know what kind of games you've been into, but getting yourself tied up with piano wire is about the dumbest

123

thing I've ever heard of."

Milo was growing more alert by the second now. Over Dr. Jansen's shoulder he saw the bustle of the emergency room personnel, saw an old black man mopping the floor in slow, rhythmic strokes. But he was only seeing it with his right eye. He reached up to the bandage over his left. *Ruined?* He wanted to cry, but Dr. Jansen's piano wire remark suddenly filtered through to his consciousness.

"Piano wire? What are you talking about?"

"Don't play dumb. Look at your feet." Dr. Edwards pulled the sheet free from the far end of the gurney.

Milo looked. The nail beds were white and the skin below the indentations were a dusky blue. And the indentations had all become clean, straight, bloody cuts right through the skin and into the meat below. His right hand was the same.

"See that color?" Jansen was saying. "That means the tissues below the wire cuts aren't getting enough blood. You're going to have gangrene for sure if we don't restore circulation soon."

Gangrene! Milo levered up on the gurney and felt his toes with his good hand. *Cold!* "No! That's impossible!"

"I'd almost agree with you," Dr. Jansen said, his voice softening for a moment as he seemed to be talking to himself.

Behind him, Milo noticed the old black moving closer with his mop. "When we did x-rays, I thought we'd see the wire embedded in the flesh there, but there was nothing. Tried Xero soft-tissue technique in case you had used fishing line or something, but that came up negative, too. Even probed the cuts myself but there's nothing in there. Yet the arteriograms clearly show that the arteries in your lower legs and right forearm are compressed to the point where very little blood is getting through. The tissues are starving. The vascular boys may have to do bypasses."

"I'm getting out of here!" Milo said. "I'll see my own doctor!"

"I'm afraid I can't allow that."

"You can't stop me! I can walk out of here anytime I want!"

"I can keep you seventy-two hours for purposes of emergency psychiatric intervention."

"Psychiatric!"

"Yeah. Self-mutilation. Your mind worries me almost as much as your arteries, Mr. Gherl. I'd like to make sure you don't poke out your other eye before you get treatment."

"But I didn't—!"

"Please, Mr. Gherl. There were witnesses. Your breakfast companion said he had just finished giving you some disappointing news when you screamed and rammed something into your eye."

Milo touched the bandage over his eye again. How could they think he had done this to himself?

"My God, I swear I didn't do this!"

"That kind of trauma doesn't happen spontaneously, Mr. Gherl, and according to your companion, no one was within reach of you. So one way or the other, you're staying. Make it easy on both of us and do it voluntarily."

Milo didn't see that he had a choice. "I'll stay," he said. "Just answer me one thing: You ever seen anything like this before?"

Jansen shook his head. "Never. Never heard of anything like it either." He took a sudden deep breath and smiled through his beard with what Milo guessed was supposed to be doctorly reassurance. "But, hey. I'm only an ER doc. The vascular boys will know what to do."

With that, he turned and left, leaving Milo staring into the wide-eyed black face of the janitor.

"What are you staring at?" Milo said.

"A man in *big* trouble," the janitor said in a deep, faintly accented voice. He was pudgy with a round face, watery eyes, and two days' worth of silvery growth on his jowls. With a front tooth missing on the top, he looked like Leon Spinks gone to seed for thirty years. "These doctors can't be helpin' what you got. You got a *Bocor* mad at you and only a *Houngon* can fix you."

"Get lost!" Milo said.

He lay back on the gurney and closed his good eye to shut out the old man and the emergency room. He hunted for sleep as an escape from the pain and the gut-roiling terror, praying he'd wake up and learn that this was all just a horrible dream. But those words wouldn't go away. *Bocor* and *Houngon* . . . he knew them somehow. Where?

And then it hit him like a blow—*The Hut!* They were voodoo terms from the novel, *The Hut!* He hadn't used them in the film—he'd scoured all mention of voodoo from his screenplay—but the author had used them in the book. If Milo remembered correctly, a *Bocor* was an evil voodoo priest and a *Houngon* was a good one. Or was it the other way around? Didn't matter. They were all part of Bill Franklin's bullshit novel.

Franklin! Wouldn't he like to see me now! Milo thought. Their last meeting had been anything but pleasant. Unforgettable, yes. His mind did a slow dissolve to his new office at Twentieth two weeks ago . . .

"Some conference!"

The angry voice startled Milo and he spilled hot coffee down the front of his shirt. He leaped up from behind his desk and bent forward, pulling the steaming fabric away from his chest. "Jesus H.—"

But then he looked up and saw Bill Franklin standing there and his anger cooled like fresh blood in an arctic breeze. Maggie's anxious face peered over Franklin's narrow shoulder.

"I tried to stop him, Mr. Gherl, honest I did, but he wouldn't listen!"

"You've been ducking me for a month, Gherl!" Franklin said in his nasal voice. "No more tricks!"

Maggie said, "Shall I call security?"

"I don't think that will be necessary, Maggs," he said quickly, grabbing a Kleenex from the oak tissue holder on his desk and blotting at his stained shirtfront. Milo had moved into this office only a few weeks ago, and the last thing he needed today was an ugly scene with an irate writer. He could tell from Franklin's expression that he was ready to cause a doozy. Better to bite the bullet and get this over with. "I'll talk to Mr. Franklin. You can leave him here." She hesitated and he waved her toward the door. "Go ahead. It's all right."

When she had closed the door behind her, he picked up the insulated brass coffee urn and looked at Franklin. "Coffee, Billy-boy?"

"I don't want coffee, Gherl! I want to know why you've been ducking me!"

"But I haven't been ducking you, Billy!" he said, refreshing his own cup. He would have to change this shirt before he did lunch later. "I'm not with Universal anymore. I'm with Twentieth now, so naturally my offices are here." He swept an arm around him. "Not bad, ay?"

Milo sat down and tried his best to look confident, at ease. Inside, he was anything but. Right now he was a little afraid of the writer stalking back and forth before the desk like a caged tiger. Nothing about Franklin's physical appearance was the least bit intimidating. He was fair-haired and tall with big hands and feet attached to a slight, gangly frame. He had a big nose, a small chin, and a big Adam's apple—Milo had noticed on their first meeting two years ago that he could slant a perfectly straight line along the tips of those three protuberances. A moderate overbite did not help the picture. Milo's impression of Franklin had always been that of a patient, retiring, rational man who never raised his voice.

But today he was barging about with a wild look in his eyes, shouting, gesticulating, accusing. Milo remembered an old saying his father used to quote to him when he was a boy: *Beware the wrath of a patient man.*

Franklin had paused and was looking around the spacious room with its indirect lighting, its silver-gray floor-to-ceiling louvered blinds and matching carpet, the chrome and onyx wet bar, the free-form couches, the abstract sculptures on the Lucite coffee table and on Milo's oversized desk.

"How did you ever rate this after perpetrating a turkey like *The Hut?*"

"Twentieth recognizes talent when it sees it, Billy."

"My question stands," Franklin said.

Milo ignored the remark. "Sit down, Billy-boy. What's got you so upset?"

Franklin didn't sit. He resumed his stalking. "You know damn well what! My book!"

"You've got a new one?" Milo said, perfectly aware of which book he meant.

"No! I mean the only book I've ever written—*The Hut!*—and the mess you made out of it!"

Milo had heard quite enough nasty criticism of that particular film to last him a lifetime. He felt his anger flare but suppressed it. Why get into a shouting match?

"I'm sorry you feel that way, Billy, but let's face facts." He spread his hands in a consoling gesture. "It's a dead issue. There's nothing more to be done. The film has been shot, edited, released, and—"

"—and withdrawn!" Franklin shouted. "Two weeks in general release and the theater owners sent it back! It's not just a flop, it's a catastrophe!"

"The critics—killed it."

"Bullshit! The critics blasted it, just like they blasted other

The Black Spiral: Twisted Tales of Terror

'flops' like *Flashdance* and *Top Gun* and *Ernest Goes to Camp*. What killed it, Gherl, was word of mouth. Now I know why you wouldn't screen it until a week before it opened: You knew you'd botched it!"

"I had trouble with the final cut. I couldn't—"

"You couldn't get it to make sense! As I walked out of that screening I kept telling myself that my negative feelings were due to all the things you'd cut out of my book, that maybe I was too close to it all and that the public would somehow find my story in your mass of pretensions. Then I heard a guy in his early twenties say, 'What the hell was *that* all about?' and his girlfriend say, 'What a boring waste of time!' and I knew it wasn't just me." Franklin's long bony finger stabbed through the air. "It was you! You raped my book!"

Milo had had just about enough of this. "You novelists are all alike!" he said with genuine disdain. "You do fine on the printed page so you think you're experts at writing for the screen. But you're not. You don't know the first goddamn thing about visual writing!"

"You cut the heart out of my story! The Hut was about the nature of evil and how it can seduce even the strongest among us. The plot was like a house of cards, Gherl, built with my sweat. Your windbag script blew it all down! And after I saw the first draft of the script, you were suddenly unavailable for conference!"

Milo recalled Franklin's endless stream of nit-picking letters, his deluge of time-wasting phone calls. "I was busy, dammit! I was writer-director! The whole thing was on my shoulders!"

"I warned you that the house of cards was falling due to the cuts you made. I mean, why did you remove all mention of voodoo and zombiism from the script? They were the two red herrings that held the plot together."

"Voodoo! Zombies! That's old hat! Nobody would pay to see a voodoo movie!"

"Then why set the movie in Haiti, f'Christsake? Might as well have been in Pasadena! And that monster you threw in at the end? Where in hell did you come up with that? I looked like the Incredible Hulk in drag! I spent years in research. I slaved to fill that book with terror and dread—all you brought to the screen were cheap shocks!"

"If that's your true opinion—and I disagree with it absolutely—you should be glad the film was a flop. No one will see it!"

Franklin nodded slowly. "That gave me comfort for a while, until I realized that the movie isn't dead. When it reaches the video

The Black Spiral: Twisted Tales of Terror

stores and the cable services, tens of millions of people will see it—not because it's good, but simply because it's there and it's something they've never heard of before and certainly have never seen. And they'll be directing their rapt attention at your corruption of my story, and they'll see 'Based on the Novel by William Franklin' and think that the pretentious, incomprehensible mishmash they're watching represents my work. And that makes me *mad*, Gherl! Fucking-ay crazy mad!"

The ferocity that flashed across Franklin's face was truly frightening. Milo rushed to calm him. "Billy, look: Despite our artistic differences and despite the fact that *The Hut* will never turn a profit, you were paid well into six figures for the screen rights. What's you're beef?"

Franklin seemed to shrink a little. His shoulders slumped and his voice softened. "I didn't write it for money. I live off a trust fund that provides me with more than I can spend. *The Hut* was my first novel—maybe my only novel ever. I gave it everything. I don't think I have any more in me."

"Of course you do!" Milo said, rising and moving around the desk toward the subdued writer. Here was his chance to ease Franklin out of here. "It's just that you've never had to suffer for your art! You've had it too soft, too cushy for too long. Things came too easy on that first book. First time at bat you got a major studio film offer that actually made it to the screen. That hardly ever happens. Now you've got to prove it wasn't just a fluke. You've got to get out there and slog away on that new book! Deprive yourself a little! *Suffer!*"

"Suffer?" Franklin said, a weird light starting to glow in his eyes. "I should suffer?"

"Yes!" Milo said, guiding him toward the office door. "All great artists suffer."

"You ever suffer, Milo Gherl?"

"Of course." Especially this morning, listening to you!

"Look at this office. You don't look like you're suffering for what you did to *The Hut*."

"I did my suffering years ago. The anger you feel about *The Hut* is small change compared to the dues I've had to pay." He finally had Franklin across the threshold. "I'm through suffering," he said as he slammed the door and locked it.

From the other side of the thick oak door he thought he heard Franklin say, "No, you're not."

"Missing any personal items lately, mister?" said a voice.

129

The Black Spiral: Twisted Tales of Terror

Milo opened his good eye and saw the big black guy standing over him, leaning on his mop handle. What was *wrong* with this old fart? What was his angle?

"If you don't leave me alone I'm gonna call—" He paused. "What do you mean, 'personal items'? "

"You know—clothing, nail clippings, a brush or comb that might hold some of your hair. That kinda stuff."

A chill swept over Milo's skin like an icy breeze in July.

The robbery!

Such a bizarre thing—a pried-open window, a few cheap rings gone, his drawers and closets ransacked, an old pair of pajamas missing. And his toupee, the second-string hairpiece . . . gone. Who could figure it? But he had been shaken up enough to go out and buy a .38 for his night table.

Milo laughed. This was so ludicrous. "You're talking about a voodoo doll, aren't you?"

The old guy nodded. "It got other names, but that'll do."

"Who the hell *are* you?"

"Name's Andre but folks call me Andy. I got connections you gonna need."

"You need your head examined!"

"Maybe. But that doctor said he was lookin' for the wires that was cuttin' into your legs and your arm but he couldn't find them. That's because the wires are somewheres else. They around the legs and arm of a doll somebody made on you."

Milo tried to laugh again but found he couldn't. He managed a weak, "Bullshit."

"You'll believe me soon enough. And when you do, I'll take you to a *Houngon* who can help you out."

"Yeah," Milo said. "Like you really care about me."

The old black showed his gap-tooth smile. "Oh, I won't be doin' you a favor, and neither will the *Houngon*. He'll be wantin' money for pullin' you fat out the fire."

"And you'll get a finder's fee."

The smile broadened. "Thas right."

That made a little more sense to Milo, but still he wasn't buying. "Forget it!"

"I be around till three. I'll keep checkin' up on you case you change you mind. I can get you out here when you want to go."

The Black Spiral: Twisted Tales of Terror

"Don't hold your breath."

Milo rolled on his side and closed his eyes. The old fart had some nerve trying to run that corny scam on him, and in a hospital yet! He'd report him, have him fired. This was no joke. He'd lost his eye already. He could be losing his feet, his hand! He needed top medical-center level care, not some voodoo mumbo-jumbo . . .

. . . but no one seemed to know what was going on, and everyone seemed to think he'd put his own eye out. God, who could do something like that to himself? And his hand and his feet—the doc had said they were going to start rotting off if blood didn't get flowing back into them. What on earth was happening to him?

And what about that weird robbery last week? Only personal articles had been stolen. All the high-ticket stereo and video stuff had been left untouched.

God, it couldn't be voodoo, could it? Who'd even—

Shit! Bill Franklin! He was an expert on it after all those years of research for *The Hut*. But he wouldn't . . . he couldn't . . .

Franklin's faintly heard words echoed in Milo's brain: *No, you're not.*

Agony suddenly lanced through Milo's groin, doubling him over on the gurney. Gasping with the pain, he tore at the clumsy stupid nightshirt they'd dressed him in and pulled it up to his waist. He held back the scream that rose in his throat when he saw the thin red line running around the base of his penis. Instead, he called out a name.

"Andy! Andy!"

Milo coughed and peered through the dim little room. It smelled of dust and sweat and charcoal smoke and something else—something rancid. He wondered what the hell he was doing here. He knew if he had any sense he'd get out now, but he didn't know where to go from here. He wasn't even sure he could find his way home from here.

The setting sun had been a bloody blob in Milo's rearview mirror as he'd hunched over the steering wheel of his Mercedes and followed Andy's rusty red pick-up into one of L.A.'s seamier districts. Andy had been true to his word: He'd spirited Milo out of the hospital, back to the house for some cash and some real clothes, then down to the garage near the Polo where his car was parked. After that it was on to Andy's *Houngon* and maybe end this agony.

It *had* to end soon. Milo's feet were so swollen he was wearing old slippers. He had barely been able to turn the ignition key with his right hand. And his dick—God, his dick felt like it was going to explode!

After what seemed like a ten-mile succession of left and right turns during which he saw not a single white face, they had pulled to a stop before a dilapidated storefront office. On the cracked glass was painted:

M. Trieste Houngon

Andy had stayed outside with the car while Milo went in.

"Mr. Gherl?"

Milo started at the sound and turned toward the voice. A balding, wizened old black, six-two at least, stood next to him. His face was a mass of wrinkles. He was dressed in a black suit, white shirt, and thin black tie.

Milo heard his own voice quaver: "Yes. That's me."

"You are the victim of the *Bocor*?" His voice was cultured, and accented in some strange way.

Milo pushed back the sleeve of his shirt to expose his right wrist. "I don't know what I'm the victim of, but Andy says you can help me. You've *got* to help me!"

He stared at the patch over Milo's eye. "May I see?"

Milo leaned away from him. "Don't touch that!" It had finally stopped hurting. He held his arm higher.

M. Trieste examined Milo's hand, tracing a cool dry finger around the clotted circumferential cut at the wrist. "This is all?"

Milo showed him his legs, then reluctantly, opened his fly.

"You have a powerful enemy in this *Bocor*," M. Trieste said, finally. "But I can reverse the effects of his doll. It will cost you five hundred dollars. Do you have it with you?"

Milo hesitated. "Let's not be too hasty here. I want to see some results before I fork over any money." He was hurting, but he wasn't going to be a sucker for this clown.

M. Trieste smiled. He had all his teeth. "I have no wish to steal from you, Mr. Gherl. I shall accept no money from you unless I can effect a cure. However, I do not wish to be cheated either. Do you have the money with you?"

Milo nodded. "Yes."

"Very well." M. Trieste struck a match and lit a candle on a table Milo hadn't realized was there. "Please be seated," he said and disappeared into the darkness.

Milo complied and looked around. The wan candlelight picked up an odd assortment of objects around the room: African ceremonial masks hung side by side with crucifixes on the wall; a long conga drum sat in a corner to the right while a statue of the Virgin Mary, her small plaster foot trodding a writhing snake, occupied the one on his left. He wondered when the drums would start and the dancers appear. When would they begin chanting and daubing him with paint and splattering him with chicken blood? God, he must have been crazy to come here. Maybe the pain was affecting his mind. If he had any smarts he'd—

"Hold out your wrist," M. Trieste said, suddenly appearing in the candlelight opposite him. He held what looked like a plaster coffee mug in his hand. He was stirring its contents with a wooden stick.

Milo held back. "What are you going to do?"

"Help you, Mr. Gherl. You are the victim of a very traditional and particularly nasty form of voodoo. You have greatly angered a *Bocor* and he is using a powerful *loa*, via a doll, to lop off your hands and your feet and your manhood."

"My left hand's okay," Milo said, gratefully working the fingers in the air.

"So I have noticed," M. Trieste said with a frown. "It is odd for one extremity to be spared, but perhaps there is a certain symbolism at work here that we do not understand. No matter. The remedy is the same. Hold your arm out on the table."

Milo did as he was told. His swollen hand looked black in the candlelight. "Is . . . is this going to hurt?"

"When the pressure is released, there will be considerable pain as the fresh blood rushes into the starved tissues."

That kind of pain Milo could handle. "Do it."

M. Trieste stirred the contents of the cup and lifted the wooden handle. Instead of the spoon he had expected, Milo saw that the man was holding a brush. It gleamed redly.

Here comes the blood, he thought. But he didn't care what was in the cup as long as it worked.

"Andre told me about your problem before he brought you here. I made this up in advance. I will paint it on the constrictions and it will nullify the influence of the *loa* of the doll. After that, it will be up to you to make peace with this *Bocor* before he visits other afflictions on you."

"Sure, sure," Milo said, thrusting his wrist toward M. Trieste.

The Black Spiral: Twisted Tales of Terror

"Let's just get on with it!"

M. Trieste daubed the bloody solution onto the incision line. It beaded up like water on a freshly waxed car and slid off onto the table. Milo glanced up and saw a look of consternation flit across the wrinkled black face towering above him. He watched as the red stuff was applied again, only to run off as before.

"Most unusual," M. Trieste muttered as he tried a third time with no better luck. "I've never . . . " He put the cup down and began painting his own right hand with the solution. "This will do it. Hold up your hand."

As Milo raised his arm, M. Trieste encircled the wrist with his long dripping fingers and squeezed. There was an instant of heat, and then M. Trieste cried out. He released Milo's wrist and dropped to his knees cradling his right hand against his breast.

"The poisons!" he cried. "Oh, the poisons!"

Milo trembled as he looked at his dusky hand. The bloody solution had run off as before. "What poisons?"

"Between you and this *Bocor!* Get out of here!"

"But the doll! You said you could—!"

"There is no doll!" M. Trieste said. He turned away and retched. "There *is* no doll!"

With his heart clattering against his chest wall, Milo pushed himself away from the table and staggered to the door. Andy was leaning on his truck at the curb.

"Wassamatter?" he said straightening off the fender as he saw Milo. "Didn't he—?"

"He's a phony, just like you!" Milo screamed, letting his rage and fear focus on the old black. "Just another goddamn phony!"

As Andy hurried into the store, Milo started up his Mercedes and roared down the street. He'd drive until he found a sign for one of the freeways. From there he could get home.

And from home, he knew where he wanted to go . . . where he *had* to go.

"Franklin! Where are you, Franklin?"

Milo had finally found Bill Franklin's home in the Hollywood Hills. Even though he knew the neighborhood fairly well, Milo had never been on this particular street, and so it had taken him a while to track it down. The lights had been on inside and the door had been unlocked. No one had answered his knocking, so he'd let himself in.

"Franklin, goddamit!" he called, standing in the middle of the cathedral-ceilinged living room. His voice echoed off the stucco walls and hardwood floor. "Where are you?"

In the ensuing silence, he heard a faint voice say, "Milo? Is that you?"

Milo tensed. Where had that come from? "Yeah, It's me! Where are you?"

Again, ever so faintly: "Down here . . . in the basement!"

Milo searched for the cellar door, found it, saw the lights ablaze from below, and began his descent. His slippered feet were completely numb now and he had to watch where he put them. It was as if his feet had been removed and replaced with giant sponges.

"That you, Milo?" said a voice from somewhere around the corner from the stairwell. It was Franklin's voice, but it sounded slurred, strained.

"Yeah, it's me."

As he neared the last step, he pulled the .38 from his pocket. He had picked it up t the house along with a pair of wire cutters on his way here. He had never fired it, and he didn't expect to have to tonight. But it was good to know it was loaded and ready if he needed it. He tried to transfer it to his right hand but his numb, swollen fingers couldn't keep hold of the grip. He kept it in his left and stepped onto the cellar floor—

—and felt his foot start to roll away from him. Only by throwing himself against the wall and hugging it did he save himself from falling. He looked around the unfinished cellar. Bright, reflective objects were scattered all along the naked concrete floor. He sucked in a breath as he saw the hundreds of sharp curved angles of green glass poking up at the exposed ceiling beams. The looked like shattered wine bottles—big, green, four-liter wine bottles smashed all over the place. And in among the shards were scattered thousands of marbles.

"Be careful," said Franklin's voice. "The basement's mined." The voice was there, but Franklin was nowhere in sight.

"Where the hell are you, Franklin?"

"Back here in the bathroom. I thought you'd never get here."

Milo began to move toward the rear of the cellar where brighter light poured from an open door. He slid his slippered feet slowly along the floor, pushing the green glass spears ahead of him, rolling the marbles out of the way.

135

"I've come for the doll, Franklin."

Milo heard a hollow laugh. "Doll? What doll, Milo? There's just me and you, ol' buddy."

Milo shuffled around the corner into view of the bathroom. And froze. The gun dropped from his fingers and further shattered some of the glass at his feet. "Oh, my God, Franklin! Oh, my God!"

William Franklin sat on the toilet wearing Milo's rings, his old slippers, his stolen pajamas, and his other hairpiece. His left eye was patched and his feet and his right hand were as black and swollen as Milo's. There was a maniacal look in his remaining eye as he grinned drunkenly and sipped from a four-liter green-glass bottle of white wine. The cuts in his flesh were identical to Milo's except that a short length of twisted copper wire protruded from each. A screwdriver and a pair of pliers lay in his lap.

M. Trieste's parting words screamed through his brain: There is no doll!

"See?" Franklin said in a slurred voice. "You said I had to suffer."

Milo wanted to be sick. "Christ! What have you done?"

"I decided to suffer. But I didn't think I should suffer alone. So I brought you along for company. Sure took you long enough to figure it out."

Milo bent and picked up the pistol. His left hand wavered and trembled as he pointed it at Franklin. "You . . . you . . . " He couldn't think of anything to say.

Franklin casually tossed the wine bottle out onto the floor where it shattered and added to the spikes of glass. Then he pulled open the pajama top. "Right here, Milo, old buddy!" he said, pointing to his heart. "Do you really think you want to put a slug into me?"

Milo Thought about that. It might be like putting a bullet into his own heart. He felt his arm drop. "Why . . . how . . . I don't deserve . . . "

Franklin closed his eye and grimaced. He looked as if he were about to cry. "I know," he said. "It's gone too far. Maybe you really don't deserve all this. I've always known I was a little bit crazy, but maybe I'm a lot crazier than I ever thought I was."

"Then for God's sake, man, loosen the wires!"

"No!" Franklin's eye snapped open. The madness was still there. "I entrusted my work to you. That's a sacred trust. You were responsible for *The Hut's* integrity when you took on the job of adapting it to the screen."

"But I'm an artist, too!" Why was he arguing with this nut? He slipped the pistol into his front pocket and reached around back for the wire cutters.

"All the more reason to respect another man's work! You didn't own it—it was only on loan to you!"

"The contract—"

"*Means nothing!* You had a moral obligation to protect my work, one artist to another."

"You're over-reacting!"

"Am I? Imagine yourself a parent who has sent his only child to a reputable nursery school only to learn that the child has been raped by the faculty—then you will understand *some* of what I feel! I've come to see it as my sacred duty to see to it that you don't molest anyone else's work!"

Enough of this bullshit! If Franklin wouldn't loosen the wires, Milo would cut them off! He pulled the wire cutters from his rear pocket and began to shuffle toward Franklin, sweeping the marbles and daggers of glass ahead of him.

"Stay back!" Franklin cried. He grabbed the pliers and pushed them down toward his lap, grinning maliciously. "Didn't know I was left-handed, did you?" He twisted something.

Searing pain knifed into Milo's groin. He doubled over but kept moving toward Franklin. Less than a dozen feet to go. If he could just—

He saw Franklin drop the pliers and pick up the screwdriver, saw him raise it toward his right eye, the good eye. Milo screamed,

"*NOOOOO!*"

And then agony exploded in his eye, in his head, robbing him of the light, sending him reeling back in sudden impenetrable blackness. As he felt his feet roll across the marbles, he reached out wildly. His legs slid from under him and despite the most desperate flailings and contortions, there was nothing to grasp on the way down but empty air.

The Black Spiral: Twisted Tales of Terror

THE BEST FISHING *EVER*

J. Knight

The best fishing? You mean this time of year, or ever? Yeah, that's what I thought you meant. I see Randy over in the corner grinning like the idiot he is. He told you to go over and ask the old man about the best fishing *ever,* right? I thought so.

Sure, I'll tell you about it, but you aren't half drunk enough to believe it. Fill your glass first. Me? No, I've been off the booze for years, since before you were born. Buy me a 7-Up. It's all I drink anymore.

Okay. The best fishing ever. It was the summer of 1946. Yes, I'm that old.

You ever hear of Butch Malone, Aerial Ace? No, I didn't figure you had. I wrote about Butch for the pulps. He was a pilot. A new adventure every month. Butch paid my bills for two years. Twenty-four months, twenty-four novels, and now they're not even a memory for most people. But that's okay, I made a living. Drove a Packard. Butch is why I moved way out here.

Los Angeles back then was a great city, but there were too many distractions, not the least of which was the booze kindly foisted on me by my fellow writers. I had to get out and so I came here, which was the boondocks back then, before they built the lodge and weekenders like you started coming out to drop a line in the water. No offense, we appreciate the business.

Look at that light there, coming in the window. See where the glass is chipped? That's why you get that rainbow pattern on the floor. It'll disappear in a minute. There, it's fading already.

Anyway, I moved out here with three typewriters so that when one broke down I had a spare and a spare to back up the spare. When I needed an idea and was tempted to find it in a bottle, I packed up my kit and went fishing. That's where I picked up the addiction, and don't let anybody tell you fishing isn't an addiction, only it isn't illegal and it doesn't fry your brain. Well, maybe I'm wrong about that last part, but it fries your brain in a good way. Meditative, like.

So I'm out at Brown Bear Lake, got a couple of lines working, and I can see that some serious weather's blowing in from the northwest. You ever seen it out here when a thunderhead's rolling in? It'll make you

The Black Spiral: Twisted Tales of Terror

believe in God, I tell you. That black mass of clouds stretching across the horizon, the rumble of thunder, and it's heading your way and there isn't a damn thing you can do to stop it or even slow it down. All you can do is find someplace dry and hunker down and wait it out and hope that a gully washer doesn't float you away.

So I packed up my gear and headed for town. Hadn't caught squat and I needed to fill my belly so I pulled up to Trish's Diner, which is what this bar used to be in the olden days. Other people had the same notion as me and the place was packed and I had to sit at the counter next to Old Mac.

Old Mac was as much older than me as I am of you. What are you, twenty-one? Okay, twenty-seven, then. Everybody looks like a kid to me now. I was thirty-two, which made Old Mac nine days older than dust. And he was crazy. Old Mac saw phantoms. You know what a phantom is?

No, a ghost is something else. A ghost is a spirit of somebody or something that used to be alive. A phantom's not even that much. A phantom's nothing, the spirit of nothing. It's the child that was never born, the life that was never lived. It's something that might've existed only, for some reason, it didn't get the chance. And Old Mac saw phantoms, which is why he was crazy. You never knew when he'd see one or what it'd be or what he'd do when he saw it. He might yell out, or he might just give it a nod and go on eating his soup. You never knew. That's why nobody liked to sit next to him. It made you tense, just waiting for Old Mac to let out a cry or maybe grab your arm and point at nothing and say, "Lookie there! You see that? Open your eyes, you blind fool!"

But like I say there was nowhere else to sit so I sat down next to crazy Old Mac and hoped that he didn't see any phantoms in my chicken fried steak.

Now I don't want to worry you but there's a spider on the wall next to your left arm. No, don't kill it. It's beautiful, isn't it? And the webs they weave, you ever see one in the morning when it's wet and dripping with pearls? He's just looking for a place to build a web, that's all. He doesn't give a hang about you. See, there he goes. No harm done.

So we're all sitting in the diner and there's the usual fish talk about what's biting where and how everybody was just about to land the catch of their lives when the storm blew in and they had to give it up. The clouds filled the sky and the world turned dark and the first few fat drops of rain began to spatter the windows. Thunder shuddered the walls and before we knew it we were in the middle of the damnedest lightning storm that I ever saw before or since.

The lightning sizzled from cloud to cloud and bolts struck the ground so hard and fast you'd think it was the last days of Man on Earth. I swear I half-expected the ground to split wide open and let loose the demons of Hell. If it had, I wouldn't have been as surprised as I was at what really happened, because at least it would have made some kind of sense and what happened next didn't make any sense at all.

You'd better fill up that glass, young man, because nobody but a fool or a drunk would believe what I'm about to tell you.

Did you notice the waitress's eyes? It's dark in here but you should see them in the daylight. They're the most brilliant green, and that's their natural color, too, not some kind of contact lens. Take a moment and look the next time she comes by. You won't regret it.

Anyway, the conversation in the place ground to a halt. You couldn't have heard anybody's words over the thunder, but nobody was talking anyhow. They were dumbfounded by the storm raging outside and thanking their lucky stars they weren't caught out in it. There are times when any words you have to say are so insignificant compared to the awesome thing that's going on around you that you just clam up, and that's what everybody did. It wasn't fear, exactly. More like respect for something that's so much more powerful than you, all your self-importance drains away like blood from an open wound. You feel like a speck, a no-account little speck, and there's nothing a speck has to say that's worth hearing.

And that's when the first one hit the window. The first what? I'll tell you in a minute. Nobody knew what it was. It just hit the window with a thump and bounced away and Ralph McKenzie, who was sitting in the booth right where it hit, said, "What in the hell—?" and jumped in his seat like he'd been stung in the pants.

"What was that, a frog?" somebody asked, and Ralph said he didn't know, but look, it left a smear on the window. The rain was already washing it away but anybody could tell that the smear was blood.

Right quick there was another thump, and pretty soon the things, whatever they were, were bouncing against the window like hailstones, only they weren't hard like hail, they were soft and blubbery and each one left a bloody smear.

The Black Spiral: Twisted Tales of Terror

People peered out the window to see what they were but the clouds made it black as night and the rain was pouring down and the window was fogging up from so many curious breaths. Nobody wanted to step outside in that mess to find out what the things were, especially not with the lightning still hammering the ground like it was.

Then some young kid—I don't remember his name, he was one of the local teenagers—pulled on his rain slicker and announced that he was going out. A chorus of voices told him he was crazy and others wished him luck and somebody held the door open for him and he stepped out into the soup with his hood clutched tight around his throat. He didn't go but a few steps before all we could see of him was a rain-hazy blur. He bent down and picked something off the ground and then he ran back inside.

Everybody gathered around to see what the thing was. The kid held it in his fist. I think he was drawing out his moment of heroism or stupidity or whatever it was because he held his hand shut for several seconds before he slowly uncurled his fingers.

You'll think I'm just some old fart spinning a tale but I swear I'm telling the truth, and you know I haven't been drinking. But that boy held an eye in his hand, a human eye.

"There's hundreds of 'em," he said, "lying around like hailstones. They're all over the ground. Hundreds of 'em."

Everybody froze for a second at the thought. Then somebody laughed and said "Good one!" and somebody else said, "You really had us going for a minute there, Donnie!" (That was it; the boy's name was Donnie. Donnie Bainbridge.) But Donnie swore it was true and said that anybody who didn't believe him was welcome to step outside and see for himself.

By now the things had stopped pounding the window and the lightning seemed to lessen a bit. Donnie put the eyeball in a glass of water and we passed it around and shook our heads over it and waited for the storm to move on. Finally it did and we went out, and damn if it wasn't just like Donnie said, only there weren't hundreds of eyes, there were thousands. Maybe hundreds of thousands. One was caught in the windshield wiper of my Packard.

You couldn't walk without stepping on them. They popped like grapes under your feet. Somebody opened his car door and a dog jumped out and started chowing down on eyeballs until the owner pulled him away and forced him back in the car.

The Black Spiral: Twisted Tales of Terror

"Maybe a twister hit an eye bank," somebody said, but that was stupid and everybody knew it. An eye bank isn't like a money bank with hundreds of thousands of eyeballs sitting around.

"Maybe they came from a hospital or something." But that didn't add up, either. Like I told you, it didn't make any sense.

The only person it made sense to was crazy Old Mac, and I'll tell you what he said. His explanation is still, to this day, the best one I've heard.

I told you that Old Mac believed in phantoms, the spirits of things that never were. Well, he thought that those eyeballs were phantoms made real, released into our world by the lightning. They were eyes that nobody ever used. They were eyes that looked but didn't see. They were eyes that had beheld miracles unbelieved, truths unrecognized, beauty undiscovered. Phantom eyes given substance by the storm.

You think I'm lying and I don't blame you. But you asked me a question and I'm answering it, and I swear the best fishing *ever* was found at Brown Bear Lake the next day and all the next week.

Three guesses what we used for bait.

* * *

ELVIS AND ME

Richard D. Weber

Something comes a knocking.

I guess it was that vacant, terrified look in his eyes, more than his trembling voice, more than his battered face, that should have warned me—something terrible was about to happen.

It all began for me on a warm summer night in June of 1964. For others, it had begun much earlier.

I couldn't sleep. I was lying in my bed, deep in thought, counting the springs of the upper bunk. Some people count sheep; I counted springs. Personal preference. My transistor radio hung by its leather strap on the headboard. The volume was down low so Mom wouldn't have a bird. It was tuned to WLS "In Chi-chaah-go ..."(their jingle). Fifty thousand watts beamed Sonny and Cher into that tiny plastic box and into my world: a country farmhouse in rural Wisconsin. Cheesehead Land. We were twelve miles to the nearest town, a million miles to modern civilization and the "Scene" or the "Happening," or so it seemed to me at the time.

As I lay in the bottom bunk, hands tucked behind my head, my mind drifted. Thoughts of what the future held for me, Robbie Donner, cascaded through the rushing tides of adolescence. Mom said I was tall for my age of twelve years and would grow to become a "good looker." However, I thought that my medusa-like curly brown hair, my elephant-sized ears, and long tapered fingers foretold of a different likelihood. Having outgrown my plump, round baby face, I'd morphed into a gangly pre-teenager: all elbows and knees and clumsy as a one-eyed three-legged mutt stuck in a mud hole. At the time I thought a career as a freak in the circus sideshow was a more likely outcome.

Nevertheless, I'd spend hours in front of the bathroom mirror, flexing my muscles, flattening my stomach. As I stood gazing into my deep brown eyes, I'd practice raising one eyebrow like Sean Connery and say in the deepest voice I could muster, "Bond, James Bond." Ms. Moneypenny would no doubt swoon in my arms. I worked out daily on my "Ted Williams" weightlifting set, measuring my biceps each time.

The Black Spiral: Twisted Tales of Terror

But tonight my insomnia was the result of a combination of things: the extra helping of Peach Cobbler I'd eaten for dinner; great notions, plans and expectations for the summer that lay ahead, and probably most of all—HORMONES. To say I was a healthy twelve-year-old boy with natural urges was like saying the Green Bay Packers was—just another football team. Blasphemy. Hell, let's face it, I was in HEAT and the "Beat Goes On." To paraphrase the song, the drums kept driven' women to my brain... Ladee dade dee, Ladee dade da-ah. And Oh, what women: Pussy Galore from *Goldfinger* and Ginger from *Gilligan's* Island, Barbra Feldon-Agent 99 and Samantha from *Bewitched*. I had it bad and the truth was . . . yes, probably even Donna Reed and Hazel stirred my juices. It was hopeless.

Okay, so I was a weird kid. But maybe no more so than any boy teetering on the brink of manhood. And certainly no stranger than some grown males who stood at the edge of that precipice their whole life, peering into adulthood but afraid to jump, reeling at the thought of responsibility and commitment. I think they call it arrested development. Perhaps, plunge-o-phobia would be more accurate. But dear sweet Jesus, I couldn't wait to plunge head first into manhood and Samantha's waiting arms. Take a hike Darrin.

Funny how boys graduate from comic books and playing Cowboys and Indians, to girls, in the tick of a second hand. But they do. I was on the verge of change. Part of me was still a kid in Toyland. But another part of me thirsted for drag-strip babes with long fake eyelashes and bullet bras that jutted from beneath tight sweaters. Thirsted for adventure: fast souped-up cars and cruising the gut, sneaking a smoke with your buddies—whatever grown-ups had told you not to do. "Don't ever let me catch you..." Man, I was confused. Too young for the good stuff, too old for the kid's stuff (you still played kid's games but kind of in secret and only with a trusted friend). But what I didn't realize until later was that part of the little boy always remains, never let's go. If you don't believe me, just ask your spouse. Although I was willing to put away some "childish things," there was one item that was sacrosanct, my dog—Elvis. A pink-nosed, white-chested, bobtailed, rusty-red, retriever mix. His father apparently played the field, and I don't mean just the hunting field. He appeared at our front door one day, lost and hungry. Mom took one look at those drooping, sorrowful eyes and christened him "Elvis."

The Black Spiral: Twisted Tales of Terror

If a man's best friend is his dog, then to a boy, a dog is the honeymoon that never ends. Unconditional love. Yup, unconditional, everlasting, arm-nuzzling, face-licking, tail- wagging, run through the woods and even, bare your soul to—LUV.

I know what you're thinking: cut the schmaltz already. But that dog kept me from being branded murderer. So, back off dick-weed. And I know they say women and horses have a natural affinity, a romance if you will. But I can't imagine a horse, even Trigger, crawling in bed with you during a thunderstorm. Dale Evans would've made him sleep on the couch with Ol' Roy and Pat Brady. Happy Trails to You—boys. Just a thought.

"The King," Mom's latest nickname for my pooch, was sound asleep on the bed at my side. Elvis was woofing and chuffing softly: lost in puppy dog dreams of pesky-wabbits and pheasants. His body shuddered, his legs made jerky stabbing motions, as if he was running in some dream woods. Then so rapt in his hound dog slumber, so carried away with the chase—he fell right off the bed.

Plop goes the furball.

Elvis let out a startled yelp, glanced about to get his bearings, then sneezed and shook his ears. I scratched behind Elvis's ears, the erogenous zone, that immediately invoked the dog's imitation of Shirley MacLaine's famous Can Can: the involuntary doggie leg kick.

Elvis heard it first, pricking up his ears at the sound: the low throaty growl of a car's engine, the sound of tires on the gravel driveway, our driveway, as it approached in the night. Then the glare of headlights washed across my first-floor bedroom window.

An eel began to squirm about in my stomach, climbed up my throat, and almost burst from my mouth. My heart trip-hammered. A thin sheen of cold sweat broke out along the nape of my neck. Elvis tilted his head from side to side as a snarl floated from the back of his throat.

I was scared shitless. In the country, people don't come a callin' at midnight. No way in hell. Visions of every monster, from every American International and Hammer Studios horror flick I'd seen while cowering in the back of our station wagon at the local Drive-In—*I was a Teenage Werewolf*; *The Raven*; *Masque of The Red Death*; *Dracula: Prince of Darkness*—flashed into my mind. And every *Famous*

The Black Spiral: Twisted Tales of Terror

Monster Mag, every Dell Comic Book (and I had stacks of them in the closet) would become a burnt offering if this nightmare would only stop.

"I do believe in ghosts ... I do," I prayed.

The car's engine died. Layered over the steady drone of crickets was the soft plinking and ticking of the mystery car's engine block, cooling in the dark breeze. More sounds. A car door slammed. Hurried footsteps crunched across the gravel drive. Muffled voices. And someone crying, no, whimpering. Sobbing.

WHAM!

It seemed as though the whole house shook, but in reality it was someone pounding on the kitchen door. More footfalls but from inside the house. Mom and Stan, my stepfather, were bounding down the hall stairs. My bedroom door creaked, then slowly began to open. As it opened a sliver of light cut the darkness, and crept across the face of Bela Lugosi whose poster hung on the wall next to my bed. Dracula's hypnotic eyes seemed to pulsate in the darkness. Then, for a moment, I was like Lou Costello in a Universal Studios horror spoof, face-to-face with Bela, imagining that undulating bat wings hovered in each pupil of the Count's eyes. A figure stood silhouetted in the spill of light. Invisible spiders crawled up the hollow tube of my spine. A whisper. "Robbie, stay in your room."

It was Mom. Thank God.

I struggled to find my voice. "Yeah, okay, Ma. Who's here?"

She didn't answer. The moment of reassurance I'd felt vanished in an instant as her form evaporated into the darkness. Elvis, his head hung low, cautiously padded out of my room and into the void. I was alone, all alone.

WHAM! More fists pounded the door.

I was up and out of that bed faster than crap through a goose. As my feet hit the floor, the icy, yellowed linoleum leached through my soles, into my bone marrow. When I rounded the corner and bounded into the kitchen, I froze. Stan held his "Stan the Man" baseball bat in a white-knuckled grip, his back pressed to one side of the doorframe. Beads of sweat dotted the hairline of his steel-brush crew cut and tracked down his temples, onto his cheeks. Next to him stood my mother, half-covered in shadow. She had turned on the porch light, which now drifted through the side windows and into the kitchen, bathing a portion of her face in its caress. Her blond hair seemed to phosphoresce. There

The Black Spiral: Twisted Tales of Terror

was something in my mother's eyes, something I didn't recognize. And now I know what was—fear.

The light reflected off the barrel of the Iver Johnson .22 revolver that wavered in Mom's hand. She was biting her lower lip, trying not to shake. It wasn't working. She was shaking like a Mix-Master eggbeater. Come to think of it, so was I.

My eyes shot back to Stan; his jaws were clenched so tight that I could see his pulse pounding in his temples, bulging. His neck was corded like a twisted rope.

WHAM! More pounding.

Stan cleared his throat and stammered, "Who is it? What do you want? I've got a baseball bat and I know how to use it." He probably should've mentioned the gun, but he was just as scared as Mom and me.

I heard a growl and looked down to see Elvis's head tucked between my legs, shielded by my body. Well, he didn't have the gun or the bat—now did he? Smart dog.

Now you're asking—why didn't they call the police. Well, we lived at the southern most tip of Beaver River County. It would have taken the sheriff a good twenty minutes to get there. No, scratch that because his name was "Speed" Willie. It would have taken an hour. He talked fast but drove like an old maid. Stan knew Speed from way back and used to joke about him and call him Barney. Good ol' "Mr. One-Bullet."

A muffled, high-pitched voice came from the other side of the door.

"Stanley? Stanley, it's me, Eddie. Open up!"

Bat turds and monkey farts! It was only Cousin Eddie. His overeducated, obnoxious self. Elvis snuffled, padded to his corner, circled twice and lay down. Why do they do that? Mom lowered the revolver and threw back the deadbolt. I appeared at her side and she gave me the—look. As if to say, "Robbie, I thought I told you ..." But then she flashed a weak smile and clutched me tight against her side.

Stan peered through the now cracked door.

He dropped the baseball bat and took an involuntary step backward. Mom shot a hand to her mouth and gasped. Propped up against Cousin Eddie's chest was Herbie. His flaming red hair and freckles matched the loud red Hawaiian shirt that Eddie was wearing. In the harsh glare of the porch light the whole thing looked like a scene right out of *The Twilight Zone.*

Herbie looked like he'd fallen into a cement mixer—pulverized. He might not make it to his thirteenth birthday at this rate. Somebody had beaten the snot out of him. His right eye was swollen shut, his lip split, his shirt torn to shreds, and when he managed a faint smile, I could see that his front teeth were missing. He was a basket case, as Mom would say. War-talk I think? When Stan grabbed Herbie by one arm, Herbie cried out in pain.

"I think his arm's dislocated, Stanley," Eddie offered. His bulging hazel-yellow eyes stood out from his pudgy round face like two sunny-side-up eggs in a skillet.

No shit, Sherlock, what was your first clue? They hobble-carried him to a chair beside the kitchen table and Mom ran to the cupboard for the first aid kit. Stan was upset. I mean really pissed. His eyes flickered with anger and his hands kept fisting. Of course, now I know why. Stan had an abusive father and the sight of the beating that had been inflicted on poor old Herbie hit a nerve. Hit below the belt.

"It's okay, Herbie. You're safe now. You hear me? You're safe," Stan whispered.

I don't think Stan ever had any formal crisis counselor training. Oh, what am I saying, there was no such thing back then. But nevertheless, Stan was right on the mark. Herbie needed desperately to understand that he was safe. Stan knew that the physical wounds would heal much faster than the psychological abrasions to Herbie's psyche. Stan hid his own scars well but not now, not under these circumstances. He pulled Cousin Eddie to one side. They spoke in hushed whispers.

Mom's eyes glazed over with that man-hater look. You know the one. It's the same look any man gets when his wife puts on a new dress, and he tells her how nice her hair looks.

"Stanley Donner, get this boy up on the table and hold him down while I set his shoulder."

Stan gave that "who me?" look of his and scurried to Herbie's aid. Then he turned to Cousin Eddie.

"You gonna just stand there like a stump, or are you gonna help?"

They held poor ol' Herbie down while he bleated like a sheep whose head was stuck in a woven-wire fence. Mom ripped up a sheet, made a sling for Herbie's arm.

The Black Spiral: Twisted Tales of Terror

Then she had me run to the freezer for some ice and a beef-steak for his eye. That's when I finally had the courage to speak to Herbie for the first time.

"Hang in there, pal. Man, you look uglier than a bull dog on a meat wagon." I forced a smile and winked.

Herbie winced with pain and looked up. "Hey, Robbie, guess they'll have to call me Timex, huh?"

"Timex?"

"Yeah, takes a lickin' and keeps on tickin'. Get it?" As Herbie said it, he laughed. But then his head rolled to one side, his face screwed up with pain.

Mom was holding the beef-steak to Herbie's eye and nodding her head. A faint smile curled Herbie's lips. Mom smiled, too. Guess she liked my bedside manner. She was a nurse, no, rather a RN—Registered Nurse with a capital "R."

Yes, Capt. Connie Wagner (her maiden name) of the U.S. Army Nurse Corps. Though I am sure neither Robert Altman nor John Irving had ever met my mother, she certainly could have been the inspiration for two of their favorite characters. She was a combination of Sally Kellerman's Margaret "Hot Lips" Houlihan from the movie **M*A*S*H**, and Glenn Close's portrayal of Jenny Fields, T.S. Garp's women's-lib-preaching mother in the film. And like Garp's emancipated mother, she could be tough as nails when she needed to. And more often than not, she needed to. But right now she was "Hot Lips" Houlihan. Her soothing voice and smile permeated the air. She had strawberry-blond hair, peacock-blue eyes and was only about thirty at the time. Some of the guys told me she was a babe, but the way ol' Herbie was drooling over her, you'd think she was a goddess. Or maybe in Herbie's case, a banana split.

Oh yeah, Herbie was sucking it up big time. But don't get me wrong. He deserved it. Poor old Butterball.

Stan and Eddie had moved further away and into the corner of the kitchen, their voices raising and lowering in sync. I had a good idea who had tromped the beejezus out of Herbie, and knew it was going to put me in a bind. Jeff Horne, my best bud, had confided in me that Herbie was a Klepto, sticky fingers. Jeff overheard his older brother, Chad, telling his girlfriend how Herbie had been boosting food from his house. Despite this, we still liked old Butterball.

The Black Spiral: Twisted Tales of Terror

You have to understand that Butterball came from a big family: eleven brothers and sisters plus him made an even dozen.

Their dad was crippled in an accident at his job. Herbie's old man was a mechanic for the city of Milwaukee, and one day, while fitting a snowplow to the front of a dump truck—he became a pensioner. The driver's foot slipped off the brake pedal and onto the gas. The way I heard it the driver was a real Doofus, and got so rattled that as the truck lurched forward, he accidentally hit the control that raised the plow. Herbie's dad got skewered like a side of Wisconsin corn-fed beef. He lost both legs.

The pension and disability amounted to doodly-squat. And certainly not enough to feed that brood of kids. If you were trying to take their family portrait, you would have to use a wide-angle lens. Remember those Ma and Pa Kettle movies? What little they had on the dinner table was vacuumed from their plates in an instant. Same here. Their mom, Margie Manson, worked as a cleaning lady at a hospital, and that's where my mom met her. Mom and I lived in Milwaukee and parts west before moving back to Grandpa's farm, the homestead.

Anyway, Jeff and I figured that Herbie and the rest of the kids learned to steal food in order to survive. It didn't make it right, but I would've probably done the same. Who knows? That's why Mom had arranged for Herbie to spend the summer with Cousin Eddie. One less mouth to feed. And besides, Eddie needed some help with the farm work.

Okay, here goes nothing and everything, I thought as my gaze bored in on Herbie. "It was Chad Horne wasn't it? He caught you at his place again, didn't he? Stealing food." I was Mr. District Attorney.

"Shut the 'f' up, Robbie. You want to get me killed?"

"Whoa, slow down, pig breath. I'm not gonna rat you out. We pinky swore, remember?"

Herbie was trembling like an epileptic Pillsbury Dough Boy. I looked down and noticed a wet stain flowering in his crotch. I backed off and sidled up to Stan. He didn't notice.

"But Stanley, the boy is my responsibility. He's staying with me for the summer," Cousin Eddie whined. "I should have kept a better eye on the lad. Chad Horne is crazy. So what if Herbie stole some meat from his freezer. You'd better calm down, Stanley. We need clear heads right now." Cousin Eddie was right but it was no use. Stan wasn't buying it. Wasn't even listening.

The Black Spiral: Twisted Tales of Terror

I could imagine that in his mind, Stan could only see the image of Chad Horne, his fists flailing into Herbie, the rage in his face, the cruel expression on his lips. And years later, Stan told me that it was an image of his own father that stood before his mind's eye that night, not Chad Horne. And Stan was Herbie, crumpled over, too small to fight back. Stan was incensed. Full meltdown.

Like my mother, there was something in his eyes. But unlike her look and the confusion it had caused me, I understood this look. I knew exactly what it was. It was hate!

Stan placed his hands on his hips, looked down at his feet, and then spun about. He snatched the revolver from the counter where Mom had placed it. He opened the cylinder, checked that each chamber was loaded and tucked the weapon into the pocket of his coat, which hung on a rack by the door.

Then he drew a Camel from the other coat pocket and lit it. Without a word, he pulled on his boots and coat, headed for the door. I yelled, "Hold on—Stan, aren't you forgetting something?" He was still in his boxer shorts. I ran to get him a pair of pants. When I returned, Mom was blocking the door, her face flushed red and her eyes were almost—iridescent—like a hellcat.

"Stan, if you step one foot out that door ... well, I'll just have to call my brother," she said.

Big threat that was—! I handed Stan his pants and started to put my shoes on. Mom's maternal instinct overrode her citizen's arrest routine. She moved from the door and grabbed me by the shoulders.

"Is this about that animal, Chad Horne? You think violence will solve this? It never does and you know it," Mom half-cried.

Stan turned to me and said, "Robbie, stay with your mother. Lock the door and see to Herbie."

I gulped hard. My mouth felt like it was stuffed with cotton balls. Elvis stirred from his corner and whined.

Stan marched toward the door like a man of purpose. A man with an old score to settle. He paused, whistled for Elvis and as an after thought, hoisted the baseball bat to his shoulder.

"Come on, Eddie. I need to have a little talk with Chad Horne. Up close and personal." With that, Stan was out the door. Eddie trailed behind like a foal following its mare, on shaky legs with a bewildered expression on his face.

The Black Spiral: Twisted Tales of Terror

"Now, Stanley, let's take a moment to consider our options here." Eddie was book smart but not very persuasive. A Dale Carnegie Drop Out.

All six-foot-two of Stan never broke stride. "Just get in the fuckin' car, Eddie. And shut up."

Holy shit! Stan never used the F-word and Mom caught it, too. But she didn't say a thing, didn't move a muscle. Herbie sat there, his mouth open wide as a large-mouth bass.

I turned slowly and slipped off to my bedroom. Tearing off my pajamas, pulling on my clothes, hopping on one leg, I fell flat on my ass in the process.

I went to the closet and fumbled for the overhead light's pull chain. Aw, screw it. Then I saw it, hiding in the corner behind my sleeping bag: my Remington .22 carbine. I grabbed it and stuffed my pockets with two boxes of shells, then quietly climbed out the bedroom window.

Chad Horne lived in a rented farmhouse just down the road next to Cousin Eddie's. If I hurried, I could get there before the action started. If Stan could take the "plunge"—so could I. **Truth, Justice and the American Way.** I just hoped Chad Horne was faster than a speeding bullet.

The Test of the Gunfighter.

As I loped across the yard, silver droplets of moonlight dappled the ground. The giant shadows of trees leaped forward, fell back, and leaped again across the grass. Phantom, my bike, was propped up against the toolshed. I clambered onto the bicycle, threaded my arm through the carbine's strap, slung it over my back, and tore down the driveway. Without stopping at the end of the drive, I banked hard to the left and onto the blacktop roadway.

I stood on the pedals, pumping so hard that I thought I could almost smell smoke pouring off the rear axle. Once I crested the incline about twenty yards ahead, it would be all down hill from there.
I was rocketing down the slope now, the wind swept like cold silk against my face. The air was sweet and clean. I could see the taillights of Stan's VW Beetle receding in the distance.

The Black Spiral: Twisted Tales of Terror

I'm sure Stan had that sucker floored, but it was such a dog that I was seriously worried ol' Phantom and I might overtake them. Well, okay, maybe that's a stretch but at the time, it sure seemed that way.

The lake and a tall stand of oak and birch flanked the road. As I soared past, the full moon appeared to hang suspended, bobbing slightly like a child's balloon grasped by the finger-like branches of the trees. Lake Maria was a dark maw, black and smooth as pooled oil.

Purple and black. Black and purple.

The roadway leveled and I pumped the pedals again, the drive chain serenading the night, along with the steady hum of the bike's tires against the blacktop. I saw the entrance to Chad Horne's farmhouse just ahead. I shot into the drive, did a side dismount, balancing by my left foot on the pedal, and rolled to a silent stop. After easing my bike to the ground, I crept like a stalking Comanche through the shrubs and sidled up to Chad's '64 **GOAT** parked about fifteen yards from the house.

Chad Horne had three passions in life: his wheels—a five-coats-of-lacquer, custom-painted, candy-apple-red GTO; his drinking, you name it he drank it; and fighting—look at him sideways and he'd like to knock your clock off. He wasn't just a mean drunk, he was cool as a cucumber kind of mean. Deliberate. And everyone, including my best bud, Jeff Horne, knew it. Sometimes Jeff stayed clear of his brother, Chad, for weeks.

When Jeff and I had let Herbie join the gang that summer, we had all pinky swore and spit, pledging never to rat on one another. Never. For us, this was a drop dead, cross-your-heart, stab-me-in-the-eyes-with-darning-needles oath. But I couldn't rid myself of that nagging feeling that this whole thing was somehow my damn fault: That Herbie got the shit kicked out of him; that Stan was about to blow Chad Horne to kingdom come; maybe spend the rest of his days locked up in Waupon State Prison making baseball bats and playing the harmonica. And it was my fault that my best buddy, Jeff, was about to lose his big brother. Of course, not that anyone but Jeff would shed a tear for Chad. Congratulations, Robbie, you screwed this one up big time.

From where I sat, crouching behind the GTO, I commanded a clear view of the farmhouse and the front door. It was a dilapidated structure with peeling white paint, weathered shingles loose and flapping in the breeze and littering the yard, a sagging porch with half its railing missing, and screens dotted with holes. A blanket of old bottles and rusted engine parts and a discarded stove and refrigerator served as lawn ornaments. The only thing missing was a junkyard dog.

The house was dark. The shades were drawn and hung tattered and lopsided in the windows like the wrinkled eyelids of an old man. I saw Stan's VW Beetle parked to one side of the house, nesting in the shadows. Then a brief flicker of eyeshine—animal eyes—floated in the darkness. I swallowed audibly.

It was Elvis, peering at me from the back seat of the Slug Bug. Crazy mutt had half-scared me to death. But where the hell were Stan and Eddie? Then came the sound of footsteps approaching, glass breaking under foot. Drawing nearer. A cough. Sounds that made greasy fingers wiggle in my stomach. I was crouched on the balls of my feet, like I was about to take a dump. And then I almost did.

I slowly reached behind me, grabbed the stock of the carbine slung over my shoulder, lifted the weapon over my head, and cradled it in my lap.

More footsteps. Another cough.

The kitchen windows lit up; a floodlight blazed to life. Pucker factor big time. I ducked. A shadow glided across the shades. I took a deep breath, closed my eyes. "Come on you big, chickenshit," I whispered to myself.

I found a morsel of leftover courage that I'd been saving for a special occasion, and peeked over the trunk of the car. Two men stood, their backs to me, outlined in the harsh glare of the floodlight's beam. It was Stan and Eddie. If I hadn't been so frightened, I might have laughed out loud. There they were—Mutt and Jeff—right out of the funny papers. Stan's frame dwarfed Eddie's who was only five feet four to begin with and about sixty pounds overweight. Eddie's Hawaiian shirt was so long it reached the bottom of his plaid Bermuda shorts. He kept rocking on the balls of his red high-top P.F. Fliers, as if that would somehow make him taller. Stan was standing so straight you'd think he had a corncob jammed up his butthole. Sgt. Friday and his partner, Baby Huey.

The lights winked out. My hands were slick with sweat as I clutched the rifle for comfort, rolling the grip of the stock back and forth in my palm. Then I saw him.

My eye caught just the slightest movement near the corner of the farmhouse. But instinctively I knew it was him, Chad. His movements were fluid and silken, a ghost dancer. For an instant, as he stepped from the shadows and into the moonlight, something about him was so strange; he was like one of those life-size cardboard cutouts that they prop next to you at the fair as they shoot your picture: A movie star—James Dean. And like the cutout, Chad's image was two-dimensional, lifeless and totally devoid of humanity.

Chad stood there, eyes glazed over. Silent. Staring. He raised his hand slightly and I caught the flash of metal in the ambient moonlight. I thought it was a pistol. It wasn't. Chad's thumb kept flicking his Zippo lighter.

Opening and closing it. Opening and closing it.

It was like the sound of a knife blade being drawn across a wet stone. Then a hollow click. A burst of flame. It was the first of two sounds that I heard that night: sounds that wouldn't be forgotten, couldn't be forgotten.

Chad's eyes reflected a spectrum of moonlight that mirrored his mood: flame red. They glowed like burning embers in the inky blackness. The full moon's radiance glanced off the zippers of Chad's leather jacket; they glimmered like cold-white sutures stitched into the fabric of the deep nightshade. And then he laughed, threw back his head and laughed. His words cut the air.

"I'm in such a mood. Such a damn good mood. I might just pretend that you two A-holes never came here tonight."

I saw Stan flinch. Eddie took half a step back.

Chad's voice grew deep with anger.

"On second thought, maybe I'm in a bad mood. Such a damn bad mood, that I should just stomp you two like cockroaches."

Stan stiffened and took one step forward. "Stomp us like you did that poor boy? You cheap punk."

Eddie crab-walked two steps from Stan's side.

Now Chad's voice completely changed in timbre and pitch. It seemed to be more animal than human—or something less than both.

"Big talk, old man. You bring the little Kewpie doll along for the ride? Or is he your date? You wanna dance, old man?"

The love chant of crickets and frog song was suddenly extinguished. Brooding silence. The night air seemed to compress, to liquefy and become like tar. So thick I couldn't breathe.

Then something flickered in Chad's hand. At first I thought it was the Zippo, but it wasn't. It was a switchblade.

The Black Spiral: Twisted Tales of Terror

    I found myself shivering despite the muggy, roiling air that swirled around me. I was drenched with fear. Shaking in my shorts. And yet, fascinated.
    All the while Stan stood tall, neither moving nor making a sound. I knew he had seen the vicious blade spring open just as I had. Why didn't he do something? I looked closer. Stan held the revolver cradled in the small of his back. Then I thought I saw his arm stiffen, his finger slowly tighten on the trigger. For a moment Stan looked like Yul Brynner's character, Chris Adams, the gunslinger from the *Magnificent Seven*. In my mind's eye—he was now dressed in black from head to toe, steely eyed, cold as ice. Watching, waiting for young Chico, not Chad, to make his move, clap his hands. The gunfighter's test of speed. But before the hands could draw close, before the smack of flesh on flesh, Stan, the gunslinger, would plant a hot slug right between young Chad's eyes. Pow.
    I silently mouthed Vin's (Steve McQueen's) tag line from the movie, "We deal in lead, my friend."
    But this wasn't a movie and deep inside, I knew it. However, it was so real, so intense, that it instantly overwhelmed my senses, sending me hurtling down a rabbit hole and into an alternate reality. A two-dimensional universe without depth, without the fourth vector: Time. God had inserted his pinky finger into the clockwork mechanism of the universe.
    Stan, Eddie, Chad, the whole world stood before me—suspended in time.
    A little boy's imagination was the only coping mechanism I could turn to. At that moment, I wished I were "THE FLASH." Imbued with super powers, able to move at near light speed. I would grab Chad Horne by the lapels, slap him silly, then snatch the gun from Stan's hands, all in less than the blink of an eye. Old Chad would come to, all trussed up in a straightjacket and seated on the floor of a padded room somewhere in Outer Mongolia. Crazy bastard. That's where he belonged.
    A tear rolling down my face, and something equally wet but ice cold—brought me back to the present. It was the pooch, Elvis, pressing his cold snout to the small of my back. He had somehow figured out a way to get the door of the VW open. So much for German engineering. I gave him a quick hug and a noogie, then raised my carbine. I steadied the rifle on the trunk lid. I figured they wouldn't

The Black Spiral: Twisted Tales of Terror

send a kid to reform school for life. But they sure as hell would send Stan's ass away forever. As I was drawing a bead on Chad, something knocked me off balance. It was Elvis again, whining, chuffing. Then he jumped on top of me. I tried to get up, but each time I rose, he'd grab a mouthful of my collar and pull me down again.

They couldn't see me—but I heard Chad's voice. "Make your move, old man." It sounded thin, icy.

A blur of fabric shot past me. Beach attire. It was Cousin Eddie running so fast you'd of thought that Dead Head had shouted, "Surfs up!" He dropped the baseball bat he'd been holding; it landed smack on my head. Never throw your bat.

I was catapulted out of my dazed—el' Ka-bonged'—state by the screeching of brakes, the slamming of car doors. Elvis and I both spun in the direction of the clamor. Clouds of dust, kicked up from the gravel drive, floated in the headlights of a car. The silhouettes of two men stood, towering like giants, in the backwash of the vehicle's high beams.

CHA-CHUNG

If you've ever heard that sound, even once, you will never forget it. Not in a zillion years. It was the sound of a 12-gauge, pump-action Mossberg. I told you there were two sounds I heard that night. This was the second. I can still hear it today and it bores like a corkscrew into my brain.

They were a sight for sore eyes: Speed Willie—*The Lawman*—and Uncle Elvin. Mom warned us she'd call Elvin, her brother. Uncle Elvin wore a denim work shirt, buttoned high at the collar just under a hardball-sized Adam's apple. His overalls were faded and frayed at the bottom of both pants legs. He had an upturned, taunting smile, and coal-black hair slicked back with Vitalis. And I guess Stan was wrong about Speed having only the one bullet. Even if he did, it didn't matter. It's really hard to miss with a scattergun. Shit, even if he did miss, Uncle Elvin would just open his big mouth and talk us all to death. If I had been Chad and had to choose between the two, I'd have to go with the shotgun—less pain and a hell of a lot quicker.

Sheriff Willie stepped out of the headlights and immediately shrunk back to Barney Fife size. But he leveled that 12-gauge right on Chad Horne. From my vantage point I saw Stan sidestep out of the BB pellet's shot pattern and tuck the .22 under his coat. He and Chad were only a few feet apart. If the sheriff hadn't shown when he did, it could've gotten really ugly, really quick.

The Black Spiral: Twisted Tales of Terror

When ol' Speed spoke, there was a slight tremor in his voice. He spat out the words like whizzing rounds from a grease gun.

"Stan, why don't ya take da' boy and get on home now. I mean, I think Elvin and I can find some 'ccommodations 'dat suit Mr. Horne 'der. Can't we now, Elvin?"

Uncle Elvin's eyes twinkled as he broke in right on cue.

"Sure, betcha we can. I was just thinkin' of a real sweet place for Mr. Jim-dandy 'der." He rubbed his stubbled chin with his large hand, pondering. Suddenly the answer washed over his face. "I got me plenty a room in 'dat 'der pighouse!" Elvin chuckled as he rolled that trademark toothpick of his from one corner of his mouth to the other, as if it were an extension of his tongue.

Stan nodded and then after chewing on Speed's words for a moment, he turned. He looked at the carbine in my hands, and then back to me. He just gave a faint smile.

Elvis panted a doggie smile and woofed, then padded across the yard to Stan and sniffed his hand. He stood there looking up at Stan as if to say, *"H'mm, very interesting. Smell something. Not chicken. Not liver. Sweat. Man scared. Lock me in car. No fun. This place smell bad. I like. Come back tomorrow. Boy, where boy? Get boy! Go home?"*

Elvis turned and bounded to my side.

Stan took me by the arm, grabbed the .22 carbine from my hand, and placed it on the floor in the rear. But as we climbed into the VW, Stan didn't say a word, not one word. Elvis crawled over my lap and hopped into the back seat. As we drove off, I saw Speed walk up to Chad. I couldn't make out what Chad said to him, but it must have been a real doozy, because that shotgun stock flew into Chad's gut quicker than a greased pig. "Too bad, sucker. That one's for Herbie," I shouted.

I was going to ask Stan about my bike, but decided to keep my big trap shut. *Don't push your luck, Robbie.* We drove into the night and all the way home in silence. I rolled down my car window, leaned outside and gazed upward into the star-punctured sky. The wind kissed my cheeks, and streamed between the spread fingers of my outstretched hand. Life filled the night. The scent of green ripening cornfields hung sweetly in the air. A swarm of insects, caught in the onrushing path of the metallic Slug Bug's headlights, looped and rolled like tiny fighter planes. A Kamikaze-style June bug flamed against the deck, stinging my palm.

The Black Spiral: Twisted Tales of Terror

When we got home, Mom was on the front porch waiting. Isn't that what moms do best? Wait and worry. She said that Cousin Eddie had called, and asked if he could bring my bike over in the morning. Stan and I exchanged glances and laughed: inside joke. Mom looked puzzled.

I learned later that Cousin Eddie hid in the woods until Uncle Elvin discovered him, cowering behind a sapling, illuminated by the harsh glare of police car's spotlight. Eddie declined Speed's offer of a lift home, choosing not to sit in the rear of the squad car with Chad. So he cobb'd my bike.

Can you picture it—a Kewpie doll in a red Hawaiian shirt, pedaling his fat buns off, as he streaks through the night? It's "THE FLASH."

I felt like I'd been squeezed through the ringer of our old MAYTAG. So I crawled off to bed. Herbie was fast asleep on the lower bunk, my bunk, no doubt dreaming of triple-thick chocolate malts and bigger-than-your-head cheeseburgers. His mouth gaped wide; his breath whistled through the gap left by his missing front teeth each time he exhaled. I shrugged my shoulders and swung up into the top bunk. Elvis snuggled in with Herbie.

As I lay there, staring at the ceiling, trying to come down off that adrenalin rush—The Beat—I remembered Stan's words earlier that night, "It's okay, Herbie. You're safe now. You hear me? You're safe."

And he was—for now. We all were.

For now.

***

FAMOUS HOUSE

Mike Rimar

"Will you just look at this house? It's beautiful!" Maggie's green eyes flashed at her husband, sparkling with excitement.

Bob Sparks kept his homebuyers poker face neutral, unwilling to give away too much. A pointless exercise. Maggie loved the place, and he could sense the realtor tasting blood. "Let's see how it looks inside."

Maggie looked at him. Her round face, framed by thick dark hair, turned sour, but she kept silent.

"Your husband is right, Maggie," Sally Newport their realtor said. Bob called her Mrs. Newport to her face. When it was just he and Maggie, she was *The Realtor*, like some comic book villain. Real estate agents were of the same ilk as used car salesmen, and he refused to get chummy with anyone whose sole purpose was to take his money.

"Let's go inside," Mrs. Newport continued. "I just know you'll both be pleasantly surprised. *Famous House* rarely disappoints." A toothy smile flashed across her unnaturally tight face. Bob suspected many commissions worth of plastic surgery.

Mrs. Newport led them along the gravel drive leading to the house. Sunlight filtered through the canopy of two gnarled and ancient oaks, covering the Greek revival-style house in dappled shadows. A twin set of glass-paneled windows complete with wooden shutters flanked either side of the double doors. A low porch spread out across the ground like a boardwalk. A balcony of equal length separated the second floor from the main, supported by four thick columns. Arched windows protruded from a sharply angled roof, *un*blinking eyes watching over the half-acre estate of fresh-cut lawn. A wood lot bordered to the east, cornfields to the south and west.

Whitewash covered the house like icing on a wedding cake. Oak leaves rustled in a warm breeze. The calm, soothing sound reminded Bob of childhood summers. Weeklong visits with Grandma Pearl. Apple pie, ice cream, and fruit juice served in the treasured Honey Bee mug she had given him.

"It looks so old—" Maggie leaned against a towering column.

The Black Spiral: Twisted Tales of Terror

She inhaled sharply.

Bob took her by the arm. "You okay?"

She placed his hand on her bloated pregnant belly. Irregular thumps vibrated through his splayed fingers.

"He's gonna be a soccer player," he said.

"Maybe, if *she* wants to be," Maggie said in a barbed tone as a broad grin curled her lips.

Bob rolled his eyes theatrically. He loved this argument. Boy? Girl? He didn't care, having deliberately chosen to not know through the sonograms, but the game was fun.

"Is this your first?" Mrs. Newport asked.

"Yep," Maggie beamed. "Just another month to go."

Bob shared in her pride. Damn, he was lucky.

Mrs. Newport studied them with a sage-like expression. "I have one word of advice. Epidural. Don't be a hero. I've had three children, and blissfully didn't feel a thing. Believe me. It's the only way to go."

"So we've been told," Bob said. He'd heard it all before. Ultimately, it would be Maggie's decision, but when the time came he would push for the drugs. Her pain was his pain.

The porch's slats creaked under his weight. "Exactly how old is this house, again?"

Mrs. Newport cleared her throat like a tour guide. "*Famous House* was built by Colonel Xavier St. Germain in the eighteen-sixties. It is reminiscent of the grand plantations of the Old South. The colonel had fought for the Confederacy and, after the war, brought the design north to Serly, Illinois. I guess, in his own way, he refused to give up the fight." She giggled. "Originally a farm of vast acreage, the land has been parceled off over the years. The woods belong to the County now, and the cornfields to neighboring farmers." She leaned conspiratorially and winked. "The first ten rows are feed corn for the cows. Go in deeper for the good stuff."

Maggie grinned and asked, "Why is it called *Famous House?*"

"Because so many famous and successful people have lived here. Colonel St. Germain's son began the local paper, which he turned into a statewide empire. He also happens to be my uncle, many greats over. Agatha Rowntree grew up here. She became a world-renown opera singer in the early twenties. Silent movie director, Malcolm Ewing, Terry Willis, a hall-of-famer who played for the Yankees, the list goes on and on. They all lived here."

"Wow," Maggie said. "Maybe some of that good luck will rub off on our child?"

"Perhaps it will," Mrs. Newport said with a smile.

Bob pursed his lips. *The Realtor* already had the papers signed in her mind. "Let's look inside." Maggie's warm hand held in his, he waited for Mrs. Newport to unlock the front door.

Something must be wrong with this place, he thought. There had to be. How else could he wrangle for a lower price, not that they could afford it anyway. As a computer consultant he made good money, but not that good.

The door swung open, and Sally Newport stepped back.

Maggie gasped. Sunlight glared from polished wooden floors. The cavernous foyer was right out of *Gone with the Wind* complete with recessed columns along the walls and a stairway that curled to the second floor. He could sense Maggie's desire. She wanted this house.

Bob stepped onto the floor as if it was glass. He sighed. *Let's get this over with and move to the next house. We can't afford this place.*

Maggie floated through the sitting and living rooms and he knew that look in her eye. She was visualizing the couch here, the television there. In spite of *Famous House's* antebellum exterior, the kitchen had been fully renovated. The wooden cabinets were sleek; the stainless-steel sink gleamed with newness. White ceramic tiles covered the floor, bright and unmarred. A wide window revealed a view of the backyard, another half acre of grass brought to an abrupt end by the southern cornfield. Bob shook his head while Mrs. Newport led them to the second floor.

Bob noticed that the house seemed to invigorate Maggie. Eagerly, she climbed unaided up the curved stairway, unfettered by the weight of their unborn child.

Damn, I should tell her now. We just can't afford it. Why was *The Realtor* even showing us this house?

The second floor didn't help, either. The master bedroom was immense, with a walk-in closet, bathroom, and an arched doorway leading out to the balcony. Mrs. Newport showed them three more bedrooms, another bathroom, and what she called a sitting room. It would make a perfect nursery.

The basement had also been worked on. Painted walls subdivided the family and laundry rooms. The utility room remained unfinished and with a well-built, albeit homemade, workbench. A new gas furnace whispered quietly in the far corner. Bob sighed again. It was time to break the bad news to Maggie.

"How much?" She asked before he could speak.

"Maggie—" he began.

"Two-fifty," Sally said without hesitation.

Bob blinked. Did he hear right? He expected a half-mill at the least.

"We'll take it," Maggie said.

Bob did a double take. "Shouldn't we discuss this first?"

Maggie faced him. "All right. I love this house. I want this house. We can afford this house. We'll take this house." She smiled.

He knew that smile, had seen it when she said, "I do," and when she said, "I'm pregnant."

How could he say no? "Can we at least talk to the previous owners?"

"They've moved to the west coast. The little boy is going to be in movies." Sally grinned as she delivered the coup de grace.

Bob took out his pen. "Where do we sign?"

"I love this place!" Bob shoved his golf bag into the closet.

"Have a good game?" Maggie lay on the couch.

"Sorry, did I wake you?"

"No, just feeling a little queasy."

He rushed to her side. "What's wrong?"

"Nothing. He's just giving me a hard time. Mother stuff." She smiled and patted her belly.

Satisfied, he stood. "I gotta tell you, there's nothing like a two minute drive to the golf course."

"Is that a pun?"

He stared at her quizzically, then laughed.

Maggie tilted her head toward the front window. "Are you going to mow the lawn now?"

"I guess I can't avoid it any longer." Bob sighed like a man given a life sentence. He walked out into the brilliant sunshine.

The lawnmower was stored in the plastic shed he had purchased shortly after they moved in, and he grunted as he dragged it out. The sun beat down without mercy, growing in intensity by the minute. Wasn't it better to mow grass in the evening? He turned to the house.

Maggie was on the porch, teetering gently in the rocking chair he

163

had put there for her.

Look at her lording over me like a rude taskmaster, he thought.

He waved to her and yanked on the cord. The mower coughed to life on the first pull. He'd procrastinated too long; the yard was more like a meadow than a lawn. After a few passes he could feel sweat rolling from his arm pits.

Maggie looked up from the magazine she was reading and waved.

Bob hid a scowl. Doesn't she trust me? No, she just knows me. As he crisscrossed the patch of grass, his mind wandered. Other than the huge lawn, it really was a great house. A real keeper. It was easy to envision himself playing catch with his son by the front porch, pushing him on a tire swing.

He paused.

His son.

Maggie had referred to the baby as *he*. He, not she.

Bob glanced at her and froze. She was doubled over, clutching her belly. "Maggie!" He ran to her.

"It's time," she said. "Didn't you hear me?"

"No. The mower was too loud. What's wrong?"

She grimaced, her face pale. "My water broke."

A month had passed.

Bob crept into the kitchen. Johnny had finally gone down for his nap. Maggie had decided that she, too, needed a rest. He agreed. They all needed a rest.

The coffeemaker was already set, and he opened the cupboard. Emptiness replaced the spot where his Honey Bee Mug usually sat. Must be dirty, he thought, but couldn't recall using it. With a shrug, he chose another mug, too preoccupied with more pressing matters. After filling the mug with coffee and two spoonfuls of sugar, he quietly made his way through the hallway and out the front door to enjoy the solitude of the open air.

He knew of postpartum depression, but Maggie's had gone far beyond his expectations.

She had become a different person since the birth. They fought all the time, when she could bear the sight of him long enough to talk. Rarely giving the baby more than minimal care, she even talked of putting Johnny on the bottle.

The Black Spiral: Twisted Tales of Terror

Bob had tried to make things better. He took care of Johnny as much as possible, even taking an extended leave of absence from work.

It was never enough. Everything the child did irritated her. Each movement, any sound Johnny made brought a scowl to her face.

He explained with fading patience, "Babies cry in the middle of the night. And yes, they poop in their diapers. It's what they do."

Maggie viewed it as some grand conspiracy.

It was a dark time, but it seemed to have passed. Maggie now held onto Johnny like a lifeline, finally loving their child like a good mother should.

Their own relationship, however, had worsened. He couldn't say exactly how. She was kind to him, and thankful for his help, but it all seemed superficial, contrived, a servant to be endured while present.

Bob pushed the tire swing he had strung up from one of the oaks the day after they returned from the hospital. Dead leaves blew in the autumn wind. A lonely scene, but he found comfort in it. It was warmer outdoors than in the house. Wherever Maggie went, a cold chill followed.

At least he had Johnny. He was great boy. Handsome, like his dad, with dark intelligent eyes. He was going to be. . . a star.

Why did he think that?

Just the whimsy of a proud father. He pushed the tire swing again. Perhaps Maggie was right. If they had switched to bottles he could have fed the boy more often. Establishing a bond with the child was important.

It wasn't fair of Maggie to hog Johnny. After all, a boy should be with his father.

"You're not doing it right," Maggie grated.

"This is the way I do it." Bob bounced Johnny on his lap, waiting for the child to burp.

"It's not the right way."

Oh, shut up and go back to bed, he thought but said, "It's worked for me so far."

Maggie suddenly snatched the boy from his lap. The child began to cry. She ignored his wails, forcing his tiny infant head onto her shoulder. Her hand drummed a constant beat on his back.

"You're hurting him." Bob reached for Johnny who squirmed in his mother's rough grasp.

The Black Spiral: Twisted Tales of Terror

Maggie spun away. "This is the proper way to do it."

"But—"

"But nothing. It's a wonder you haven't killed the poor thing. Really, the ideas you get." She shushed Johnny, trying to calm him.

Where do you get your ideas, television commercials?

Johnny's pudgy little hands reached out, looking for his father's familiar warmth.

Sorry, kid, the wicked witch of the Midwest has you now. Reluctantly, Bob left the nursery. She was his mother. Who was he to argue with maternal instincts?

Johnny continued to wail. He wanted his father, not her.

For the first time since they had met, Bob wished Maggie would just disappear.

"The basement is soaked," Bob said around a mouthful of ham sandwich.

"So? Clean it up." Maggie poured a cup of coffee for herself.

"The spring thaw flooded the basement. The damage isn't too bad, but the carpet is water logged." He opened the kitchen cabinet. His favorite cup was still not there. "Where's my Honey Bee mug?"

"I broke it."

"Broke it? You broke my mug and didn't tell me?"

"It was an accident. It happened months ago. I'm sorry, okay. Grow up and pick another." She absent-mindedly flicked a strand of dark hair from her forehead.

You insincere, little . . .

Grandma Pearl had given him that mug. He was going to give it to Johnny. Maggie continued drinking her coffee, oblivious of his growing rage. He grabbed another mug, shoveled in two heaping spoons of sugar and filled it with coffee. He stirred, clinking the edge of the spoon loudly against the side.

Maggie didn't look up. Sensing their conversation for the day was complete, he stomped down the stairway.

When had things gone so wrong? They weren't in financial trouble. They had a healthy boy, and a beautiful house. Yet they were on the cusp of divorce, and he didn't have a clue why.

That wasn't true. He had a clue. The woman sitting at the kitchen table was not the same person he had married. That person disappeared and, he feared, would never return.

The Black Spiral: Twisted Tales of Terror

He set his mug down and retrieved the Wet-Vac from the utility room. After an hour of sucking water from the carpet, he began his search for the source of the leak. A small puddle formed by the west wall. The paint was stained dark. The drywall was spongy to the touch. He ripped the drywall away to expose a hairline fissure in the foundation. He ran a finger along the concrete. It crumbled easily.

Bob scowled. This was beyond his expertise. He drained his coffee and grimaced. His stomach burned. The basement was cool and damp, yet he was perspiring.

I need more exercise.

Bob watched with mixed feelings as Maggie's compact car backed out of the driveway. His SUV remained, a testament that he was alone.

This was good, he kept telling himself. They needed time apart.

Maggie's mother had become ill, and she had to take care of her. Maggie, however, seemed too happy to go, too eager to be away from him.

He hoped she felt the same as he, that a few days away might help bring them together. But it would hurt to be away from Johnny. He already felt his son's absence, but he needed the time to fix the basement.

His stomach burned and he popped an antacid. Why did Johnny have to go? Bringing a baby into a sick woman's house wasn't wise. He could've taken care of him, and fix the cracked foundation. It would have been fun.

Yeah, right. He'd never get any work done, and it was good for Johnny to see his grandma. After rooting around a minute in the storage shed, he found his pick and shovel.

"Hello?" A strange voice called out.

Bob walked out of the shed. An elderly gentleman stood in the yard, hands stuffed in the pockets of his worn denim coveralls. He was thin, with a thick bushy moustache, which was yellowed at the edges. Gray hair, long and wispy, hung freely to his shoulders.

"Can I help you?" Bob asked.

"Name's Joe. Joe Tinker from up the road. Just thought I'd drop by and say hello."

Bob laughed. "After a whole year?"

Tinker blinked once. "Been sick, and heard you had a baby."

Bob, you're an ass. "Sorry. I'm just a little out of sorts. I'm

The Black Spiral: Twisted Tales of Terror

Bob Sparks. Would you like a beer?"

"Thanks, but no. Don't drink alcohol. Coffee would be nice, if you're having some."

"Coming right up." Bob invited Tinker into the kitchen.

"Place looks different since I been here last," Tinker said.

"The renovations were like this when we bought it. The rest is mostly Maggie's stuff. She's my wife. I have lousy taste in furniture, or so she tells me."

Tinker chuckled dutifully. "Tell her she has a good eye."

Bob grunted. "So, you've been in here before? I mean, before we moved in?" He handed a cup of coffee to the old man.

"Yep. Used to visit Mrs. Simmons all the time."

"Really?" Hopefully he didn't plan on visiting them all the time, Bob thought as he spooned sugar into his own cup.

"Used to do odd jobs for her. I see you like your sugar."

"Sweet and black." Bob gave a good-natured wink, and offered the sugar bowl to the old man.

"Sweet and black," Tinker whispered back. His piercing gray eyes stared out the kitchen window as if lost in thought. He made no move for the sugar bowl.

"Uh, Mr. Simmons was a bit of a klutz then? Is that why you had to help?"

Tinker's eyes met his. "No. He died."

"Died?"

"Bad heart. Collapsed while cutting the lawn."

Bob nodded in understanding. He definitely was going to buy a riding mower. "I heard the Simmons family moved to the Coast."

"Mrs. Simmons and her son, Billy. About a year after Archie died."

"Really? So tell me, exactly how did little Billy get into the movie business?"

"Movies? Not sure. Just happened. The boy had talent, though. Wasn't too surprised to hear it." Tinker fumbled at the words, as if speaking them for the first time.

"Mr. Tinker—"

"Call me Joe."

"Joe. Do you know anything about fixing foundations?"

Tinker smiled. "Sorry, my thing is fixing stuff above ground. Foundations and the like I leave to the professionals." He paused briefly then asked, "The Missus take the boy away?"

"How did you know?"

"Saw them drive away." Tinker frowned, as if he disapproved. "Boy should be with his father."

Bob stared, wide-eyed, at the man's audacity. "He's off to see his grandmother," he said, loathing his defensive tone.

"Sorry. People talk. Just hate to think she might not be coming back."

Bob paled. "Why wouldn't she . . . of course she's coming back."

Tinker nodded and stood as if sensing it was time he left. "Didn't mean to be nosy. You know, I raised my boy alone. It was hard, but it was worth it."

"Mr. Tinker, we are a family, and will stay a family. You can tell *people* that."

Tinker smiled, a thin line barely exposed by his drooping moustache. "That's good to hear, good to hear."

Bob escorted Tinker up the walk, then made his way to the back the house. Earlier, he had marked the spot where he suspected the leak originated. After popping another antacid, he began to dig.

His thoughts trailed to Tinker.

Curious old man. Busy body, too. He paused. Maggie *was* coming back. She had to. He checked his watch. She would still be on the road. He would call her mother's after a couple hours. Just to be sure.

Sure of what? That she hadn't lied? That she wasn't on her way to anywhere to get away from him?

The shovel's blade vibrated, followed by a hollow thud. Using the blade to clear away dirt, he exposed a wooden door buried under the sod. It was nearly rotted to pieces. "It's a wonder no one has fallen through," Bob spoke aloud.

He found a rusted iron handle and pulled. The metal ripped out of the wood. Next he reached for the pick and whacked at the door with it. The brittle wood splintered, revealing a small room. A foul stench rose from the opening, and Bob nearly gagged. His stomach lurched, he downed more antacids.

It was dark inside the hole, but he heard the distinctive sound of debris plopping into water. "Must be some kind of storm cellar." He paused and grinned. "Stop talking to yourself, you nutbar."

The Black Spiral: Twisted Tales of Terror

He returned from the shed with a flashlight, stepladder, and the waders he had bought thinking, since he was now a country boy, he would take up fly-fishing. He aimed the flashlight's beam through the gap in the splintered door. As was suspected, no stairs led to the bottom. Dark mold and pale fungus blotched the fieldstone and mortar walls. Brackish water flooded the floor. The stench nearly overpowered him. He fought his nausea with more tablets.

This was the source of his flooding problems. He had to go down for a closer look. Resigned to the job, he lowered the ladder into the hole.

The water was almost to his knees, cold as ice. He swung the flashlight, illuminating the wall nearest the house. His teeth chattered like castanets. The mortar had eroded badly, leaving large gaps between the fieldstones. He hated to think of the wall's condition below the water line.

Something bumped against his leg. He lowered the flashlight. Bones floated in the water. The initial shock sent ice-carved dominos toppling down his spine. With a nervous laugh at his foolishness, he managed to calm himself. As if to prove a point, he reached down and fished out a bone.

Small and too thin to be human, it was probably from a small bird. Some sort of preservative, like enamel, covered the bone. He dipped his hand into the dark water and pulled up another bone. Thicker and softer, it wasn't a bone at all, but the stubby end of a pioneer-style tallow candle. Nearly a dozen other candles floated among the bones, wood splinters, and other debris.

"Very strange." The small enclosure dampened his voice. Birds must have gotten themselves trapped in here and died, but since when did birds have varnished bones? As interesting as the mystery was, the bones and candles took a back seat to the problem at hand. He stuffed the bone in his pocket, and surveyed the flooded floor. It was going to be a bigger job than he thought.

Back in the kitchen, standing at the counter, Bob opened the phone book. He'd have to call in professionals like Tinker had said. He thought of the room. It looked old, probably as old as *Famous House*. And completely unknown.

He closed the phone book.

Like a whisper, Tinker's words echoed in his mind. *Boy should be with his father.* They sounded familiar, even before the old man had spoken them.

Raising a child alone wasn't hard. He had practically done it himself during Maggie's postpartum depression. He had the child. The hard part was already done. And it wasn't like Maggie was much of a wife to him anymore.

Bob gave his head a quick shake. What was he thinking? He poured himself a cup of coffee and popped two antacid tablets into his mouth without thinking.

He took the chicken bone from his pocket, lips pursed in thought. It was time to learn more about *Famous House*.

Serly's public library was surprisingly modern, with two small computers, and archives dating from pre-civil war days.

He remembered Mrs. Newport, the realtor, mentioning Xavier St. Germain's son had started the local newspaper. He found the first couple of issues, but they didn't turn up anything significant. He sighed, and put the papers away. Research was never his strong suit.

He approached the librarian, a middle-aged woman with a kind smile. "Excuse me. This might seem an odd question, but do you have any information on one of your local characters. A Colonel Xavier St. Germain?"

The librarian's smile broadened. "You're the one who moved into *Famous House*."

"That's right. Bob Sparks. How did you guess?"

"They always come looking for information on the house."

"They?"

"The previous owners. The house has a lot of character. I guess they want to know more about it. Isn't that why you're looking into it?"

"Yes, it is." Bob saw no point in telling her about a room full of bird bones. He followed her down one aisle, then another.

She pulled out a book. "Here, this is the complete history of Serly, and all it's well-known residents. Many of them have lived in *Famous House*. That's why we call it that."

"Yes, I know. Thank you, very much."

"Just put the book back when you're done. I'm afraid you can't take reference material out of the building." The librarian smiled again and shuffled away.

Bob seated himself at a table. Looking at the copyright page, he noticed that the publisher had updated the book every five years. He flipped to the index, looked up Xavier St. Germain, and turned to the appropriate page.

Born in Louisiana, St. Germain was a plantation owner with a large stable of slaves. He had fought for the South during the Civil War, which was no surprise. When the war ended, he moved to Serly and built his house, a miniature version of his plantation home in the bayou. He had one son, Pierre. Xavier's wife had died shortly after Pierre's birth.

A black-and-white picture of the man stared back at him. He wore a Confederate uniform. Penetrating eyes glared fixedly into the camera lens; his face creased with a dour expression. There was something odd about the man. Something familiar.

St. Germain had a full round face, a thin taunting smile. On a whim, Bob placed his index finger across the gap between St. Germain's nose and upper lip, like a moustache.

Joe Tinker's moustache.

It couldn't be. His stomach churned. He reached for his roll of antacids, but he had eaten the last of them during the drive into town. Flipping rapidly through the pages of the book searching for Joe Tinker's name, he found it. Tinker was indeed a farmer, and he, too, had lived in *Famous House*, moving out soon after his wife's death. His son had become a politician. Both Joe and his son had died shortly after the Second World War.

Bob frantically combed through the book, seeking the other names Mrs. Newport had mentioned: Agatha Rowntree, Malcolm Ewing, and Terry Willis. All had led successful lives, but in each case, either the mother or father had died shortly after the children's births.

His stomach twisted. He winced in pain.

It was a frightening connection, but it didn't give him any answers. He needed to find out more, anything to bring reality to his growing nightmare.

Perhaps Mrs. Newport would have them. Didn't she say she was related to St. Germain?

Sally Newport lived in a large home outside Serly. He had phoned earlier and, like any good realtor, she was happy to see him.

"Hello, Bob." She greeted him with her ever-present smile. "How's *Famous House* treating you?" They stood in the entry hallway. She didn't invite him further into her home.

"All right, I guess. The foundation is leaking though."

The Black Spiral: Twisted Tales of Terror

"Oh dear. Are you feeling all right? You look a little pale."

"Nothing to worry about. I've been doing a little research on your ancestor, Colonel St. Germain."

"Oh?"

"And Joe Tinker. He came over for a visit today." He watched her closely.

"You've met Joe?" Her smile broadened. Then, her lips skinned back revealing a flash of teeth, giving her a hungry look. "If Joe met with you, then it must be time."

"Time?"

"Time for you to decide."

"Decide what?"

She took a deep breath, as if debating whether to continue, then her face smoothed, radiating warmth, sympathy. "You want the best for your child, don't you? We all do, all parents do. If you think about it, it's what we all live for—what we die for. Our children must succeed us, or else we are failures as parents. However, with success comes sacrifice."

"Sacrifice?" Bob grasped the word, trying to follow her thinking. She was talking nonsense, but he couldn't concentrate. His stomach raged like an inferno.

"Yes, Bob. Sacrifice. *Famous House* can give you what you want, give your son what you want for him, but it wants something in return. Do you understand?"

Spikes of pain lanced through his abdomen. "No," he gasped.

"I guess you know my great-uncle originally came from Louisiana. Voodoo country. At the time, he was one of the few whites who practiced black *magick*. When the war ended badly for the South he moved here, but not before he killed every one of his slaves."

"Every last one?"

She nodded. "He drained their blood, bottled it, and when he came here, he consecrated the ground of his new home with it. *Famous House* is built on the blood of two hundred slaves.

"And it hungers for more. It needs. It desires. Its rewards are bountiful. All it wants is a little thing. A life, perhaps."

"A life?" His head spun. Voodoo. Images like newsreels flashed through his mind. *Old black women with gunmetal-blue skin, slick and glistening with sweat, sat cutting the heads off chickens.* The images swirled, changed. *Bird bones floating with candles in a murky-*

red miasma. Mrs. Newport's strange babblings; Joe Tinker; the bones; the candles—all pointed to one thing. The room was a shrine. A church of Black *Magick*. He reached out and clutched the door jam for support, winced and lowered his head.

"Are you sure you're all right, Bob?"

"Yes. No. My stomach hurts." Bob's head snapped up. He tried to focus on Sally Newport's smiling face. "It's the house, isn't it? It wants me, trying to kill me?"

"My heavens, no. That's not how it works. The house wants a sacrifice, but it does not kill. Besides, Xavier visited you, as Joe Tinker. He wants *you* to be the parent. Don't you see? You can be there, when your boy achieves his greatness. His success will be your success."

Bob shook his head. "You're mad. I'm going to the police."

Mrs. Newport barked a laugh. "And tell them what? *Famous House* is haunted? That it's alive? That a ghost visited you? Come to your senses, Bob. Uncle Xavier has made you a fair proposition, and I've heard things are not going well between you and your—"

"Shut up! You just shut up." Bob took a step forward, but his knees nearly buckled from the effort. He had to get out. He had to get back to the house. If what Sally said was true? He swallowed back coppery bile.

If what she said was true . . .

Lurching out the door, he bolted for his SUV.

"Better see a doctor, Bob," Sally Newport called after him. "You don't look well at all."

Bob didn't look back, tried to ignore her insanity. Everything was insane. He wanted to go home. Everything would be all right if he could just rest. Hastily, he backed the SUV onto the street, nearly hitting a light stand. He needed some antacids. That was all, just something to cool the fire in his stomach. He brought his handkerchief to his mouth and coughed, a wet rattling sound. Red flecks mixed in with his spittle stared back from the kerchief.

The drive to *Famous House* was only ten miles, but it took him nearly thirty minutes. The big vehicle swerved all over the road like a drunken beast, and he almost ditched it twice. A cloud of crimson floated before his eyes. And in it, he saw the faces of Xavier St. Germain, and Sally Newport. They floated in a bloody pool filled with chicken bones. Then another body floated in the pool, pale and bloated like a corpse long drowned. Long dark hair splayed out in thick clumps around

The Black Spiral: Twisted Tales of Terror

Maggie's face.

He thought of the secret room. The voodoo shrine. He could cover it up again. He could get Maggie to walk around the house. Ask her to get something. It was easy to fall in. There would be nothing to stop her, just some sod, and maybe a thin brittle board. He could do it, and he would have his boy. The house would be sated.

He could be there when Johnny becomes—someone.

"Boy needs to be with his father," he said.

He pulled into the narrow drive of *Famous House* and stomped on the brake pedal, nearly ramming Maggie's car.

She had come back to him. She was on the porch, sitting in the rocker. Johnny was in her arms, small fingers entwined in her dark hair. She looked at Bob quizzically and laughed. Her face brightened. He remembered how it was, how it could be again.

His guilt caused more pain than anything his stomach had given him so far. How could he think those thoughts? His life would be empty without her. He needed her; he needed his family.

It was the house. It got into his mind, warped his thoughts. He was not a murderer. The house put those ideas into his head. They had to get away before it consumed them all.

"Maggie." He opened the door. Vertigo overcame him and he nearly toppled onto the grass. She waved once, stood, and stepped off the porch. Johnny wriggled in her arms as she headed for the side of the house.

The hole!

"Maggie," he called again, but she continued as if she didn't hear. He coughed, a long hard spasm, and disgorged a glob of sticky blood that flew to the sod. He gasped for air, horrified, staring in disbelief as the blood seeped into the ground and disappeared. Get Maggie, his mind screamed. Get Johnny. Get his family away.

With his left arm wrapped around his belly, he stumbled between the giant oaks. Their gnarled limbs seemed to stretch down, reaching for him. He brushed away at branches suddenly too low, ignored the knots of pain that wrenched his stomach with his every step. He rounded the corner of the house.

Maggie was there, holding Johnny, and peering into the subterranean room.

"Maggie, we must get away from here."

"What are you talking about?"

"This house." He groaned and clutched his stomach. It felt like knives were grinding his innards to pulp. "It's . . . evil . . . voodoo . . . haunted. All those people. The famous ones. Their parents die." The pain was intense. His legs folded beneath him. He reached out to Maggie pleading for help.

She stepped aside smartly, watching him fall to his hands and knees. "All parents die eventually," she said and turned back to the hole. "So that's where it is."

"Maggie, my stomach." He coughed. Blood spurted out. "My God, Maggie. Look!" He pointed to the red blotch. The earth drew it in like a sponge.

Her eyes studied the ground. "It hungers—"

"What? Maggie, help me."

"I can't."

"Maggie." Blood flowed freely from his mouth, dark and viscous. His vision blurred and he curled into a fetal position.

His wife looked down at him as if inspecting a bug. "Joe Tinker said you would try to steal Johnny away from me. You were going to kill me weren't you?"

Just then, the old man appeared behind Maggie. He placed a withered sun-leathered hand on her shoulder, a thin smile half-buried beneath his moustache creased his face.

"No. . ." Bob said. A simple word, but it meant so much. No, I didn't want to steal Johnny. No, I still love you. No, that isn't Joe Tinker; he's the devil himself. Bob was too tired to say any of it.

Xavier had talked to her first, meant her to be the surviving parent, convinced her in the midst of her depression, when her mind was weakest. Yet Xavier had talked to him, too, had filled his head with just the right suggestions. Why? To play both sides, of course. The winner got Johnny. The loser fed the house.

"No," he repeated.

"Don't lie." Maggie hissed back. "Joe told me. So, I struck first. I ground up the glass of your stupid Honey Bee Mug into a fine powder. Just like sugar. You shouldn't take your coffee so sweet. Still, it took longer than I thought. Every day I waited for your stomach to grind itself to mulch. Waited for you to die.

"It's for Johnny. The house is going to make him a star. But there is a price, Bob." She crouched down low. "It's better you pay that price. After all, a boy needs his mother."

The Black Spiral: Twisted Tales of Terror

Bob coughed out another gusher of blood, feeling the icy clutch of death closing in on him. He tried to focus on Johnny. His boy. His son.

A star.

He rolled on the grass, once, twice, then felt a floating sensation, like falling off a cliff, as the earth beneath enveloped him in its dark hunger.

A small price for fame.

The Black Spiral: Twisted Tales of Terror

MEGAN'S SPIRIT

Nancy Kilpatrick

The cup had just touched Megan's lower lip when the ghost drifted into the living room. Her hand jerked, splashing Colombian coffee onto her flannel pajamas.

The nearly transparent man in worn Levis, black tank top and open black leather jacket had the sensitive face of a thirty-something Gordon Lightfoot. His blond hair was slicked back into what used to be referred to as a "duck's ass." He paused. Megan set the cup and saucer on top of the unopened carton precisely marked "Living Room—Entertainment Unit—Third Shelf—CDs."

She held her breath.

The apparition eyed Megan slowly from head to toe, his pale masculine eyes troubled. Then he strode through the room as if in a hurry, his knee-high boots silent against the rugless hardwood. As he passed through the wall into the awkward space she used as a dining room, Megan wondered why he didn't just go through the door.

She ran into the room. No sign of him. She entered the stainless-steel kitchen—empty. This was the second time she'd seen him. Yesterday, when she was moving in, he'd made his presence known as if staking out territory. While normally she wasn't prone to hallucinations, the stress of moving made her write the incident off as just that—stress related.

But seeing the ghost again was a shock, an intrusion into her orderly existence, and she was concerned that she might begin responding to him as if he were a normal part of her routine. Then she chided herself. "Not on your number-crunching life!" She was practical, not the imaginative type. Alan, her ex, had confirmed that self-assessment often enough, as did Frank, the head accountant at work. Seeing a ghost was not like her at all.

But others had seen "Gordie," the nickname she'd conferred on her personal apparition. The two guys who moved her; they wrote Gordie off to the fog that came with the rain. She was happy to do the same thing until she discovered that the previous owners knew about him.

The Black Spiral: Twisted Tales of Terror

When Megan phoned about the key for the basement door, she'd casually brought up the apparition. Helen MacIntyre dodged her questions but finally confessed that she and her husband had researched past owners, and hadn't uncovered much. "They say, though, that the place has always been a wee bit haunted. But don't you be worrying yourself. We've seen nothing. And besides, I think he likes women," and she hung up.

Megan was furious. She'd worked hard to get out from under the debts Alan had saddled her with. Finally she could afford the minimum down payment on this tiny house—her first—and she didn't want to share it with any male, living or in any other state. It doesn't matter, she'd almost convinced herself.

But honesty forced acknowledgement that had she known, she probably would have passed on the place, even though it was perfect in every other way. At least now she understood why the price was so low. And why the MacIntyres were in such a hurry to sell.

She unwrapped the kitchen clock and hung it above the refrigerator. The ghost had come at twelve both days and she suspected he wouldn't be back until noon tomorrow. At least Gordie's reliable, she thought. A lot of men aren't.

"You think I should call a *ghostbuster*?" Megan asked.

Frank crossed his arms over his chest. "All I said was, Alice and I saw this TV show about a local guy who dehaunts houses. If old Gordie's such a threat, do something about it. Look, if you had termites, you'd bring in an exterminator, right?"

"A dehaunter? I think I should call a debunker," Megan snapped. She'd been so upset she'd blurted everything out to Frank, something she ordinarily would have been too circumspect to do. Now she regretted it. She'd forgotten how annoyed he got when anyone resisted his ideas. Still, he *was* her boss. They had to work together.

"I'm sorry, Frank. It's just that this is so wacky. A ghost exterminator. It's like something you'd read about in a flaky New Age magazine."

"So is having a ghost."

"Good point." She raised her mug in his direction, hoping to change the subject. He nodded and handed her his cup.

As Megan walked to the coffeemaker for refills, she tossed Frank's suggestion back and forth in her mind. Quirky as it was having a cute and innocuous spectre who appeared on schedule, Megan knew she wanted him out. It was her house. Her home. The world outside her door was frightening and uncontrollable enough, everything from murders and sexual assaults to AIDS—is there such a thing as safe sex, she'd often wondered? She was a woman, alone now, not that she really hadn't been alone through the long and painful years of her marriage. Everyone, she reminded herself, is entitled to a secure retreat. She needed to lock the door, close the blinds and block it all out. This dehaunter, or whatever he called himself, was expensive, although it might be worth the price if she could be free of Gordie, not that she thought it would work.

As she handed Frank his coffee, he said, "I'll pay. Consider it a house-warming present."

"Doctor" Randolph arrived Saturday. "You may call me Latern," he said in a British House-of-Lords accent. Then, "My associate, Mrs. Reisman."

Megan shook hands with both of them. Latern, sixty-something, reminded her of Alistair Cooke. Megan thought Mrs. Reisman, older, grayer, much shorter, could double for Dr. Ruth, when she wasn't eradicating spooks from people's homes.

Latern carried an old-fashioned black doctor's bag, but Megan had the feeling the title in front of his name was honorary. "Where does the lingering soul manifest?" he asked, looking around soberly. Mrs. Reisman appeared to be preoccupied.

"He always comes through the wall on that side of the house and walks through this room, then through this wall." She led them into the main room.

The "Phenomenologist," as his card identified him, tapped the wall beside the dining room door. "Undoubtedly this was, at one time, a larger doorway. Perhaps leading to a second bedroom. Not unusual in a modest, older home."

Mrs. Reisman moved around the living room, one hand stretched before her as if she were blind and feeling for objects in her path. A weak sound came from her lips, something between a hiss and a sigh.

"She perceives his essence. On the astral plane, of course," Latern said.

Megan wished she'd had the nerve to insist that Frank be here. After all, it was his "gift," having these people invade her privacy.

The Black Spiral: Twisted Tales of Terror

Latern sat his case on the coffee table and opened it. Megan peeked inside. Fat beeswax candles and thin colored ones, bunches of dried herbs—she didn't have a clue what—wooden tongue depressors, string, a large box of table salt.

Latern removed a white candle and a branch of one of the herbs and lit both with a pocket lighter. The aroma of sage filled the air, reminding Megan of Thanksgiving.

"Can I get you anything?" she asked, feeling cynical. "Coffee or tea? A candle holder?"

He shook his head. Megan got the feeling she was in the way.

Latern followed on Mrs. Reisman's heels. They wandered the length of each freshly-painted wall, Latern holding the candle above his head and blowing the strong-smelling herb down in front of Mrs. Reisman's face.

Megan perched on the couch watching, feeling a bit like a voyeur. At one point Latern said, "It is imperative we purify the corrupted space. Male apparitions frequently enjoy tormenting a woman without a mate, if I make myself clear. The herbs will, shall we say, dampen his fervor." Megan nodded; although she had no idea what he meant—Gordie had been about the most polite ghost she could have wanted, if she'd wanted a ghost, which she didn't.

At two minutes to twelve, Mrs. Reisman began to hyperventilate. Both hands trembled as they extended in front of her. Megan jumped up, alarmed, but Latern waved her back. "He's near, oh yes he is. Can you hear me, then?" he called in a loud and somber voice.

"I hear ya!" It was Mrs. Reisman, but not her voice; at least Megan didn't think so. So far Mrs. Reisman had only made sounds; the nasal tone might in fact be perfectly natural.

"She channels, a living necroscope, if you will. I am merely the reassuring voice with which the near-departed communicate," Latern advised in a stage whisper.

Megan checked her watch. "It's only..."

"Shush!" he instructed.

Mrs. Reisman's eyes rolled up into her head, which fell back. Her body began to convulse.

"What is your name?" Latern asked.

"Hershel. Hershel Seinfeld," Mrs. Reisman replied.

Megan's eyebrows shot up. Gordie might not be her ghost's name, but she definitely couldn't see him as either a Hershel or a Seinfeld.

"Why are you haunting this house, Hershel?" Latern asked.

"I live here, if that's okay with you!"

"I'm afraid it is not. This is not your home anymore. It's Megan's. And you are no longer living. You're dead, and you are frightening Megan. Your being here is an impropriety."

Mrs. Reisman's voice grew loud and panicked. "Dead! You say I'm dead? *Kaput*? Can't be!"

"Yes, Hershel, you have become spirit, not flesh. You have passed on and must continue into the beyond. The astral plane. Along the tunnel and into the light."

"Nah! Not the light. I'm scared of the light. It makes me *meshuga*!" Mrs. Reisman's arm jerked up to protect her eyes.

"The light is nothing to fear. There, pleasures await you. Anything you desire, Hershel. More than you could obtain in this accursed mortal realm. Isn't there something you've always longed for?"

Mrs. Reisman and/or Hershel thought for a moment. "A new Harley. Yeah! Five hundred CC's. Mine was trashed in a crash."

Megan sighed. She had described to Latern on the phone how her ghost dressed. He was obviously a rebel. She supposed he *could* be a biker, but it was disappointing. She thought Gordie—Hershel—had more class.

"What else do you want, Hershel?" Latern asked.

"Beer's my poison. Bud!"

"It shall be yours. Is there more, Hershel?"

"Blondes. Like Megan. But dozens of 'em. Shapely. Not too bright. Fun to be with, know what I mean?"

While this conversation continued, Gordie appeared. Dressed as always, he strode into the room purposefully, glanced at Mrs. Reisman and Latern who did not notice him, then turned his sad and frightened eyes on Megan. She felt accused.

"Walk into the light!" Latern ordered, pointing toward the bay window. "There ye shall find all that ye seek."

"Yeah, the light. It ain't so bad, I guess. It's, like, callin' me. Hey, there's my shiny new bike! And a couple cases of brew. I'm goin'," Mrs. Reisman called, her voice growing softer, as if she was farther away.

The Black Spiral: Twisted Tales of Terror

Gordie turned toward the dining room.

"I'm goin'," Mrs. Reisman whispered, heading toward the window.

Gordie passed through the wall.

"I'm gone." Barely audible. Mrs. Reisman's fingers touched the glass.

There was silence. Megan tried to digest what had just occurred.

Latern led the exhausted Mrs. Reisman to a chair. She looked drained, lips pale, brows furrowed, but she'd come out of the self-induced trance. "Would you be so good as to bring Mrs. Reisman a cup of tea?" he asked. "Camomile, if you have it. Loose, not bagged."

"Sure." Megan headed to the kitchen.

Gordie stood in the doorway to the kitchen. Her first thought was to call for help. Her second to run. He stared at her with those forlorn eyes. Eyes that talked about loneliness and pain. About betrayal. About loss. Although she had never been this close to him before, she didn't feel frightened. He looked like a hologram.

Tentatively, Megan reached out. Instead of meeting his face, her hand passed through empty air. That unnerved her and she jerked her arm back. But he looked so vulnerable that she relaxed and tried again. This time the air felt textured. Emotional. Emotional? she thought. What made me think that?

"Can you speak?" she asked. His lips did not move—it was as though he couldn't hear her. "What about writing?" She edged past him and took a pen from the holder by the sink, tore a sheet of paper from the pad magnetized to the refrigerator door, and handed both to him. He reached out, but his fingers went right through the solid objects.

Frustrated, she tossed the pen and paper onto the counter behind her. "Great!" She turned back to him, saying, "How can we have a relationship?"

Latern, clearly visible, walked through Gordie's subtle body. Apparently he did not see the ghost. "Perhaps we are dealing with a resident incubus," he said.

Gordie vanished like steam from a kettle.

"Why don't you try sign language?" Frank suggested.

"I guess I could," Megan said tentatively, wishing he hadn't brought this up again—of course, Frank had wanted all the details, figuring, no doubt, that he'd paid for them. "It would have to be simple signs."

"Me living," Frank pointed to himself, "you dead," he pointed at her.

Megan felt belittled.

"Maybe," Frank was really getting into this, "you can coax him to merge with the chips inside your PC. He can send you insider messages in e-mail form about the stock markets of the other world."

Boss or no boss, she didn't have to put up with this. "You're not taking me seriously."

"What was your first clue?"

"You think I'm losing it, or making all this up, don't you?"

Frank, who'd been pressing his desk calculator's on/off button, sat back in his swivel chair and stared at Megan. "I think *you* think you're seeing the ghost of Gordon Lightfoot who, I should remind you, is still living—"

"I didn't say he *was* Gordon Lightfoot. I said he *looks* a little like a younger version of him."

"Looks like, is, what's the difference, Megan? You're talking about a supernatural being. You're playing a game with yourself; you need to get out more. It's been a year since Alan. You're probably lonely. And after everything that's happened, nobody would blame you for being gun shy. It's natural. But you're an attractive woman. Very attractive. You shouldn't be alone."

Megan found all of this attention embarrassing and intrusive. She made some excuse about an unbalanced balance sheet and escaped.

Gordie was staying longer. Yesterday he'd been in the dining room—obviously his favorite room—for two and a half hours before he'd entered the kitchen and faded. Today, the clock over the stove in the kitchen said four p.m. and he showed no signs of evaporating.

Megan had tried various methods of communication: hand signs; written notes; words on the computer screen. She had no idea whether he couldn't read or couldn't see the letters. Maybe she and her world were as hazy to him as he and his world were to her.

She wasn't sure if he heard her, because he did not respond, but Megan told him about herself. Of twelve painful years of marriage to a man who not only nearly destroyed her financially but had been unfaithful on more occasions than she cared to count. The divorce had made all that public and humiliated her.

    She also told Gordie about her fear of having to face the world alone. A world that had altered considerably from when she had been a young single woman. And of her terror of nudging forty and no longer being as attractive as she had been. She certainly was not as naive and trusting.

    As she spoke, Megan reached out slowly. Her fingertips were becoming fine-tuned to his ethereal body. She sensed the cool electric energy as if it were solid. Her hand moved into his chest. The translucent particles vibrated and parted, and her skin tingled up to her arm.

    It was like running underwater in slow motion, the liquid charged. Alive. Solid in an odd way. Struggling to stay separate and yet to meld with her skin.

    His melancholy eyes sang to her. He was lonely too, trapped; she felt that to the core of her being. She moved her hand down his chest, further inside him. Heart-level, vaporous light pulsed and radiated, making the texture of her hand more porous and changing the color of her flesh to a pinker shade. The particles warmed her skin like dry ice.

    Megan became aware that she had been holding her breath. As she let it out, fear filled her. The sensations felt too erotic. Too real. This is not right, she told herself. I'm spending all my free time with the dead. Caressing the incorporeal. This isn't healthy. He's a *ghost*. Fear swirled up her backbone as the implications of that word crystallized in her mind. She became acutely aware of a solid, other-worldly silence. The texture of the air sharpened.

    She backed away, and he reached out. Megan panicked. It was the first time he had touched her. Terror of the unexplainable glued her in place. His arms encircled her body, passing through her shoulders, his chest melted into hers. Flesh dusted by a purple passion plant, she thought. Her body quivered slightly, a leaf touched by a breeze. A leaf that had not been touched in a long *long* time.

    No! This is crazy, she thought. Very sick. I'm losing my mind completely. I need help. Fast! She backed across the room trembling.

    Suddenly the temperature plummeted. An odor clogged her nostrils—hair cream. Frightened, her body turned clammy and her skin sprouted goosebumps. The silence became a living entity and crushed hard against her eardrums. She clamped her hands over her ears and squeezed her eyes shut, terrified. Every orifice felt assaulted. Something was trying to invade her.

She wanted to flee the house, race out into the streets and scream for help. But the twilight outside her door felt more threatening than being inside, and that paralyzed her.

And then a sound—like wind sighing. A not-quite human breath, seeping through the barrier between worlds. A breath that sent a shiver up her spine, that carried a word—*Megan*!

She stared at Gordie, startled. His form was like a pulsing mist, on the verge of dissipating, or solidifying. On the verge of erupting. His spectral face held a terrifying predatory quality. He was hungry; starving. He reached out for her again.

Megan darted from the room and raced upstairs to her bedroom. She locked the door. In bed, she drew her knees to her chest and pulled the duvet over her head. Tears of rage and fear welled out of her. She felt caught between a sob and a laugh. *I am fated to be alone. Lonely. Vulnerable. My life insubstantial. I am barely a shadow, fearfully skirting life. Never experiencing warmth and love and companionship. Destined to live with phantoms. A phantom myself.*

She cried loud and long, cursing fate, despising the fears that kept her locked inside. Finally she tumbled into the black hole where dreams usurp reality.

The impression of stillness. Her flesh throbbed, a large mouth hungry for life. Diffuse brilliance from every direction coated her, from nowhere she could identify. Density crushed her body, the weight of a leaf floating on air. She could not breathe; a scent both comforting and intimidating filled her.

A wispy cloud passed along the skin of her breasts and paused at her nipples. She trembled in fearful ecstasy. Something wafted down, through the skin and muscle of her belly, penetrating organs and swirling deep into the cradle of her pelvis. Her marrow opened to buoyant clarity. Fire swelled down to her groin and roared back up, scorching her. It was as if she were in the grip of an inferno. Suddenly, she burst into white flame and cried out.

Suspended in the white light, Megan felt Gordie in and around her. She had never experienced such luminescence or felt so secure. Instinctively she understood everything: he could be there for her, as no man had ever been. As no man could be. He would live inside her, and she would give him the world, through her eyes, her ears, her flesh. In protecting themselves, they would protect each other. By opening, they could both be free.

Two minds fused realities: *the world in which you exist is only frightening if you're alone. You'll never be alone again. We're one now.* His voice, so clear, deeper, more confident than she imagined it, brought her to awareness of their joining. She felt caught in this new half-life like an insect in amber. Already, her needs and desires were far more intense than in the full life she had now. She sensed merging with her was more concrete for Gordie than his ethereal soul-prison. A prison that, in a sudden horrible flash she knew had come about because of no sad act of fate, but was a form of punishment he had been relegated to. A punishment for what, she did not know, but her intuition told her that she might soon find out.

Megan struggled, but it was too late to resist him. *Everywhere. Always. Together. You'd better get used to it!*

As if her body were being moved by invisible strings, Megan watched herself climb out of bed. She stripped off her clothing and stood before the full-length mirror. Her body looked slimmer, more "male." The hands fondling her so roughly felt unlike her own.

The thought came to her that she would need new clothes. A leather jacket, boots. She pulled back her hair to see how it would look cut short, just a tail at the nape of the neck. She would need to buy hair cream.

Megan felt herself crying and looked again in the mirror; the tear ducts were blocked by spectral plugs and no liquid leaked from her haunted, terror-streaked eyes. But that, she knew, was irrelevant, because the voice swirling through her could not have been more adamant, more possessive: *You'll learn to play, Megan. My games!*

* * *

THE GARGOYLE SACRIFICE

Tina L. Jens

The gargoyle's red eyes sparked. Its distended belly seemed to pulsate as its tongue flicked the air. Marissa would have sworn the gargoyle was watching her. Its body was sterling silver, its belly a ruby-colored stone the size of an egg. Smaller rubies were embedded in the creature's eye sockets. Finely-engraved talons stretched to form the sides of the collar necklace. Marissa imagined what it would feel like to clamp those claws over her shoulder bones.

She wanted the gargoyle, wanted it badly. But it was trapped in the display case, just as surely as she was trapped in the Sun King's Occult Curiosities store.

She'd come at Rudy's urging.

After hours, Pharaoh, the store manager and the Sun King's servant, did body piercings, tattooing and pagan earth ceremonies in the back room. He also provided drugs and booze for a small fee.

By day, the place was a bookstore and magic shop, but in all the times Marissa had walked by the store, she'd never seen anyone in the place before sundown. Sometimes Pharaoh didn't even open up the shop at all, just waited until closing before he unlocked the back door. Marissa wondered if the Sun King knew.

Probably not, with him in jail. Sometimes she wondered if the Sun King really existed at all, or if he was just some joke Pharaoh and the older kids had made up.

They said Pharaoh was blood-bound to the Sun King, and with the proper ritual, the Sun King could possess his servant's body. The older girls claimed they'd slept with both the master and the servant, and could tell when Pharaoh was possessed, because the Sun King was a better lover.

They also claimed Pharaoh saved all the blood from the sex and piercings as a sacrifice for the Sun King, to increase his power. And, that one day, the Sun King would be so powerful he could summon the dark gods of Egypt.

The Black Spiral: Twisted Tales of Terror

Marissa's excursion into the front room was a brief reprieve. Any moment Rudy would come to drag her back for her turn in the chair. He wanted her to get her nipples pierced, promised to buy her a gold chain to suspend between them. Probably wanted to yank on it while he was doing it to her.

She wouldn't mind having a gold chain. But she didn't see how he could afford it when he'd begged ten dollars off her that afternoon to help pay last month's rent. She'd taken it out of her old man's wallet. With any luck he'd be drunk before he noticed it was missing. He didn't hit as hard when he was drunk, though sometimes he tried other things. Sometimes when he was drunk he'd get confused, would think Marissa was her mother, though her mother had died years ago.

Marissa rubbed her hand over her breast, the flannel softly comforting her. It would hurt. Last week Mindy had cried for half an hour after her piercing. It had taken forever to stop the bleeding. When she'd finally left, the whole front of her shirt was red with blood.

The ruby eyes flashed again. The gargoyle was laughing at her for being such a chicken shit. Marissa turned away from the display case.

Maybe she'd have *one* done, see how it felt.

She pulled her worn leather jacket tighter around her and drifted down the aisle. She scanned the Ancient Egyptology book section, then turned away in boredom. The next counter held incense and candles. She wrinkled her nose, disgusted at the smell. Still, she liked the little brass burners, they were dainty, delicate.

She heard the beads in the doorway clacking. Probably Rudy looking for her.

"Come on, Marissa. You're going to lose your turn."

Marissa studied her boyfriend. He wasn't much to look at. Tall and too thin, with dirty brown hair that fell past his shoulders. But, he was one of the oldest guys in the group and he could French inhale his Camel cigarettes. Marissa had to be careful, a lot of the girls would be happy to steal him.

"I'm comin'," she said, shrugging. Her leather jacket squeaked loud in the silence. "Wanna show you something first."

She led him to the counter and crouched down in front of the display case. He hunched down to see what she was pointing at.

"Isn't he beautiful!" Marissa whispered.

"'s okay." He pointed to the card sitting beside it. *For Display Only.* "Means it's expensive." He sounded more interested now.

"I heard about this necklace," Rudy told her. "The guys were talkin' about it. It's supposed to be magic. The last piece the Sun King made. The night before he went to jail, they had this big midnight ceremony, took a blood sacrifice from all three of his kids."

"That's why his belly glows," Marissa murmured.

Rudy laughed. "They're full of shit!"

"What'd the Sun King go to jail for?" Marissa asked.

She'd just turned fourteen and started coming to the store. She was too young to have met the storeowner. Rudy was eighteen. He'd been coming here a long time.

"Bunch of stuff," Rudy said casually. "Statutory rape, animal mutilation, possession of controlled substances. That kind of thing. Got twenty years. But the Sun King's got connections. He won't be in long."

He stared at the necklace thoughtfully. "Those are supposed to be real rubies and silver," he said slowly. "I bet it's worth some money."

"Would it cost more than a gold chain?" Marissa hinted.

"Doesn't have to."

"I already checked," Marissa said, the disappointment heavy in her voice. "The case is locked."

She felt Rudy's arm snake around her waist. He leaned close and whispered in her ear. "Look baby, I'm short on cash tonight. I was going to have you pay for the pierc—"

Marissa jerked away and glared at him.

"Hey! I was gonna pay you back," Rudy said defensively.

He pulled her body back to him. "I got a better idea, now. You can get both your nips pierced *and* get the necklace—free of charge." With a flip of his head he tossed the hair out of his eyes.

"How?" Marissa demanded.

"Tell Pharaoh you want to make alternate arrangements for payment."

Marissa shook her head. "Pharaoh's not gonna trade the necklace for alternate arrangements. Besides, the card says it's not for sale."

She stroked the glass, wishing desperately she could pet the gargoyle. She would have sworn it's belly was glowing, beckoning to her.

Rudy's breath tickled her ear again. "He'll make arrangements for the piercings. If you keep him busy long enough, I'll do some arranging of my own."

"I don't know," Marissa said slowly.

The Black Spiral: Twisted Tales of Terror

"You want the gargoyle don't you?"
She nodded.
He shoved her toward the beaded door. "Remember, get the hoops. They'll work better with the chain."

Marissa whispered "alternate arrangements" in the Pharaoh's ear. He grinned a fat, greasy smile and led her to the reclining chair. She stared at the dozen faces that had gathered around the chair to watch.
Around the room teenagers were flopped down on ratty furniture, drinking cheap beer and smoking rolled cigarettes. A New Age music tape was blaring from a portable tape player, the sound heavy with flutes and wind chimes. Clouds of incense hung in the air.
Marissa's head was swimming.
"Want a shot?" one of the older boys asked.
She nodded and he poured her some whiskey in the community shot glass. She choked it down, coughing.
"You'll be alright," the boy told her.
Pharaoh sat beside her. "Rudy tells me you want hoops."
Marissa nodded dumbly.
"I am just the Sun King's servant," Pharaoh said, as he fumbled with the buttons on her gray flannel shirt. "But I think he would approve."
He pulled the material away and caressed her. "Very nice," he hissed, rolling her nipples between the thumb and finger of each hand.
A sea of faces nodded in agreement.
Marissa swallowed hard, forcing back the bile that was welling up in her throat. The incense and whiskey were making her sick. She stared at the Pharaoh's blood-spattered shirt.
It was bad enough to be pawed in front of everybody. She tried not to think about what would happen when the piercing was done. Pharaoh would take her to the bathroom for that part.
A crack rang out, loud as a gun shot in her ears. It was just Pharaoh at the ice tray. She moaned and tried to concentrate on the image of the gargoyle, as he advanced toward her wielding an ice cube and a carpet needle.

Marissa huddled against the brick wall under the El tracks, and stroked the gargoyle's red belly. The necklace seemed to emit its own heat lying against her skin. It comforted her in the chilly night.

The Black Spiral: Twisted Tales of Terror

She let her fingers stray down to her breasts. They still ached from the piercing. It hadn't helped that Rudy had kept trying to pinch them.

She'd rushed straight out of the shop after she'd paid off Pharaoh. Ran the whole five blocks to the alley where she and Rudy always met. He was leaning against the wall looking smug when she pulled up panting. He wouldn't tell her if he got the gargoyle. Demanded that she show him first. She'd opened her jacket and unbuttoned her shirt, displaying herself for his approval. The cold had turned her nipples hard, making them ache even more.

He'd wanted to pull on them, play with them. He started pouting when she told him to knock it off. But he stopped her when she tried to button her shirt. Marissa saw the gargoyle's eyes flash as Rudy pulled it out of his coat pocket. The metal should have felt cold in the night air, but it was warm as Rudy slipped it on her.

Marissa stroked the gargoyle's belly, again. She thought she could feel its heart beating.

Rudy had wanted to screw her. Had wanted her on her back right there in the alley. Said he'd even put his jacket down under her, though he didn't like it getting scuffed up. Said he wanted to play with her new piercings as he screwed her. Said she could wear the gargoyle while they did it, if that turned her on.

But, one fat humping pig a night was enough. Of course, she hadn't said that to Rudy. After twenty minutes of trying to force her, he'd stalked off in a huff.

Marissa was glad he'd left. Except, she'd been counting on sleeping over at his place. She wanted to avoid the old man for a few days.

She'd be all right under the tracks for the night. It was early spring, still cold enough to be uncomfortable, but not cold enough to be dangerous. The cold would protect her. The drug pushers would stay in their cars, and the street people would be fighting over the heating grates. She had her leather coat and the gargoyle to keep her warm.

From the flush in her face, she knew she also had a fever, either from the booze or the piercing. Either way, it felt good in the chill night.

She sat with her back against the brick wall, soaking up the heat absorbed by the bricks during the day. She was getting hungry. Marissa unwrapped and ate the other half of a candy bar she'd stolen out of a vending machine.

The Black Spiral: Twisted Tales of Terror

She pulled some old newspapers out of a Dumpster, spread them out into a nest against the wall, then leaned back and closed her eyes.

Marissa slept fitfully. The cold bit at her. The El rumbled overhead. Awful images filled her dreams. Fat old men pawing at her naked body ... Rudy, forcing her down on all fours, whipping her and dragging her around by a long gold chain ... Her old man backhanding her across the room ... pulling her across the kitchen by her hair ... grabbing her by the throat and bending her backwards over the kitchen table ... choking her, tighter and tighter.

Marissa jerked awake, gasping for breath. The nightmares were gone but the vise-like grip on her neck remained. Cold tears leaked from her eyes as numb fingers fought to unzip her jacket. A sharp pain shot across her neck, as the gargoyle sliced through her skin. She tried to wedge her hands under the metal collar, but it was sticky and her fingers kept slipping. Rivulets of blood seeped down her chest and back.

She felt the gargoyle move. Its claws dug deep into her shoulders as it slowly climbed up her chest. She felt its hot breath against her skin. Heard a chittering in her ear. Then more pain, as its teeth ripped her earlobe.

"You've done well," the Sun King said to his fat, ingratiating servant through the Plexiglas pane in the prison's visitation room.

Decapitated body discovered at Lawrence Street El, the newspaper clipping said.

"The as yet unidentified girl is just another suspected casualty in the mounting gang war over the Uptown territory," the Sun King read aloud.

"Is the necklace back in your possession?" he said suddenly.

"No, but soon," his servant assured him. "The alley was still cordoned off as a crime scene when I went by this morning. But the police will be gone by the time I return. It shouldn't take me long to find our little pet. It won't have gone far."

The Sun King nodded and dismissed the man then signaled to the guard to escort him back to his cell. He had a much more important visitor to meet there.

The cell door clanged shut and the echo of the guard's boots slowly faded away. He turned to face the shadowy figure lurking in the corner. It had not been there moments ago.

The Black Spiral: Twisted Tales of Terror

The Sun King suppressed a shiver. It would not do to show his true feelings toward the beast who reeked of sulphur and spoke with the voice of an angry rottweiler.

"That's thirteen," the creature barked.

"No, sixteen," the Sun King said firmly. "You persist in forgetting my children. Surely this one meets—exceeds—our agreement. I'd be paroled after twelve years, fourteen at the very outside."

Sounds of snuffling filled the corner, and the form of the dark shadow shifted. The Sun King was glad he could see no more than a vague outline of the figure. The unnatural protrusions of the nose and ears, seen in the shadows on the wall, were enough to convince him to look no closer.

"The gods of the underworld do not bargain. The deal was one soul for each year of your *sentence*," the shadowy figure growled. "Deliver seven more... and we'll both be free."

* * *

The Black Spiral: Twisted Tales of Terror

PICNIC

Kevin Anderson

"Do you think we'll find some treasure, Dad?" Ethan asked as he heaved another pile of sand from the knee-deep hole.

"Ya never know, son." Carl Johnson arched his sore back and stepped out of the pit.

The boy stopped digging. "Did you ever find any treasure?"

"Well, not treasure. But I did find a bunch of old coins once."

"Wow! Were they pirate coins?"

Carl smiled and started to contrive a little story about the rusty coins in order to make the find a bit more interesting for his ten-year-old son. The Johnson family had been alone at the isolated picnic area on the central California beach for almost an hour. The spot was so infrequently used it had only one picnic table, one barbecue pit, and a single trashcan, which was probably only picked up once a month.

Carl had chosen this picnic spot for its beauty, tranquility, and the seclusion it provided from other road-weary vacationers and tourists. It required taking two desolate sideroads off the main highway to find it. And the last was nothing more than a narrow, gravel road.

Having finished his long tale, Carl turned to leave. Then suddenly, from the corner of his eye, a flicker of light caught his attention. Turning quickly, he caught a brief blur of motion as a vehicle came to rest next to the family Bronco. It's mile-wide windshield blazed, reflecting the harsh sunlight and concealing the car's driver.

He wondered why he hadn't heard it approaching. The first sound that registered was the crunch of tires coming to rest on the loose gravel. It was as if the driver had cut the engine and coasted in.

Jeez, Carl thought. *All I wanted was a nice afternoon with the family. Is that too much to ask?* Carl continued to stare at the car for a moment, and then turned to Ethan. "I'm gonna go see what your mom is up to. Ya comin'?"

"Nahh," Ethan replied as he thrust his child-size shovel into the hole. "I've got lots of work to do." He brushed a shock of blond hair from his eyes and smiled with a gap-toothed grin.

"Okay kiddo, but don't overdo it and mind the rules." As he studied the car, Carl fought the urge to take up sentry duty at the side of his Bronco, standing guard over their luggage—and a canvas bag that lay nestled in the back compartment. It was a strange-looking car. Dark in color and old in design. A station wagon with tinted windows, shielding the occupants from view. And the longest station wagon Carl had ever seen, appearing to have been modified. As he pictured the vehicle with white lacy curtains in the back windows, the image transformed into a hearse.

Forcing the picture from his mind, he shook his head and joined his wife and daughter, Cindy, at the picnic table.

Carl leaned over and whispered into his wife's ear. "There goes our quiet little afternoon."

"Oh now, hush up," Mandy said in her East Texas drawl.

Working many years in finance, Carl had the look of a banker: perfectly groomed hair, manicured nails, and even his khaki slacks had a knife-edge crease. He'd also managed to shed his small-town Texas accent and so far, it hadn't been passed down to the kids. Mandy on the other hand, was a proud and stubborn woman who wasn't about to trade in her Southern drawl or her big Texas bouffant hairdo no matter what anyone thought, especially Carl.

"I was just hoping for a quiet afternoon," Carl murmured as he watched the station wagon's four doors open with uncanny uniformity, as if rehearsed.

A tall, slender woman with long black hair stepped out of the passenger side. She had creamy white skin. And a velvety afghan draped over her shoulders. Noticing the Johnson family eyeing her, she waved and smiled, baring two rows of polished teeth.

Without hesitation, Mandy waved back.

Carl glared at her. "What are you doing?"

"I'm being polite," Mandy replied. "Don't you want to set a good example?" Mandy turned to her daughter, who was unwrapping the paper plates. "Honey, what's rule number nine?"

Cindy thought for a moment, her brow furrowing. Then her green eyes sparked. "Try, try, try, with all your might, it's always rewarding to be polite."

Mandy put her arm around Cindy. "That's right, sweetie." Then they both turned toward the station wagon.

A teenage girl climbed out and slammed the door fast. Her black lipstick matched her dark tattered outfit. She was shrouded in the Goth style of dress brooding teenagers seemed to gravitate toward.

The Black Spiral: Twisted Tales of Terror

"Wouldn't be able to attend Tyler High dressed like that," Carl scoffed aloud to himself.

The driver, a man in his mid-forties, got out quickly and moved to the rear door of the station wagon. As he reached into the back compartment, another young girl emerged from the car. She was seven or so, a redhead, and wore a dark blue dress.

Carl shuddered as the young girl caught his gaze. In the blink of a moment, he swore her eyes flashed—eyeshine—like an animal caught in the beam of a spotlight.

Before he could point it out to Mandy, the little girl scrambled to the rear door and began to help the man pull something from the back of the wagon. As they lifted out a large, folded mechanical-looking devise, the little girl started fussing with its latches and knobs. She twisted a lever and it unfolded abruptly, like a black widow extending its legs from a recoiled position. It was a wheelchair—slightly customized, but a wheelchair all the same.

While the little girl started to flip up a large piece of canvas, designed to cast constant shade on the occupant of the chair, the man sidestepped to the rear passenger door.

With strong and caring arms, he reached in and carried out a fragile-looking boy, then placed him gently in the chair. The tall woman removed her afghan and placed it over the boy's lap.

"Oh, that poor dear is crippled, bless his heart," Mandy whispered to her husband.

"I think there's more wrong with the kid than that . . ." Carl said, arching his eyebrows. "He looks dead."

"Carl, you evil man. The Lord will hear you," Mandy scolded as they watched the teenage girl pull a picnic basket from the rear of the car. She seemed to be asking the woman where she should set the food.

The tall woman, who could have been Morticia Addams's twin, looked around.

Mandy's jaw dropped wide in an expression of understanding.

"Look, Carl. They have a picnic basket."

"So?"

"Well, we're occupyin' the only picnic table and the only bit of shade under this here tree."

"That's because we got here first. Early bird, Mandy. Early bird."

197

The Black Spiral: Twisted Tales of Terror

"There's room enough at this big ol' table for all of us. Just look at those dears out in the sun," Mandy said as Carl sighed deeply. "And isn't that why we are on this trip? To show our little darlin's new places and meet new and interestin' people?" Turning to her daughter, she asked, "Cindy, what's rule number twelve?"

Cindy's gaze shot upward, as if searching the sky for the exact words. "Twelve, uh… likable people are always…"

"Caring," Mandy offered.

"Filled with good cheer," Cindy continued, "and always sharing."

Carl rolled his eyes and gave in. "All right, but I don't have to be nice."

"You can be a first rate horse's pah-toot for all I care, Carl Emit Johnson. My mother brought me up to be a hospitable—"

Carl finished her sentence. "—Southern woman. I know, I know. Just spare me the speech and call 'em over."

Mandy stood on tiptoe and kissed Carl's neck. Then yelled out, "Hey Y'all, please come on over and join us; there's plenty of room."

The newcomers exchanged confused glances. It seemed for a moment that the family was going to ignore the Johnson's invitation, then the wheelchair started to move. It whined as the fragile boy twisted its control lever, steering it toward the picnic table and the shade. The rest of the family fell in line behind him and within moments, both families were staring at each other across the picnic table.

It was as though each family were sizing up the other, like two rival gangs in a Mexican standoff. Carl focused on the scars decorating the teenage girl's forearm. He didn't need to be a high-school crisis counselor to recognize the signs of self-mutilation. *Jesus, what an unpleasant and frightening lot,* Carl thought.

Silence hung thick over the table. In an attempt to end the awkwardness, Mandy put on her Martha–Stewart hostess smile, blotted the perspiration from her hands on her red apron, walked around the table with her hand extended and introduced herself.

But when she turned to introduce Ethan, she noticed he was still digging. Placing her hands on her broad hips, she called out, "Ethan! Come over here and say hello to these nice people!"

The slender dark-haired women took Mandy's hand in an elegant if not archaic fashion and smiled. "I'm Agatha. Very nice to meet you."

The Black Spiral: Twisted Tales of Terror

Mandy's eyes widened in disbelief. "My great-grammy's name was Agatha."

"Is that so?" Agatha said.

Mandy turned and bent over the boy in the chair. "And who is this beautiful boy?" The boy's soft gray eyes met Mandy's.

Agatha said, "This is Dante."

"Well, good afternoon to ya, Mr. Dante." Mandy proffered her hand. Dante slid his ghost-white hand off the chair's controller and grasped hers.

"Very nice to meet 'cha. Are ya hungry?" Mandy asked.

"Yes," Dante said quickly.

"Well, we have cherry and pumpkin pie. Can I set ya up with a slice?"

"We don't mean to intrude," Agatha cut in.

"Oh, don't worry yourself about it. There is plenty of room here. Make yourselves ta' home." Mandy gestured to the table, then turned back to Dante. "Now, which kind of pie do you like?"

Dante studied her with half-dead eyes, pondering. Then as a broad grin creased his face, he said, "Pumpkin."

With that single word, the ice was broken, and the two families became one at the table.

Agatha introduced her husband, Hilgard Black, teenage daughter Camilla, and Dante's twin sister, Guinevere. For the next two hours, the families shared food, spirits, stories, and family history. The Johnsons hailed from Tyler, Texas and were in the middle of a three-month vacation, zigzagging across the United States. The Blacks were on their way up the coast to Mendocino, were they'd rented a house for a month.

When the meal was finished, Mandy stood up. "Well, I guess I should start straightening up. We Johnsons even have a little rule about cleaning, don't we, sweetie?" She turned toward her daughter Cindy.

"Yes, we do," Cindy said. "Rule number four. . ." She cleared her throat. "When the deed is done and you have had your fun, do your best to clean up the mess."

Agatha smiled. "How charming."

"Carl and I have made up little rhymes to help the children remember all the important things they need to know," Mandy said proudly.

"I think we could use a few rhymes in this family." Agatha nodded and winked at Dante.

Her husband, Hilgard, rose suddenly, his eyes narrowed as if admonishing Agatha's comment. "Well, it's getting late. And we had better get a move on if we want to get to Mendocino by dark."

"All right." Agatha stiffened slightly and rose. "You pack the car. I'll help Mandy clean up."

"Agatha, if you don't mind me asking ... about Dante."

"It's okay. He has a mild form of XP, Xeroderma Pigmantosum"

"I'm not familiar with that."

"It's very rare. Only about a thousand people in America have it. Cretins call it 'Koontz's vampire disease.'" Agatha lowered her gaze for a moment, eyes glistening. "It's a genetic disorder that causes extreme sensitivity to the sun. We try to keep him covered as much as possible."

"Is it like an allergy?" Mandy asked.

"No, but it makes him very weak. That's why the chair. He can walk, you know."

"Oh, that's a blessing," Mandy forced a smile that soon faded. "I swear, I wonder what God is doin' sometimes."

"What?"

"If God can do that to a child," Mandy paused, doubt lacing her voice, "I just ... well, it makes me wonder."

"Every day is a gift, my dear. The reason why there is suffering is so far beyond ..." Agatha's voice trailed off as she struggled to blink back her tears.

Mandy leaned forward and put her arms around the taller women. Agatha returned the embrace and the two stood motionless for several moments.

Hilgard interrupted the scene with a honk of the car horn. "Let's shake a leg, crew!" he shouted. The two women separated, and Agatha wiped away a tear. Looking around, she said, "Now where is Guinevere?"

"Last I saw, she was digging in the sand with Ethan," Mandy said.

"Guin baby, let's go," Agatha called. As Guinevere came running, the two women walked arm in arm toward the Black's car. "Now, you are gonna send me that Pumpkin Pie recipe?"

Mandy smiled. "First thing I'll tend to when we get back to Tyler. Y'all should get it in about a month or so." Within a few minutes, all had said their good-byes, and the doors on the Black's car thumped shut.

Carl strode up from behind Mandy and placed his arms around her waist. "Now they are an odd lot, huh?"

"Stop it. Not everyone is cut from wholesome stock like us," she said. "Besides, that little crippled boy is so darlin'. Bless his heart." A tear began to well in Mandy's eye and she brushed it away with the back of her hand. "I swear, if it was up to you, Carl Johnson, I'd never get to meet anybody interestin'."

Carl puffed his cheeks. "I'm just saying they were a little peculiar, that's all."

Mandy was staring off toward the road. He gently took her hand and smiled sheepishly. "C'mon, let's check on Ethan."

Ethan tugged at Carl's trousers. "Dad, can I get *it* out yet?"

"No, son. You know, rule number two."

"Uhm . . ." Ethan squinted his eyes and pursed his lips. "Oh, I remember. Eyes are everywhere so roll up your sleeves, never a witness should you leave."

Carl nodded and shifted his gaze toward the dark station wagon as it faded out of sight through the trees and down the gravel road. Carl turned back to Ethan. "Okay, now. Go ahead."

Ethan spun on his heels with the excitement of a child scrambling to see his Christmas presents. He ran to the back of their Bronco where Cindy was already waiting.

Cindy reached up and pulled open the rear door. Together they reached in and grabbed a big, white canvas bag. Their cheeks flushed red and arms straining, they jostled the heavy bag from side to side gradually inching it out.

The bag fell to the ground with a smack, and dust rose around it like morning mist. As Ethan reached down to grab the bag, he stopped and pulled back quickly. A sudden movement, like drowning cats squirming in gunnysack, came from within the bag.

"Dad," Ethan called as Carl came rushing around the back of the Bronco.

Carl kneeled down and punched the bag. A muffled whimper came from the bag. He shook his head. "Now kids, I'm glad this happened. It's a good lesson. What's rule number six?"

The Black Spiral: Twisted Tales of Terror

"I know," Cindy shouted. "Sometimes they come back. When this happens, pick up a shovel and whack, whack, whack." Cindy turned to Ethan and the two giggled. The words seemed to tickle Cindy's tongue.

Carl drew a shovel from the back of the Bronco. He raised it over his head and brought it down hard on the lumpy bag. Another soft whimper. Carl pounded the bag again and again. With the third blow, came a concave, cracking sound. The bag lay still. Silent.

As if on cue, the children both picked up a corner and started dragging the bag to the sandy area. When they reached Ethan's hole, Cindy released the bag and slipped backward into the pit.

"Careful, honey," Mandy said as she joined her family at the rim of the hole.

"I'm okay, Mom," Cindy said while she steadied herself and began to climb out. "Hey, is this hole deep enough?"

"Don't know, sweetie. What's the rule?" Carl pushed the bag into the hole with his foot.

"When all is quiet, begin your toil, and bury the leftovers under at least four feet of soil," Cindy said.

"That's definitely four feet. Maybe even five," Ethan said proudly.

"Great job, son." Carl believed that positive reinforcement was just as important as punishment when it came to being a good parent.

"And what's the most important rule of all?" Mandy asked as she swept her baby girl into her arms.

"Rule number one: God has chosen us to make the herd thinner. We're on a sacred mission to kill each and every sinner," Cindy said with a growing smile.

God's work done, they cleaned up the picnic site, leaving it spotless, and headed east in search of more sinners.

***

MINIMUM HUMAN INTEREST LEVELS

Thomas Deja

"(There were) other things that we will never know about in our lifetime including, perhaps, an invisible cloud of evil that circles the world and lands at random in Germany, Cambodia, possibly Iran and Beirut, maybe even America...."
--Spaulding Grey, *Swimming to Cambodia*

The lights flashed and fizzled, blinding the couple as they were led outside the courthouse. It seemed strange now, the beautiful blonde couple with their sparkling eyes and too-white teeth now handcuffed and hiding their faces. The reporters closest to them could hear the wife's sobbing.

"Is there going to be an appeal?" shouted one of the reporters from the sidelines.

"It was an accident!" wailed the wife. One of the guards took her arm and helped her into the prison van. The husband followed, his movements stiff and unnatural. And the horror show moved on . . .

"You're telling me there's something in the air, Mr. Delphi?" Jenny had had doubts that the man before her knew anything about the Brynecki murders when he called. Now that she was sitting in his trailer in the wilds of New Jersey, those doubts had increased exponentially. The place was littered with television parts: wires, circuit boards, some vacuum tubes from prehistoric times, channel knobs, antennas—all contributed to a surreal carpet of technology that crunched wherever Jenny walked. On one wall, Delphi had installed industrial shelves, upon which sat rows of picture tubes. As Jenny passed them by, her black-and-gray reflection met her gaze, distorted by the fish-eye quality of the glass. The effect was akin to being studied by some monstrous Japanese insect.

Sane men did not live in places like this.

Delphi pushed a clump of greasy black hair back from his forehead and nodded. "Yeah. Come on over to the monitor and I'll show you."

Jenny carefully made her way through the carpet of television spare parts—decorated in spots with pizza cartons—to stand beside him. Mr. Delphi appeared to be one of those rare souls who simply didn't care that he was smaller and slighter than she was; if anything, his posture in front of the jury-rigged equipment he was operating at the moment made him look smaller still. A smell like stale pepperoni came off him.

He was typing furiously away at a keyboard as Jenny came up behind him. The monitor had a medusa's riot of wires sticking out of it every which way. "This tape was recorded off a weather satellite feed I came across five weeks ago, about the same time the Brynecki's son was found at the bottom of that lake. And over here," he added, pointing at a bluish-gray mass somewhere over California, "is an anomaly the likes of which I've never seen before."

"What the—"

"As far as I can tell, it a EMF that screwed up the satellite's recording equipment. You'll notice a shadow exists from where the thing was last over here, which seems to indicate a noticeable level of radiation."

Delphi pointed to an area bordering Chicago. "Familiar?"

"Arlo Jackson."

The man strode into the Sears Tower lobby like a toy soldier wound up too tight. His right hand was buried deep inside the canvas carryall slung over one shoulder. Despite the bone-numbing chill just outside, sweat beaded his forehead. His smell, stale and suffocating, permeated the air of the busy lobby.

Jimmy Delmonico manned the security desk that day. The guard was busy thinking about a date. It had taken him a whole month just to get her to agree to go out with him. The woman was tall and dusky and had a solidness to her that made Jimmy weak.

When the man passed Jimmy without showing proper ID, the guard snapped out of it. Jimmy stepped out from behind his desk, a gentle hand on the visitor's shoulder.

"Excuse me, sir, you need a pass—"

The Black Spiral: Twisted Tales of Terror

The man pulled a gun out of his carryall, a massive chrome hand cannon Jimmy had only seen the likes of in Arnold Schwarzeneggar movies. The man's face showed no emotion as he squeezed the trigger.

The steel-jacketed hollow-point bullets disintegrated Jimmy's face at the same time as the screaming stopped.

The man didn't notice. He got into the elevator, closed the door, and reloaded. He had a busy day ahead.

"The pattern next moves north, passing over the Great Lakes—there was a drowning, nothing that got past the local news—into Canada, then falling back over Vermont like so."

Delphi tapped at his keyboards, prompting a stuttering display of the shadow's movements along the top of the continent, into the outskirts of Toronto and landing in New England. Its dark, staticky form was at odds with the dreamy blue and white streaks of the clouds and air currents. Finally, it stopped, swirling into a whirlpool pattern over a particular small town Jenny knew all too well.

"Heuvelman."

"Exactly. I've extrapolated its movements from as far back as ten years ago, and I'm sure you could tell me what happened at each exact point where it stopped."

"So what are you telling me?" There was a hint of impatience in her voice.

The sheriff put himself between the crowd and Irwin Mellish. It was his job.

The crowd agreed that the sheriff was secretly a Zionist. That was the only reason why he protected Mellish from their rightful wrath, even though in reality Mellish hadn't raped Earl's daughter and buried her in a ditch after snapping off two of her fingers.

Fourteen broken bones, the papers whispered. Anal penetration, the crowd passed amongst themselves.

Dogs had gotten to her, Kelly Gifford swore. Kelly had found the body, and was considered an expert on the case.

No Zionist was going to protect one of his own kind, the crowd agreed. Irving Mellish had to pay for sodomizing and mutilating poor Earl's daughter.

He had to pay that night.

Which is why the crowd returned armed.

"I'm telling you this—this psionic lifeform is out there, maliciously or inadvertently causing havoc because we demand it." In the glow of the monitors Dephi's face was lit a dim blue. Jenny reached into her purse and activated the minirecorder. "I'm listening."

"I trust a woman with your experience in unusual phenomenon knows about psychometry."

"The alleged psychic ability to 'read' impressions off of inanimate objects."

"That's one way of putting it," Delphi continued. "Others believe that what a psychometrist does is read the electromagnetic echoes left behind by the living thing that last handled it."

"Pardon?"

"Every living thing has an electromagnetic field . . . it's very low-level, but it exists—sharks track their prey through a sense organ refined to detect them. What if our electromagnetic fields are interacting with the EMP created by television transmissions? What if all that interference melded together into an interactive electronic 'program,' if you will. Hell, our imprint comes from a sentient being; what if enough of those 'sentient' imprints get mixed up with that program, directing it to seek out and stimulate what the source needs."

"That's an awful lot of ifs, man," Jenny replied.

Delphi turned away from his monitors and faced Jenny. Away from their glow, she was struck by just how pale and sallow he really appeared. "I pieced together the rumors on the 'Net, Ms. Hargrove. I know your reputation for dealing with the unnatural. This,"—he motioned to the screens, the pixilated light throwing reflections on his skin—"this is as unnatural as it gets. Whatever it is, lifeform, presence, an amalgam of our viewing consciousness . . . all it really wants is to provide for its parents what it thinks we want."

"Violence."

Jenny took a deep breath. She thumbed the recorder off. "Isn't that laying blame a bit too thin?"

"Not if it's the truth." Delphi turned away from the monitors. Reaching below a undersized desk to retrieve a small keyboard, he started tapping in data. One by one, the monitors switched from tracking patterns to channels—network channels, cable channels, satellite feeds, international channels from far-off sites . . . and in the center was stringy haired, owl-glassed, pathetic Delphi. Car crashes dueled with cartoons, which fought for attention with talking heads deep in debate. As Delphi turned his attentions back to Jenny, his sallow complexion came alive with a kaleidoscope of cathode ray reflections. "Look at this, Ms. Hargrove! THIS is what we choose to beam into our homes, twenty-four hours a day. This drowns out what little compassion and love and emotion we allow to squeeze through."

"You're a soft touch at those public television marathons, aren't you?"

Delphi advanced on her, pointing at the screens franticly. "This is all that presence knows of its parents...a hunger, a desire for blood. And it seeks to please Mom and Dad by providing us with an acceptable level of violence. It wanders from place to place, interfering with the electromagnetic impulses of our own brainwaves, throwing that little switch in the back of random people's heads, triggering an irrational response . . . madness, death . . ."

Jenny threw her hands up, "I understand what you're saying, Mr. Delphi, but you have to admit, I'd have problems selling this to my editor."

"Oh, I know he'll can this piece, just like he canned the other ones." Delphi turned back to his viewscreens, staring up at their electron-streamed pictures with a holy hermit's fervor. "But you've found ways to stop all of the bad things you uncovered—every zombie, every magician, every killer. I know you can find a way to stop our child before he kills again. And this time you *have* to, Ms. Hargrove. Who knows if it's even now bombarding some new schlub with radiation, hoping to produce a Ramsey, a Simpson, a Brynecki ... some kid like Cunanan who's going to go on a murder spree for *no reason whatsoever*. We're not manufacturing our monsters fast enough for its taste, so it's making them for us. You've got to stop it."

Jenny reached into her purse until her fingers wrapped around the pepper spray. "You've got to admit to how crazy this is."

Delphi's eyes flickered to a spot over Jenny's head, where a monitor showed some Chinese warlord deafening a complaining subject. "I've shown you all the proof."

Jenny started inching toward the door. Snapshot images from the various glass screens imprinted themselves on her retinas. "Then print out your proof, let me go over it, go to a couple of experts I trust . . . let me try to validate your theory. If there is any validity, I'll help you."

The Black Spiral: Twisted Tales of Terror

Delphi tore himself away from the screen he was watching. From a distance, he had the bone-tired, wasted appearance of the seriously ill. "I don't have the time," he stated weakly.

"*It* know*s*, Ms. Hargrove. It's sensed my eyes watching it, and it's watching back. It's begun to affect my thought processes. I've been having thoughts, terrible thoughts."

By that time, Jenny was out the door and halfway to her car.

The store window was badly spider-webbed from the bullets. Jenny flashed her press pass to the nearest officer and explained why she was here. After the man radioed inside, she was let though.

The store smelled of cordite, burnt plastic, blood and ozone. The glass shards crunched under Jenny's feet. Counselors and paramedics led the survivors of the massacre past Jenny, their wails and comforting words shrouding her in a white noise blanket. The rising and falling whine of ambulance sirens came closer.

One of the plainclothes detectives, a friend of her boyfriend, recognized her. "No reporters, Hargrove," he said, coming up to her. "There'll be a press conference when we're done."

She took in the carnage. "Cool your jets, Ray," she replied in a stunned voice. "We're on the same side this time. I knew the guy."

A tall officer with spiky hair came up behind Ray. "It's okay, sir. The skel's note mentioned her."

The body lay under a sheet behind her, sprawled in front of the television display. Each and every monitor had its screen shattered. "How many?"

"Still assessing, Hargrove. You can find out—"

"—at the press conference, right. On second thought, I don't think I want to know." She turned to go.

"Did you know him, Hargrove? We'll need you for identification."

"His name's Paul Delphi," Jenny replied. She refused to look at Ray, at the body, at the mess. "If you can't find a relative, call me."

She heard ray following her. "Don't you want to know the details, or find out what the note said?"

Jenny stopped. She scanned the damage of Delphi's rampage. Taking her silence as an assent, Ray continued. "He wanted you to know he held out as long as he was able to, but a presence overpowered him. Does that mean anything to you, Hargrove?"

The Black Spiral: Twisted Tales of Terror

She tried to imagine how long "as long as he could" meant. Red lights flashed through the broken windows. Already, she could see the first wave of her fellow reporters arriving in their cars, looking for someone, anyone to talk to.

"Word of advice, detective?" Jenny sighed and hoped she was going to be able to practice what she preached.

"Take up reading."

* * *

The Black Spiral: Twisted Tales of Terror

ORGANIC

Sara Merlene

"I like this color," Eve said. "It's a nice light tan." She ran her finger over the sample page. "Adam, what do you think?" Her voiced cracked slightly as she met her husband's warm brown eyes.

"Let's go for a slightly lighter shade," Adam said. "The brochure states that the lighter tones may not fade as quickly. We can always change it later."

Eve nodded, faining agreement. Maybe he was right. Maybe they shouldn't try to replace what was lost and simply let go of the past.

Taking the catalog from Eve's lap, Adam stroked his chin as he flipped the pages. He shook his head and sighed. "It's no use. I wish we could see the actual models."

He took Eve's hand, squeezing it tightly. Searching the showroom floor, he said, "Where's that salesman?"

"Be patient, honey ... be patient," she said. Her green gold-flecked eyes glistened slightly as she nervously brushed a long shock of auburn hair from her brow.

Eve studied her husband, took in his dark wavy hair, his soft smile. Were they really ready? It had only been two months; maybe they should wait a little longer.

Turning, she scanned the other couples seated on matching sofas about the showroom. Their eyes glowed with a childlike wonder as they smiled and pointed to different items in the catalogs, which were clutched firmly in their grasp.

The room seemed to be designed to create a subdued and claming effect. Done in soft pastels and neutral beiges, from the carpet to the formless images that decorated the walls, the scheme seemed to exert a faceless conformity. A blank slate. However, it had the opposite affect on Eve. It was too artificial, as though it was struggling to imitate life and failing miserably.

As Eve turned her attention back to Adam, pain seized her heart. His face once smooth and youthful was now creased with worry lines. Crow's-feet etched the corners of his eyes. *If only I could reach up and caress his face, place a soft kiss on his lips, hold him.* But outward signs

The Black Spiral: Twisted Tales of Terror

of affection were outlawed—dangerous. They could indicate forbidden passion.

The salesman's voice interrupted her thoughts. "Have you folks picked a model?"

"How accurate are the color samples in the pictures?" Adam asked.

The salesman smiled wide and said, "There will be a slight variation in color. It's an approximation of flesh tones." The salesman was slick. His gray pinstripe suit perfectly tailored, his hands meticulously manicured, his hair groomed. Polished, finished, and ready to help couples achieve their dreams. Eve wanted to feel at ease with him, but he lacked one essential element—humanity.

"Just the same, we'd like to see some real-life samples," Adam said. Eve turned to Adam in disbelief. It was all happening so fast, too fast.

The salesmen shifted his feet and finger-combed his hair.

"We don't normally allow that in the early stages, but considering your *situation* . . . let me check with my Manager." As the salesman left she thought—*of course, their situation.* The words forced Eve and Adam into separate silences. He rose from the sofa and began pacing. Eve glanced at the other couples; they were checking boxes on order forms.

"Honey, do you think we'll be able to bring one home today?" Eve whispered with a slight edge punctuating each word.

"Maybe, because of our . . . *situation,* he said. Sometimes, the models are ready to take home." Eve's pulse quickened. Even though the words were said, the question asked, she hadn't really considered bringing one home today. Everything was ready at home, everything but her.

The salesman returned, his face beaming. "Okay, folks. Right this way." They walked side by side through the double doors and down a sterile white hallway.

"The models are down this hall at the end. Are you ready to make a decision, today?"

After stealing side-glances at one another, they answered in unison.

"Yes!"

"Good, then you'll be taking one home today?" the salesmen asked. She swallowed audibly and nodded. As they stood before a

211

massive stainless-steal door, the salesman punched a code into an adjacent keypad. Cool air washed over them as the door swung open.

The salesman made a sweeping gesture as he said, "Ladies first."

They took an involuntary step through the doorway and into a vast warehouse.

The warehouse held row after row of children in different stages of growth. They hung suspended in glass animation tubes. Their eyes closed as if in sleep, waiting to be awakened, to be claimed.

"Perhaps I'd better explain the process," the salesman said. "The large tubes attached to their abdomens function as umbilical cords, supplying nutrients. Electrode pads at each temple stimulate nerve growth in the brain, educating all the children to their age level, making full use of their genetically enhanced brains. Perfection of the species. No disease, no aberrations. No rolling of the dice, no organically conceived offspring. No unsanctioned breeding! No 'Organics.'"

The hushed silence which followed was drowned by the pounding rhythm of her own heartbeat, seemingly beating in syncopation with the hundreds of tiny heartbeats, each murmuring in the seedbed of darkness:

"Take me, take me, take me . . . "

Eve was drowning in the sound. It washed over her in waves, enveloping her and triggering a vision. Her son, Cody, was clutched to her breast. His sandy cloud of hair pressed to her cheek, the fresh soapy sent of a just bathed child. Then *they* came, ripping him from her arms. He was an *Organic*. Conceived out of love—but a mutant in the eyes of the government.

The salesman's oily voice pulled her back to the present. "Well folks, do you want to have a look around? Or do you have some specific attributes you're looking for?"

Eve searched Adam's face; she could see the helpless look in his eyes. Eve steeled herself and said, "We'd like to look around, by ourselves."

The salesmen shrugged. "Of course, feel free to browse. On the outside of each Gen-Tube, you'll find all the information on the Gen-Child inside. Sex, I.Q., eye and hair color, projected height, likely future occupation, and of course—age.

"The babies are immersed the artificial Gen-Wombs, the front five are available for immediate delivery. However, I think the age range you may be looking for is on the far left. Not many couples like to look at specimens over the age two, but older couples and people in your *situation* prefer the older Gen-Children."

There it was again, their *situation. I guess that makes us some sort of criminals.*

They'd given birth to an *Organic* child, which was against the law in a society where even sex was legislated. To *conceive* an *Organic* child by artificial insemination was considered acceptable: it was a contribution to the grand plan. But to engage in sexual intercourse, to actually give *birth* was illegal, and once discovered, the *State* rushed in and confiscated the child.

A chill crept up Eve's spine as she remembered the doctor's exact words. "Within the first eight weeks of pregnancy the embryo is removed for genetic encoding by the Department of Chromo Molecular Study. From there the DNA is mapped, stem cells reproduced, and the desirable transgenetic information removed from the genome. The transgenes are then taken and inserted into the chromosome of a Gen-Embryo to produce a Gen-Baby, a made to order eugenic designer baby grown to the specifications of the parent."

She'd wanted another child, needed to fill that loss, that vacuum in their lives. But now as she stood there, about to see the fruits of the State's cold harvest, doubt and heartache filled her.

Eve found her voice and clenched Adam's hand. "NO. We want to look at the babies."

The salesman's brows knitted together, then a thin smile creased his face. "Well ... now you've got the spirit! We have a fine selection of specimens to choose from. The latest advancements in production technique. If you'll just accompany me—"

She tore free of Adam's hand.

"I'll meet you over . . ." Her voice broke. She hesitated, regained control. "I need use the restroom."

"It's to the left, the door on the—" the salesman called to her, but Eve had vanished around the corner. Disoriented, she fought to stare straight ahead, marching down the aisle without looking at the children encased in Gen-Tubes on either side of her. As she turned to the left, she saw two identical doors.

"Well, I guess I'm lost," she whispered to herself. She reached for the doorknob to her right. Stepping cautiously into a cold dark room, she searched for the light switch. Her hands fumbling at first, she found it. The room blazed to life with hash, blinding light forcing her to shield her eyes.

When she lowered her hands, she saw that she stood in another warehouse, filled with row after row of frosted Gen-Tubes. An overhead sign read: **Harvesting Room**. For a moment she stood frozen, lost in a forest of glass. The deafening silence was marred by the steady click of her high heels on the concrete floor as something pulled her, guiding her to the second row. Suddenly she stopped. Her eyes rose, taking in the towering Gen-Tube before her.

She read the label:

Organic 1258940

Sex: Male
Age: 5
Harvested: March 12, 2075

The date leaped out at her. That was the day *They* came. The day *They* took Cody. Eve reached out and frantically rubbed the outside of the glass with her palm. The image of a child's face slowly formed: familiar little lips and even the freckle just below her left eye. She looked closer straining to see. A scar zoomed into focus. A tiny little scar only a mother would notice right at the child's hairline. A scar that her Cody had gotten falling down the cellar steps at grandpa's house.

Her hands hammered the frosted glass of the Gen-Tube. She clawed. She screamed. "Cody, it's mommy ... Cody!"

Then finally exhausted, her throat raw and tears clouding her vision, she slumped forward slowly, sliding to the floor. She knelt there, her hands caressing the cool glass hoping to coax warmth from her child within.

* * *

The Black Spiral: Twisted Tales of Terror

PREVIEW STORIES FROM
NEKRomantik
EROTIC TALES
Coming in 2004

THE SERPENT SAID

William D. Gagliani

Yesterday I was duly afflicted by the curse of the snake, and I fear there ain't no redemption in sight.

Let me how it all started. But beware a' my words, brother—they'll chill your *precious* souls.

It was the thirteenth day of the month and a Friday both, a devil's day as you ignorant people would have it. If I truly believed that claptrap, I would've done my best to refuse this ... this blasted *power* I didn't go lookin' for but was granted over any woman I chanced to meet in this Indiana Bible "chastity" belt backwater.

The Black Spiral: Twisted Tales of Terror

Excuse me a sec . . . I need to spit. There, that's better.

Now where was I . . . Oh, ya . . .

I shoulda refused the power, turned my back, packed up and hunted me up a new line, but I didn't. God help me, I surely didn't. The curse was strong, and I was weak. Ain't it always like that?

Pride is the greatest sin, even *I* know that, and *my* pride is strong, mighty strong. You see, I was born poor enough to learn at a young age that you don't turn away what is freely given. It's how I kept me in this business so long.

See, Molly's my up-front girl, been with me for three hard-luck years and never looked past the low cash pay, the grimy little offices, the run-down hotels, or even the late-night escapes. Maybe she's enjoyin' the risk. The danger of getting caught. But she never made a move on me, my Molly, and I never did on her. Our arrangement was strictly business, understand?

So Molly suddenly starts starin' into my eyes with those large, kinda watery pupils of hers. It plain surprised me no end. I asked her if she had just learned of some death in the family, then I got sidetracked onto a rant: why wasn't my new bottle open and stashed behind the makeshift pulpit of my latest low-rent storefront office, like always? She just stared at me and I stared right back.

Fact is that Molly can turn heads, yes indeed, when she puts some time into the endeavor. She's a dumb hillbilly in one town, but passes for one of them Vegas chippies out for fun in the next. Brush that chestnut hair, slap on cheap mascara with a heavy hand to make those wide eyes of hers downright huge, and slather bright red onto those lips, which already tend to impress with their wanton fleshiness. Her slight overbite does the rest to most men, sure enough.

Yesterday my Molly decided to go chippy, and when I entered the dim office and spotted her, my first thought was to inquire as to the health of her rotten scoundrel of a no-good husband—she sure was dolled up as if ready to attend his funeral, oh happy day. But surprise stole my words right from me.

Our eyes locked for a few seconds and then she looked down, at the elongated wooden box I carried, and then up again at me. She seemed about to speak, maybe to greet me, but paused in the very act of opening her mouth. She cocked her head to the side, like she was listenin' intently to a voice I couldn't hear. I noticed the faint line of moisture above her perfectly penciled upper lip, that morsel now quivering in its fiery glory.

The Black Spiral: Twisted Tales of Terror

Damnation! Suddenly I felt downright inclined to lick that sweat off her downy upper lip. I confess, I was weakened by the sight, so I leaned back into the door I'd just shut and reached around with a free hand to turn the latch, assuring our privacy. I don't know what made me do that, you see?

The box vibrated in my hand and I felt its weight bear down sharply into my elbow. I sensed its movement, imagined it a slitherin' away in there. I shuddered like I was feverish or somethun. The solid door behind me propped up my clumsy body to face that sudden vision of sultry femininity, Molly—my sweet Molly!

She parted bloated lips and poked the thin, delicate tip of her pink tongue right out from between them, leaving a glistening trail wherever it traveled and lingered and traveled again. Her eyes continued to probe mine, but I admit I couldn't focus entirely on them—no sir, I chose to admire those fleshy lips just a writhing before me, now curling upward, and I felt my manhood untangle and curl upward, too. The longbox vibrated softly in my hand. Another glimpse of silent movement through the cross-shaped cut-out centered on one of the lids. The tiny brass lock swung with exaggerated slowness. Indeed, everything was flowin' at the speed of molasses.

Oh, what strange magic potion filled the sultry summer air! Bit of a poet I am, I reckon.

"Ned," she whispered with a voice so low it sounded not like hers at all. "My Ned."

I blinked both eyes slowly and somehow missed her approach, and when I opened them again Molly stood mere inches from me, looking up into my bearded face like a schoolgirl. I wanted to speak, but my vocal cords froze up on me. Then her head disappeared and I felt a sure, gentle tugging on the outside of my trousers. I looked down and beheld those widened pupils gazing into mine, her lips all puckered up like she was about to whistle, and one slim hand parting the folds of fabric which held me prisoner no longer, the buttons undone as if in a dream. Yes, I was free, tinglin' and hot to trot.

I tell you, her touch was cool, yet blazing.

"Molly," I managed. "Oh, my sweet, Molly."

Things got kind of dizzy like, my old knees were weak. I'm tellin' ya. That girl could suck a pickled egg clean through a straw, if ya get my drift.

I set the longbox down on the tiny table which held the guest book, placed my hands in her hair, and felt each movement until finally I felt the shiver building, snaking up my spine as she moaned in rhythm. Then she wiped the corners of her mouth with a prim, slender finger following the curl of her smile. Moments later she fixed her ruined lipstick and left me to cover myself—and recover—as best I could. We didn't say a damn thing. No, sir, not one damn word.

Oh, don't judge me with disapproval, you dim-wits!

You'd a-had no more strength than me, if the roles were reversed. Molly's a good girl, a swell actress and valuable ally: a real lady in the parlor but to my surprise—a whore in the bedroom. When she returned to her desk, she winked at me and licked her lips and—for a moment, mind you—I missed the small-town Molly I used to know. It was like she'd got herself a cat-house education that afternoon, and I'd written the curriculum.

Frenzied knocking at the locked door set me to righting my trousers and buttoning the fly. I was thankful for the yellowed blinds that screened out the afternoon sun and kept visitors from pryin'. Sweat stung as it dribbled into my eyes.

"Are you goin' to get that, Reverend?" Molly asked in her sweetest voice. She was my up-front girl again and looked no more forward to me at that moment than any church secretary.

"Uh, yes," I stammered as I fumbled at the door. "I believe I will."

I'd no sooner unlatched it than it flew open as if shoved by northeaster.

"Well well, lookie here!"

I studied the loud, lanky visitor. A Woolworth's suit, a wrinkled white shirt, and shoes that hadn't been polished since the War. A crushed fedora tilted over flat, uninteresting features. I could see a dented black Packard parked outside.

"Look, Sister Molly, if it ain't a member of the local journalistic industry!" The words welled up before I could stop them, but it didn't matter because the flat-faced man had flashed his press card at me even as I spoke. I can spot a newspaperman by the cheapness of his clothes, the stench of rut-gut whisky on his breath, and by the hyena gleam in his bloodshot eyes.

"John Molinaro, Reverend. News Gazette. You *are* the Reverend Jim-Bob Wallace?" He extended his hand experimentally.

I took his hand close to his wrist, holding it long enough to pretend cordiality and far up enough to escape a vise-grip that might have strangled a camel, had it found purchase. "C'mon in out of the heat, Mr. Molinetti."

"Molinaro," he corrected, smiling crookedly at Molly behind me. "Ma'am," he said, leering. His gaze switched to me and went flinty. "I'm real sorry to come callin' so soon after your arrival in town and all, but you know ..."

I swung the door closed behind him, catching sight of the guest book and the longbox on the table. "Not at all, Mr. Moli—I've had a day to unpack and prepare for my ministry. What can I do for you, sir?"

He smiled. "As you might imagine, your arrival here in Hadlyville has caused quite a stir." He wagged his head back and forth like it was hinged. "Quite a stir. Word's been spreadin' for the last day or so that you're part of one of those *special* Christian groups." He had a pad out by now, and a stubby pencil.

"We're all Christians here in Indiana, sir," I pointed out. "Ain't we?" I made sure I was smilin' like an idiot. Behind him, I saw Molly look away.

"That's for sure, Reverend Wallace. You've put your finger on a basic truth around these parts." He nodded and scratched some symbols into his notebook. "What is the name you go by, uh, the name of your ministry?"

He was tauntin', pronouncin' *ministry* like a cussword. I wondered if I'd set my sights a bit too high this time around.

"I'm ordained by the Holy Highway Church of God," I explained slowly, so he could jot it down. "I'm here to spread news of the power and the glory of the Lord."

"No doubt, no doubt. And your first service is tomorrow? Is that right?"

I'd made some calls and my contacts were coming through, one by one. Next evening at eight the local Pentecostal church, housed in a bungalow on the outskirts of town, would host about three dozen worshipers and a delegation of preachers from in and around the county, and we would handle serpents for the glory of God.

And for the glory of the donation plate. *Praise the Lord.*

"It is indeed, Mr. Millitaro. Ya'll come by and witness to our *Savior*? You can report in your paper the holy love that'll be pouring out of each of us."

"What about the snake handling? Can I report on that?" He grinned at me as if we were sharin' a joke. Maybe we were.

"There will be serpents handled, yes, symbolizing our mastery over the Great Serpent, the Evil One."

"You know snake handling is illegal here in this state, don't you?" he drawled with a smirk.

"The laws of man hold no sway over those of the Lord," I said, bringing my hands together and gazing downward. I've found that most reporters get edgy when faced with piousness. I'm pious right often when there's a journalist in the room. Played just right, their stories help swell the donations. Wrong, and we're headin' out of town just ahead of a lynch mob.

He looked around, measurin'. "Not a lot of money in your calling, is there?"

That's another tactic, attempting to goad some blasphemous response from a man of God. I'm careful not to let my finances show in my surroundings.

His gaze fell upon the longbox. "Is that what I think it is?" he asked, stepping closer. He bent over the table and jumped a small step back when the box moved of its own accord.

"That is a serpent, yes sir," I said. "A full-grown, poisonous rattler we'll be handling tomorrow, safely under the protection of our Savior." I imagined the disgusting scaly skin, rippling and slithering inside the box, visible through the cross-shaped cut-out. He stared at it. "You're welcome to handle the serpent yourself, Mr. Moli— …"

"I'll leave that to you and your flock, Reverend," he said, runnin' a nervous grin. And takin' another sidelong glance at the longbox.

"They're not my flock yet," I pointed out, trying for modesty. I looked at Molly for some support, but she was facing away from us. Usually she's part of the act, drivin' it home.

He headed for the door. "I'll be here tomorrow," he said. "You can count on it."

I smiled. "Prepare yourself to witness miracles."

I heard his mocking laughter even after he had left.

"What the hell were you doing?" I shouted at Molly. "You gone crazy?"

Before she could answer, the door flew open again and smacked against the wall. I turned and faced this new intrusion with my quick temper, which faded when I saw that it was a striking woman in a serious Sunday dress. Her features were as severe as the cut of her clothes—

sharp and not altogether unattractive, though pinched and devoid of any cosmetic embellishments. You coulda cut yourself on her chin and nose.

"May I help you?"

"I'm here on behalf of my husband, the Reverend Horton. He has the parish down the street a-ways, Holy Redeemer. I've come to plead with you not to taint our community with your blasphemy!" she said in a high-pitched, nasal, nagging voice.

This was not turning out to be a good day, despite that display of Molly's unexpected expertise in matters carnal.

"Mrs. Horton," I began as smoothly as I could muster, "let me assure you that . . ." I trailed off.

Her eyes had left mine and wandered downward, fixin' my groin area with a bizarre stare. I followed her stare and saw that my trousers had somehow remained unbuttoned. *Had Molinaro noticed?* As I made to hastily correct the matter, the Reverend Horton's wife suddenly sank to her bony knees, reaching out to prevent my escape.

"Yes," she whispered, voice gone real husky, not nearly as nasal. Answering a question, a demand, only she could hear. "Yes! I am honored, my master!"

A lifetime later, the minister's wife stood, her eyes again blazing into mine. "You be there tomorrow night, you hear?" Her tone had slowed to a drawl, completely unlike how she sounded upon her arrival. Carnal and raw, it was the voice of a demon.

I said, "Yes, ma'am!" But she was already storming out the door. Molly left immediately after, speaking not a word, leaving me alone in my disheveled clothes, a strange soreness setting into my abused groin. I sagged to the floor and felt tears squeeze from my eyes. Surely, you would think I'd struck a golden vein in this new and bizarre tendency for women to offer their mouths and tongues to me, but I sensed the onrush of some sort of end, a final twist to my strangely sweet-sour torture.

The door opened before I could stand to slip on the latch, and my newest visitor looked down upon me with a mixture of amusement and false pity. Thin and wiry, he was dressed in black and wore a sort of beret on his nearly hairless head. A devilish goatee stained the lower reaches of his chin. He grinned with crooked brown tooth stumps.

"Well, man, what have we here?"

Under the circumstances, I declined to answer.

"Ned Potter, I presume?"

"I'll have Riley's money in a week," I said, gathering my legs under me. "Ten days at the most."

"Sweet, but not good enough." He gritted the stained stumps. The pain must have been severe. "Riley wants you to know, he's in a hurry, man. He's sweated up over this little problem you and he have between you."

"No need, not at all. Seven days—" I was nearly up now, and focusing on his groin, where my boot would land when I had regained enough of my balance.

The beatnik was no idiot. He leaned forward and stepped on my leading foot and—while I shouted in blue pain—snatched something long and metallic out of his pocket. I saw the glint of the blade even as I heard the *snick* of the mechanism, and then the tip of the dirk was probing my left nostril.

I half-stood very still as his nicotine-and-rot breath washed over me.

"Don't sweat it yet, Daddy-o," he said with a snort. "Riley wants to get paid, so you're a nothing to him dead."

"No argument from me," I whispered carefully. The blade was cold inside my nose.

"However, you can still pay while maimed."

I nodded very carefully.

"Two days," he said. "Forty-eight little hours."

His free hand gripped my left ring finger before I could contemplate moving it out of range, and with a crisp yank upward he broke it, pain lancing from the joint up my arm and flashing into my brain as he bent it back over my wrist and then twisted it sideways. He cut off my croaking scream with his hand.

"Work your little scam, Preacher Man. I'll be watching you from real close, and if you try to skip I'm going to take particular pleasure in breaking every one of your fingers, and then stuffing your dick down your throat. Then maybe I'll put you out of your misery, or maybe not. You got that?"

I nodded through the tears. His repulsive face cracked into a brown smile and pulled back, and then I slid to the floor while he slammed the door.

No respect for a man of God.

I lay there a while, then crawled to the lectern and drew myself upright. I ground my teeth to keep from screaming again while I splinted and taped my broken finger, feeling the knucklebones scrape together like shards of glass.

Sweat trickled off my brow as I checked the longbox, just to see the movement inside. The diamond shapes oozed wetly past the opening. I listened carefully, almost not breathing, but no sounds came from the serpent. No sounds except the gentle slithering of scaly skin on rough wood. No voices. I put the longbox down on the pulpit and scrabbled about for my bottle. Two long pulls dulled the pain a little. A third almost killed it.

"What the hell's happening?" The occupants of the trick longbox ignored me and my strangled wail. I drank more. Maybe it was time to pack it in. Maybe Indiana wasn't the best place—back to Kentucky, where women were unlikely to worship my groin before I said a word, or spent a dime.

Riley and his money. Fleece the natives, as planned, or meet the beatnik's blade one last time? I drank some more.

An hour later I felt little pain. Still no sign of Molly. But I sensed visitors. Or maybe the longbox was feeding me images like spoonfuls of sugar.

You see, I was soon to understand that there was not a woman who could resist the call of the serpent. Young and old, pious and fallen, the lookers and the ugly—the serpent spoke to them all, and he spoke in a tongue they heard well.

How did I know?

Yes indeed. So thirsty. Let me have some of that water, would you? Thanks so much. And a cloth to wipe the sweat from my eyes. It's sure as hot as an open bonfire, ain't it? Maybe that fire's just for me.

Molly's *unusual* behavior was just the start, you see. The spreading news brought more visitors from around the county. That's what I wanted. At least, that's what I wanted *before* the serpent went and started speaking to those that came by to see the new preacher boy.

First was another matron, perhaps a neighbor of the minister's wife, a Mrs. Alma Wellers. Then Sue Ann Barton, a young and untouched maiden who left still unblemished and yet very, very worldly. And Mabel Smyth, who came to curse but knelt instead to "pray," stuttering answers to questions only she could hear. A fat and hairy farm wife named Hildie, and several of her neighbors. And at last I pushed two lusty cross-eyed farm-bred teenagers and their lustful mothers out and locked the door, but I could sense them and others outside, waiting.

The Black Spiral: Twisted Tales of Terror

A line of celebrants, apparently called—*to punish me?*—by something I could not fathom. Lordy, was I depleted, brother!

Today, the same. Another mother and her full-figured daughter, maybe one of those from yesterday, stopped to pay their respects, so to speak, kneelin' together.

You like that?

Yea, I say unto thee, my children: listen to the voice of the serpent, for he hath spoken. I feel the bite of insanity comin' on, I do, and there's nothin' to be done about it.

I see you all there now, starin' at me. I see you all, judgin' me. Self-righteous hypocrites the lot of you!

When it came time for the service, I was as empty as my whisky bottle, and yet I saw the women staring at my privates and licking their moist, painted lips—some painted for the first time, I am certain!—with snaking tongues. I delivered a sermon the words of which meant nothing and went nowhere, but not one of them noticed because the night heat and the serpent's words were like an injection of raw lust. You men seemed not to follow the words, and you women all swallowed me with your lustful eyes.

Don't turn your eyes from the truth, now!

When I took the longbox from its shelf and felt the movement inside, I swear I heard the Lord tellin' me to take up the serpent right then, to praise His name and His mastery over the evil one. I saw Molly in the corner of my eye, her face a blur. In the far corner, Mr. Molinetti—whatever, pencil and pad in hand and a smirk on his face. Near the door, the beatnik, here to guard Riley's recent investment in my professional gambling career. No running for me, not today. I knew my collections would suffer greatly without the passion and the rattler. I listened to the voice I heard, and I told them all:

"Here I will take up the evil one and fear no harm, for my faith protects me! For He said, 'Behold, I give you authority to tread upon serpents and scorpions, and over all the power of the enemy, and nothing shall hurt you!'"

It's my biggie out of Luke, and it set all them locals to swayin' and speakin' in tongues. Several hicks strummed instruments while others sang or hummed "When the Roll Is Called Up Yonder." I snapped the clasp off the left side of the longbox, reached in, and took out the limp forty-inch rattler that lay coiled within. Carefully, I set the longbox down on the lectern behind me, where no one could see the identical lid on the right side, and the other serpent shape it hid. A bit of sleight-of-hand, harmless in nature, and necessary for the illusion.

The rattler's muscles rippled beneath my fingers as it awoke panicked and attempted to roll. I held it up over my head in both hands, the tail high on one side and the pointed head on the other, its cold reptilian eye starin' at me with no expression. Its thin, forked tongue flicked out at me as the beast sensed danger. The tail rattles started their chatter and blended in with the screams—both of fear and of ecstasy—comin' from the thickly packed congregation. I heard them speakin' in tongues, their voices raised in a babble straight from Hell, and my voice joined theirs in a moment, for the serpent had truly awakened and I saw when it gaped open its hinged jaw that the fangs were fully exposed and that the venom sacs were in place.

No! How could they be?

I found Molly's eyes in the crowd around me, and saw a foreign emotion there, a steely glare I'd not seen before. Her stare spoke volumes. *She* had switched reptiles—the other compartment now housed the de-venomed rattler, while I held aloft the one whose fangs even now drooled poison into my eyes.

Before I could react, heave the serpent from my grasp or at least send it spinning to the floor, the head rolled lazily backward and then struck, fangs flashing in the poor light.

Once.
Twice.
And again.

The first and second strikes in my right forearm, the third in my shoulder, and almost immediately I felt the cold heat of the poison as it entered my blood like twin rivers mixing into one channel.

I dropped the serpent and saw it slither under the lectern, while around me the congregation continued their celebration, blissful and unaware of what had happened. *Ignorant!* I lowered my arms and felt the paralysis begin, the cold-hot invasion roiling through my veins like millions of tiny twirling serpents. My eyes met Molly's and she licked her lips and whispered some words I could not hear, but I felt my arousal begin even as I sagged slowly to my knees. I knew then—knew without a doubt—that she was speaking to the serpent, replying to his requests.

The beatnik's leering face loomed over me, and the first slug from my boot derringer tore through that vile mouth and showered the congregation with blood and bits of his brain. I lay back, ignoring the sudden quiet in the room, and put the second slug through the rattlesnake's forehead, quieting that voice forever.

Still, they hear voices. You hear voices, don't you?
Don't you?
I don't hear them, but I know they speak of me.

I saw Molitano—whatever there, too, and I lifted the derringer one last time and pulled the trigger, but it was a two-shot and empty. But seein' him hug the floor and piss his pants almost made the whole thing worth it, it sure did.

I know I've been babbling, but my throat is dry. Bone-desert dry. The paralysis is a commencin'; the light's fadin' from the outer edges of my vision.

And now I lay among you clods, awaitin' the moment, blind and powerless. And thirsty, so very thirsty.

The serpent said it would be so. And he was right, wasn't he?
So right . . .

THE DANCE

L. Marie Wood

The room was a sauna, oppressive. My sweat-dampened clothing clung to the small of my back. The air hung heavy blue with cigarette smoke and pheromones. The Plasma Club spanned three levels, each jam-packed with a feeding frenzy of dancers and watching wallflowers. The Reggae room occupied the top floor, over the Goth and R&B rooms; pulsing waves of sound washed across the floor and down the stairwell. I had just wandered up from the Goth room when I saw her.

Her body teased as she drifted like hot, sultry smoke across the floor. Dark silken hair danced across the middle of her back as she swayed, her shapely hips rolling rhythmically to the pounding beat of the music—with gyrations slow and hypnotic—at one with the bass. Small but ample breasts rose and fell delicately, almost still.

She turned, scrutinizing me from head to toe. And her dark liquid eyes were wide and unblinking, like eyes in a portrait. The women's generous lips parted in a sensual smile. A smile more confusing than the feelings stirring within me. Did she like the way my eyes blanketed her body? Exploring, searching every inch of her.

As my lips parted, mimicking her, the room swam out of focus until only her image remained. My cheeks flushed red, embarrassed. A tingling sensation swept upwards from my groin, knotting in my stomach, and finally spreading across my lips. Lips that hungered for hers.

She continued to stare, her gaze unwavering.

God, could she read my mind?

Dazed, I drifted in a fog, blocking out everything but the sensual curve of her hips as they undulated beneath the glistening fabric of her dress.

I licked my lips. My heart kicked against my ribcage. She turned toward me again. I looked closer. In the pulsing strobe light her eyes seemed transparent as glass. Suddenly she broke her gaze.

Her eyes were closed as she twirled, her mouth gaped wide in satisfaction.

As she whirled about, her raven's wing of hair took flight. It seemed to float. Whipped by invisible updrafts of sound. And the music pulsed: louder, sharper, the bass pounding through my body, hammering into my soul.

    I felt it.

    I felt her.

    I felt her just as though she were moving in my arms, her hot flesh trembling, smoldering. Perspiration beaded my forehead as I imagined touching her moist skin. I knew it wasn't real, even as I traced the imaginary round of her breast beneath my sweaty palm, almost feeling the warmth from her body on my fingertips. The nagging question was why. Why was I thinking this way? Why did she, this stranger, rouse such feelings in me?

    She stopped and turned, her hair gently settling on her shoulders. Wisps of dark strands webbed her face, covering her eyes like a veil. Eyes that held me. Ruled me from a distance. Understood my turmoil.

    And she liked it.

    She flipped her hair away from her face gently. Teasing. Her Mocha-ice skin glistened in the dancing spotlights. Come to think of it that described her perfectly: a tall glass of molten-kava but with a certain frosty edginess about her—Ms. Mocha-ice. I wanted to touch her hair. Run my fingers through it. I wanted to run my hands down her spine, clench her firm buttocks. Rove my hands over her upstart breasts. Feel her thighs press against me, grinding.

    Instantly, the spell was broken when she pulled a man from the wall, drawing him with the sheer magnetism of her eyes alone. Their bodies melted together, probing with first gentle then ever harder thrusts. Faster and deeper thrusts. My face, my hands steamed hot; my breath became quick and ragged.

    He held my sultry vixen by the small of the back as she bent backwards to touch the floor with an outstretched hand. As her breasts perked skyward, I could almost see the supple flesh. Screwing up her face in a sly and wicked smile, she shifted with her partner then slowly turned, rubbing her buttocks against his genitals. I nervously met her stare.

    Then she began to touch herself as she danced. After pulling the hair from her face, she slowly ran the back of her hand down her swanlike neck, edging lower and lower to her breasts, provocatively tracing their shape as her fingertips caressed the shimmering fabric.

    I watched as she played.

    I wanted to play, too.

The Black Spiral: Twisted Tales of Terror

He tightened his hold around her waist as the line of his jaw imprinted itself on her tender, brown skin. As her eyes locked on mine, she flashed a taunting smile, conveying gratification as her partner's groin pumped and probed from behind. She wheeled about, resuming the dance, and breaking eye contact with me. And still I watched.
Ms. Mocha-ice never looked my way again.

Disappointed, the spell broken, I realized I was parch dry and headed downstairs to the bar. The lounge was warm, cozy. The air laced with laughing voices, the odor of stale malt and hops. Voices amplified by liquor, amplified by ecstasy and cocaine. Clouds of blue-gray cigarette smoke hung in the air like mourners hovering around a freshly dug grave. It was a Goth hangout. Black was the color. There was a black lacquered bar along the right-hand wall, about twenty small black tables circled the dance floor, and a row of black faux-leather rounded-Vegas-style booths along the left wall. A long expanse of mirrored wall covered the back of the bar. Endless rows of onyx-colored glasses, stacked on glass shelves, were backlit with the pale-blue glow of fluorescent light.
   The bartender was a good-looking predator with cobalt-blue eyes, and moussed hair. A pincushion of flesh with a pierced nose and eyebrow, and about seven earrings decorating the edge of his ear. He wore contact lenses, which transformed his eyes into the elliptical shape of a reptile. Snake eyes.
   I ordered a drink.
   With my back to the club and my eyes glued to the glass in front of me, I tried to forget that face, that body, those eyes. I tried to forget the inviolable stirrings she summoned within me. "Time to ease off the booze," I lied aloud to no one in particular, knowing full well I'd only had one *virgin* Bloody Mary. Yes, I lied because I couldn't face the truth. The woman had awakened feelings in me I didn't know I had, didn't know I was capable of having. It was just as frightening as it was incredible. But the emotion I couldn't quite bend my mind around or fathom was how deeply I wanted it to be so. To touch, to taste her supple body, was that so wrong? So what if her skin was *darker* than mine.
   I had to see her one more time.
   I made my way back upstairs. Another reggae song, only much slower, beckoned to the crowd, which soon fell under its spell, its promise of the press of warm flesh . . .

The Black Spiral: Twisted Tales of Terror

I scanned the room, searching for a glimpse of my mystery woman. I saw the man she had been dancing with standing in the hallway talking to someone. Someone hidden in shadow. Slumping, I resigned myself to the fact he was talking to her and that he was getting her phone number. But why did that bother me?

Frustrated, I turned and scrambled down the steps, jostling couples as I moved.

I stood at the bar. My hands were fisting at my sides in anger.

A voice like velvet fog interrupted my thoughts. "Anything good mixed with that soda?"

I turned to see her standing next to me. At five foot seven, I was more than two inches taller than her, which meant she had to tilt her head slightly. I liked that for some reason. As she stood there with her hair tousled, her face flushed, and slightly winded, she was breathtaking.

"Just plain old soda," I said, unsure of the timbre of my voice.

"Oh—" A provocative smile curled the corners of her lips. I could almost taste the sweetness of it. "Can I buy you something with a little more kick?"

I shrugged and sighed.

"No. This is about all I can handle right now. But thank you."

She smiled again, revealing a trace of lipstick on her teeth. Seemingly sensing it, she ran her tongue along those perfect ivories and over her full upper lip. I envisioned my mouth on hers, kissing her passionately. Because she conjured visions of danger, of the forbidden, the thought both frightened and intrigued me.

"Do you like reggae music?" she asked, catching me off guard. She dabbed her forehead with a napkin from the bar, looking at me all the while, waiting for me to respond.

"Yeah. Why do you ask?"

"Because I saw you watching me while I danced."

"I like the way you move," I heard myself say.

"Thank you." Her words carried the faint trace of an accent, maybe Caribbean. The sound was bewitching.

The sparkle in her eyes hinted that she knew I was admiring more than her dance moves. A man elbowed his way closer to the bar, forcing her to press tight against me. Her body heat rose in waves, her perfume scented the air. I stood rigid, captivated.

"Would you like to dance with me?" she asked, her voice no more than a whisper.

The Black Spiral: Twisted Tales of Terror

"To reggae music? I think people would look at us a little strangely, don't you think?"

"Don't be shy, Blondie. I'll teach you a few steps."

She was dangerously close.

"I don't know—"

"Well, if you don't want to—"

She started to walk away. Panic welled within me.

"I didn't say that. I just don't know about dancing with *you . . . here*." Even as I said it, my mind reeled, the words echoing in my head. It went against everything I thought I knew about myself. Everything I thought I was. But the truth of my feelings was undeniable. Maybe despite my claims to being a liberal, I was a bigot after all. Had my façade crumbled with that one simple question?

She smiled and picked up another napkin. She took a pen from the bartender and wrote down her name and number.

"Give me a call when you feel like dancing, Blue-eyes."

She tucked the napkin into my hand and slowly curled my fingers around it, never releasing her gaze. Then she whirled around, made for the stairs. The sway of her hips as she walked away tantalized. Like the lurch in your gut as a roller coaster plunges over the crest, a rolling wave of nausea overcame me.

Determined not to make the same mistake twice, I bounded for the staircase. I caught up to her just as she was merging into the crowd, moving her body to the swelling reggae cadence.

My legs moved of their own volition, following her as she moved deeper and deeper into the crowded dance floor. She faced me as I approached her, her eyes gliding up and down my body, watching. Although self-conscious, I kept moving steadily toward her. I slid between couples, as they stood apart, tempting one another with an outthrust hip for him, a cleavage baring stoop and shudder of the shoulders for her. "You can look but you can't touch," their eyes said, resembling peacocks circling each other in a mating ritual. I saw them but didn't. They made up the clutter of my peripheral vision. My eyes were honed in on her. And hers on me.

As the reggae rhythm moved me, covering ground I didn't feel beneath my feet, I navigated the dance floor until I stood directly in front of her. Her face and chest were filmed with perspiration; the ends of her hair matted against her cheek. The glistening line of her cleavage was exaggerated by the light of the strobe, the tops of her round breasts peeking through, pushed up by the under wire of her bra. I followed the plunging scoop neck of her dress, the soft swell of her breasts, fancying I could make out the nipples, slightly erect, beneath the sheer material. My own nipples hardened at the thought. I took a deep breath to clear my mind.

We stood inches apart, our breath mingling, blowing wisps of hair across each other's faces. She tilted her head the slightest bit upward, toward mine. Her hair fell from her shoulders and cascaded down her back. I wanted to put my hand in it, to smooth it against her skin, to feel its silkiness between my fingers. Instead I stood still, unable to move, spellbound.

She said nothing as she drew closer. I backed away on contact, suddenly aware of my surroundings. *People are staring at us.* My face flashed hot as I thought of them watching. What must we look like?

Two women undressing each other with their eyes in the middle of the dance floor.

I imagined them pointing and snickering at our public display of affection, certainly deemed gratuitous by the straight couples in the room. I would think as much if the shoe were on the other foot, I admitted to myself. Even a casual touch, a knowing glance from one partner to another was enough to make me leave the room.

This was happening so fast, all so new.

She pushed closer, until our bodies touched through our clothes. Her hands rested on my hips, the slow grind of her hips growing salacious. Then she caressed the outline of my hips, her hands tracing from waist to thigh, from outer to inner, as she danced. I soon forgot my concerns and fell under her control, moving my body against hers, and feeling pleasure in the contact. Her breasts rubbed against me, just beneath my own, her nipples as aroused as mine as they pressed. She smiled as she fondled me, enjoying my reaction as the façade I had lived under all my life melted away beneath her fingertips.

As we danced, I pressed my pelvis hard against her. She pulled my trembling hands to her and guided them over her body: over her hips, the tops of her thighs, up and down her ribcage, and each time teasing me with the fleeting brush of her breasts. I was throbbing with desire, my heartbeat rising in my throat. She brought my hands around to her buttocks and held them there, spreading my fingers so that both of my index fingers danced along the edge of her cheeks. I felt her move beneath my hands as she danced. I pressed closer still to her warmth, longing to taste her skin.

More than anything, I wanted to make love to her, to give her what she seemed to be asking for, begging for. The realization floored me, but I set it aside.

The music, the tang of her sweat, the heat of her soft breath enchanted me. Blotted everything out. I no longer sensed prying eyes, no longer heard chattering voices around me. It was just the two of us standing there now, on the brink of coition.

Her firm hands were on my neck, pulling me toward her gently, as her hot, sweat-drenched bosom sandwiched against mine. Her flickering tongue grazed my neck and sent shivers down my spine. I shuddered as her tongue lapped the dew of perspiration from the hollow of my neck. My mouth opened, slack from excitement. I leaned into her, wanting more. She nibbled at my neck, suckled it. I stood allowing her to do as she would, willing to experience anything she wanted me to.

She spoke in the softest of tones at the base of my neck, her voice so quiet.

"What did you say?" I sighed, inebriated by her touch.

"I asked if you remembered my name. Do you?"

My mind grasped for an image of the scribbled napkin. Her name and number. The letters floated in the fog of arousal, I couldn't remember whether they were cursive or printed, or even the color of the ink. All I could see was her. All I could feel was her.

"Do you?" she asked again, more insistently this time, her mouth hovering over my neck as she spoke.

With my eyelids squeezed tight, I commanded my mind to clear itself, if only for a moment. Terrified and afraid she'd cast me aside if I couldn't answer this one stupid little question. *Jezzus, think!*

And then it came to me. I saw the napkin, her flowery, calligraphic handwriting and a name—Vanessa.

As I opened my mouth to say it, I felt her soft lips upon my skin again.

"Van—" I started.

But before I could finish, something sharp pierced my neck. My eyes flew open. I gasped. My hands reached out for Vanessa and found her shoulder, taut now as she held me in place. I struggled against her superhuman strength, my own deluded by ever growing waves of terror-filled ecstasy. A muted cry bubbled from my lips, resembling queer little animal sounds of panic and desperation. I was bombarded by sensations: my neck burned poker-hot; my hands grew icy, fish-cold. And finally the roar of rushing blood pounded against my eardrums as she suckled noisily, wildly.

As instinct took hold, I scanned the room, desperately seeking help.

But the men and woman who, only minutes before, were so normal, dancing to the music, sipping their drinks, and making small talk, were all staring, their faces now more like wild beasts than human, or some strange combination of both. And when they laughed, their lips skinned back as thick tendrils of saliva dripped from razor-edged incisors. Fangs. Others stared proudly, watching the display with an air of nobility. Their faces contorted with a greedy edge; it was a needful look in the eye for some, a gaping maw for others.

A hunger.

A need to—feed.

Vanessa drank her fill and once finished, pushed me away. Her rich laughter fanned the air, the sound buffeting my ears. I looked at her, at the blood—my blood—which coated the front of her dress and filmed her heaving breasts. Even then, with her bloody fangs protruding over her bottom lip, her yellow cat's eyes glowing in the dim light, she was gorgeous.

In a languid motion, I raised my hand to my neck. My fingers probed the puncture wounds tentatively; I cringed from the touch. My vision clouded over as I stood among the **undead**, before the woman who would take my mortal life. My legs weakened and I sank to the floor. I sat looking up at her. Tears blurred my vision as I faltered, what was left of my blood seeping from my wound and down my blouse. I saw her walk toward me as I laid my head on the dance floor. Vanessa knelt before me and brushed a lock of damp hair from my face, smoothing it with her delicate fingers.

Her eyes held a profound sadness as she watched me die. The warmth of her hand burned my face as she touched me, growing hotter and hotter against my chilled skin. Then, she entered my open mouth with a probing finger. Seeking to aggravate the wound, she thrust it deep into my throat causing me to gag, then choke on my own blood. Once done, she removed her hand and closed my mouth gently, caressing my chin as a lover would. Again, Vanessa spoke, her voice tender and sweet:

"Do you love me, Candace?"

The Black Spiral: Twisted Tales of Terror

    With my last breath, I managed a feeble, gurgled response, "Y . . ." And so I lay dying with Vanessa's face looming before me, and the smell of my blood wafting from her lips.

    I blinked my leaf-dry eyes and swallowed hard, my throat raw and desiccated. Pushing off the floor with my hands, using muscles that now felt invigorated and strong in a way they had never felt before, I stood. Vanessa stood with me, her face proud, glowing. I studied the faces of my new family and saw respect and rivalry roiling within them, just beneath the surface of their fragile skin, as I stood in front of their one true love—Vanessa. I peered deep into her eyes and said:
    "Yes, I do."

The Black Spiral: Twisted Tales of Terror

LIGHT REIGN O'RE ME

Sephera Giron

Her body craved him, ached for him but she didn't know how or if she could ever touch him.

Oh, to feel the press of his flesh against hers, to feel him deep inside, cradled into her warmth ....but wishing wasn't going to make it so.

Lilah breathed in the sweet pungent curls of rain-scented incense that spiraled lazily before her. The small altar consisted of several red candles, incense and a few crystals arranged in a circle. Through her window, the full moon bathed the darkened room with silvery streaks, glancing along the stones, giving them a polished glow. The musky scent of rain filled her senses. She could smell him, she could taste him and soon she would see him once more.

The warmth of White Light caressed the top of her head, searching for the entryway through her thick expanse of hair. That first feeling when light burrowed down from the heavens at her call, dancing along the room until it found her, caused her heart to race, for she knew that she would be on her way once more. She guided the ray gently to her crown chakra, feeling it press against her hair. She savored the sensation for a moment, waiting as the warmth grew into heat, and light burned into brilliance beyond white.

She breathed in deeply, letting it penetrate her. Light broke through, filling her head with spinning vibrations. She breathed again and dizziness passed into a rush that no drug had ever given her. Light slipped through her mind and spread into her physical being. Every limb and organ greeted the energy as it washed through her in a wave. She shuddered, enjoying the delicious sensation. Her physical body prickled with goose flesh, her nipples hard as bullets, her groin swelling slick with anticipation.

Then, her body was no more as she hurtled through a corridor of darkness. The journey was short and she emerged intact into a golden crest of light.

Brimming with energy, she opened her eyes and saw her spirit guide, Rayn, before her. His blue-green eyes sparkled with the knowledge that he had yet to share with her. His shaggy brown hair and tousled bangs made him human but the glow of energy beaming from him was a kaleidoscope nearly painful to look upon. Lilah often wondered if she created his beautiful form in her own vision of her ideal lover, or whether he had truly been so handsome in his time on earth. His straight white teeth gleamed and his firm young chest was teasingly covered with a red satin robe that slipped open, exposing a nipple. She yearned to lick that hard little nugget of flesh, even as she returned her gaze to his vibrant eyes.

"Come with me," he beckoned, taking her hand into his strong warm one.

She went. Traveling through places that now held memories, as though saved from a dream. They visited familiar meadows and streams, a market place rife with crowds, animals that spoke like humans. They watched a distant tornado sweep across a milky horizon, twisting into itself until it was nothing. They scooped up sand from the beach where a turbulent aqua ocean that twinned Rayn's eyes slapped at their feet.

When at last they rested, she found herself in an enormous palace room complete with gilded walls, high arching ceiling and abundant satin pillows. As she languished across one pillow, wondering if she would ever taste the delights that lay beneath Rayn's robe, he lay across from her, his eyes still burning with unspoken secrets as he rested and watched her.

She was grateful the day he appeared as her spirit guide. It was not so long ago that she didn't get the hang of meditation at all. Now she visited these places as if they were down the street from her home, speaking to people who seemed more like friends then anyone in her real life, and of course, there was always the draw of this handsome young man to lead her.

Before she found the light, her life was mired in boredom and repetition. No matter how she chose to fill her lonely nights, it was never enough. Her job as an accountant lost its challenge a couple of years after graduation, and she felt sure that she would never meet a man she felt enough passion for to actually consider settling down. As far as she was concerned, at the age of thirty-five, she was settled down, with her job and apartment and tiny circle of friends.

Then Rayn came into her life.

The first time she saw him, he was but a hazy form, lurking in her dreams, daring her to step outside of herself to taste the next level. She ignored his call for a year or two, forgetting it immediately upon waking. But bit by bit, his insistence at getting her attention leaked into her real life, and she educated herself to understand how to respond.

His form was never concrete in the early days. Maybe he was a glow of color, or a figure shrouded in robes, taking his place with the other dream shadows. His face was unrecognizable as such, but she knew it was him, that he was one constant, by the soothing ring of his melodic voice.

He spoke in short patient tones during her fledgling visits, words she could scarcely understand. Sometimes he would hum or sing softly to draw her attention, and she grew to recognize the unique vibrato in his voice. She wondered what he would sound like on earth. Just a mass of humming quivering vibrations, or would he make the transition in a way humans could decipher?

She watched him, hoping for his robe to slip open further along his well-muscled thigh. She wondered if he knew what she was thinking, and she knew that he had to know. Spirit guides knew all, did they not?

Her thoughts stopped completely, as if blocked by a door slamming. She felt an urge to look beyond Rayn, almost as if someone was commanding her to look, though she heard no voice.

Her eyes were drawn to a narrow door, set in along the gaudy gild molding. She was certain she had never seen it before.

"What lies behind there?" Lilah asked Rayn. His mouth curved into a mocking half smile.

"It is not for you to know."

"Oh, come on. I'm familiar with this game."

Lilah pulled herself up from her pose and marched over to the door. She wrapped her fingers around the long, cold golden handle and pressed down. She gently wiggled it, she pushed harder, her fingers clenching. Despite her most vigorous attempts, the handle simply would not give.

"It is not your time," he said.

"Oh, Rayn. I've come a long way," she said, exasperated.

"The spirit is willing, but you have nothing to give."

"Give?"

"The portal is a gateway to the Maze of Delights. But the taste of such pleasure does not come without cost. To continue the journey, sacrifices must be made."

"Sacrifice?"

The Black Spiral: Twisted Tales of Terror

Rayn stood behind her, stroking her bare arms with his strong warm hands. She melted back into him and the walls echoed with her sighs. A glaring white light burned her eyes and in that instance, she felt the shudder of delight in true essence. How she thrilled to the quiver of pleasure that filled her very being from the outside in. She was flying and drowning in the same moment, her nerves painfully stretched and teased, a rolling thunder of wonder undulating from her crown to her clitoris. The moment was eternal, yet in a second and he was gone.

When she woke back in her room, the incense burned out, the smell of rain still clinging to her nostrils; her body glowed with a pale luminance that was almost, but not quite, unearthly. She felt the stain of Rayn, of his words echoing down through the layers of consciousness. She wondered what the sacrifice would be and hugged herself as she remembered the brief, oh so brief, glimpse he had given her, of what true pleasure would be with him.

And her hunger grew.

Work filled up the time between meditations and provided the means to buy endless candles and incense. She sometimes felt Rayn around her even when she wasn't thinking about him, which was not often to be sure. Her lust for him continued to grow until she was aching at all hours of the day with unreleased desire.

Yet, she was flesh and he was spirit and no matter how well the meditation and spiritual awakening might be going, the bottom line was, they could never truly fuck.

The first darkness of depression mocked her. Where the brilliance of light had brought her joy, she now let it wash across her with pain. Each time she saw his face, her heart grew colder, for she knew she was in a terrible place. Even the memory of his hands stroking her that one time when she asked about the door was not enough to sustain her, for the reality of the whole thing was, she was starting to believe she could never have him.

She HAD to have him, or she would go mad.

Again they lay on the pillows in the palace, his eyes narrowed as he watched her. Lilah stared at the forbidden door.

"I want to go there," she said.

"I know."

"So, what do I do?"

"You need more light," he said softly.

"More light? How?"

"You can get it."

"But it is hard enough to find the light that I have."

"You must bring others." His words were simple but Lilah frowned as she tried to envision it.

"Other people here?" she asked.

Rayn laughed, his eyes flashing as he threw his head back. Lilah resisted the urge to lean over and lick the long expanse of exposed neck and instead gazed at him with wounded eyes.

"Why are you laughing?"

"Nothing is simple or easy or straightforward around here. You know that by now."

"Do I ever. So what is it that I need to do?"

"You need to collect more light from the earth plane and bring it here. To me."

"Just to open the door?"

"Yep."

"And how do I collect this light to bring to you?"

"You'll think of something."

"And how do I know if it's worth it?"

"It's worth it." Rayn grinned, his smile a little too wide.

"Can I have a hint?"

"Bring me light," Rayn commanded. His hands reached over to cradle her face. He tilted her head until she was looking into his eyes, mere inches away. Her lips parted dreamily and she felt like a sunflower absorbing the sun's rays. His lips were close, she could feel his breath on her face. She reached up to touch his hands with hers and pulled them down across her breasts. The heat of his touch seared through her and she gasped at the intensity. She stared back into his eyes and found herself drowning in an aqua sea. Her body trembled as she fell back into White Light and on towards home again.

The little taste of him inspired her to seek out what he wanted. When Lilah returned to work the next day, she was amazed to find herself able to see people's auras. She had been trying for the longest time to achieve such a goal. Squinting her eyes, staring at people in darkened movie theaters, stared at herself in the bathroom mirror late at night. And now, suddenly, whether it was all her practicing or something else, she could see the electric energy that made up each human being around her. She felt like a blossoming flower in a darkened field of glowing fireflies.

"Good morning, Lilah. You look happy today." Roger from down the hall nodded at her as he walked past her desk. Lilah stared at him, stunned, amazed by the halo of brilliance emanating from the top of his head, even more amazed at the orange tinge that flickered like a fire when she caught his eye.

Orange meant horny, did it not? She tried to remember from her readings, but decided it did not matter. For in that brief moment, she knew how to find light for Rayn.

Roger and Lilah lay in Lilah's double bed. His lips hungrily sought out her nipples and she let him, dreaming of Rayn and her together at last.

For "the maze of delights" must mean the most exquisite of erotic pleasure, mustn't it? And if she served Rayn, then surely they would be together. He knew, had to know, that was what she wanted most of all.

Lilah barely noticed that Roger was sliding his cock into her until he started rocking hard against her. She didn't hate it, actually she quite enjoyed it, but she was not with the one she truly desired.

She watched Roger's aura pulsate, watched the light flicker and dance as he rocked in pleasure. She stroked his blond curly hair, and drew her fingers along the edge of his aura. It was hot under her touch, flashing orange and red and yellow as passion gripped him.

Lilah pursed her lips and sucked in. She saw the light waver. She spread her legs wider and with every push of Roger's hips, she willed his light into her body.

Light tickled her vagina, filling her uterus, and spread along her body. The sensation was warm, like a tide coming in. Slowly, deliberately, orgasm grew imminent for both of them.

Roger pushed into her one last time with a moan and Lilah inhaled the last of his light. She cried out as an earthly orgasm tingled through her. She clenched herself around his pulsing cock, sucked in, held in light and fluid so as not to lose it. She twitched and moaned, slipping off of him, rolling along the bed, her body not feeling like her own any more. She didn't even notice that Roger lay very still.

The Black Spiral: Twisted Tales of Terror

"You have done well," Rayn grins, his smile a little too wide, his eyes incredibly bright.

"How can you have it?" Lilah asks, feeling as though she might throw up. The foreign light, Roger's light, roils through her, like oil trying to penetrate water. It is not of her own making, it is Roger's essence and it rebels against her theft.

"Get it out of me," she begs. "It's like a parasite, eating away at me."

"Nonsense," Rayn laughs. "You are just too full. But you won't be for long."

Lilah shudders as he takes her hand and leads her towards the door. Her steps are heavy, she is waddling as though she ate a gallon of chili washed down with a keg of beer.

Lilah stands before the door and touches the handle. It is not cold anymore, but warm and giving. Her hand relaxes and the door swings open.

Tears fill her eyes as she stares out across the sea of yellow. A million giant sunflowers turn their heads towards her in welcome. They rustle, whispering greetings with their thick, long stalks and large broad leaves. The power of their love swells towards her, enveloping her in a wave. Lilah runs out into the field, staring up at the flowers as they coax her further and further inside. They nod and sway, dancing to an unheard melody. The door is gone but Lilah does not notice.

She holds her hands up to their large yellow and brown faces, feeling light glowing at her. The ground beneath her feet rumbles. The vibrations tickle her toes and the earth shifts a bit. She stares down at the ground in wonderment until she hears Rayn's laughter.

He stands in the sunflowers, his ruby robe gone, as is hers. She runs to him and throws her arms around him. He hugs her and for a moment, flesh presses against flesh. His long hard cock pokes against her belly, her erect nipples rub against his, and she covers his mouth with her own. He kisses her, hard and soft, tongues dancing, his passion ebbing through him and into her.

At last, he gently removes his mouth from hers.

"They told me it couldn't be done." His eyes brim with tears, shining like sapphires. He cups her face in his hands, stroking her cheeks softly with his thumbs. "But it can."

"What?"

The Black Spiral: Twisted Tales of Terror

        "That two humans could meet and fall in love on the spirit plane."
        "Humans?"
        "I am human too, like you. I found you when I was dreaming one night and I had to have you. I kept coming back, wishing and hoping that one day, we would meet in the flesh, but I didn't know who you were or where you lived or even how to find you."
        "You aren't dead?"
        "No. And now I am with you and you feel so real!" His lips suckle her nipple. She feels extra light seeping from her into his mouth.
        "So what was with the extra light?"
        "We needed it to get through here. I had to get it too."
        "Who told you?"
        "My own spirit guide. I was told that once we found the path in, we would be together, forever."
        "Forever is a long time."
        "What is time?" Rayn grins. "Time spent on earth is time wasted from here."
        They fall into sunflowers, lips and hands rubbing and stroking each other, exploring creases and pockets of flesh that were once dreamed about but now a reality.
        "Why can't we just exchange addresses and meet each other, in the flesh?" Lilah asks.
        "It doesn't work that way. You know that."
        Their mouths press together, their legs intertwine. Lilah runs her fingers along the smoothness of Rayn's back, Rayn cups her ass with his hands.
        The ground rumbles again. A stalk shoots up through the earth, snaking along the ground until it finds Lilah's vagina.
        At first, Lilah closes her legs, but the root is persistent. It strokes her as Rayn watches. A moan escapes from Lilah's lips, speaking of pleasure she has never experienced. Rayn kisses her and the stalk enters her body. She trembles, anticipation of all that came before and all that ever will be spinning through her mind like a kaleidoscope.
        A cloud sinks from the sky in a foggy puff, enveloping the couple in its warmth. Rayn squeezes Lilah's breast and more light seeps out. The cloud rolls dark and heavy over them, undulating waves of smoke shielding the flowers from the sun.

The Black Spiral: Twisted Tales of Terror

Lilah, lost in the pleasure of the stalk, closes her eyes, to enjoy the penetration more fully. Her breasts are warm with the light dripping and leaking, she feels her groin swollen and aching and she yearns for release. When she opens her eyes again, she is so very tall, and so very strange. She sees that Rayn is gone, but she doesn't think to worry.

Lilah is a strange sort of sunflower, staring up at the sun. Her body twitches and writhes, for the pleasure is endless, constant edginess but not complete. She moans and feels the stalk growing wider inside of her, filling her so completely from her vagina up and out of her crown chakra. Light circles her, fanning the pleasure faster as each nerve ending, both new and old, craves the release.

Above her, she sees a storm cloud rolling closer. Light whips faster as thunder rumbles, the deep vibration adding to the pleasure that burgeons on the edge of pain.

Suddenly, the cloud is above her, and lets loose with a storm that pounds rain down onto the flowers all around. It beats on her sunny yellow face, it dribbles inside her mouth, it flows down her body, into her crown, through her being. As the rain touches her body, she shudders and writhes, twisting in the wind, her cries accenting the pleasure coursing through and around her.

As she twitches with orgasm after orgasm, she realizes that she has truly received her wish. She will spend eternity in the maze of delight, tasting rain, drinking rain, Rayn washing her from the inside out.

The Black Spiral: Twisted Tales of Terror

AUTHOR BIOGRAPHIES

MORT CASTLE has written or edited 14 books, including the novel *Cursed Be the Child,* about which Rave Reviews wrote ravingly, ... a classic of its kind, and the essential reference work Writing Horror: The Handbook of the Horror Writers' Association. He's published 500 or so shorter things, mainly stories, in anthologies and magazines and is the only living author to be included in all five volumes of the acclaimed Masques series edited by J.N. Williamson. He's won or been nominated for the Bram Stoker Award, the Pushcart Prize, the International Horror Guild Award, the Emerson Fiction Award, the DeMarco Prize, and others. He has had several dozen stories cited in Year's Best compilations in the horror, suspense, fantasy, and literary fields; has been honored by Argentina's prominent Galaxia Cthulhu literary society as Number Five in a ranking of writers of the world's Top Horror Tales; and has been recognized by numerous universities, institutions, and magazines as one of America's outstanding writing teachers on both the secondary and college levels.

A musician and entertainer, Castle is widely acknowledged as the best Horror writing bluegrass banjo player in his height, weight, and age division. Castle frequently performs his work, accompanied by the acoustic band, *Seeking Employment.* Castle and his wife, Jane, a bona fide Boneyard Woods Egyptian, live in Crete, Illinois.

His latest story collection is the Bram Stoker award nominee **NATIONS OF THE LIVING, NATIONS OF THE DEAD**, from Prime Books.

RAMSEY CAMPBELL, born in Liverpool England, is one of the most highly respected and widely published horror writers on either side of the pond, with over some twelve novels, two

245

hundred short stories, numerous anthologies and fiction collections ... the vast opus of his career is staggering. His most recent novel *The Darkest Part of the Woods* is available from TOR in hardcover. He has won two World Fantasy Awards and three British Fantasy Awards. **Peter Straub** when speaking of Campbell's mindset said, "The world Ramsey Campbell takes for granted is the world of our darkest nightmares."

F. PAUL WILSON, who grew up in New Jersey glued to the boob tube, is a man of many talents. In his spare time he is a practicing physician. His forte is medical and horror thrillers. THE KEEP and THE TOMB both appeared on the New York Times Bestsellers List. WHEELS WITHIN WHEELS won the first Prometheus Award in 1979; THE TOMB received the 1984 Porgie Award from The West Coast Review of Books. His novels and short fiction have appeared on the final ballots for the World Fantasy Award, the Nebula Award, and the Bram Stoker Award. DYDEETOWN WORLD was on the young adult recommended reading lists of the American Library Association and the New York Public Library, among others. He is listed in the 50th anniversary edition of Who's Who in America.
Over six million copies of his books are in print in the US; his work has been translated into twenty-four foreign languages.
F. Paul Wilson resides at the Jersey Shore with his wife Mary where he is working on a new
"Repairman Jack" novel. "Repairman Jack is one of the most original and intriguing characters to arise out of contemporary fiction in ages. His adventures are hugely entertaining.
Dean Koontz
When discussing making a contribution to this anthology, Paul said, "... stories of revenge? I've written many but this is one of my all-time favorites."

NANCY KILPATRICK lives in lovely Montreal, Canada. She is an award-winning author and has published 26 books, 14 of them novels, the latest *Eternal City*. Her alter ego, Amarantha Knight, deals with the erotic side of horror and has penned one

The Black Spiral: Twisted Tales of Terror

half of those novels. Nancy also edits anthologies and is currently editing her 8th, with writer Nancy Holder—*Gothika* will be published by Roc/NAL in 2005. She is also the author of the non-fiction book *The goth Bible: A Compendium for Lovers of Darkness*, to be published in 2004 by St. Martin's Press. Her novel *Near Death* has been optioned for film by C8 Productions. Visit Nancy at: www.nancykilpatrick.com

SEPHERA GIRON is a best-selling horror novelist with Leisure Books. Her titles include *House of Pain* and *Borrowed Flesh*. *Eternal Sunset* from Darktales Publications was recommended for a Bram Stoker Award. She lives in Toronto with her two sons and two cats (probably familiars). Visit her online at www.sff.net/people/Seph

TINA L. JENS is a three-time Bram Stoker Award nominee (given by the Horror Writers Association) for short fiction in 1999, for producing the Twilight Tales reading series in 2001, and now for Best First Novel *The Blues Ain't Nothin'* from Design Image Group, which was also an International Horror Guild nominee. Here's what **Peter Straub Author of** *Black House* **(with Stephen King) and** *The Hellfire Club* has to say … "Exactly like the music in which it is soaked, The Blues Ain't Nothin' jumps, sings, soars, sighs, and exalts. This novel is bursting with energy and charm." Tina's two stories *Elvis Can't Dance* and *The Gargoyle's Sacrifice* are updated and revised reversions now appearing in The Black Spiral for the first time. Visit Tina at
www.tinajens.com

ROBERT WEINBERG is the author of over twelve novels—*The Black Lodge* from Pocket Books and *The Devils Auction* and *The Armageddon Box* from Leisure books to name a few. And as if that wasn't enough, like a character in one of his comics, he somehow manages to stretch time—imbuing him with the power to write volumes of short stories faster than a speeding bullet, leap into editing numerous anthologies, and write tales for Moonstone Comics that are more powerful than a locomotive. Read what the **best-selling novelist Dean Koontz** has to say

The Black Spiral: Twisted Tales of Terror

about Bob's latest book ***The Science of Superheroes*** from John Wiley & Sons co-written with Lois H. Gresh. "I found this book to be a hoot from beginning to end. Ms. Gresh and Mr. Weinberg must have spent some time in institutions for the deranged, because well-balanced minds could not have conceived of this project. But thank God for their derangement, for they have produced a package of pure fun from first page to last. If, like me, you admire superheroes from a distance, or if you are a hardcore fan of them, you will enjoy this book as surely as you would enjoy waking one morning to discover that you are invincible, able to fly, and in possession of a totally cool costume behind which to hide your true identity." --Dean Koontz, from the Introduction. Visit Bob at www.robertweinberg.net

TIM LEBBON was born in London in 1969. His novella *White* (MOT Press, 1999) won the British Fantasy Award for Best Short Fiction, as well as being shortlisted for an International Horror Guild Award. It was recognized and listed in The Mammoth Book of Best New Horror, and Ellen Datlow's The Year's Best Fantasy and Horror. He is a member of Leisure Book's stable of noted horror novelists. The Leisure edition of *Face* was released in April of 2003 and optioned by the BBC in March of 2003. His novella collection *Fears Unnamed* will be published next year. He is delighted to announce that *The Nature of Balance* was also optioned for the screen. Tim is vice president of HWA Horror Writers Association. In the summer of 2003 he became the proud father of a baby boy. Visit Tim at www.timlebbon.net/

JAROSLAV KNIGHT and his alter ego, Jan Strnad, live in Los Angeles. His work has appeared on HBO, Fox, CBS and ABC. He occasionally performs as an actor. Pinnacle Books will release his first novel ***Risen*** in January of 2004. His boyhood love of comic books has been realized by writing for the Dark Horse Comics' series based upon *Star Wars* and *Straship Troopers*. Visit J. Knight at www.AtomBrain.com

The Black Spiral: Twisted Tales of Terror

KAREN SANDLER collected an impressive stack of rejection letters before she finally sold her first romance novel in 1997. She has since sold several others and is currently a member of Harlequin's stable of romance writers. In a total departure from the romance genre, her short story Mom displays her hidden gift for creating dark, nail-biting terror while weaving an intricate web of horror and suspense. Also a screenwriter, she has written and produced two short films and also works with L.A. producers on feature film projects. Visit Karen at http://www.karensandler.net/

THOMAS DEJA has lived and worked in New York City all his life, which may explain why most of what he writes is horror fiction. From his earliest work for the seminal humor 'zine Inside Joke to stories in magazines like *Creatio ex Nihilo, After Hours, Rictus, Bare Bone* and *Not One of Us*, as well as the short-story anthologies *The Asylum Volume One: The Psycho Ward*, and *Decadence*, he has continued to deliver the message that runs through all his work: the nature of life is changing, and it hates you. His work has received Honorable Mention in The Year's Best Science Fiction and Fantasy, and has been published in four languages. Mr. Deja's most well-known stories, however, are those that have appeared in the Marvel Comics paperback anthologies *The Ultimate Hulk, X-Men Legends and Five Decades of the X-Men*. Presently, he is preparing to undertake an original dark science fiction novel called *The Jefferson Doctrine*. **Mr. Deja** has a long-standing relationship with *Fangoria* magazine; from his highly controversial *X-FILES* Episode Guides to his author profiles and book reviews, his work always generates talk. In 2001, he was appointed Fiction Editor for *Fangoria's* "Frightful Fiction" section, accessible on the magazine's website www.fangoria.com This has led to his writing a series of articles on how to get published for Scavenger's Newsletter, his editing of the debut issue of Underworlds, and upcoming ventures with the print publisher **Cyber-Pulp.**

The Black Spiral: Twisted Tales of Terror

WILLIAM D. GAGLIANI's story *Icewall* shared a spot in the 1998 anthology *Robert Bloch's Psychos* (Pocket, ISBN 0 671-88598-7) with Stephen King's own "Autopsy Room 4" and made the Preliminary Ballot for the Bram Stoker Award and was named an Honorable Mention in The Year's Best Fantasy & Horror (11th ed.). It's still Bill's proudest moment as an author, though some of the upcoming publications come close. His debut novel *Wolf's Trap* was just released by Yard Dog Press. Bill hails from Milwaukee, Wisconsin. He graduated with an MA in English in 1986 from the University of Wisconsin at Milwaukee where he later taught Creative Writing and Composition. He dedicates his story "The Serpent Said" to The Belleview Cult 1979-1980.

RICHARD D. WEBER was formerly a U.S. Foreign Service Officer, Special Agent in Charge of Dignitary Protection with the U.S. Department of State's (DSS) Diplomatic Security Service. He protected the late Princess Diana and Prince Charles, the Secretary of State, and has traveled extensively. He roamed the hallowed halls of Foggy Bottom, various embassies, and the Pentagon. During his tenure with the DSS, he was chief editor of the Foreign Service Newsletter. He's a graduate of University of Wisconsin and a member of HWA. Richard currently resides in the Dallas, Texas Metro Plex area where he is hard at work on his new novel *Boyhood's End,* and putting the finishing touches on his euro-thriller screenplay/novel *The Sampson Project.* His current novel *Protocol-17: A Conspiracy Thriller* is a Bram Stoker Award recommended work and has enjoyed top-seller ranking. He has interviewed such notables as Doug Clegg and Tom Piccirilli for publication. His latest works will appear in *BLACKOCTOBER MAGAZINE,* and *Cthulhu* Issue 17 Vol.II. When not writing, he is an adjutant teacher of creative writing and an editor with Cyberpulp Publishing. Visit Richard's website at www.darkprotocols.com

L. MARIE WOOD was born in Monsey, New York in the early 1970s. Being an only child, she often entertained herself by concocting imaginative storylines and writing them down. With the upcoming publication of her debut novel **CRESCENDO** in

The Black Spiral: Twisted Tales of Terror

November of 2003, a life long dream has been realized. She has written screenplays and short stories in the Horror/Suspense genre. Ms. Wood has also written poetry— thirteen chapbooks of it— under the pen name Elle Wood. She has penned several short stories that have been printed in anthologies and on websites such as Erotic *Fantasy: Tales of the Paranormal*, and *Horrorfind*. To learn more about her visit her website: www.lmariewood.com

KEVIN ANDERSON has been an advertising and marketing professional for the last thirteen years, and has written award-winning copy for TV and radio. He has been published in *The Harrow, Champagne Shivers, Writer Online, the Canadian monthly anthology – Thirteen Stories (issue #6 and #8), Black Satellite (issue #6), Twilight Times, and Rogue Worlds*. Kevin has recently won John B Ford's Top International Horror 2003 contest. His story *Third Shift*, along with other winning stories, will be published in Rainfall Book's Top International Horror 2003 anthology coming out this fall. Although Kevin concedes that his wife is the most "tolerant" woman on the planet when it comes to his long hours spent writing, he feels that she should have had a premonition of things to come, especially since they were wed on Halloween. Visit Kevin at www.kevin-anderson.net

MIKE RIMAR is yet another Canadian writer, Ontario to be specific. Describing himself in a Lemony Snickett fashion, Mike lives over there with no intention of moving here. His wife thinks he's married and his daughter calls him Daddy to his great confusion. Most of his day is spent doing things, unless he isn't, in which case he must be writing. All kidding aside, Mike lives with his charming wife, Kathleen, daughter Hayley, and Clifford, The Big Red Cat. Mike says the idea for *Famous House* came from a news broadcast concerning moving an historical monument from one location to another: ". . .they will move the famous house on Tuesday. . ." And a story was born.

SARA MERLENE lives with her two sons, two Boston Terriers, two leopard geckos, demonic hamster and a horde of dust bunnies in the Dallas area. She is currently at work on her second novel. Sara says the demonic hamster, Boris, provides the muse for her dark-work writing. However, the inspiration for her story Organic came from a bit of undigested kibble late one night as she tossed and turned in her bed. She's originally a native of Oklahoma, which is the setting for her debut novel *The Haunting Lullaby* released July of 2003. Visit Sara at www.hauntiglullaby.com

JULIE NOVAIS received her bachelor's degree from the University of California, Santa Barbara. She currently resides in a suburb of Dallas, Texas with her husband and three children. She spends her days working for an insurance company and her nights working on her first novel. Inspiration for *Gillian's Eyes* came from a friend's recent experience with corrective eye surgery coupled with the author's fascination with dark fiction.

The Black Spiral: Twisted Tales of Terror

Author and Editor Richard D. Weber

The Black Spiral: Twisted Tales of Terror

Printed in the United States
29059LVS00003B/181-183